In Praise Of

AS HOT AS IT WAS YOU OUGHT TO THANK ME

"Nanci Kincaid has written a sizzler of a novel – a compelling story of a community in crisis told by the brightest, sweetest, most honest and down-to-earth teen narrator I've encountered in years. Nanci Kincaid is a wonderful writer, and she is at her peak in this compulsively readable novel. Sex, religion, place, and class are all factors as Berry tries to figure out who she is in this surprising, fast-paced novel with mystery at its core."
– Lee Smith, author of *The Last Girls*

"Snakebites, chain gangs, wayward preachers, exploratory sex, a tornado, RC Cola – this is just the sort of novel Harper Lee would proudly claim as her own." – T. R. Pearson, author of *A Short History of a Small Place*

"As you read along, the wonderful, clear narrative voice enables you to see the world afresh, as if for the first time – through the eyes of a young woman whom you'll come to love in the way we should all love ourselves."
– Clyde Edgerton, author of *Walking Across Egypt*

And Its Author, Nanci Kincaid

"Kincaid's exuberant female characters seduce with bouncy charm and then – *thwack* – come at you from left field with gritty insights about life and love." – *Elle*

"Part of the beauty of Ms. Kincaid's art is that she tells plain truths about serious subjects, yet does it with a light, deft hand, in a story that is compelling and entertaining. . . . Kincaid's fiction belongs on the shelf with that of Lee Smith and Anne Tyler."
– *Winston-Salem Journal*

Also by Nanci Kincaid

Crossing Blood

Pretending the Bed Is a Raft

Balls

Verbena

AS HOT AS IT WAS YOU OUGHT TO THANK ME

A NOVEL

NANCI KINCAID

BACK BAY BOOKS
Little, Brown and Company
New York Boston

Back Bay Books / Little, Brown and Company
Time Warner Book Group
1271 Avenue of the Americas, New York, NY 10020
Visit our Web site at www.twbookmark.com

First Edition: February 2005

The characters and events in this book are fictitious. Any similarity to real persons, living or dead, is coincidental and not intended by the author.

Library of Congress Cataloging-in-Publication Data

Kincaid, Nanci.
As hot as it was you ought to thank me : a novel / Nanci Kincaid. – 1st ed.
p. cm.
ISBN 0-316-00914-8
1. Teenage girls – Fiction. 2. Fatherless families – Fiction. 3. Hurricanes – Fiction. 4. Prisoners – Fiction. 5. Florida – Fiction. I. Title.

PS3561.I4253A8 2005
813'.54 – dc22

2004016659

10 9 8 7 6 5 4 3

Q-MB

Printed in the United States of America

For my brothers, Roger, Wayne, Frank, and Paul – and my sweet sister, Lucy. I thank them for all the ways they made the journey easier – more intense, more interesting, more important.

The lie is a condition of life.
– Friedrich Nietzsche

The truth is cruel, but it can be loved.
– George Santayana

AS HOT AS IT WAS YOU OUGHT TO THANK ME

We had a yard cat. It was like a yard dog, only it was a cat that couldn't come in our house or any house, just roamed the sandspur yard, all hot day and all hot night, looking for a dark spot in the world that might be cool, like dark meant cool, but it never did, not even under the car, or under the chinaberry tree, or under the house by the dripping faucet, or under the cement steps that led up to the porch. Not even the nights with the icy-looking stars sprinkled overhead were cool, because cool was only a thing we dreamed, all of us, something we heard about once or read about some-place and decided to believe in. It was such a fine thing to be-lieve. Better than heaven. Like standing in the open refrigerator door, feeling that one second of crisp air until the kitchen heat got it, until Mother yelled, "Close that door. You're letting all the cold out." That kind of believing.

But our yellow cat had never been in a house, never seen the light go on in the refrigerator and felt the good shock of a cold second, never finding a cool spot anyplace, because there wasn't one, not ever, just stalking the yard, looking for small things to eat – not mice, we didn't have any mice that I ever saw, just snakes mostly, small ones, poisonous or non-poisonous, it didn't matter, she would get one in her mouth, paw it to death, then drape it on the back porch steps for us to see, white-bellied sometimes, the kind of dead you can poke with a stick, the lifeless snake lying in wait, belly up, making our mother scream when she saw it.

If it was small enough our mother swept it up in a dustpan and threw it in the trash barrel out by the fence where our neighbor burned his trash every week or so. If it was bigger she let us bury it – my brothers, Sowell and Wade, and me – in a sandy patch beside the house that Mother insisted on calling a flower bed.

Our mother didn't believe a dead snake was ever really dead. "I've seen many a snake come back to life," she warned. But Sowell and Wade made it their job to test for death authenticity. They put the limp snake through assorted life-or-death maneuvers – slinging it back and forth across the yard like a boomerang that had lost its arc, pinning it to the wire fence with a clothespin clamped on its tail, clearing a place in the sand like a clean slate and twisting the dead snake into alphabet shapes all the way to Z, dropping it in the bowl of cat water that sat beneath the spigot to see if it could float – before declaring it officially dead and fit to be wrapped in a paper napkin and buried beneath the morning glory vine that clung to the side of our wooden house.

Sometimes our cat sniffed us and clawed at our legs while we laid the snake carcasses to rest. Sometimes the burial was complete with a Popsicle stick cross and a memorized Bible verse, like maybe I would say, *Make a joyful noise all ye people, come before the Lord with gladness,* or something religious like that. Our yellow cat sat on my lap and let me pet her while Sowell and Wade dug a deep hole with kitchen spoons. It seemed right that our yellow cat, the killer of these snakes, should want to, should have to, watch them be buried. *Amen,* we said.

Snake killing was one of the many nasty cat habits that made Mother declare our yellow cat a yard cat. Another was clawing the back-door screen until it was in shreds. I thought this meant that our cat wanted inside the house with the rest of us, that she wanted to be a house cat. I imagined letting her sleep at the foot of my bed, listening to her purr, stroking her yellow fur until she fell asleep. But Mother said, "That cat is too wild, Berry. It would feel like an innocent prisoner locked away in a jail, a stray cat trying to live in a house, scratching everything to pieces. Houses are good places for people, honey, but they're like prisons to cats and dogs."

My daddy had been raised on a farm and it had made him hate animals. "If you'd butchered as many hogs, rung as many chicken necks, shoveled as much manure as I have, you wouldn't be an animal lover either," Daddy said. But it wasn't true. I would be. "You just be grateful I let you keep that cat for a yard cat," he said. "Don't start begging me to let the cat in the house, Berry. You hear me?"

Our cat didn't have a real name. We just called it *our yellow cat.* Where is *our yellow cat?* Here are some leftovers to feed *our yellow cat.* Like that. From out of nowhere our yellow cat had just wandered up to the yard one day looking starved half to death and sunbaked too. Her eyes were crusted over. It made me think of the hobos that came to our back door, who migrated through Pinetta just as sure as any flock of birds, called out to Mother through the screen door, "Sister, can you spare a bite to eat?"

Mother stopped her ironing and came to the door and looked at them the same way she had looked at our yellow cat that first day. She gave those hobos a tuna fish sandwich, or last night's meat loaf, or once a slice of Sowell's birthday cake and then usually the men, who looked like somebody had painted them with grime, like grime was the color of their hair and skin and clothes and even their eyes, and who were sun-hardened, turned nearly reptile-skinned the way the Florida sun did people who were not afraid of it, who lived out in it until they looked like something tough and overdone, maybe used to be tender, but not anymore, then those men said, "Grateful, sister." The sun had tattooed them all over, except their hair, which was sometimes turned golden on their heads, like angel hair, underneath the grime.

"You can wash your hands at that faucet." Mother pointed to the spigot on the side of the house. "Wade, go in the bathroom and get the man a bar of soap."

It was a pleasure to watch a grown man wash his hands and face with a slippery bar of soap out in the yard, sticking his whole baked head under the faucet, making it seem like steam was coming off him, getting his shirt dripping wet, wiping his clean hands dry on his dirty pants.

"You need to comb your hair," I said once. The man's hair was as long as mine. He made his fingers into comb teeth and raked his hand through his hair over and over again. "How's that, girlie?" he said.

"Good," I told him.

The hobos sat on the back steps, like yard dogs, like yard cats themselves who could not come inside houses where clean people lived. They sat and ate the plates of food Mother gave them and drank the Kool-Aid from her Tupperware cups and Sowell sat beside them, and so did I, and Wade too. We watched the men eat, some slow to make it last, some fast like they were worried Mother would change her mind and come back outside and snatch their plates away. We drew with sticks in the sand,

and ran our feet over the sand pictures to erase them, and asked the men questions. "What's your name?" we said.

They said Little Willie or Petey-boy or some other happy-sounding name that made us laugh, like little boys' nicknames stuck onto grown men, who seemed suddenly friendly when you knew how harmless their names were.

"Where do you live?" we said.

"Nowhere," they might say. Or "Anywhere." Or once a man said he was from Georgia. "Live on the road," they all said.

"But where do you sleep?" we asked.

"Wherever I can find a cool place," one hobo said. But we knew there were no cool places.

"I guess you must sleep in somebody's refrigerator then," Sowell said. "Only cool place around here."

"Cherry Lake is cool," Wade said. "At night. At midnight."

"He don't sleep in no lake," Sowell said.

"He *doesn't* sleep, Sowell," Mother said. "*Doesn't.*" We hadn't known she was standing there, waiting to hand the man an orange. An orange. She embarrassed me doing that. Why would anybody give a Florida hobo an orange when he could just about get all the oranges he wanted for himself? Just pick them up off the ground or off a tree. I wished she'd had an apple for him. I think he would have liked that better. She set the orange down on the steps beside him and went back into the kitchen.

"I sleep under a car sometimes," the hobo said. "In a ditch on the side of the road. Lay out some palmetto leaves, make me a good spot. Heck, sometimes I sleep up in a tree."

"You don't sleep up in no tree," Sowell said.

"You ever seen snow?" Wade asked.

"Many a time," a hobo answered. "Seen it. Slept in it. Eat it. I done it all, son."

"What's snow like?" Wade sat close by the man like he was falling in love with him, like he'd been separated from him at birth by endless questions and now, at last, here came the answers.

"Cold," the hobo said. "That's all. Snow, it's right pretty one minute, nasty the next."

"You ate some?"

"Sure I did."

"What did it taste like then?"

"Nothing," he said. "Don't have no taste."

"You got any kids?" I asked the man. His stringy hair was slicked back behind his ears in little greasy ropes. His beard looked like a fistful of Spanish moss stuck onto his chin. His teeth were yellow except where they were missing.

"None that claims me," the man said. "And none I claim."

"Too bad," I said.

"Is that a saying out of the Bible?" Wade asked. "None I claim?"

"You want more Kool-Aid?" Sowell said. "Give me your cup, mister. I'll get you some more."

We loved it when the hobos came, when out of the string of little white Pinetta houses they picked ours, with our T-shirts and underpants hanging on the clothesline, our tire swing hanging from the chinaberry tree, our rusty bikes slung to the ground up next to the house. It was like they could just look around at the six white shoebox houses, all of them just alike, and know we had the nicest mother living in ours, that she was sure to come up with something good for them to eat. It made us proud of her. And sort of surprised too. Like a vote of confidence.

We had neighbors, the Burdetts, with a store-bought swing set in their yard and other neighbors, the Ingrams, with the only television set for miles around, a scarecrow of an antenna stuck up on the side of their house saying so. The Ingrams were not rich, but now that they had a television set it seemed like they were and everybody was nice to them because we wanted to get invited over to their oven of a house to watch their fuzzy television and listen to the fake audience laugh at things to let us know they were supposed to be funny. It was like a signal – here's where you laugh – and so we did.

There were six children in the Ingram family. Five girls older than me and one boy, Jimmy, my age. Jimmy was known all around Pinetta as the boy who wore dresses. Even I did not wear dresses, except on Sundays. But Jimmy, with his buzz haircut and bare feet, wore a dress practically every day of his life, hand-me-down dresses from his sisters. He didn't seem to know it was unnatural.

"Why you wear them dresses?" Sowell asked him once.

"Because" – Jimmy hardly dignified the question with any explanation – "I want to."

When we were little stay-at-home kids, too young for school, it didn't seem to matter that Jimmy wore dresses. I got used to it and didn't think it was a bit odd after a while. Jimmy was my main friend. We made forts in the weeds, played war with the water hose, caught roly-polies up under his house and set fire to anthills like we had received a divine calling. I knew firsthand that Jimmy was just as mean and normal as any other little boy – dress or no dress.

Besides, I don't think I ever wore a shirt until I started school. I am not proud of this fact, but in all our family photos I am standing in the yard in my underpants, bare chested as my brothers. Sometimes I have on some shorts and sandals, but that's usually all. My hair is white and cut short, giving my head the look of a misplaced snowball. These are mostly before-glasses photos. I was always smiling then. So a girl who never wore a shirt shouldn't have been laughing at a boy who wore a dress. It was like we were too little to understand who we were or what we were supposed to be. Like nobody had bothered to tell us yet. I wish Mother hadn't let me go around bare chested like that, but when I said so, she said, "Berry, for goodness' sakes. As hot as it was you ought to thank me."

She says that now.

"Wearing those dresses is going to confuse that child for the rest of his life," Mother told Daddy one night after supper. She had invited Jimmy to eat Spam sandwiches with us, after which we had all rushed outside to play swing the statue until it got too dark to see anymore and the bugs took over. Mother and Daddy sat on the bumper of our car, sipping their iced tea and counting out loud while the rest of us hid from whoever was it.

"Jimmy is a sweet boy," I heard Mother tell Daddy, "but he's in for a rough time if Mrs. Ingram sends him to first grade dressed up like a girl."

It was Daddy that finally – weeks later – went over to the Ingrams' and told Mrs. Ingram that when Jimmy started Pinetta School he was going to have to dress like a little boy. He said there were rules against boys wearing dresses to school. Mrs. Ingram said she understood that. She said she had no intention of sending the child to school in his sisters' old clothes. She didn't mention one thing about Daddy letting me run around half naked nearly every day. She didn't say, "There are rules about little girls starting school wearing nothing but their underpants." Mrs. Ingram was more sophisticated than that.

"You know children mess up their clothes roughhousing

around outside," Mrs. Ingram said. "I didn't see no sense in buying Jimmy good clothes just so he could tear them up playing in the heat of the sun all day. I thought, well, just let him mess up something that's already messed up. What difference does it make then?"

She promised to buy Jimmy his own clothes when he started school and she did – navy blue shorts with elastic waistbands. I thought he looked foolish in them at first. He acted embarrassed too. He cried when we all laughed at him, his legs showing, looking as startled as a couple of people, like two legs who knew how foolish they looked hanging out of a pair of shorts, who knew they looked finer when they hung out of a too-big hand-me-down dress. Jimmy looked like a ridiculous stranger in those brand-spanking-new boy clothes.

"Oh, you are handsome, Jimmy," Mother told him, wiping his wet eyes with her skirt tail. "You are about the handsomest thing I have ever seen, all dressed up in those nice boy clothes. Isn't he handsome, Berry?" she said.

"Yes, ma'am." I nodded.

After that nobody laughed at him and he seemed like he had made the transition just fine.

The Ingrams had a big car parked in their yard too. Jimmy and I liked to play like it was either a rocket or a wagon on a wagon train. There was no way for a stranger to know it wouldn't run, hadn't run for a few years, just sat there looking like you could get in it and go someplace, but you couldn't. You'd think a hobo would pick a house like that – the Ingrams' – where the people might hand out a plate of cold fried chicken or a piece of pie, but no, hobos picked our house. They picked us. Our house didn't even have a car in the yard during the day because Daddy drove it to work. He was principal at Pinetta School. Mother said people treated Daddy like he was half preacher and half policeman. She told us, "There are two things I never wanted to be, a preacher's wife and a policeman's wife."

Jimmy was always jealous when the hobos came to our back door. He tried to entice them to his house with promises of RC Cola or boiled peanuts. "You can sit in my daddy's car and eat," Jimmy said to a really old hobo who had a dirty white beard and was skinny as a paper clip.

"He looks like Santa Claus's evil twin," Sowell whispered to me. "Don't he?"

"Come on over to my house, mister," Jimmy pleaded. "My mama will give you some marshmallows."

"Can't do it, son," the hobo said. "Got a train to catch."

"You don't neither," Jimmy said. "There ain't no train."

"There is if you know where to look," the man said. "Got to know where to look."

We had never seen a train, but we knew about them.

"Where?" Jimmy said.

The man laughed.

"They let you on a train?" Sowell asked.

"They don't have to let me," the hobo said. "You can jump on easy when the train slows to a crawl. I been clear to California and back on a train, saw the entire United States of America and I can tell you firsthand it is a fine, fine country – this US of A."

We didn't believe he'd really done it, but we liked his patriotism.

After a hobo had eaten everything Mother could scrounge up, he politely yelled, "Thank you, sister." Mother did not allow a hobo to come in the house, but she might allow one to take a nap in our yard, under the chinaberry tree, ordering us not to worry him to death. Some hobos can sleep on a bed of nails. They can sleep in a smoldering fire or on the roof of a fast-moving car. They can even sleep through three kids who are dedicated to their not sleeping at all. By the time they ate a plate of our personal family food and answered our hundred questions and took a nap under our climbing tree, we were hanging on those hobos acting like they were our best friends and we just found out they had to move far away to another state and it was tearing our hearts out. Or like they were our uncles and we loved them and wished we could go with them because they knew a lot of good jokes and might take us bowling or to a drive-in movie. Especially Sowell acted this way. I swear it made him sad to see a hobo go on his way. He walked with him out to the mailbox, then just stood there and watched until the man evaporated in those waves of heat coming up off the gravel road.

"Wonder where he's going," Sowell said. "I wish I knew."

"Could be to hell in a handbasket," I said. It was something I heard Daddy say once about a hitchhiker. Daddy did not believe in picking up any hitchhikers unless they were dressed in a military uniform, preferably the army.

"Could be going to Madison," Sowell said. Madison was the closest thing to a town anywhere near us. "That lucky dog."

So that's why we got to keep our cat, because Mother could not resist a hungry creature. It's like they chose her, so she chose them back. Even our yellow cat, which was mostly my cat because it preferred my company to anybody else's in the family. I never participated in the death authenticity that Sowell and Wade specialized in. I think the cat must have known that and respected me for it – that I was more scared of snakes than I was of death. I'm pretty sure about that. I liked to pick our yellow cat up and take it off someplace away from the rest of my family and away from our neighbors, who you could not really get away from because they just showed up wherever you were, even if you thought you were hiding someplace.

I liked to sit in the Ingrams' big car that wouldn't run and hold our cat in my lap and just think about things that I could not think about in the company of others. I laid down in the backseat. It was so hot it burned my skin at first, until I got used to it and started to sweat and sort of slid around like a slippery fish in a greased skillet. Our yellow cat finally couldn't stand it, not the heat, not my hands trying to hold on to her, trying to make her stay with me and love me the way I loved her, and she jumped out the car window and ran off. So I got out too and went home. My hair was wet to my head and I was so beet red it made Mother feel my forehead and say, "Berry, you look on fire. Have you got a temperature? Where've you been?"

"Nowhere," I always said, because that was the truth.

~

Our house looked like a startled white face with two bewildered windows for eyes and a wide-open door for a mouth. There were five other houses with the same shocked face lined up on the gravel road leading away from here in both directions, houses like sextuplets who were only different by what went on inside their heads. Inside each house was a living room, a kitchen, a bathroom and two bedrooms. We had five in our family. Other families had more.

I shared a room with Sowell and Wade, who slept on bunk beds now. Sowell, even though he was the oldest, slept on the bottom bunk and hung a sheet from Wade's high mattress, making his bunk like a private white cave. He always slept like that, hidden from us, as if we cared anything about watching him sleep. I had a single pink-sheeted bed by the window, the one I wished our cat could sleep on the foot of. Mother told Daddy that before long I would have to have a room of my own. Daddy said, "We'll see," which was his favorite answer for nearly anything anybody at home – or at school – asked. He called it diplomacy. An answer that could mean both yes and no at the same time and generally kept people from repeating the question.

Already I had stopped taking baths with my brothers. Used to be we would all three get in the tub like a can of worms spilled into shallow ditch water. We'd swim and splash and scream. Mother would make us devil horns out of shampoo suds and let us play in the tub until our hands and feet were wrinkled like hamburger meat. Sometimes to keep us entertained she put Tupperware containers in the tub and we pretended they were boats – except Wade, who pretended they were bombs. Mother's idea was to let us get accidently clean while we played in the soapy water. It was Mother herself who taught Sowell and Wade to shoot the soap out of their hands like it was a slippery bullet. They could shoot the soap out from their underarms and from between their knees and even the cracks in their butts.

But Daddy gave us our baths military style – *Okay, everybody on your stomach* – and we would lie still in a smashed row while he went at us with a soapy wash rag – *Okay, everybody roll over* – and we did, silently, our heads bobbing no-foolishness style while Daddy washed our fronts, sometimes tickling us, sometimes rubbing so hard the washcloth left red streaks on our skin – *Arms up, left feet in the air, now right feet, okay, good job.* Afterwards, when we got out of the tub it looked like a mudhole, the silt settled on the bottom, the water the color of weak tea, us polished to a high pink gleam, standing in a row for Daddy to inspect us. My brothers' flopping penises making me think of tiny elephant heads, small and helpless, but sort of wild-looking.

Then one day Mother noticed the nickel-size knots on my sun-browned chest and announced that I was getting too old to take baths with Sowell and Wade anymore. I was shocked and deeply ashamed. It was about that time that Daddy bought the bunk beds and Sowell started hanging a sheet to make himself a sleeping tent and we divided off into two boys and one girl.

The neighborhood houses were spread out, not bunched up, and it was like we shared an endless backyard that went from patches of grass sprigs in the sand to a sea of weeds to a tangle of briars to the woods full of pine trees and scrub oaks and palmetto leaves and some said – quicksand.

The threat of quicksand kept us mostly close to home. We had heard the stories, the way men with guns gone to round up snakes, or to hunt deer, had disappeared and never been heard from again, leaving a worried wife and too many crying children to fend for themselves and the mother got sick and died and the children grew up to be criminals or to marry criminals and everything had gone from bad to even worse. Offspring of these men sucked to their deaths by quicksand went to Daddy's school. He knew some of their stories. How one year later maybe somebody would find one of the men's missing boots, which had floated to the top of a swamp like a warning to others, like the proof everybody was looking for. Like quicksand could suck anything down and later spit up what it didn't want. A man's skeleton, a man's gun barrel or eyeglasses or pocket watch.

Mother said she wasn't sure that quicksand swallowed up as

many men as people claimed. She said she bet a good portion of these men just up and ran away, went by the swamp first and threw in some identifiable object, a favorite shirt, a whiskey jug, a fine-tooth comb, something that would dignify their disappearance when it was found later. Something to save their families from disgrace.

"But why would a grown man want to run away?" we asked.

Mother bent over and kissed the tops of our sweaty heads.

~

Almost year-round we slept with the attic fan roaring. It sounded like we thought a train might sound if one went through the middle of our house. It pulled in hot air from outside and stirred it into the hot air already inside the house, like making the air into a night soup. The fan made the air move where it didn't necessarily want to go and as loud as it was it didn't always block out the screaming crickets or the whistling bobwhites or the owls hooting their endless questions into the dark. Night felt like something heavy melting over us, like if the black sky could melt like wax and coat the world in hot darkness. Sometimes you thought you couldn't breathe. You thought you were under water at Cherry Lake, had been there too long, forgotten to come up for air, won the holding-your-breath contest and lost your life. You kicked the wet sheets off you, like unpeeling a cotton skin, and lay still in a puddle of sweat that felt like if you'd been shot and maybe were bleeding to death.

Every night you had to find ways to trick yourself into going to sleep. You had to think of a game you could play in the darkness or a story that you could let go out of control in some coolish cave in the darkest part of your mind.

* * *

At night the mosquitoes were big as bees and just as mean and knew how to sneak through the screens and circle your head in a halo track, around and around, making you go crazy. We were all thoroughly night bitten, like a ritual, knowing we would wake with fresh welts on our necks and feet, on the sides of our faces or even in our hair. Some nights Daddy came in our room with poison and sprayed it around the edges of the windowsill and it smelled good, like gasoline, and sometimes he sprayed the poison on our feet too, just for good measure, and it felt as greasy as Jergens Lotion. It was probably wrong to love poison the way we did. We took comfort in it and hoped, every time, that it would kill off the night pests, stop the music they were making, the rhythm so hypnotic and compelling that it could make you offer up your flesh, your untasted arms and legs, like sacrifices to a bunch of small, angry gods.

Some nights I could hear Sowell, his breathing almost like a snore but faster than that as he rocked in his bed, behind his white sheet, and above him on the top bunk Wade was as still as a sleeping or a dead boy, but Sowell – just his breathing – shook the room. It was a long time before I understood that he was touching himself, trying to love himself, before Wade, overhead, twisted himself in his sheets some way, then kicked them loose and Sowell's sheet wall collapsed on the floor like the remains of a ghost and I saw that Sowell was holding on for dear life. Like he was riding a slow elephant through the jungles that surrounded us, the swamps and quicksand, and it made me go perfectly still, barely breathing, pretending to be asleep, until at last he stopped. When he went to sleep afterwards I could hear him fall into it, the sleep. The quiet had a loud ringing to it.

* * *

Certain nights our yellow cat would leap suddenly from the flower bed outside onto the windowsill that was right beside my bed, nothing but the screen between us. She would curl up there and lick herself, her paws, her belly, then her paws again. She would look at me, her eyes like two glowing headlights, and I could hear her motor going and hoped she knew that I had done my best on her behalf. Our cat would sleep stretched out there, maybe suddenly slapping at a firefly, but mostly just sleeping hard, making me watch for her belly to rise and fall so I could be sure she had not died.

I prayed a lot at night, just for something to do.

I thought of praying as a test. I wanted to see if God could pass it.

~

We still don't know what Mother was so mad about. Not exactly. We woke up because she yelled for us to come to breakfast. Her voice was as sharp as a lawn-mower blade, like you wake up because you hear it, somebody roaring around, cutting things to bits. "What's wrong, Mama?" Sowell said.

"Hush," Mother told him. "Sit down and eat your breakfast. All of you."

Daddy was already at the table. He was eating his eggs, which he liked scrambled in bacon fat. We wouldn't eat our eggs that way because we didn't like the looks of all the brown bits mixed in with the yellow. It looked like bugs in there. Mother always scrambled our eggs in plain butter. But this day she gave us Rice Krispies and toast and jelly. We sat in our metal kitchen chairs like folded things that had not unfolded yet, like notes that nobody could read because we were so folded in on ourselves, all the words on the inside. Wade's morning hair was stuck straight up on end. I had my elbows on the table.

"Take your elbows off the table, Berry." Daddy was swirling his toast around his plate, sopping up all the remaining egg bits. He looked at Mother with a certain smile on his face. She would say later that it had not been a smile. It had been a smirk.

"What are you looking at, Ford?" she said.

He looked down at his plate and began to shake his head like he was thinking of something funny but it was too private for him to talk about.

"Say," Mother said. "What are you looking at?" She picked the coffeepot up off the stove and walked toward him. Her slippers flapped against the linoleum. I loved the smell of coffee. It meant, *Here we go, another day, everybody alive and accounted for.* It meant, *Life is normal, we are normal drinking this coffee right here, when you grow up you will be normal too.*

Daddy lifted his empty cup and held it out to her absentmindedly. "Good Lord, Ruthie," he said. "Look at you."

"What about me?"

"When is the last time you looked in the mirror?" he said.

Mother stood beside him with the coffeepot in her hand like it was a small flag she was waving. But not a surrender flag. She looked at him like she didn't know how he had gotten in the house, like she was going to turn to the three of us, and demand to know, *Who let this man into our house?* And we would be punished for it.

"Whatever you do, Ruthie," Daddy said. "Don't look at yourself on an empty stomach. It's bad enough I have to do that every morning."

Then with the three of us watching, but not Daddy, Daddy

still with that smile on his face that meant, *I can say anything I want to and I think I have just proved that,* Daddy looking down at his plate, swallowing his last bite of toast, still holding out his empty cup, like a beggar with a bad attitude – and Mother, she just lifted the coffeepot up over his head like it was a torch and she was the Statue of Liberty and she tilted the pot and poured hot coffee on him.

It happened fast, but I remember it slow. Daddy screaming like a scalded cat, leaping up from the table, his chair crashing to the floor behind him. Sowell and Wade, spitting out their mouthfuls of Rice Krispies, their chairs scraping across the linoleum as they stood up, their arms lifted to cover their own heads, as if they thought Mother might go at them next. I had never heard Daddy shout with pain. "What in the hell are you –?" His sentence hung in the air like a bird that dies with its wings spread, airborne that final second before falling to its graceless death. Mother was walking toward him with the coffeepot still aimed, like she had a gun in her hand, and Daddy was backing up, his pajamas coffee-stained, bloody-looking, his hands in front of him. "Whoa," he said, "What are you . . . ?"

"Get out," Mother said.

"Have you gone crazy, Ruthie?"

"Not yet," Mother said. "Get out." She waved the coffeepot at him. Coffee sloshed out on his leg and Daddy shouted and jumped back, felt for the door handle behind him and got out of the kitchen just as Mother slung the coffeepot at his head, missing him, hitting the kitchen door, where the metal pot sounded like a satellite crashing to Earth and black coffee flew everywhere. It made me think of a bomb. Mother hurried over and locked the kitchen door, then turned to look at us, her full-time audience, the watchers she had brought into this world only to find that her every move was being watched day in and day out by us, her children, her jury, the witnesses to her life, witnesses who never went off duty – no vacations, no time out – watching her now, like always, watching, watching, our questions suspended in midair like a swarm of annoying insects who only occasionally bite but always threaten, whose presence alone was the annoying thing.

Our questions were the silent kind. The kind that you can swat at and miss but that will disappear as if they'd been hit – for a while, at least – and then you will spot them darting around the room again, daring you. The kind of questions that are fully capable of playing dead when they have to but never, never, never die. All our questions started with *why?*

Sowell began to laugh. His laughter sounded like that fake stuff they have on television shows that tries to trick you into laughing too.

Mother looked at him. She was leaning up against the door, like Daddy might try to push it open and she wasn't going to let him.

Sowell laughed louder and swatted at Wade and made Wade smile. "What did that remind you of?"

"What?" Wade said.

"Red Skelton."

"Shut up, Sowell," I said.

Daddy pounded on the door. "Ruthie, let me in. Come on. I got to go to work."

"Go ahead," she said.

Daddy pounded on the door like he had a hammer in his hand.

"Sowell," Mother said. "You take Berry and Wade into your room and you three stay there until I say different."

"Let him in," Sowell said. "He's sorry."

"Go to your room, Sowell," Mother said. "Right now."

Sowell shoved us toward our room and we obeyed his shove. We heard Mother go over to the sink and run the water. I looked out to see her washing down the wall where the coffee had splattered. She was not crying or anything.

Daddy came around to our bedroom window. "Sowell," he called. "Let me in."

"Mama said no."

"Berry, go unlock the door," Daddy yelled.

"She won't let me." I looked out the bedroom window where Daddy was standing. He was outside in his pajamas and the sun was coming up good. Soon the neighbors would see him and wonder what he was doing. They would wonder why the school principal was outside in a pair of wet pajamas, trying to climb in a bedroom window like some kind of criminal who has to break into his own house.

"I've got to get dressed, Berry. Tell your mama to come here a minute."

I yelled into the kitchen, "Mama, Daddy wants you."

"Your daddy wants a lot of things," she said.

"She won't come," I told him.

"What's she so mad about?" he said, like it was one of the mysteries of this world. "She like to burned me bad. Look . . ." He pulled at the neck of his pajama shirt to show me the red place on his neck. "See that? What you think about that?"

Daddy began to circle the house, knocking first on the front door, then the kitchen door, then yelling in our bedroom window. "I've got a dollar for whichever one of you opens the door," he called to us. "Wade, son, you want a dollar, don't you?" But we just sat there on Wade's top bunk, looking out where Daddy stood, wishing Mother would let him in. Sowell still laughing at Daddy, saying to us, "Look at old Red Skelton out there."

When Mother had washed down the kitchen walls and washed up the breakfast dishes she came to our room. "You three get dressed," she said. But we had already dressed. "I'll tell you when you can let your daddy in."

"Hurry," I said. "People will see him out there."

"Good," she said.

Minutes later she came out of her room with her usual sleeveless housedress on and her hair combed and lipstick on. She was rubbing lotion on her hands. "Okay," she said. "You can let your daddy in now."

We sprinted to the kitchen door and Daddy bolted inside the house like something was after him. "Ruthie . . . ," he said.

"Don't talk to me." She turned away from him. "Don't say a word to me."

So Daddy went in his room and got dressed and loaded us into the car and we drove the gravel roads to school. We were late. But other than that, Daddy acted like nothing out of the ordinary had happened. And so did we.

~

It was not that much fun to be the principal's daughter. People thought that I could get away with murder, but the truth was that I couldn't get away with anything. Hardly anybody could. It was Daddy's job to see to that.

Even before I started school, when I used to stay home with Mother and Wade, our daddy would come driving home midday with a boy sitting in his car. "Got some trouble," he would tell Mother. "Caught him smoking cigarettes again." Mother would look out the kitchen window at the boy sitting like a statue in the car, staring out at the small piece of the world directly in front of him. "Got to run him home," Daddy would say. "It's the Greene boy, again. His mother can't control him. But I got to talk to her anyway."

Sometimes Daddy would drink a glass of Kool-Aid or eat a quick sandwich Mother made him before setting out to drive the boy home, which was usually way out in the country somewhere, the kind of place you had to know where it was to find it, you had to have already been there once and remember the way, because the silent boy beside you was not going to give you any directions. You could say, "Right or left?" He would look straight ahead and shrug his shoulders.

Daddy knew where every kid at Pinetta School lived – there were less than a hundred kids in grades one through twelve – he'd been to every home, and lots of times took us with him, his three good-example children hanging out the car windows, wind-whipped and wide-eyed. That's how Sowell and Wade and I found out for sure that we were not poor – because we saw the people who were.

While Daddy discussed with Mother what steps he was going to take to deal with the cigarette-smoking Greene boy, Wade and I went out on the porch and stared at the boy who sat in Daddy's car. The Greene boy was so sour he almost had a smell to him. He was not the kind of boy who talked. "What you in trouble for?" we yelled. "Say?"

The Greene boy was sort of pretty, I thought. If he had been a girl, people would have smiled when they looked at him. They would have fixed their eyes on him and studied his face every chance they got. They would have talked to him in a sugar voice and reached into their pockets to find something nice to give him, a nickel, a stick of chewing gum, a rock that you might could believe was an arrowhead. His hair was more white than blond. His skin the color of the tobacco in one of his Camel cigarettes. His hair home-cut and unwashed, his clothes too small, his open eyes trained to *not see.* I'd learned his kind of eyes early on, seen them on women at church, on men with hunting guns in their hands, on barefoot kids begging for gumballs at the filling station store. They were the kind of eyes that were disappointed in themselves, wished they knew how to see something better than what they'd seen so far, but had given up, felt sort of cheated that they weren't born blind so they could just stumble through life, bumping into things, slapping their way along, not knowing what they were missing. Then there might be a little mercy to this world. Eyes like that. The Greene boy looked at Wade and me like we were a couple of invisible kids. Like if we were fools enough to think that we were real, well, then that was our problem.

"You been smoking at school?" we yelled. "Did our daddy catch you?"

The Greene boy trained his eye on our yellow cat, watched it stalk around the yard, looking for something to pounce on.

Daddy slammed out of the house and patted us on our heads and got in his car, saying to the Greene boy, "Okay, son. Me and you gonna ride out and have a talk with your mama. Let's go. You ready?"

The Greene boy did not answer Daddy, but he didn't jump out of the car and run away either. He just sat there like it was someplace to be. Like as long as he had someplace to be, he didn't care where it was.

"Bye," we yelled to the Greene boy. He slumped down and rested his head on the seat back, no expression on his face.

~

I was only seven years old when some boys drew naked women across the front of Pinetta School in white chalk. They drew tits that looked like the eyes of God on flimsy, unsubstantial body faces. Tits were the main thing. The bigger, the nastier. One of the drawn women had chalked drops of milk coming out of her tits. They did not have faces, the drawings, just tits and open legs and tiny round heads with corkscrew hair sticking out.

When Daddy drove us up to school on a Monday morning, we saw it first thing, the tits, the spread-legged women. Daddy stopped the car right in front of the building and stared at the mess scrawled everywhere. "Look at that," he said.

"Who did it?" Sowell asked.

"Somebody sorry – who's about to be sorrier." Daddy slow rolled his car into the teachers' dirt parking lot. I could see Daddy's mind racing ahead of the moment, scanning the possible culprits, imagining what form justice might take. Daddy was the nearest thing to a policeman that Pinetta had and this was definitely a police moment. Daddy looked at Sowell and me, his eyes blazing with the thrill of it, tits all over the wall, big tits, and somebody guilty striding the hall of his school, somebody wild, somebody bold and vulgar who needed to be caught – stopped – so that decency could triumph. So that a moral lesson could be learned by all.

"Y'all keep your ears open – you hear me?" Daddy said. "Nobody in Pinetta can keep a secret. Folks around here have to talk, have to tell everything they know sooner or later. So you two listen out. Tell me if you hear anything about who did this. You understand?"

"Yes, sir," we said.

* * *

Boys had all their lives to get used to penises. But girls – we had to spend years waiting for breasts, dreading them or longing for them. They were more interesting to me than any other body part. I didn't know if they were beautiful or hideous. I didn't know if I would be comforted by having them – or ashamed. I had never seen any breasts except Mother's once, when she was getting into her bathing suit at Cherry Lake. She mostly ignored them. But in her bathing suit there they were, small, pointed and sharp, pressed into her suit like a couple of innocent prisoners under false arrest waiting to make their escape. I thought of them like things that wanted to be set free – like they had their own little brains or something, like they dreamed dreams. It gave me the creeps in Mother's case.

But my teacher, Mrs. Freddy, who was also my vacation Bible school teacher in the summers, had large white breasts. We knew they were white because the edges of them showed at the neck of her dresses, like scoops of vanilla ice cream on a brown sugar cone wrapped in a napkin dress. During the day Mrs. Freddy shook Johnson's Baby Powder down the front of her dress between her breasts and little clouds of powder puffed out when she patted her hand across her bosom. Then she put powder on her hands and patted it on the back of her neck where her wet hair curled and lay pasted against her skin.

I thought Mrs. Freddy was beautiful even if she did wear glasses and even if she did have fingernails chewed to the quick – because she had those white balloon-size breasts that made her seem so exotic and kind. Some nights I dreamed of Mrs. Freddy's breasts. I dreamed that she let me see them and touch them and held me close against her naked self with my face pressed into those creamy white pillows of flesh. I was in love with Mrs. Freddy. If she had said, "Berry, do you want to run away with me? Be my own girl?" I'd have said yes. I wouldn't have stopped to think it over. I would not have worried that it might hurt Mother's feelings. I spent hours at night imagining just those sorts of scenarios, where it was just Mrs. Freddy and me alone in the world, having one adventure after another. I ached for Mrs. Freddy to love me back.

"Did you see what somebody did?" Jimmy asked me the minute I walked into the classroom. He sat beside me in Mrs. Freddy's second grade. There were second-graders at two tables on one side of the room and first-graders at two tables on the other side of the room. "They drew on the school," Jimmy said. "Nasty stuff."

"I saw it," I said.

"Is your daddy mad? What's he going to do?"

"Find out who did it."

"I know who did it."

This was almost too easy. "No, you don't," I said.

"I do too."

"Don't tell me. I don't want to know." I was not being psychological. I was being honest. I didn't want to be the one to have to tell on anybody.

"Guess," Jimmy said.

"I don't want to."

"Just guess."

"No."

"Sowell," Jimmy said.

I looked at him like a person looks at a roach sneaking across a clean floor. I wanted to stomp on him and listen to him crunch, his insides white as cream of wheat. "Shut up," I said.

"My sister told me."

"Your sister lies," I said.

"Not Rosemary. Rosemary loves Sowell. She says she's going to marry him."

"Well, she's not," I said.

"She said Clyde Greene and Meritus Moore and those Wilmont brothers, you know, that live out by the highway – they did it. And Sowell was with them. They dared him to. She said that way if they got caught, your daddy wouldn't be so hard on them – since Sowell did it too."

"It's not true," I said. "Rosemary doesn't know everything."

By midmorning it was already so hot that our fat pencils were slipping in our sweaty hands, and our wood-chip gray paper with its highway-like solid lines, broken lines, was wet from the sweat dripping down the sides of our faces, our chins and necks, so that any erasures became rips and even the most neatly drawn words were smeared and ugly. I kept messing up my paper and having to start over. When my paper got too wet my pencil wouldn't show up on it – it was like writing with an invisible pencil. When I was in first grade sometimes it would make me cry – just the messiness of everything. By second grade I was more used to it.

Mrs. Freddy's hair was wet around her face and she had dark perspiration rings under her arms. When she moved her arms you could see the lace of her slip and she kept clutching the front buttons of her blouse, sort of tugging at them in quick, jerky motions like she was trying to stir some air that way. It made her breasts bounce. She closed her eyes sometimes and said, "Mercy." She patted a handkerchief across her forehead and took off her glasses and wiped them with the same handkerchief. I could see the red spots where the glasses sat on her nose. Sometimes if Mrs. Freddy saw me watching her, she would smile and wink at me.

She had a husband. He was a farmer named Bye Freddy who could also fix electrical wiring and small appliances. He didn't deserve Mrs. Freddy. I knew that. I wondered if she let him watch her take a bath.

Mrs. Freddy had been Sowell's teacher too. She had taken some of Sowell's artwork and taped it up on the wall in her classroom, a collage he had made out of pine twigs and gumballs and those starfish-looking gum leaves. He had made an under-the-sea picture using land items. Mrs. Freddy used it as an example to inspire the rest of us to try to make something out of nothing too, to look at things and see them as something else besides what they really were. Sowell was always really good at that. Daddy said Sowell could look at a dog and see a cat. "It's called an imagination," Mother said in Sowell's defense. "You've heard of imagination, haven't you, Ford?"

Mrs. Freddy was also the one that first took Sowell's doodles seriously. The one who told Mother she should save the paper napkins and gum wrappers Sowell doodled on. Now Mother had a shoebox full of Sowell's artwork, which she kept under her bed. Thanks to Mrs. Freddy.

I wondered if Sowell had watched Mrs. Freddy the way I did now. Watched her sweat. Watched her hair curl into little ringworms all around her face. Watched her breasts live secret lives under her blouse like a couple of perfectly matched white mules pulling the plow of her whole self through the hot days of this life. Had he lay in bed at night thinking up stories where she took off all her clothes? Maybe it was true – what Jimmy said.

Maybe those were Mrs. Freddy's tits drawn all over the front of the school. Maybe she looked at them and recognized them – and believed those drawings to be the work of Sowell Jackson.

Maybe Sowell was in love with Mrs. Freddy like I was and that's what made him draw her naked all over the school. Love. It made people do crazy things, right?

As far as I knew, our daddy had never killed anybody – not even some of the problem kids at Pinetta School I was pretty sure he would like to have killed. Instead of killing kids, he mostly just scared them to death. That's how he did us. He could say, "I love you," so that it sounded like he was threatening our lives. But I think he meant it. Sowell liked to act like he was not afraid of Daddy – but he was. He was afraid of Daddy's words more than his belt. Sometimes I think it would have been a great relief to Sowell – to all of us – if Daddy had just hit us and hit us and hit us instead of saying the things he said.

If Sowell, who was supposed to be a good example, was guilty, then I didn't know what Daddy would do. I didn't know who could save Sowell then.

My stomach was in such a knot from contemplating all this that I told Mrs. Freddy I was sick and needed to go home. She hugged my neck and felt my forehead for fever. She smelled just as sweet as a baby's butt with all that powder on her. "Berry, honey," she said, "you don't have any temperature."

"It's my stomach," I said, rubbing it.

"Why don't you go ask your daddy what he thinks," she said. "Let him decide."

"Yes, ma'am." I looked at Jimmy as if everything was his fault. "Now look what you have done," I mumbled as I left the classroom, rolling my eyes at him. He looked bewildered. In a hateful moment I imagined him as a sideshow at the carnival.

Fifty cents to see the dress-wearing boyfreak. "I hate you, Jimmy," I said.

I was not crazy enough to go to the principal's office. I was afraid Daddy would look at me and become instantly suspicious. He was trained in suspicion. He would say, "Okay, Berry, girl, what are you hiding?"

"Nothing," I would say. How do you tell your own father that it is possible he has raised a sick and nasty son, a boy whose mind was on tits – even mine sometimes, which back then were nothing more than future projections? Still he liked to touch them, rub his hand over my nipples like they were a promise that was made but not kept yet. It was not what you should tell your father, was it? A man who named his firstborn son after his own daddy and who in return for the compliment expected something really fine from him – not just a bunch of drawings under his mother's bed or on front of the schoolhouse. "Nothing," I would say. "I'm not hiding anything."

Then he would hand me a Bible and say, "You want to swear to that, Berry? Raise your right hand and say, *I swear.*"

There was nothing for me to do but sneak out of the school and walk home. It wasn't that far. I'd done it lots of times, walked to school and back with Mother. If I could get past the teachers' parking lot with nobody seeing me, then I could get in the trees along the edge of the road and nobody would notice. So that's what I did.

Even from there I could see the chalk drawings. They were elaborate – like somebody had put work into them. Nothing slapped up on the wall in a big hurry. Anybody across the road at the Methodist church – that sad wooden box that needed painting in the worst way, needed it as bad as missionaries needed to go to Africa, as bad as the piano needed tuning, bad,

bad – anybody at the Methodist church could look at Pinetta School, see those chalk tits and wonder what the world was coming to. The preacher could make a sermon out of it and probably would.

Daddy had until Sunday to get those walls washed, but even then everybody would know everything about it because in Pinetta everybody always knew everything. Mother said that the reason everybody in Pinetta knew everything there was to know was because there *wasn't* anything to know.

I didn't have many choices. I could walk home and make Mother ask a million questions. *What are you doing home this time of day? Why didn't your daddy call me to say you were coming?* She might say, *Tell me what's wrong.* And I was afraid I would.

I could go to the filling station store and get a cold drink, except that I didn't have any money and besides, Mr. Longmont would ask questions too. He would call Daddy on the phone and say, "What is your girl, Berry, doing over here at the store on a school day?"

I could find a good place at the edge of the woods and wait for school to let out and then catch Sowell when he started walking home – catch him and tell him what Jimmy was saying about him. Tell him that if Rosemary wanted to marry him, he should not let her – ever – the way she lied. Beg him to tell me that Jimmy and Rosemary were wrong. Just because they had a television set didn't mean they knew everything.

I sat down in a shady hot spot in the thick trees beside the Methodist church. I made a lot of noise first so if any snakes were around they would know I was coming and be afraid of me like people always promised me they were. I wanted to sit under the picnic table in the churchyard, where it looked cooler and less snaky, but I was afraid somebody would see me. I sat with my back against a pine tree and began to tear a palmetto leaf into strips so that I could weave the strips into something, sort of like a leaf pot holder. While I was concentrating on it I kept my eyes back and forth on the school and the church, sort of waiting for something else to happen. Suddenly it occurred to me that I truly loved my brother Sowell. The thought of his being in trouble was unbearable to me. I felt sort of swollen up with love for him. It was something I had hardly noticed before – this love.

It didn't surprise me when the preacher, Pastor Butch Lyons, came up the road and walked into the church. He had grown up in Madison, a town boy, then gone off into the army, where he got discipline first and then religion, in that order. Now he was back being the Methodist preacher and volunteer basketball coach at Pinetta School. Just because he was tall, a lot of people acted like he was handsome. I watched him enter the church. I could hear his footsteps on the wooden floor all the way where I sat. He opened a couple of windows to let in some air. People called it fresh air, but what they meant was more hot air.

It surprised me when I saw Mother and Wade come into the churchyard minutes later. Mother had on her everyday dress and Wade was trailing along behind her, bored. I watched them go up the wooden steps and into the church. One minute later Mother came back out and sat Wade on the steps and gave him a fan with a picture of Jesus holding a lamb in his arms and another one with Jesus nailed to the cross – I knew those fans by heart – so Wade could fan himself to keep busy while he waited. Then she went back inside.

I knew Wade would turn those fans into airplanes. I knew he would have them crashing into each other and be conducting his own personal war with them in no time, bending back the fan corners to make wings, slinging them up in the air just for the pleasure of watching them wreck. That's how Wade was. All the way where I sat I could hear him making the sounds of bombs and guns, those fans flapping like two warplanes whose pilots had bailed out, stirring up something in Wade, even if they weren't stirring up any real breeze.

I could hear Mother playing a few stanzas of a hymn on the piano. It meant Mrs. Moore had been called to go look after her mother in Madison again. Mother was the backup piano player on Sundays. She could barely read music, so she had to meet with the preacher and practice ahead of time. He had to be sure he picked out songs she could play by ear. It was pretty to me, hearing the music, knowing my mother was making it. If she had noticed the chalk women drawn on the school, she wasn't acting like it. *He walks with me and talks with me and tells me I am his own.* The music came out of the church like a startled flock of doves taking flight.

Now Wade had found something sharp and was carving his name into a wooden plank on the face of the church. The wood was so soft, you could almost carve it with a fingernail. Rotten was what it was. Some people loved the church this way, old and weather-beaten but, *praise the Lord, still standing.* Some people had been going there all their lives and were used to it, moisture in the wood, leaks in the tin roof, wasp nests in the eaves, hymnals with mildew on the covers, the pages falling out, the sweet smell of decay all around, everywhere the ghostly presence of old times back before people thought of them as *good* times. The church was surrounded by a sand yard and a circle of huge oak trees with gray moss hanging like an old witch's hair. The moss was full of red bugs, but it was still beautiful in a spooky sort of way.

One year ago the Baptists across the paved road suddenly got holy and built themselves a brick church with a real steeple and a tiny fellowship hall out back with a stove and refrigerator and folding tables and chairs in it. It was modern. It looked like not even a hurricane could knock it over. So now lots of Methodists were dissatisfied. They comforted themselves by saying their church was the oldest one in Pinetta – for years had been the *only* one. Some people said all we needed to do was replace a few planks, slap some paint on there and plant a row of azaleas beside the steps. Other people said it was time to tear the thing down and start over – build something we could be proud of. Maybe get an organ. The Baptists didn't have an organ, did they? But the conversation always came back to the same thing – where would the Methodists get the money for that?

Jack and Jewel Longmont owned the gas station store. They were the only people in Pinetta with any money. And they were Baptists. Which was why the new Baptist building was named Longmont Fellowship Hall.

In a while I saw Mother come out of the church with the preacher. They were laughing. She had her hands in the pockets of her dress. Her skin was shining with heat, her face flushed. She paused on the porch and lifted her hair up off her neck, just held it up on top of her head a minute, like she was trying to allow cooler air to reach her – but there was no cooler air. I couldn't hear what the preacher was saying to her, he was talking so quiet, but she smiled at him the way she smiled at one of us when we did something right.

Then she said, "Come on, Wade, honey." Wade stood up as slow as Christmas and walked down the steps one at a time like the object was to take as long as he could to do it. Daddy always said Wade had only one speed and it was reverse. Mother and

Wade walked across the churchyard to the road. Preacher Lyons stood on the steps, watching them, watching Mother, I thought. She looked like a woman dragging a heavy load and that load was Wade.

I knew the minute Mother noticed the naked women chalked on the front of the school. She stopped and stared like she had never seen – never mind been – a naked woman before. It was like I could see her neck go red. She glanced back at the church, where the preacher was standing like a man in a trance. She waved to him and he waved back. Then she crossed the dirt road and started home and Wade followed her with a stick in his hand.

Minutes later the preacher closed the windows he had opened and put on his hat and started his own walk home. When he got to the chalk women he stopped and stared. If you ask me, he overdid the staring. Then he took his hat back off and walked inside Pinetta School. I knew that was a bad sign.

I don't know why I did it, but as soon as the preacher disappeared into the school I snuck over to the church and let myself in. It was like entering God's oven – like I was accidentally sacrificing myself. I walked to the front pew and sat down. In front of me beside the piano was the attendance board. It said thirty-two for last week's attendance. The paper numbers were slipped into the wooden tray nailed to the wall. If I tried I could probably name all thirty-two people who'd been at church last week. Mrs. Freddy and her husband, Bye, were two of them. Add my family of five, made seven right there. Mrs. Ingram came every Sunday, but she didn't always bring Jimmy and his sisters. She never brought Mr. Ingram. I think she just liked a couple of hours out of the house every week without all six children underfoot, so she could pray for them in peace. She usually cried during the hymns.

The pulpit where the preacher stood on Sundays was bare, just a wooden elbow rest. The collection plates sat on a chair behind the pulpit. Heat shimmied through the place and the glass in the windows looked hot to the touch, like it was alive and writhing. There was a wasp near one window trying to escape, hitting the glass head-on, again and again, mystified and determined. And there were several greenheaded flies circling the pulpit. They made me think of angels – tiny, ugly ones. What if that was what flies really were – angels in disguise, sent to watch over things? I bet people wouldn't sit around with flyswatters in their hands then, slapping at what they thought was a nuisance.

I liked having the church to myself. It felt like being inside the wooden bones of a big person, like the pews were ribs and I was swallowed up inside there. Like I was the heart of it. I decided that as long as I was inside the church, I would pray for Sowell. Pray for his soul. Pray for his nasty mind. I laid down on the front pew and stared at the ceiling with its two lightbulbs hanging down overhead. *Dear God,* I said, *if Sowell was a house . . .* I didn't say it in words, I said it in feelings that just shot up out of me. It was God's job to catch them and make sense of them. *If Sowell was a house he would look small from the outside, a cottage-sized boy, but if you ever got inside you would find out he had a whole castle in there. He was so much bigger on the inside than on the outside that it was like magic. He had rooms inside him that I bet even he had never entered. There were parts of him he kept locked closed too, just so his life wouldn't be too big to handle, so big he could get lost inside himself, wander for days, for years, looking for the door leading back out to this small real world.*

Maybe one of the rooms he had unlocked was the cool, dark dungeon where he kept Mrs. Freddy a prisoner. Maybe he kept her there on a cot with starched white sheets and all she had to do was read in bed and take naps anytime she felt like it. Maybe she liked it and was happy, hidden away in that special part of Sowell's mind – where she had a maid to clean up after her, and her meals were carried to her on a tray. All she had to do was let Sowell look at her, let him touch her white skin. And not run away.

There was no welcome mat laid out in front of Sowell's house self. There was just an average-looking door that you could knock on if you wanted to and take your chances on getting him to open up. If I was not his sister, I wouldn't know any of this. My house self in the same neighborhood with his house self, with Wade's house self. Our yards touching, overgrowing the boundaries, unfenced, so that they spread together into one yard where trespassing was allowed. We knew something about the way each other's houses were laid out, about the trapdoors, the loose floorboards, the odd rooms – too big for a closet, too small for a bed – the wasted space, the attic jam-packed already with stuff that should be saved and stuff that should have been thrown out. Sowell was a castle boy living in our Pinetta white shoebox house. He was like a prince with an inadequate kingdom – just his half of the bed he shared with Wade on their side of our small bedroom.

And another thing. Sowell would kill a snake, but he would not kill a bird. I told God this. He would tell a lie to keep himself out of trouble but not to get somebody else into it. If Mother cried, he cried too. If Daddy made him tell the truth, he usually did. He took his licks for it. He didn't cry though, he got stony and retreated someplace within his interior castle with all its secret passages, surrounded by a throbbing moat of his red boy blood.

If you pray long enough, it starts to feel like emptying a suitcase. Next thing you know, you can carry it with one hand, then pretty soon there is nothing in it you need anymore, so you can just throw it away and travel light, so light, you are just like something floating. Like a prayer yourself.

I didn't want Sowell to be shamed. I didn't want people thinking he was worse than he really was, nastier than a normal boy. Especially not Daddy, since we had to live in the house with Daddy. We had to love him because that was the right thing to do. And we did. I swear. I thought of Daddy taking his belt out after Sowell, making him lie on the bed with his pants down while he lashed him with the buckle end of his belt and maybe made me and Wade watch – just so we could get the spillover from the lesson he was teaching Sowell. I could hear that slapping sound, like when Mother slapped hamburger meat into patties in the kitchen, it had a sound to it, meat to meat, *slap, slap, slap,* that you could recognize without seeing what she was doing. And I hated to see Sowell's bare butt, the bloody places where the buckle stabbed him. And just thinking about it made my stomach begin to churn. It was too hot in the church. I was so hot that the blood down around my guts was starting to boil and then – I tried not to, I really tried not to – I vomited up a lot of yellow-looking nothing all over the church floor. I got so dizzy I just laid still on the pew and closed my eyes. People said hell was even hotter than this, but I didn't see how.

Religion was the main sport in Pinetta. We had just two teams, the Methodists and the Baptists – and we kept score. This was mostly Bye Freddy's job. He got to church early to count cars in the parking lot. This was easy since the two churches faced each other with a gravel road like a dividing line between them.

Daddy drove us to church every Sunday, and Mrs. Ingram drove too, even though we could all easily walk. We did it because we wanted a good Sunday car count – everybody did. Bye would instruct us to park in such a way as to appear to have a full lot of cars. There was an art to it, the parking. When the actual service began Bye would announce, "Well, they beat us by two pickups and a blue sedan." It was rare when we Methodists won the car count. Or the attendance count either. But on any given Sunday we could win the hymn contest, which was based primarily on volume. We'd hear the Baptists sing a hymn and when they were through, Pastor Butch Lyons would lift his hands as a signal for us to stand. He'd shout out a page number. We'd thumb through our hymnals in a hurry, Mrs. Monroe or Mother would start hammering on the piano, and we would belt out that hymn with little regard for anything but enthusiasm. It was not singing as much as divine shouting. When we were through, Pastor Butch Lyons smiled and gave a little thumbs-up sign, saying, "I believe they heard that! I believe we got them there." Oh, like all good Christians, we loved healthy competition. The men especially loved it. Even the ones who couldn't actually sing a lick, who hated singing, belted out the gospel with souls afire. We took pride in our small numbers and strong lungs. We made that joyful noise like the Bible said to. God heard us too. And even if he didn't, the Baptists across the street certainly did.

Lying on the hard plank pew, I was either singing or dreaming, I'm not sure which. I know whichever one it was, I was going at it wholeheartedly in my mind. *How sweet the sound, that saved a wretch like me.* I'd lost any sense of time. I'd lost any sense of place. My prayers had led me first to puke, then to a peaceful place where redemption was possible. I was right at the edge of it too, the sea of righteousness. I dreamed I was drowning in righteousness, my clothes soaked, my skin slippery wet.

When my daddy was growing up on the farm he used to call the pigs by saying, *Sukeeeeeeee.* That was the way he called me too. *Berreeeeeee.* My name came to me, broken like that. *Berreeeeeee.* I could feel my name wrap around the corner of the church building, trying to get in. I could hear it the way you hear a snake rattle its tail. When I opened my eyes I didn't know where I was at first. It was dark out. My own name was the darkest thing of all.

It was like I had to unpeel my sleeping skin from the wooden pew, like I had gotten stuck there – glued – and it hurt to peel loose. I fumbled up and felt my way down the aisle toward the door. "Here I am," I said, but no sound came out.

When I pushed the church door open I saw Daddy in the road by the school, yelling my name into the night. He had a rhythm going, the way a loud cricket does.

"Here I am," I said. "Over here, Daddy."

Before I could stumble down the steps Daddy broke into a run and seeing him come toward me took my breath away. I felt like a girl under water. Daddy picked me up off the steps and shook me to see if I was real, then he hugged me against him so hard, so long that it scared me. "Where have you been?"

"I fell asleep," I said.

"What are you doing here, Berry? You scared us to death. Your mother is worried sick."

"I threw up," I said.

All this time Daddy just held on to me – hard – like he wanted this to be a moment imprinted on both of us. "Thank God," he said. "Are you all right?"

"I got sick," I said. "I laid down in the church."

"Why are you crying?" He looked at me hard. "Say?" He took my face in his hand. "Look at me." He put his face right in front of mine and he was red-eyed with fear. "What's wrong?"

"Where is Sowell?" I asked.

"Sowell?" Daddy stepped back. "What's Sowell got to do with this?"

"Nothing."

He took my hand and led me across the churchyard toward home. "You got a lot of explaining to do, missy."

Mother was on the porch and saw us walking up. "Thank you, Jesus," she said. "Berry, child, where on earth have you been?"

"Found her at the church," Daddy said. "Sleeping."

"At the church?" Mother sounded like she didn't believe it.

"Said she got sick. Threw up."

Mother took over from there. She pulled me away from Daddy and took me straight into the bathroom and closed the door. She wet a cloth in the sink and began to wash my face. "What is this all about?" she said. Her touch was so gentle, like she was lifting a Christmas tree ornament out of its box, not like somebody scrubbing the burned place off the bottom of a pot, the way she sometimes washed a bedtime face. "Mrs. Freddy said you disappeared from school today, Berry. Nobody had any idea where you were. Is that any kind of way to behave?"

"No," I said.

"Don't you think your daddy has enough to worry about without his own child worrying him half to death?"

"Yes, ma'am."

"I hope you're ashamed of yourself."

"Yes, ma'am."

"Get on your nightgown. When you've got a good explanation for this, I'd like to hear it."

As I walked out of the bathroom Mother said, "Berry, do you need some milk of magnesia?"

I shook my head no.

"Okay, then," she said.

"You're back," Sowell whispered when I went into the dark bedroom to put on my nightgown.

"Where were you?" Wade whispered.

"Nowhere," I told them.

There were lying still as two dead boys, flat on their backs, with the sheet pulled up to their bare chests.

"Mother thought one of those hobos kidnapped you or something," Sowell said. "She thought you fell in some quicksand."

"Daddy didn't eat his supper," Wade said. "He went to all the neighbors' houses and was yelling your name everywhere. He kept saying, 'This is not like Berry.'"

"Yeah," Sowell said. "He said, 'This is like something Wade would do.'"

"Shut up," Wade said.

I peeled back the sheet on my bed and laid down. I could hear Mother in the kitchen, fixing Daddy a plate of supper. They were talking, but I couldn't hear the words. I kept thinking about how Daddy had grabbed me, hugged me like something he loved so much he might have to crush me to make his point. I saw that love in his eyes. It was him almost crying that made me cry. Now I just wanted to be left alone, to go back into that sleep I had been in earlier – to get there and stay there.

Our yellow cat was not in the window sleeping. I remember the absence of the yellow cat that night, how I needed it but had no name for what I needed, so I looked at the windowsill right beside the head of my bed, wishing, but there was nothing there.

Just when we thought it was safe to fall asleep, Daddy came into our bedroom and turned on the light. "Berry," he said. "There is a consequence to every action. You know that, don't you?"

"Yes, sir."

"I'll deal with you in the morning." Then he turned off the light and left.

"Now you're in trouble," Sowell said.

Before breakfast the next morning, before we were even dressed for school, Daddy came into the bedroom with his belt in his hand. "I wish I didn't have to do this, Berry." He stood in the doorway like a roadblock in case I should try to make a run for it. That was what Wade usually did. Make Daddy chase him down first – then he got it twice as bad.

"She won't do it again," Sowell said. There was panic in his voice, not like when he got licks himself and just went rock quiet. "She's sorry."

"Sowell, you and Wade sit right there and don't you speak unless spoken to." Daddy's eyes hypnotized them into obeying. "This hurts me as much as it does anybody, but your sister here needs to learn that the same rules apply to her that apply to anybody else."

"What are you going to do?" Wade said.

"Three licks." Daddy rolled the belt around his hand.

I could hear the coffeepot percolating in the kitchen. I could smell the bacon frying and hear Mother setting the table, the sounds of plates and silverware settling into proper place. But she didn't come into the bedroom to see.

"Don't use the belt," Sowell said. "She's a girl."

Daddy looked at Sowell.

"Just use your hand," Sowell said, as if it were his job to instruct Daddy on punishment techniques. "Not the belt."

"If I want your advice, I'll ask for it. You want me to use this on you?"

"No, sir."

"I didn't think so."

I was not scared. I was not scared, because I was not really there. I was off someplace else, up, like a cloud or something. Like a not-human thing that just gets above the trouble, a bird maybe or an airplane heading for Miami Beach. "Take down your pants, Berry," Daddy said.

But I was a not-human thing.

"Take your pants down or I'll take them down for you," he said. I didn't look at Sowell or Wade, because I knew they were going blind like I was. I was a bird some boys had blinded with a BB gun, an airplane with all the windows busted out. I looked toward Sowell and Wade, but they were not there, just like I knew they wouldn't be, which was how I knew I wasn't there either. I did it. Pulled my shorts and panties down around my ankles. I did it like the good girl Daddy was trying to make me be.

"Lay across the bed," he said.

So I did. Laid down on my belly and closed my eyes.

"Three licks," Daddy said. "Is that fair, Berry? Do you think the punishment fits the crime?"

I nodded yes. *Yes* was the right answer. My eyes clinched shut like fists full of money.

I heard Daddy's belt drop to the floor, the noise the buckle made when it landed. Then I felt a lash across my skin. It was his bare hand. *Merciful God.* I jumped and a cry came out of me accidentally. The sting of it. "One," Daddy groaned. Then another hit. "Two." It was like slow motion. Each time I felt myself slam down into the mattress and my breath go out of me. Another hit. "Three."

Then there was nothing. Just my face buried in the bedsheet and Daddy's hard breathing. "Okay," he said. "Let this be a lesson to you."

I was playing dead.

"Get dressed and come eat your breakfast," Daddy said. I heard him pick up his belt off the floor. "Get a move on."

~

The chalked women were still on the front of the school. They were still naked. Like maybe somebody might draw some clothes on them while we were waiting for the guilty party to confess or be found out.

I sat in Mrs. Freddy's classroom all day with Daddy's handprints on me. Pink handprints, which would later be purple handprints. Mrs. Freddy said once that purple was the color of royalty. I wondered if she knew Daddy's handprints were on me. I wondered if it would make her change her mind about me. "You sure had people worried yesterday, Berry," was all she said.

Jimmy said, "Where did you go yesterday?"

I said, "None of your business."

It was Sowell's job to walk me home after school now, to make sure I went straight home and didn't wander off again. He did it like he was getting paid.

"Next time you decide to just leave school and walk off someplace and not tell anybody – maybe you'll think twice," he said. Sometimes Sowell imitated Daddy. But I could recognize when he was being himself and when he was being the son Daddy wanted him to be. I could tell the difference.

We were walking home by ourselves, which rarely happened. Usually Jimmy and his sisters walked with us because Rosemary always wanted to be around Sowell. Sometimes the Burdett kids walked with us too. But this day Daddy made us come by his office before we started home so he could lay his eyes on both of us and know for sure that the world was in its proper orbit.

I didn't like to walk through sandspurs, but Sowell didn't like to walk on the gravel, so we were walking home right along where the two met at the edge of the road, like walking with a haphazard dividing line between us.

"Did you draw those naked women on the school?" I asked.

"Me?" Sowell said. He kicked a pinecone. "No."

"Jimmy said you did."

"Since when does Jimmy know anything?"

"He said Rosemary told him."

"I didn't do it," Sowell said. "But I know who did."

"Don't tell me, then."

Sowell smiled. "You thought I did it?"

"Jimmy said."

"You've seen me draw." Sowell grinned. "You know I can draw better than that."

It was Thursday before Daddy called the whole school into the lunchroom first thing in the morning and announced that three boys had confessed to defacing the school. The Greene boy – Clyde, of cigarette fame – and the two Wilmont brothers. Earl Longmont, whose parents owned the gas station store, had confessed only to being there but swore he didn't touch a piece of chalk. He was guilty only by association. Guilty by witness.

"These boys have made a serious error in judgment," Daddy announced with the four boys standing in a lineup in front of the lunchroom. "They have been disciplined by the school and will be turned over to their parents for further discipline." Daddy paused as if he were waiting for the audience to burst into applause.

"These boys owe us all an apology," Daddy said. The boys stood with their hands in their pockets or behind their backs, looking mostly at their feet. Clyde Greene had on his usual high-water britches and no socks on in his too-big, hand-me-down shoes. Something about the looks of him made me think he wasn't really sorry.

Daddy said, "I offer these boys as an example of failure – failure to respect themselves or others, failure to respect school property, failure to use the good sense God gave them." Daddy turned and glared at the hang-neck boys. "Do any of you have anything to say to your fellow students?" he asked.

They all shook their heads no. Never took their eyes off the floor.

On Saturday Daddy took Sowell and Wade and me with him up to the school, where the boys were being brought by their parents and made to wash the front of the school with mop buckets of soapy water and old rags.

The parents – except Clyde Greene's mother, who didn't have a car and had sent him with the Wilmont brothers – stood around discussing what the world was coming to. This was Daddy's favorite subject. Mrs. Wilmont brought sweet tea for everybody as a way of showing how sorry she was about what her boys had done. Just because something terrible had happened, there was no need for people to stand around and be thirsty.

Wade and I sat in the grass like Daddy told us to, but not Sowell. He was pacing around like a cat on a rat's trail. "Why don't you sit down?" I said. But he wouldn't.

I don't know when the exact moment was when I realized that more than anything, Sowell wished that he *was* guilty. Even though the other boys were older than he was, Sowell wished to be one of the boys in trouble, getting publicly punished, humiliating himself in front of his own kind. It was killing him – this longing to confess to an uncommitted crime. It was like I could see him making the personal decision never to let such an opportunity get away from him again.

The naked women washed away pretty easily. They seemed to sort of melt off the building once the soapy rags started scrubbing their exaggerated shapes. It was like seeing a bunch of brazen women go right down the drain, sort of puddle around the bare feet of those boys. It was like instead of washing away sins, they were washing away the sinners too. Tits and all.

I watched them like I was drawn on that wall too – me – my shorts drawn down around my knees, and the boys at school dedicated to getting rid of me, just erasing me right out of the world. By the time the wall was cleaned off and all the parents were satisfied and the boys were forgiven and ready to go home, I felt really funny – like they had all put their hands on me.

Like they had touched me.

~

When I got glasses I didn't want them. Mother said she got worried about me the way I was always squinting and miscalculating what was in front of me. She said to Daddy, "Berry moves so timidly. Watch her." Those were her exact words. She said she could tell by the way I ran that I could not see where I was going or what I was about to run into. And it was always something, an ant bed, a water sprinkler, a barbed-wire fence, a clothesline, dog shit. At the time I had no idea there was more to the world than what I could see. What I could see seemed plenty enough.

The day I got those glasses – and I cried getting them because I knew it meant I was even more imperfect than I already felt – I knew people would all know how imperfect I was now when they saw me with those pink glasses on my face, my eyes magnified until they looked practically like the eyes of God. I stared at myself in the mirror for days afterwards, my eyes were about twice their normal size. They were about all there was to me.

Years later Mother would confess to me that when I was born they had given her some kind of knockout drug that was supposed to kill her pain during delivery and later they found out that it affected the eyesight of the baby when it was finally born. So she blamed herself for my glasses, but I never knew it. I was busy blaming myself.

"Four eyes!" Sowell had called me when I came home that first day with those glasses precariously balanced on my nose.

Daddy had hauled off and swatted Sowell so hard he fell to the ground on his knees. "That's no way to talk to your sister, son," he said. "I better never hear you talk like that again."

And nobody ever did hear Sowell say it again.

For days after getting my glasses I would not come out of the house. Mother had to try and bribe me with Popsicles and little cans of Vienna sausage, but it didn't work. Even her promises of trips to Cherry Lake to swim didn't put a dent in my resolve to stay indoors the rest of my life.

I didn't want Jimmy to see me, for one thing. Or anybody else. But another thing was, I didn't know for sure if I really wanted to see other people clearly for the first time in my life. Like Jimmy, for example. I was used to the pleasant blur he was, like a voice with hair on its head, with arms and legs that didn't show every mosquito bite he'd scratched into a scab, every strand of his black sweat necklace, every cavity in his open mouth when he ate a peach. Now I could see the rotten spots on my bananas and I didn't hardly like bananas anymore. I could see the gnats on sores and the flies on dog shit and the blink of the eye when somebody was lying. It was better before.

That was what was hard for Mother to understand, that it wasn't all about not wanting to be seen, but also about my not wanting to see. It felt like too much. Just lying in my bed, looking at the Sears and Roebuck catalog, was one hundred times a more powerful experience than it had been before. I could see the details. I could see the expressions on the models' faces and their fingernails and count the buttons on their dresses. It changed everything, being able to see.

This was what I believed. That my glasses were magic and when I had them on I could see more than nearly anybody around me. I could see things that nobody else could. At first I really hated that. But pretty soon I was locked into it.

At night when I took my glasses off, it felt like turning the world loose, removing myself from it to float in the sweet heat and darkness, excused from not understanding things. But when I put my glasses on each morning, it was like being allowed to know again. Well, actually, it was like being forced to know. People thought they could look right through those clear glasses on my face and see me, Berry Jackson, ordinary girl. But they couldn't. Those glasses were like a dimension, with the world on one side and me on the other. In my glasses I felt like the fourth dimension in a three-dimensional world.

~

"Your mama has got a pair of legs!" Daddy yanked up the hem of Mother's dress like he was going to show everybody what he meant. Like he was going to prove it.

Mother slapped his hand and said, "Behave yourself, Ford Jackson." Then she continued around the kitchen table, serving us chocolate pudding for dessert and pouring more iced tea.

"Come on, Ruthie," Daddy teased. "Show these children your beautiful legs. Give them a thrill."

We laughed because we could tell Mother was enjoying the teasing, that in this instance when she said, *Behave yourself,* she really meant, *Don't.*

"I know your mother raised you to act better than this, Ford," Mother teased. "If you keep it up, I'll just have to call her and tell on you." This made Daddy laugh. It was almost like he hoped she really would – just call his mother and tell on him. Tell her everything rotten he had ever done. Private things. Personal things.

Nights when Daddy was in a good mood like this at the supper table, nobody knew what he might do next, volunteer to wash the dishes, let us skip our baths, let us play outside long after all the lightning bugs and mosquitoes were battling each other for the night – winner takes all – read to us a chapter out of *David Copperfield* or *Huckleberry Finn,* which he believed gave us a full understanding of what lucky children we were, sneak us some cake after Mother plainly said we couldn't have any more. When he was happy like this he would take charge of things and just let Mother do what she wanted to, read a *Ladies' Home Journal* in the living room, put a red-tea rinse on her hair at the kitchen sink, go over to the Ingrams' and watch a Perry Mason television show, clip her toenails, or just sit out on the porch and stare at the night sky for as long as she wanted to, just barely bouncing back and forth in her low-slung metal chair, thinking something.

When Daddy put us to bed, after he kissed each of us, before he turned off the light, he would say, "You are the best children in the world. You know that, don't you? Don't think for a minute that I don't know it too." Then he would close the door to our room and we would be swimmy-headed in what he'd said, as drunk as children could get off a father's love. Intoxicated on his spoken word.

Then he would go find Mother, search the world over if he had to, and the next thing we would hear would be her laughing. It was like we thought heaven would be if we made it there – our Mother laughing like that.

Mother only wore shorts inside the house. If she had to go anywhere else, then she always put on her everyday dress. She thought this was ridiculous. But Daddy thought it was not right for a principal's wife – any more than a preacher's wife – to go around barelegged in shorts. He liked to be the only person who stared at Mother's legs when she went around the house doing her work, bending, lifting, squatting, kicking – her bare legs like a second pair of arms.

Once Jimmy's daddy, Mr. Ingram, came over to our house looking for Jimmy and he saw Mother standing at the stove, frying green tomatoes in her shorts, and he whistled at her. She smiled and was the nicest she had ever been to him, because usually she didn't like him much.

His whistle brought Daddy in from the living room, where he had been reading the *Tallahassee Democrat* and smoking cigarettes. It made him happy, I think, and mad too, Mother getting paid attention to by another man.

~

Every family in Pinetta invited Daddy to supper at least once a year. They had to, since he was the school principal. It would be too rude not to, no matter how poor you were. The Millers were always our favorite family to eat with, partly because they were so raw-boned and dirt-poor, it made them pure fascinating. We'd been going to their house once a year for as long as we'd lived in Pinetta and we'd come to look forward to it. There was not one thing normal and boring about the Millers. I think they were proud of that too. Daddy said they were the kind of family every place needed because they proved to the rest of us that no matter what we thought about our own circumstances, we were not that bad off – comparatively speaking. There should have been some comfort in that. But the way the Millers went at proving this point was unusual, because when they were through talking their old-fashioned talk, displaying their neediness and lack of everything – instead of feeling sorry for them, you were dead jealous. It wasn't just me. It happened to everybody. Whatever the Millers might lack in worldly possessions they made up for in pure excitement. I swear. You'd drive home to your nice house in your nice car and think, *I wish I lived in a kudzu-covered shack like the Millers. I wish I didn't have indoor plumbing or decent shoes or good sense.*

There were terrible rumors about Mr. Miller, of course, the violent lengths he went to to keep his kids in line – especially Rennie, now that she had grown into a beauty without his permission or cooperation. Neither poverty nor pain could keep her from shining out like a flash of lightning. Nothing the Bible said made her ashamed of her beauty either. She did not long to repent and be saved. That was the thing. Rennie was known to prove all the ugly rumors true by showing bruises, scrapes, and cuts – sometimes human bite marks – under her clothes. She was famous for these revelations and displays. People would have paid good money to see the evidence – if anybody had had good money. Consequently, Rennie Miller was as near as Pinetta had to a hometown actress. Her sense of drama transcended anything the rest of us could ever dream up on our wildest day – if we'd ever had a wildest day, which for the most part we had not. None of us.

We first developed more than a passing interest in Rennie and the Millers about a year and a half ago when Rennie, out of the blue, stopped coming to school. Ordinarily, Daddy did not allow anybody to stop coming to school. He went out to the Millers' to investigate her absence and Mr. Miller swore that Rennie had run off and nobody knew where to. All Mrs. Miller did was rock back and forth in her straight-back chair and cry.

"What you mean *run away?*" Daddy'd said. "There's nowhere out here to run to."

"That girl is wild as a buck," Mr. Miller said. "Probably run off with some no-count boy."

"That don't sound like Rennie," Daddy said. "She wouldn't go off and worry her mama like that." He looked at Mrs. Miller, tears running down her tired face. "Would she now?"

Mrs. Miller shook her head no, but didn't speak a word.

"Those are not alligator tears you crying, are they?" he asked.

"She don't do nothing but sit around here and cry all day

long," Mr. Miller answered for her. "She gets like that whenever she's in a family way."

"That right, Mrs. Miller?" Daddy asked. "I guess I ought to congratulate you then."

She just looked at him with hard eyes and never nodded either yes or no.

When Daddy got home that night he was shook up. Mother made him some iced tea with whiskey and lemon and they sat outside in the dark of night in those rusty yard chairs, talking. We had gone to bed and Wade and Sowell were dead asleep, but I could hear broken bits of sentences coming in the window where our yellow cat sat licking her paws.

"They tried to say Rennie has run away," Daddy said. "Shoot, I hope to God they hadn't gone and killed her or something."

"Lord, Ford, you don't think they'd really do that?" Mother said.

"I wouldn't put it past them," he said. "Strange as they are. You've heard the stories."

Rennie didn't come to school the rest of the year. And nobody saw her all summer long either. Then next thing you know, it's the first day of the new school year, still hot enough to bake biscuits on the hood of a car, and here comes Rennie Miller in her black dress and men's box shoes, carrying her book satchel. Her hair was springing loose from the knot she had it in, curls escaping in the humidity, giving her an uncorked look. She showed up with some of her brothers and nobody much remarked on her return. Nothing the Millers did ever really surprised anybody. When Daddy called Rennie into the office to question her on her whereabouts, he said her only explanation was "I just run off for a while. That's all. I'm back now."

"Run off where?" Daddy asked.

"I stayed with some people you don't know."

"I know everybody around here," Daddy insisted.

"It wasn't around here. They live off," she said.

"You set yourself back a year, Rennie," he said. "You won't graduate with the others now."

"I wouldn't come back at all except for the baby. Mama's baby."

"Cadell told me your mama had a newborn. She doing okay?"

"Her milk didn't come down," Rennie said. "She's had a rough time out there with only Daddy and them boys to do for her."

"Well, it's good you're back," Daddy said. "Don't you go off like that again without alerting the school. You hear me? Lots of people around here were worried about you."

"Yes, sir." Rennie nodded.

At supper that night when Daddy was telling this, he said, "Rennie is a mystery. You can't believe but half of what she tells you. But it's what she don't tell that puzzles me."

"I guess she's got her reasons," Mother said.

"Her reasons. That's what interests me," Daddy said.

It interested me too. But I, for one, knew we'd most likely never know Rennie's reasons. Maybe it was best if we didn't. But I didn't say that to Daddy.

Since she came back, Rennie had been as regular as clockwork at school. She got her homework every day and her grades were up. Her tales of beatings and such kept right on like always, which intrigued and satisfied people. And things were back to normal.

* * *

Daddy knew where every soul in Pinetta lived. It was like a point of pride with him, finding houses that were especially designed not to be found – such as the Miller house. You had to know where you were going out in those woods. Mother said she guessed Daddy was part bloodhound. There wasn't a child or a family in all of Pinetta that could hide from Daddy.

Sowell and Wade and I washed up and put on clean clothes and loaded into the backseat of the car, fighting over who got to sit by the windows. I never won. I always sat on the hump.

Mother had curled her hair and she sat in the front seat with a cake she made herself wrapped in tinfoil on her lap. It was a devil's food cake with seven-minute icing. Because she had fixed her hair, she wouldn't let Daddy or us roll down the windows much since it would blow her hair to bits and then she would have to be in a bad mood all the rest of the evening. So we cracked the windows just enough for a wasp to escape in case there was a wasp loose in the car. Daddy sat behind the wheel in a white short-sleeved shirt with a necktie knotted loosely around his wet neck. We all sweated in anticipation of the supper looming before us out at the Miller house, not because the supper would be good. It would not. It was usually something left over from the morning and served to us cold, like cold sausage, cold grits, and cold greens. Even the biscuits, if there were any, would be cold. And no butter. Water to drink, which Mrs. Miller sent one of the boys after, out to the pump beside the chicken pen, which hardly had any chickens in it, with a bucket in his hand. We drank out of canning jars.

The Millers had nine children in all, mostly boys older than us. When we pulled up in front of the house it looked like nobody lived there. It was an old, unpainted house with its front porch falling off. The roof was patched with tar paper and scrap lumber. If a house was a person, then this one would be suffering from a broken heart to go along with all the rest of the brokenness. In the summer the Millers let the kudzu grow right up the sides of the house and onto the roof. The house looked deserted, left to the loving embrace of those green vines the way a dying carcass is left to the loving advances of buzzards.

"Why do they let the kudzu grow up over the house like that?" Mother said. "You know there's a world of snakes tangled up in that kudzu."

"Mr. Miller claims it keeps the house cool," Daddy said.

If it weren't for the dogs coming out from under the porch and barking like maniacs, you would not believe human beings actually lived there. But as soon as Daddy got the car stopped, here came Mr. Miller with the biggest smile on his face. He was wearing work pants and an undershirt and suspenders and his hair was greased and parted with a couple of strands hanging loose in his face. He was tall and dark eyed. I had the feeling that if he could ever get totally clean, he might be almost handsome. It was mostly his bad reputation that ruined his looks.

"Hey, there, Mr. Miller," Mother sang out.

Out the lopsided front door that hung open, not a dozen paces behind Mr. Miller, came a string of his sons, tall and lanky all, dark haired like their daddy. They had good faces mostly, nice teeth, big hands like their daddy too and either bare feet or shoes with no socks. Either shirts or no shirts. They looked half washed, like somebody had made each of them slap some water on his face so he could call himself clean.

"Y'all come around back," Mr. Miller said. "Mrs. Miller is around to the back." He led us on a path around the side of the house. The dogs sniffed us with wild excitement. They sniffed me right between my legs and would not stop. I had to slap the fool out of them.

"Hey there, boys." Daddy pounded the Miller brothers on the back. He had had every one of them in Pinetta School at one time or another – still had most of them. "Been staying out of trouble, I hope," he said, even though he knew better.

"We got us a ball game going out back," one of the boys said. It was Cadell. He seemed like the only one who talked. The rest made me think of a herd of spindly-legged deer. They were skittish like that. And sort of pretty eyed. And grinning too.

I trailed along directly behind Mother, who held that cake out in front of her like it was a crown on a tray intended to make Mrs. Miller feel like queen for a day. "Look where you step, Berry, honey," Mother said to me. For a path it was pretty overgrown. I guessed the Millers had just as soon we didn't all stomp through their house just to get to the backyard. They probably didn't want us to see inside their so-called house. All that wall-to-wall nothing they had in there.

Around the back of the house was a swept yard. It was like colored people do their yards in Tallahassee and Alabama. The sand was so smooth you hated to walk on it and mess it up. Underneath a shade tree sat Mrs. Miller in a straight-back chair. She was a plain woman. You know, one of the plain people, whose religion makes her be plain – even plainer than necessary. The Millers went to the Baptist church though, whenever they went to church at all, and the Baptists did not insist on plainness in their women. Just the opposite. Take Jewel Longmont, for example, she was as decorated as a Christmas tree. At least that's what Mother always said. "She looks like something that needs to be plugged in," Mother said, always studying Jewel's clothes down to the very last detail. Mother always knew better what Jewel Longmont had on than what she had on herself. Lots of women in Pinetta were like that. I personally thought Jewel Longmont was as glamorous as Elizabeth Taylor and only married once, at age sixteen to Mr. Longmont, who owned everything in Pinetta. Now she was older than Mother and had a bunch of kids, but still there was nothing plain about Jewel Longmont. She had more pride than to let herself completely go like that.

In fact, Mrs. Miller was the only woman I'd ever seen, religious or not, who was dead serious about plainness. She wore a black dress that came all the way to the ground. She wore a pair of men's black shoes. Her hair was parted in the middle and pulled back into such a tight knot it looked like her eyes wouldn't blink. She wore an old-timey bonnet that was so embarrassing to see her in, made her look like somebody just off a wagon train west. It made her look one hundred years old, like she was supposed to be from the olden days but had somehow got mixed up and ended up in present-day Pinetta and didn't know the difference. She stood up when she saw us, peeled that bonnet off her head – which we all appreciated – smiled at Mother, took the cake from her hands, saying, "Honey. But you ought not to done this." She handed the cake to her daughter Rennie, who peeled back the tinfoil and studied it closely, then took it into the dark house, carried it like you carry a newborn baby.

"Y'all sit down," Mrs. Miller said. She motioned to a couple of cane-bottom chairs and a homemade bench clustered underneath the sprawl of a chinaberry tree. She picked up a palmetto leaf that she was using as a fan and waved it to chase flies off the bench. "The flies is bad this year," she said.

Mother sat down and smoothed the skirt of her dress. She

crossed her legs, then uncrossed them. Sowell and Wade and I stood practically in a straight line, like three soldiers waiting for our orders – or waiting for somebody to say, *At ease.*

"Y'all boys want to play some ball?" Cadell yelled to Sowell and Wade. He was climbing over a fence that lined a pasture with two worn-out cows in it, bony-backed cows, grazing on sandspurs. "Your daddy give us this baseball," Cadell said. "It come from over at his school."

"Is it all right?" Sowell made the question out of his eyes.

"Go ahead." Daddy nodded. Sowell and Wade took off after Cadell.

"Take your shoes off first," Mother yelled. "No need to scuff up your shoes." She looked at Mrs. Miller, who sat gripping that palmetto leaf. "You know how hard boys are on shoes."

Mrs. Miller smiled. Her boys were almost every one barefooted – or else had on shoes not much better than make-believe.

Sowell and Wade left their shoes and socks at the fence like crime evidence. Their feet looked strangely pink for a minute, like something so private and personal we shouldn't be looking at them. But no sooner were they over the fence and running across the pasture than the sand coated their sweaty feet and made them look right again, normal.

"You come on too, Mr. Jackson," Cadell yelled to Daddy. "You ain't too old."

"Too old?" Daddy grinned.

"If you ain't too old then," Cadell yelled, "you come on and prove it."

"Did I ever tell you boys I played some baseball in the army? Say? Did I ever mention that to you boys?" Daddy sat down on the bench beside Mother and took off his shoes and socks and rolled up his pants legs. Mother was smiling at him like he was doing something truly remarkable. There they were, his own two pink feet with those yellow toenails that bothered me to look at them.

"Those boys think I'm hobbling around with a cane?" Daddy said. "Is that what they think?"

"You be careful now, Ford. You hear me?" Mother smiled. This was one of those rare moments when it was clear that Mother actually loved Daddy. She could have passed a lie detector test right at that moment if she had to.

Next thing I knew, Daddy was climbing over the fence into the pasture and Cadell yelled to Mr. Miller, "Come on, Daddy. You got to play. Thataway we got us a old man on both sides."

"I'll show you old man," Mr. Miller yelled. He was already barefooted and he leaped the fence like he was a boy instead of the daddy of six boys.

"Mother." I nudged her quietly. "Can I play too?"

"Berry, sweetie." She reached for my hand and pulled me down beside her on the bench. "You visit with Mrs. Miller and me, why don't you."

Rennie came out of the house, carrying her baby sister with her. The baby had that sleep look folded into her face like children do when they wake up but haven't come all the way back to life yet. "Hey, sweetie," Mother said to the child. "You're a precious little angel, aren't you?"

"This is Babygirl," Mrs. Miller said.

"That's a healthy-looking baby," Mother said.

Babygirl stared at Mother with a blank face. Rennie bounced her up and down, trying to coax her to life. "Say hey, Babygirl. These people come for supper. You be nice and say hey." Babygirl looked like a cherub out of the Bible. "She's spoilt," Rennie said. "Can't nobody make her do nothing she don't want to do." Rennie said this like it made her so proud she didn't hardly know what to do with herself over it.

"Where's Little Sister?" Mrs. Miller asked Rennie.

"I told her to come say hello to the company, but she acts like I told her to stick her foot in a fire." Rennie shifted Babygirl to her other hip, where she hung on like a little plump pink monkey.

"Oh, that child is a puzzle." Mrs. Miller shook her head. "Scared of her own shadow."

"Little Sister is real timid," Rennie explained. "The school said they's something wrong with her head but there ain't. She is too bashful to talk to folks is all. Her head is plenty good."

As if on cue, Little Sister came walking down the back steps – which was a stack of cinder blocks – and first thing a black dog came over to her with his tongue hanging. She held on to the fur on his neck and took the steps one at a time, slow, slow, trying to make us give up on watching her, I guess. She had dark hair like the boys and it was in tight plaits. She had on a black sack dress with a tear in it. No shoes.

Little Sister had been in first grade with me a long time ago – on the rare occasions when she had actually come to school. Mrs. Freddy had given the class a talking-to about being extra nice to Little Sister, about going the extra mile and helping her get used to us by showing her how kind we could be. Mostly we did, except some boys who said, "You ain't none my little sister. Why don't you get you a real name?" Mrs. Freddy had to snatch them up by the necks of their shirts and drag them outside for a second dose of talking-to. Next thing you know, Little Sister just stopped coming to school altogether. Seemed like there was nothing much Daddy could do about it. Daddy had told Mother, "We don't have the answers for a child like Little Sister."

"Hey, Little Sister," I said. "Is that your dog?" But she just kept on working her way down the steps like she was a little deaf-mute child, which she was not. That was how she had been at school too. Pretending she couldn't see nothing, couldn't hear nothing. She was my age, but she acted like she wished she was Babygirl's age, like she was planning to go backwards all her life instead of forward if she had a say in the matter.

"Little Sister," Rennie said, "you come on over here and say hey to Mrs. Jackson and Berry."

Little Sister made her way across the swept yard and stood beside Mrs. Miller, rubbing one foot all over the other, like she was standing in an ant bed. "Scoot over, Berry," Mother said. "Make a place for Little Sister." So I did. She sat down, just like a little dark ghost.

It was Rennie that had my attention. I couldn't hardly take my eyes off her. She dressed plain too, but it didn't look as bad on her as it did on Mrs. Miller. She had on a long black dress like her mother, but hers was loose like a slip with sleeves in it. She was barefoot and her hair was knotted behind her like her mother's, but it was shiny and strands had sprung loose and curled around her head like ribbons. She was not plain, no matter what she didn't do. Rennie was the kind of girl who could not be plain under any circumstances. The kind of girl I wanted to be.

"They won't let you play, will they?" she said to me. "Them boys."

"I don't want to play," I lied.

"It's a stupid game," she said. "Hit a ball with a stick and then run around in a circle like a chicken with its head cut off. What kind of game is that?" Rennie looked at me and smiled.

We could hear the boys shouting in the pasture. It was nonsensical, their yelling, but it gave off a good feeling – not like shouting usually does. Sometimes it was Daddy's voice that came to us the loudest of all. "Run, Sowell, son," he'd yell. "Touch the base. Attaway. Attaway. Okay, Cadell. Batter up. Batter up."

"Mrs. Jackson brought us a cake, Little Sister," Rennie said.

Little Sister's face twisted into a smile. She rubbed her feet together and looked at Mother.

"You like chocolate, Little Sister?" Mother asked. "I made seven-minute icing."

We hadn't been there long, but already I had to go to the bathroom. The trouble was, the Millers didn't have a bathroom. I remembered that from all the other times we'd come to supper. Their outhouse was a long way off too. On the ride out here Mother warned us, "Don't any of you dare ask to use the bathroom tonight. In the name of decency, do not make the Millers tell us – again – they don't have a bathroom. I mean it now. We're not going to be rude about a thing like this." We said okay. Then her last words to us right before we got out of the car were "I don't want to hear the word *bathroom* spoken. You understand me?" We nodded yes, that we understood. "Sowell, you and Wade just step quietly into the woods if you need to pee. Don't draw attention to yourselves. And, Berry, honey, don't you drink any water if it's offered, just try and hold on until we get back home."

But I couldn't. Now Mother was mad. "Berry, for heaven's sake," she said when I told her.

Rennie saw me squirming. "Come on with me," she said. "I'll walk you to the outhouse."

Mother smiled. "That's nice, Rennie." She looked at me with no smile.

We walked along a wire fence beside the baseball game. "I hate baseball," Rennie said. "For the life of me, I don't see the fun in it."

"What do you like to play?" I asked.

"I don't like to *play* nothing, honey. I like to do *real* thangs."

"Me too," I said, although I had no idea what real things I was talking about.

It was like Rennie knew immediately I was lying, just looked at me and knew, so we just walked along without saying anything until we were out of sight of the house. "I hadn't seen Little Sister in a long time," I said, just to interrupt the silence.

"Daddy's got Little Sister messed up," Rennie said.

"Why?" I asked.

"Daddy likes to mess with people – especially his own family. Look at Mama. She proves the point. If I had a gun, I swear I'd shoot Daddy. I mean it." She held back a blackberry bush so I could get by without my legs getting clawed. "You got the nicest daddy I know anything about," Rennie said. "He treats people decent."

"Thank you," I said. It was not a subject I was in the mood to explore.

"I'd give anything if I had your daddy for mine," Rennie said. "Me and you'd be sisters."

Before I could enjoy thinking about this splendid notion, Rennie as my sister, she said, "Look out for snakes now." She stooped down to pick up a stick and I saw that it was a stick left especially in this spot for especially this purpose. She began to beat the stick along the path, right and left, the way a blind girl would use a stick. "This warns snakes we're here," she said. "I stepped on a snake out here once. A rattler big as my arm."

I kept quiet because I didn't want to hear the details of it.

The outhouse was made out of some boards nailed to three trees. Inside was a hole dug in the dirt with a couple of boards hammered over it. Before I even got inside I started gagging. "You go ahead," Rennie said. "I'll wait for you right here."

It was dark inside. If snakes were in there, you'd never be able to see them. My plan was to hurry up and get this over with. I pulled my panties down around my ankles and pinched my nose to stop the awful smell and squatted over the hole. Pee ran down my leg and I tried my best not to get my shorts messed up. I pulled my panties up and came out and felt like I had just done something brave and athletic – something at least as complicated as baseball.

"Okay," I said. "We can go back now."

"Not yet," Rennie said. "Follow me." She led me down the path behind the outhouse, slapping her stick at the ground as she went. I followed her into a clearing and then across the clearing to where a muddy stream ran through a patch of trees. In the fork of one of the largest trees was a tin can. Rennie used her stick to pry the can loose and it dropped to the ground at her feet. She picked up the can and reached inside and pulled out a crumpled pack of cigarettes. "You can't tell nobody," she said. "Sit down over here."

I followed her to the stream and we sat on the bank and she put her bare feet in the water. She pulled a small box of matches out of the cigarette pack and put a cigarette in her mouth and lit it. "You want one?" she asked.

"No," I said. But I did. I just didn't know how to do it – smoke. I didn't want her to see that.

She sucked on that cigarette so hard and her cheeks caved in so pretty, like dimples, but better. Then she blew the smoke out long and slow, and it came out her nose too, and it was really a very beautiful sight.

"Who gave you those cigarettes?" I asked.

"You wouldn't believe me if I told you," she said. "It's somebody you know too."

"Who is it?" I asked. I was thinking it might be Sowell. Once Daddy had taken a pack of cigarettes from Clyde Greene at school and Sowell had stolen them and hid them in the hole in the weeds where he liked to smoke them when he thought nobody was looking. Clyde Greene's mother had had the gall to ask Daddy to return those confiscated cigarettes to her, since they were paid for and rightfully belonged to her. "Somebody could use those cigarettes," she insisted. When Daddy went to get them he couldn't find them. Mrs. Greene acted like she didn't believe him for a minute. Daddy finally put her in the car and drove her to the store and bought her a new pack of Camels. I know because I rode with them, got a pack of cheese crackers and a grape Nehi. Daddy did it partly because Mrs. Greene was a widow with a sad story and a badly behaved son she could not control. She needed a scrap of pleasure in her worn-out life. While he was at it, he bought her a loaf of Sunbeam bread and a carton of eggs and a quart of milk. But it was the cigarettes she appreciated most. "Don't you let Clyde get hold of these," Daddy told her. "If I catch him with cigarettes again, I'll take them away again. Next time I won't replace them either."

She opened the pack of cigarettes and lit one. She blew smoke and picked a piece of tobacco off her tongue. "Clyde is a good boy," she said. "I'm proud of him."

"If you didn't love your boy, what kind of mother would you be?" Daddy said. We drove back to where Mrs. Greene caught a ride home with one of the Miller boys.

Now Rennie was sucking her cigarette the same as Mrs. Greene had. Getting that scrap of pleasure from it. "I didn't think plain women were supposed to smoke," I said to Rennie.

She laughed. "Plain women ain't supposed to do nothing."

"What'll they do if they catch you?"

"Nothing they ain't already done a bunch of times."

"Whip you?"

Rennie laughed the sweetest laugh. It was not bitter, like a laugh that is not really a laugh because it is full of poison. Sometimes Mother laughed that way – like she thought we wouldn't notice all the poison in her laugh. No, Rennie's laugh was real. "If whipping me would help, then I'd be near about perfect by now. I'd be a angel." She smiled. "Whippings don't scare me."

"They scare me," I said.

"That's 'cause you ain't had enough to get immune to them. You know what I do when my daddy whips me? I laugh."

"Does he make you pull down your pants?" I asked.

"Oh, he tries to," she said. "But I ain't scared of him. You know what I say when he starts whipping me? I say, 'Okay then, Daddy, I'm gon find me a boy and run off and marry him and you ain't never gon see me again.' Oh, he goes crazy. He does like a wild man."

I tried to picture Rennie getting a whipping. What could she do that was so bad her daddy would want to whip her? Smoke cigarettes? Was that it?

"I'm not gon be plain all my life," Rennie said. "No, sireee, God and Jesus, I am not. I'm going to have me some dresses like Mrs. Longmont wears to church. I'm going to have perfume and stockings and earbobs and everything I want. I know it like I know me and you are sitting here in this ditch. I just know it."

"Me too," I said. I could picture what she was saying. I could see it easy.

"You know what else?" Rennie said. "I'm going to marry a rich man and move away from here, maybe off to Jacksonville. They got lots of soldiers over in Jacksonville. I might marry me a soldier. The government pays them good."

"My daddy was a soldier," I said. It was a stupid thing to say.

"I'm gon live in a fine house with fine furniture and curtains everywhere and have me lots of babies and maybe send for my mama to come live with me. She's gon have her own room and she can stay plain if she wants to, or she can change – it won't matter to me."

Rennie was so beautiful saying this that I couldn't stop staring at her. How did she think these things up? I wanted desperately to be like Rennie, dreaming things, swearing they will happen, letting no amount of whippings kill the desire in me for a big surprise of a life. Rennie's face was pure radiant, like those angels lit up by halos painted on the fans at church. God loves Rennie. That's the thing. I swear, you can see it plain as day. Anybody can. His love for her.

"I'll be wearing high heels and dancing to all that rock and roll music." Rennie closed her eyes and smiled, then looked at me. "I already know how to dance. Nobody showed me how, I just showed myself. I can do it pretty good. I think about wearing a bought dress, you know, and dancing with a boy and him twirling me all over the place, saying compliments right and left, you know, just being real wild about me and all, and I don't know how to explain it, but I know it will happen like I know I'm sitting here. So my daddy can whip me every day of my life if he wants to, but he can't stop me from running off when I'm good and ready."

"What about going to hell?" I asked. "Don't that scare you?"

Rennie tapped her cigarette ashes into the creek. "I believe I am going to like hell, honey." She smiled at me.

"Your daddy don't seem that mean," I said. "He don't seem so hateful."

"He's mean as that snake I stepped on that time," she said.

"He don't seem like it," I said again.

"I hate him. I wish he was dead."

I went silent then because Rennie was saying the word *hate.* Mother tried not to let me and Sowell and Wade say we hated things. It wasn't actually that she minded if we hated things, because some things needed to be hated, they were meant for hatred – but it was just the saying of it that Mother objected to. What we *felt* was mostly our own business, but what we *said* was Mother's business. She had been known to swat us if we said, "I hate this, I hate that. . . ."

"There's going to come a day when you'll be talking just like I'm talking, Berry Jackson." Rennie smiled. "I recognize it in you. See, Little Sister is not like me and you. She is soft as a feather, just blow on her and she is all over the place. She's the fall-apart type because Daddy has done ruined her. But me and you are not like that. We're hardheaded. That's what's going to get us out of here for sure, out of Pinetta, Florida. Ain't that right?"

"Yes," I said. But I didn't believe it. I didn't understand sureness – what it was or how you got it. I didn't think I was a bit hardheaded. I thought I was about as sweet as I knew how to be and already I was just about exhausted from trying to be so sweet all the time. But whether it was true or not was not the point. The point was, Rennie thought I was like her, and God knows I wanted to be. It seemed like just sitting there at the creek, watching her smoke that cigarette, I was falling in love with her just the way she was planning on falling in love with a nice boy as soon as one came along.

First Mrs. Freddy. Now Rennie. Was I going to fall in love with everybody in the world who was fun to look at and halfway nice to me?

"You're beautiful, Rennie," I said.

"Not yet," she said. "But I will be. You wait and see."

"My daddy thinks you already are," I said. "He's mentioned it before. Mother too." Now this was not exactly the God's honest truth, but it was close. Maybe they didn't actually remark on Rennie's beauty, but they noticed it. I saw it today and I'd seen it lots of times before. People look at beautiful people with such forgiveness in their eyes. They have more hope for them, more vision for what their lives should be.

"You daddy has always been kind to me," Rennie said, blowing smoke. "Your mama too."

We didn't see Mr. Miller come over the rise behind us. It wasn't until he hollered out that we knew he was there. "Rennie, that better not be a goddamned cigarette you got in your hand." Just the sound of his voice sent a chill down my spine and I flinched.

"Oh shit." Rennie snuffed out her cigarette. She didn't turn around and look at him. "Berry, if he gets after me, you run away, you hear? Get to the house as quick as you can."

I was trying to think if I could even find my way back to the house. I had just followed along with Rennie, not paying any real attention to where we were going. I was likely to run in the wrong direction, likely to get lost. The thought of quicksand crossed my mind.

Before we got up from the creek's edge Mr. Miller was down the hill and taking almost a running dive at Rennie. She sat still, frozen in place. "Get yourself up from there, girl," he shouted. His eyes were blazing like a fire.

"You go on, Berry," Rennie said. "Now."

My legs were shaking so bad I could hardly get up off the ground. But it was like Mr. Miller didn't even see me. He was so set on Rennie. He swooped down on her like a hawk and snatched her arm so rough she let out a little scream. "What you telling this girl?" he said. "More of your damn lies?"

"Nothing," I whispered, but he didn't seem to hear me.

"Don't you believe nothing this girl says." He was talking to me, but not looking at me. "She's a liar. Ain't that right, Rennie? You a goddamned liar, ain't you? Tell the girl what a liar you are."

"She wasn't lying," I said, but I'm not sure my voice had any sound to it.

"Stand up." Mr. Miller yanked Rennie to her feet. The look on her face was awful. I saw the fury there. I saw that she had lied to me about not being scared. She was scared.

"Go on, Berry," Rennie said again. "Go home."

"You can't believe nothing this girl says." Mr. Miller's fiery eyes were fixed on Rennie.

I saw her try to pull away from Mr. Miller. "Let go of me," she said. It was like she was spitting at him. "Turn loose of me."

He hauled off and slapped her face, hard.

I screamed. But she didn't. "Stop it," I yelled. "Don't." My stomach flipped and I felt vomit move up to my throat.

Rennie wrestled with him for a few seconds, trying to pry herself loose from his grip. She was kicking at him with her bare feet and her face had gone red with rage. She clawed at him and bared her teeth, biting her own lip hard. I watched Mr. Miller sling her to the ground like a sack of something. She hit hard, her head bounced backward and the breath went out of her. Her face went pale and she made sounds like the time Wade had the croup and sucked air so loud and desperate I was scared he would die. Now I was scared Rennie would.

Mr. Miller straddled her and held her hands to the ground. She was thrashing wildly, trying to get some air. The inhale sound was like a scream turned inside out. I thought he might kill her with his weight on her ribs like that, and me standing there, watching. I don't remember telling myself to scream. I didn't know it was me making the shrill, throbbing noise until I saw Daddy and Cadell and the other boys come running over the rise, sweaty and loud from their baseball game – their wide startled eyes on me. Daddy saw Mr. Miller on top of Rennie just as he backhanded her across the face, hard. "She can't breathe," I screamed. "He's killing her."

Daddy hollered, "Good Lord," and ran to where Mr. Miller was pressing Rennie down into the dirt. Daddy went at Mr. Miller, pushing him off Rennie, shouting, "What the hell you think you're doing?" Mr. Miller swung at Daddy, his fist clenched, his teeth clenched, his hair flying across his face. Daddy kicked him in the belly, hard, so hard that Mr. Miller hollered out and fell back. Rennie was trying to get up and get away. She was scrambling. "Get her out of here, Cadell," Daddy yelled.

Cadell and the others grabbed Rennie and pulled her to her feet. "Come on," they coaxed, as if she needed to be convinced to go with them. "Come on, Berry," Cadell shouted at me. "Get out of here."

I stood paralyzed, watching blood gush from Daddy's nose where Mr. Miller had hit him. "Sowell, y'all get your sister," Cadell shouted. "Bring her here."

Sowell ran to me, grabbed my wrist and yanked me along. "Come on, Berry."

Rennie was bent over, her head at her knees, still trying to get her breath back. She was wheezing, walking along bent in half that way, her hand on her belly, trying to run but stumbling instead. I ran to her. "You okay, Rennie? You okay? You okay?" I guess I said it a thousand times.

She grabbed my hand and squeezed it so maybe I would hush. We walked back to the house like that, holding hands, her struggling to breathe, two of her brothers holding her up, walking along with us in silence. Sowell and Wade walking beside me, but staring back at Daddy and Mr. Miller, two grown men fighting like a pair of tomcats. I shook like a leaf, my heart kicking so hard it hurt.

Cadell and the other boys stayed back with Daddy. Daddy's lip was busted and bleeding all over his shirt. His sweaty hair was messed up and wild-looking. Mr. Miller made it up on his feet and lunged at Daddy, making a low growling noise before going down on all fours. "What the hell is wrong with you?" Daddy yelled at Mr. Miller. "Are you crazy?"

Crazy. The word echoed for miles.

When we got close to the house Mother saw us coming and came running. "Oh, my God," she said. "What happened?"

Mrs. Miller, sitting with Babygirl in her lap, stood up and looked our way a minute, then turned and scurried inside the house, leaving Little Sister sitting all by herself on that bench in the yard, staring at us, swirling her feet in the dirt.

"Rennie didn't do anything," I told Mother. "It's not her fault."

Mother put her arms around Rennie, saying, "It's okay, honey. It's okay."

It was dark and the crickets were shrieking before Daddy and the other boys came back to the house. Mr. Miller was not with them. By that time we had Rennie sitting in a chair in the yard, her face washed off with a wet rag, and she was sipping some cool well water, her hands nervous and clumsy. Mrs. Miller was standing in the dark house, peering at us from the doorway. Whenever Mother called to her she refused to answer. She was giving us the creeps.

"Get the children in the car," Daddy barked at Mother when he walked up.

"Where's Daddy at?" Rennie asked, her voice hoarse and raspy.

"Gone," Cadell said.

Rennie looked like she might cry.

"Is your daddy bad to drink?" Daddy asked.

"Naw. That ain't it," Cadell said.

"What had him so upset, Rennie?" Daddy looked at her pleadingly, like she held the key and could unlock the mystery of her daddy's craziness if she just would. Daddy's shirt was ruined. His face was smeared with blood and dirt. He didn't take his eyes off Rennie until she answered.

"I was smoking a cigarette," Rennie said.

"Daddy's got a bad temper," Cadell explained. "Rennie – he gets mad with her."

"He was calling her a liar," I said. "But she wasn't lying. I swear."

"Don't swear, Berry," Mother said.

"Get in the car, Berry." Daddy's eyes darted from face to face where we were clustered in the dark. "You boys too." He nodded at Sowell and Wade, who had gone silent witnessing the sorry events of the day.

"What if Mr. Miller comes back?" I said. "And goes after Rennie again?"

"Y'all can't leave me here," Rennie sobbed quietly. "Please." She stood up and limped toward Mother, who reached for her. "Let me go with you," she whispered, looking hard into Mother's eyes. "He'll mess with me bad."

Daddy turned to Cadell. He wasn't the oldest, but he was the leader of the brothers, the only one who really talked much. "Is your sister safe here, son?"

"Naw." He shook his head. "Not till Daddy cools off."

"Let me go with you," Rennie begged.

"Get in the car," Daddy barked. "All of you. Go on. Rennie, you too." We could hardly get to the car fast enough. Wade got in the front with Mother. Rennie got in the back with Sowell and me. There was not a word spoken.

Daddy looked at Cadell and the others. "Son," he said, "you boys look out for your mama and sisters. If your daddy comes back . . . if there's any more trouble . . . somebody go for help."

"Yes, sir." Cadell nodded.

Daddy glanced toward the doorway, where Mrs. Miller stood camouflaged in the darkness, only her pale face and the fear in her eyes visible. "You going to be okay now?" Daddy hollered the half question, half command and waited for her reply, but she didn't answer.

"Look out for her," he said to the boys. They nodded.

Daddy got in the car and slammed the door shut. He started

the engine and we all held our breath as we snaked down the dirt road through the thick, steamy woods, the car lights flashing around nervously at every curve. Nobody took a breath until we finally reached the two-lane gravel highway.

"He's going to be mad," Rennie said. "Y'all taking me home with you."

"You don't worry about him," Daddy said.

"Thank you," Rennie whispered.

On the ride home you could about suffocate on the fear inside that car. Rennie looked out the window the whole ride – at nothing. The rest of us looked straight ahead and thought our own small dark thoughts. I chewed my fingernails to the quick. I drew blood.

That night Mother made Rennie a bed on our living room sofa. She fixed her a glass of sweet tea with lemon and gave her one of my clean cotton nightgowns to sleep in. Rennie was the quietest I'd ever seen her. Sowell and Wade and I wanted to huddle around her in the living room and stare at her and ask questions, but Mother said, "Leave the girl alone. She's been through enough for one day." Daddy made Sowell and Wade go to bed, but I had a minute to go in and say good night. Rennie was sitting up on the sofa, looking at one of Mother's *Ladies' Home Journals*. I sat down next to her and said, "You were right about your daddy, Rennie. I hate him." She patted my leg and smiled halfheartedly.

"Now it's not just me talking," she said. "I got witnesses."

"It looked like he was going to kill you," I said. The scene kept flashing across my skull over and over like a slide projector.

"Ford saved my life," she said. "I owe him too."

I had never heard Rennie call Daddy *Ford.* Nobody called him that, except Mother. Even the neighbors usually called him

Mr. Jackson. But Rennie was too upset to correct under the present circumstances.

Daddy came in bringing Rennie two aspirin like Mother told him to. "Berry, you get on to bed now. Rennie needs to get some rest."

Rennie stayed with us for the next two weeks. It was like our living room became Rennie's own private room. She kept the door closed on and off, so you had to knock before you could go in. Every morning she got up and dressed in something of Mother's that she'd laid out for her. Not a bit of it was black and even if it didn't fit right, Rennie still liked it, no matter what it was. As soon as she was dressed she set out to help Mother get breakfast on the table before Daddy drove us all to school.

People noticed. They saw she was coming and going with us every day, wearing clothes that belonged to Mother. If people didn't know the real story, then they made up one just as good – which was the custom in Pinetta.

After school Rennie tried hard to help Mother. It made me look bad, Rennie offering to finish ironing Daddy's cotton shirts, or to hang Sowell's and Wade's dungarees on the line, or to peel the potatoes for supper, or set the table, or scrub out the tub and toilet, or mop off the back porch and water Mother's potted plants or sweep the yard. I tried to tell Rennie that we were not the kind of people who swept the dirt. "Don't do that," I said. But she liked doing it, swirling the broom through the sand, making designs and giving the sand an organized look.

"Don't that look better?" she said afterwards.

"It looks like colored people live here," I said, which was sort of mean of me and I was sorry right away.

Jimmy was excited about Rennie staying with us too. He

stuck around our house like a fly on flypaper. You could not run him off. Anything Rennie did, he wanted to do too. If she shook out a rug, he wanted to shake one. If she opened an ice tray, he begged to open one too. If he was wearing a dress and she said, "Jimmy, how come you're wearing that dress?" he didn't even mind the question. Usually it made him go crazy, somebody asking the obvious. But to Rennie he said, "My mama don't want me to mess up my school clothes." It was the sort of answer Rennie understood better than most people. He sensed that, I guess. If Rennie said, "Jimmy, you need to go on home. We got to eat our supper now," he would fling himself down in the sand in the backyard and act like she had just shot him dead. He would roll around in the sandspurs or the red ant beds, trying to get us to take pity on him. Jimmy tried his hardest to get himself invited to supper every night, no matter what we were having, and sometimes Mother gave in and set him a place, but mostly she didn't. She would insist he go home, speak to him in a firm tone and for a minute or two he would act like he was minding her. Then later, after supper, we would see he had climbed the chinaberry tree and was hanging there like a monkey, trying to see in our window and watch us eat supper. It was bad enough that he was the oddest boy in Pinetta, but when he got to be a nuisance too, it was just too much. "I feel right sorry for that boy," Rennie said. "They's something wrong with him." It was a hard point to argue.

At supper Rennie would not take any food until after everybody else had theirs. She took such a tiny bit on her plate that Mother would remark, "Rennie, honey, you got to eat more than that. That little bit won't keep a bird alive." But Rennie never took more. Mother had to reach over and scoop her out some more corn or beans or a chicken thigh – whatever. Anything Mother heaped on her plate, Rennie said, "Thank you, ma'am," and proceeded to eat every bite of it. She cleaned her plate without anybody having to remind her to do it.

When supper was over Rennie insisted that Mother go sit outside in the yard, or go over to the Ingrams' and watch TV, or read one of those paperback books on her bedroom shelf. Rennie shooed everybody out of the kitchen, which wasn't too hard. I never heard of anybody wanting to clean up the kitchen and wash the dishes and put them away. But Rennie did. Sometimes I helped her because I wanted Mother to appreciate me like she appreciated Rennie, but mainly I wanted to be near Rennie, to be like Rennie. Rennie washed the dishes and she wasn't in any hurry about it either. I dried them but she wouldn't let me put them away, even though I was the one who knew where everything went. She liked to put them away herself, because she liked the chance to look through our cabinets and see what all we had stored away in there. Little by little she had gotten the cabinets cleaned out and reorganized – which made Mother crazy happy, since she herself did not have those sorts of organizational tendencies. And neither did I. I watched Rennie unload a cabinet, read the labels on things she didn't recognize, wipe things down with a soapy rag and put things back, just perfect. She was not doing it to show off or win Mother's love either. I swear I think she just had excess curiosity and a deep longing to make things clean and neat. Really. It was like a sickness.

As much as Mother admired Rennie's desire to help, Daddy admired it more. When he was home he sat and watched her fold the quilts off her sofa bed, or hang out bedsheets on the line, or mop the kitchen floor without being asked, or knot his black socks and line them up in his dresser drawer and he was impressed. "Rennie has a work ethic, Berry," Daddy said. "It wouldn't hurt you to learn the value of hard work."

His admiration of Rennie was killing me. I would try for a while to be as helpful as she was, but somehow Daddy never seemed to notice my small contributions to the household the way he noticed Rennie's. At night he praised her for all the ways she was helpful. And Rennie, she ate that praise up too. You could tell. I got worried that maybe Rennie would try to stay with us – you know, forever. She acted like she was applying for a job – that of being the daughter Mother and Daddy really deserved instead of me. She was starting to scare me. At night after Sowell and Wade and I were sent to bed, Mother and Daddy would sit in the living room with Rennie and discuss her problems. The list was long too. They shut the door so we couldn't listen. Sometimes Mother got tired of prying the ugly details out of Rennie night after night, hearing her tell her terrible story over and over. She had her limits. Mother has never really prided herself in giving people advice like Daddy did either. So she would hug Rennie and excuse herself and go to bed. Hours later you could hear her go back in the living room and say to Daddy, "Ford, come to bed. For heaven's sake, even if you think you don't need any sleep, poor Rennie does." And Daddy would apologize and follow Mother to the bedroom.

It was only after everybody in the house had finally gone to bed, fallen asleep, that Rennie would sneak into the bathroom, which did not require sneaking, and run herself a hot tub of water and take a long, slow bath. She did this like it was something she could get arrested for if she ever got caught. "What's she doing in there?" Sowell asked me one night when we woke up to the sound of the water running.

"She likes to take baths," I said.

"This time of night?" he said.

One night I woke to the sound of Rennie splashing around in the bathtub and I had to get up and go to the bathroom myself. I didn't want to. I had to. So I went to the closed door and tapped. "Rennie?"

"Who is it?" she called quietly.

"It's Berry," I said. "I've got to use the toilet."

"Come in, then," she said. "Close the door behind you."

I sat on the toilet and stared at Rennie sunk low in the hot bath. Little puffs of steam were rising up, the water was so hot. "You gon scald yourself," I said.

"I like to get clean," she said.

"I never saw anybody stay in the tub so long. I start to worry you've drowned in here."

Rennie laughed her little laugh.

Mother tapped on the door and stuck her head in the bathroom. She had pin curls in her wild hair and her faded robe on. She was squinting from the bright bathroom light and there was husky sleep in her voice. "Y'all get to bed, Rennie. It's too late to take a bath, honey. You're waking up the whole house with the water running and the lights on. Berry, you too."

The minute Mother scolded her, Rennie sprang up from the bathtub and grabbed one of those flowered towels Mother collected from the detergent boxes. It was a flimsy and cheap towel and Rennie tried to cover herself with it, but it was too puny. "Sorry, ma'am," Rennie said, clearly panicked. She held the towel first over her breasts, then over her belly, but we saw what it was she was trying to hide. I saw the startled expression on Mother's face. She closed the door and went back to bed. I stood up and flushed the toilet. Rennie stood naked just inches from me, patting herself dry, trying to hurry into my borrowed cotton gown, yanking it over her head. All across her belly and breasts the skin was bright pink and stretched, red veining, like tiny scars.

I don't know what my face said, what my eyes told her, but she looked at me and shook her head *no, no, no.* Did she mean, don't ask? Or was she just wishing she could erase a piece of history that was forever documented in her flesh?

"Night, Rennie," I said quietly and patted her arm. I hurried back to bed and left her alone in the bathroom. In minutes she cut off the light and I heard her tiptoe across the floor to the living room sofa. I lay wide-awake all night long, just thinking about Rennie's naked body. I swear, her skin looked like maybe Mr. Miller had set fire to her or something.

The next afternoon, when we came walking home from school, Pastor Lyons was at our house. I saw him sitting out on the porch with Mother, drinking a bottled cold drink. Mother was dressed nice, her hair brushed to the side with a clip. She was wearing an ironed dress and good shoes. We could hear her alternate between laughing and whispering with Pastor Lyons. When we got to the door Mother stood up and said, "I made lemonade. Y'all help yourself in the kitchen." She was acting like this was a daily occurrence, which it was not. It was like she was showing off for Pastor Lyons, trying to make him think this was the kind of mother she was, pretty and cheerful, always thinking of small happy ways she might serve others. The way Pastor Lyons was staring at Mother, I'd say he was pretty easy to fool.

"Rennie." Mother took her hand. "Honey, actually Pastor Lyons is here to see you."

Rennie looked startled, a worried expression crossing her face like a gray cloud. "Why?" she said, diverting her eyes away from his.

"He just wants to talk to you, honey," Mother said. That's all."

Rennie didn't argue. She shrugged and nodded okay. Pastor Lyons smiled and followed Rennie into the house. While the rest of us sat at the kitchen table drinking our lemonade, Pastor Lyons and Rennie shut themselves away in the living room, where all we heard was whispering and now and then Rennie letting out a little sob or blowing her nose. He was making her cry. Several times Mother knocked on the door and went inside with glasses of lemonade or Fig Newtons on a plate. Once she took Rennie a box of Kleenex. She'd stay a minute or two, survey things and come back to the kitchen, shaking her head.

This went on all afternoon until Daddy got home from work. He saw Pastor Lyons's car parked out front and it was like just the sight of it flew all over him. When he walked in the house he was already annoyed. "What's the preacher doing here?" he asked.

"I called him," Mother said. "I thought it would do Rennie good to talk to him."

"What's she going to say to him that she can't say to us?" Daddy asked.

"He's a preacher," Mother said. "He's trained to counsel people."

"Bullshit," Daddy said. "He's trained to preach. I don't think a sermon is what Rennie needs right now."

"Ford, for heaven's sake, she needs all the help she can get, doesn't she?"

Daddy put his briefcase on the kitchen table and walked right into the living room without knocking. Pastor Lyons was sitting on the couch next to Rennie with his arm around her and she was crying into his handkerchief. Her eyes were swollen into two pink eggs. It was like they hardly noticed Daddy barging in. "Rennie, you okay?" Daddy asked. It was like he suspected the preacher was torturing her or something.

She nodded and began to blow her nose into the wrinkled handkerchief.

"Hey there, Ford," Pastor Lyons said.

"Hate to interrupt this prayer meeting going on in here," Daddy said sarcastically.

Mother rolled her eyes. She knew that whenever Daddy got rude like this, then things usually got messy. She would have to go in there now and try to out-polite his rudeness enough to maybe strike a balance. The sharp edge in her voice said everything. "Ford, I thought maybe Pastor Lyons might be some comfort to Rennie."

"Rennie, why don't you go in the bathroom and wash up a little," Daddy said. And she stood up and did what he said.

Pastor Lyons stood up too. "Rennie is a good girl," he said. "In a situation like this, a girl needs her church family."

Daddy glared at Pastor Lyons. He didn't bother to point out that we were not her church family. We were Methodists and proud of it. Rennie and the Millers went to the Baptist church, when they went at all. But the details seemed lost on Daddy. The way he looked at Pastor Lyons with his eye twitching and his nostrils flared, it crossed my mind that he might get in a fistfight with Pastor Lyons too, that it was going to be his new hobby, fighting over Rennie, fighting over who was going to be the one to comfort Rennie best, advise her wisest, save her most heroically. I was about to get mad at Rennie over it too.

"Butch," Mother said, "would you like to stay for supper? We've got plenty."

Lord, no, I thought. Was Mother crazy? Didn't she see how aggravated Daddy already was?

Pastor Lyons paused as if he was thinking it over. "I better get on my way," he said. "I'm thinking I might drive out and talk to Rennie's daddy. See if I can talk sense to Mr. Miller."

"That won't be necessary," Daddy said. "I'll handle Mr. Miller."

Rennie came out of the bathroom then, her face fresh-scrubbed, her wet hair pulled back into a neat ponytail. She looked cried out and suddenly shy.

"You sure you won't change your mind and stay for supper?" Mother said again.

"Ruthie," Daddy said. "The man said he can't stay. No need to keep after him."

Mother shot Daddy a poison-dart look.

"Before I go," Pastor Lyons said, "I'd like us all to say a little prayer together. That okay, Rennie?" He glanced at her standing like a girl caught in a briar thicket. She nodded and bowed her head.

Mother stood between Daddy and Butch Lyons, took each of their hands in hers. I stood between Rennie and Daddy. Sowell and Wade hid out in the bedroom the minute they heard any mention of praying. It wasn't Sunday. I was hoping Pastor Lyons would keep it short. Rennie's hand was sweating in mine.

By the time Pastor Lyons got Rennie prayed for and Mother wrapped him a plate of pork chops and sliced tomatoes in waxed paper and he smiled good-bye at everybody and left, the evening was spoiled. We sat down and ate our supper, but Mother was so irritated with Daddy that nobody could enjoy a bite of food.

After supper I helped Rennie clean up the kitchen. She was subdued, like she had been ever since she came to stay with us.

I liked her better the other way, loud and show-offy. Now she was trying so hard to be polite and helpful that she was making me sick. "Berry," she whispered, "if anything were ever to happen to me . . ." Her voice trailed off.

"What? Like if you died?"

"Or if I went off someplace, or something bad happened to me, I got sick . . . would you . . ."

"What?" I said.

"Look out for Babygirl. I don't want her messed up like Little Sister."

"Sure," I said. "I guess."

"Just don't forget about her out there," she said. "Mama might not can save her."

"Okay." I would have promised Rennie about anything. Even the impossible.

That night we went to bed and tried to fall asleep, listening to Mother and Daddy argue in their closed bedroom. I hated it when they argued. I hoped Rennie was happy.

Two days later Mr. Miller showed up at the school. I thought maybe he had come to kill Daddy. But he was cleaned up some, had shaved his face and held his hat in his hand nervously. He looked humble. He went to the office to discuss his desire to bring Rennie home where she belonged. Cadell saw him pull up in his tin-can truck, and went with him to Daddy's office. Next thing you know, Rennie was called to the office too. She went like a girl walking the plank, knowing she is about to be fed to the sharks and jellyfish.

Nobody knows exactly what was said or done. But that night when Daddy came home he was like a soldier who had won every battle but still lost the war – and he said that Mr.

Miller spoke of changing his ways, not being so hard on Rennie and the boys. Daddy said he got his Bible out and made him swear to it. At the end of it all, in spite of crying a river, Rennie got in the truck with her daddy and Cadell and the other brothers and they took her back out to the woods and the life she was born to live. She didn't throw a fit either. She just stared out the window at all the nothing everywhere. Steam was rising off the asphalt road when the truck pulled out on the road. It was hot as Hades everywhere you looked.

If you ask me, Daddy looked stricken, watching them drive off. He looked half furious and half fearful. Either he was feeling like he had handled things successfully or else that he had failed miserably. It was hard to tell. Mrs. Freddy put her arm around my shoulder and said, "Berry, there's nothing your daddy can do. Rennie's situation is just one of those sad accidents of birth. We all wish her a different life – but this is the life God gave her."

It seemed to me that God ought to do better by Rennie. Either He was all-powerful or he wasn't. The Bible needed to clarify that. I expected a lot more out of God than I did Daddy – even though in this particular case it seemed like Daddy was trying a lot harder. Even if God's mysterious ways allowed Him to overlook Rennie's mess of a life, I knew that Daddy's mysterious ways did not.

Word flew through Pinetta that Daddy had given Rennie back to her rightful owner. Some people respected that. Some shook their heads and cursed Daddy. When Jewel Longmont stopped by the house to question Daddy's logic, he said, "Sometimes you have to do what you have to do, Jewel. The legal thing is not necessarily the right thing – but still you got to follow the law." It was like he was trying to convince himself. It was clear he did not convince Jewel Longmont.

"The law, the law . . ." She waved her hand like she was dismissing Daddy's weak argument. "This is not about the law, Ford Jackson. You know that as well as I do."

But maybe he didn't. Night after night at the supper table Daddy set out to explain himself, although none of us in his own family were really asking for an explanation. "Rennie might be better off staying with us, Berry," Daddy said one night, "but she don't belong to us. She's not ours. See? We can't just take her away like that – not even for her own good. She belongs with Mr. Miller until she turns eighteen or gets married. You understand that, don't you?"

I didn't know why he was explaining things to me. I hadn't asked him any questions about it. I didn't demand a detailed account. I wasn't blaming him or feeling disappointed in him, because he was so busy doing that to himself.

"If I could take Rennie away from Mr. Miller, I would." Daddy slathered a piece of cornbread with butter. He went at it like he was icing a cake. "If it was legal, I would. I'd go out there right now and get her. Right this minute." He bit into the cornbread and crumbs fell everywhere.

~

Jimmy and I were laying up under the car in his yard. I was petting our yellow cat, who was lying on her side as still as a rock, like a dead cat. Jimmy was digging halfheartedly for roly-polies with a Popsicle stick. Mother said Mrs. Ingram must be feeding Jimmy better these days since he was growing like a weed. He was half a foot taller than me now, all arms and legs going everywhere. We were too old to lay up under a parked car, but there was nothing else to do. His sisters acted like they owned the TV, so we were not welcome to come inside the house to watch it.

Mother didn't like us banging around in our house either, so we had limited choices. Ride our bikes. *We already did.* Walk up to Longmont's gas station and get a Popsicle. *We already did.* Climb the chinaberry tree. *We already did.* Spray each other with the water hose. *We already did.* Spy on Sowell or Wade. That was boring because Sowell and Wade never did anything interesting. Their idea of a big time was still mostly killing snakes. Sowell liked to catch them first, play with them a while – poisonous or not-poisonous didn't matter – before he killed them. It had gotten to where whenever the neighbors came across a snake, they called Sowell to come get it. Sowell went around Pinetta like he thought he was Tarzan, king of the jungle, snakes – dead or alive – looped over his bare shoulders. It was the proven truth that Sowell was not afraid of snakes. Wade still preferred his snakes dead. He specialized in death and post-death rituals. Elaborate animal funerals were his primary interest.

Neither did that witch's nest of sisters Jimmy had ever do anything interesting enough to spy on, unless you call putting a permanent wave in your hair interesting, unless painting their fingernails was interesting, or laying in the sun until they were red as a pot of steamed lobsters with moods to match.

Jimmy was as near as I had to a best friend. I knew things about him that nobody else did – like for example, that he was always reading stuff. He was ashamed of this and only did it locked into the bathroom or late at night when everybody else was asleep, or sometimes out in the hole in the weeds when he was there alone. He read books from the school library that had bad parts in them. He memorized the bad parts and told them to me – nobody else. Also, he showed me Mr. Ingram's calendar with the undressed women, one for each month. Mr. Ingram kept it in an old gas can in his tool shed. It was more interesting to me than it was to Jimmy. He had probably seen enough of that at his own house.

"Sometimes I wish Rennie was still staying with y'all," Jimmy said. "She was nice. Different from most girls."

I guessed he was talking about his sisters – since I didn't think he actually put me into the girl category. Besides, I was so nice I completely hated myself. I thought you would be hard pressed to find anybody in Pinetta who would say I, Berry Jackson, was not nice. Nice was my middle name. Nice was my curse. "You were in love with Rennie," I accused. "You made a fool of yourself over her. Everybody said so."

"I liked her," he said. "They was something about her."

"Well, maybe you liked her, but she thought you were strange as you could be. She used to look out the window at you, going around in those dresses, and a shiver would go over her. She said so." Even though this was sort of a hateful thing to say, I said it very nice. My tone was harmless.

"I don't care," Jimmy said. "I hate your daddy for sending Rennie back home. Them Millers is like insane asylum people out there. They all belong over at Chattahoochie. Except for Rennie and Cadell. They're about the only two decent people in Pinetta."

"No, they're not," I said. "You just like them because they take people's mind off how odd you are. That's all."

"I rather be odd than ordinary – like you. You are so ordinary it is pure sad."

This hushed me up because I recognized the truth in it. That the reason I had to be so nice all the time was because – Jimmy was right – I was so ordinary. I had no choice in the matter – it was nice or nothing. Whereas Jimmy, as odd as he was, was excused from having to be nice. Nobody expected a oddball to act right. For a minute I was jealous of him – and he knew it too.

"I hate you sometimes, Jimmy," I said. "You are so mean."

He smiled. "You can't hate me, Berry. Not since I'm the only friend you got."

Mother had always wanted me to make better friends with Jimmy's older sister Rosemary, and for a split second I wished I had. But I didn't like Rosemary. She was always trying to make me tell her stuff about Sowell. *Did he like her? Did he ever talk about her?* No was my answer to anything she asked me. When I saw Rosemary coming I just looked right at her and said, "No, Rosemary," before she even asked me the first question.

"You just hate Rosemary because she's pretty," Jimmy said once.

"Pretty is as pretty does," I'd insisted. (What the heck does that mean anyway?)

"Well, at least she's not boring. Like some people," Jimmy said.

"Too bad they don't give prizes for that," I snapped. "Not being boring."

"What's the matter with you?" Jimmy asked. "Why are you so mad about everything?"

Jimmy – of all people – asking me that. Brother.

I wasn't pretty. Nobody had to tell me so, because I could look in the mirror and see for myself. I was not the kind of girl that made teachers automatically call on me to give the right answer – even though I often knew it – or the kind of girl who inspired old men to fish through their pockets for a piece of chewing gum to give me. That was the kind of girl I wanted to be. Rosemary was sort of that kind. Her hair was curly and everybody acted like that was a big accomplishment. So was Marie Longmont pretty – only she was also nice to go with the pretty, which was totally voluntary on her part and so like a two-for-one bonus. I would have been Marie Longmont's best friend if she'd wanted me to, but she didn't. Marie already had all the friends money could buy. Rosemary claimed she was Marie Longmont's best friend. So I settled for Jimmy. No matter what mean stuff he said, he didn't care how I looked and I knew it. He was easy and indifferent around girls. And he had decent sister skills, which worked just fine with me.

That spring Mother had let us camp out in the backyard with Sowell and Wade. Jimmy and I worked all day on our campsite, which was the huge hole in the weeds that connected our backyards and which none of us knew the origin of, but all of us had contributed to over time, digging with our fathers' shovels, or our bare hands, until the hole had the feeling of a topless cave, with little compartments dug out along the walls. It was red clay mostly – the hole – and more than once we had tried to make pottery out of the red clay when it rained, tried to imagine ourselves as Seminoles, although Daddy later told us that the Seminoles never came anywhere near Pinetta and we should pretend to be Creek or Cherokee if we wanted to pretend something. We shaped muddy statues, bowls and coffee cups all afternoon, then sat our handiwork out on a metal cookie sheet in the sun the next day, not just in the sun, but in the sun in the middle of the tar and gravel road in front of our house. That road got so hot that the tar melted over and over again, only the most powerful bare feet could stand up to it, and all of us had had the annoying task, the painful task, of peeling hot tar and raw skin off our half-cooked feet. Time and time again our pottery failed. The Indians knew something we didn't. Our bowls crumbled like sand to the touch. After a day baking in the sun we had what looked like a cookie tray full of dirt dobs – that's all. But we never gave up on it.

The hole in the weeds inspired us in other ways too. It was where we played until long after dark, where we plotted and confessed and the boys repeated dirty jokes they'd heard at school from other boys who'd heard them from uncles or fathers, and where we went when one of us needed to cry a river. You could lie down in the hole and nobody could see you, especially no parent, no nosy, well-meaning adult.

So when Mother said we could camp out in the hole, it was thrilling, like if she'd said we could sleep on the roof of the house, which we had also begged to do, but she had never let us. "Don't be ridiculous," Mother said. "You will roll off the roof and kill yourselves."

In the red clay hole we slept on some big tractor inner tubes Jimmy's daddy kept for when they went to Cherry Lake to swim. We each had an inner tube and a bedsheet or tablecloth our mothers did not care if we ruined, since the ones they let us have were pretty much already ruined. We had a pickle jar of ice water and a box of graham crackers and that was all we needed. Our yellow cat had ventured out to see what we were doing and I caught her and was holding her under the spread, petting her so gentle, trying to get her to relax and fall asleep beside me. She seemed like she might cooperate.

I am telling this to explain about not being pretty. The proof, as if I really needed any. By the time the night was in full bloom, just a purple night full of insects and stars and the gaudy orange electric lights of houses with their porch lights on, drawing moths from miles around, we were all settled in the hole good, in a circle more or less, all our heads bunched together and Jimmy said to Sowell, "Rosemary says she's going to marry you."

"I think I got some say in that," Sowell said. "Who I marry."

"You don't love her, do you?" Jimmy said.

"No, I don't love her."

"What's wrong with her?" Jimmy asked.

"I didn't say there was nothing wrong with her."

"She's pretty, isn't she?"

"I guess so."

"I don't see why you don't love her," Jimmy said. "She loves you."

"Naw, she don't," Sowell said.

"She says you are beautiful. Doesn't she say that, Berry?"

"I'm not beautiful," Sowell said. "I'm handsome. It's a difference." He said it like he was confessing to a bad quality, like crooked teeth or something.

"My mama says you got your mama's good looks," Jimmy said. "Wade and Berry here, they look like your daddy."

"What does that mean?" I said. Our yellow cat began to stir. "Does it mean we are not beautiful?" I asked. "Say?" Our yellow cat struggled to get free, but I had a stranglehold on her.

"I don't want to be beautiful," Wade insisted.

"I didn't say that," Jimmy said.

"You said I look like my daddy." Our yellow cat dug her claws into my arms and went stiff, but I held on even tighter.

"My mama said that, Berry. Not me."

"Admit it," I said. "You don't think I'm a bit pretty. Just say so."

"I wasn't even talking about you," Jimmy said. "Good grief, Berry. I was talking about Sowell."

"There's more important things than being pretty," Sowell put his two cents' worth in, pushing the hair back out of my face like he was somebody's granddaddy or something. "You know it."

"I don't know it," I said.

"You got good character," Sowell said. "That's a heck of a lot better than being pretty."

"You're lying through your teeth," I said. "I don't have good character."

"You do, Berry, honest," Jimmy said. "You have the best character of any girl I know."

"What are you talking about?" My voice jumped the tracks mid-sentence. "You don't even know what character is. So how do you know I have it?"

"What are you so mad about?"

"Because," I shouted. "I don't want character. Don't ever say I have character again."

"It was Sowell that said it. Not me."

"I think you're sort of pretty, Berry. A little bit," Wade lied. I thought about slapping him, but I could not let go of our yellow cat, her claws like little nails hammered into me. "Mama says you're going to be real pretty before it's over."

"Before what is over?" I shrieked.

"I don't know," Wade said.

Our yellow cat let out an ugly sound and sprang loose, scratching my arms with her barbed-wire paws, leaving red parallel lines all over me, like little bloody roads leading to someplace – to someone – that was not me.

See, I could not trick them into saying I was pretty. I could not make them guilty enough to say it. I could not get them to lie just to soothe me and so I always think of that moment, that night, the three boys who loved me most in this world – the only boys who loved me – and not a one of them thought I was anything close to pretty, which I already knew but did not want to give in to knowing, like I was holding out hope that I was wrong about this and it would be brought to my attention, to my surprise, that in fact I was a pretty girl after all. But this night was when it was supposed to happen if it ever was going to and it didn't – they just told the truth, which I hated them for. I thought if they really loved me, if they had a shred of love in their hearts, then they would have at least cared enough to lie.

Afterwards they felt bad. I was not pretty. Okay. Okay. Our yellow cat had scratched the hell out of me, trying to get away. Nothing was like I wanted it. Sowell moved his inner tube so he was right next to me and he put his arm around me real tight and Jimmy got on the other side and put his arm around me too and they made me into a girl sandwich. Wade just laid in his regular place and sort of watched this sympathetic spectacle. Sowell wrapped around me, tangled his legs with mine, and put his hand over my heart right where my breast was beginning and the heat of his hot body made me start to sweat. It was like his pitiful way of saying he was sorry that he had turned out to be the beautiful one, which was a nuisance for him but which would have done me a world of good. He seemed so genuinely sorry about it all. Wade seemed like he thought we were both crazy and he wasn't going to take sides. He just laid there as neutral as Switzerland.

Jimmy liked to do things that Sowell did, so he snuggled up next to me too, saying, "Berry? You're not mad at me, are you?" He rubbed his hand on my hip, like he was petting a dog.

If I'd thought crying would have helped I'd have done it. They had made it impossible for me to fool myself anymore. Did they think good character gave me comfort? And now, all of a sudden, they were acting so sorry – like they really just loved me to death.

~

When Mother saw that Pastor Lyons was walking up to our house she made a dash for the bathroom and ran a comb through her hair and put on lipstick. Then she ran into her bedroom and took off her shorts and put on her housedress. When he knocked, she took her time getting to the door, then acted like she didn't have any idea in the world who it could be surprising her like that.

Pastor Lyons was upset. I could tell by the look on his face and because he forgot to act friendly like he usually did. He usually tried to be nice to people's children even though he didn't really like children all that much and everybody knew it and frequently commented on it. He had always been nice to us though, because he liked Mother and being nice to us was his way of showing it. "Can I talk to you a minute, Ruthie?" he said.

"Come in," Mother said. "I got coffee on."

He came in the kitchen and we stared at him. He was big and it felt like he took up all the air in the house. He set his hat on the table, pulled out a chair and folded himself into it. Sweat was rolling down the side of his face, which he wiped off with a handkerchief.

Mother got him a cup and saucer and poured his coffee and set it before him on the table. "This sure is a surprise," Mother said. "A nice surprise."

"A pastor is not a perfect person. You know that, don't you, Ruthie?" He looked at Mother so hard she practically turned into a statue, like his eyes froze her into place.

"Sure I do," Mother stared back at him. "We're all sinners."

Pastor Lyons shook his head and looked into his coffee cup like he thought he might find his next sentence floating there. "I'm afraid I got to cancel church services on Sunday," he said. "Something has come up."

Mother pulled out a chair and sat down at the table across from him. "Is something wrong?"

"Jack Longmont is asking everybody in the community to join him at the Baptist church for Sunday service," he said. "I've agreed to it."

"That's mighty unusual, isn't it?" Mother said.

"I thought it would be a good time for me to go to Madison and see about my own family over there. Hadn't been home in a while."

"Is somebody sick?"

"Nothing like that." He looked around at Wade and me, who were enthralled with his presence in our kitchen. He was as close to a God-like creature as we knew of. We had the feeling that it was practically God himself sitting there drinking coffee with our mother. At least I did. God coming to our mother with his problems, hoping maybe she could make things right. We could see right off why Daddy didn't like him.

"Ruthie," he said. "You got a forgiving heart. You are blessed that way. So I'm going to need you to lead the others, you know, in forgiveness. The church is facing a trial."

"I'll try." Mother looked confused.

Pastor Lyons blew into his cup and took a sip of coffee and just stared across the room.

"What's wrong?" Mother said. "What is it that needs all this forgiving?"

"We got a mess on our hands," he said.

* * *

When he was ready to leave the house he hugged Mother right in front of us. She looked truly shocked and by the time he let go of her Mother looked as worried as he did. "You're sure you're okay?" Mother said.

"I'm counting on you, Ruthie," he said. "You're special to me, Ruthie. God knows. Special to all of us at the church. I'm going to be counting on you." He hugged her again, and this time he held on and bent his head down to her shoulder and I thought for a minute he might cry.

"Tell me," Mother said. "Please."

But he looked away and mumbled, "Thanks for the coffee," which he had hardly touched. He walked out of the kitchen, across the porch and out into the yard. He carried his hat in his hand, not even bothering to put it on his head. Instead, he slapped it against his leg as he went. He was headed toward Jimmy's house, where I guessed he'd say to Jimmy's mother, "Mrs. Ingram, can I talk to you a minute?"

After he left, Mother was not herself. She watched him walk over to the Ingrams' and watched and waited for him to leave there and walk on down the road to who knows where. He had a nice car, but he was walking instead, slapping himself with that hat.

As soon as he was out of sight Mother made a dash across the yards to the Ingrams' and she and Mrs. Ingram stood on their porch and talked for a long time.

When Daddy got home that afternoon, Wade said, "The preacher came to see Mother."

"Is that right?" Daddy said.

We didn't tell Daddy the preacher was hugging her too.

~

When Sunday rolled around we dressed for church like always and then walked with the Ingrams over to the Baptist church, which felt completely unnatural and also sort of exciting. For this occasion Mrs. Ingram brought Mr. Ingram and Jimmy and all his sisters. Nearly every family in Pinetta was going to be there, but nobody seemed to know exactly why. People who had not been to church in a month of Sundays – or ever – showed up on this day. The Longmonts had sent out word that they wanted to make an important announcement to the entire community, Baptist and Methodist alike. Free refreshments afterwards in the fellowship hall. Nothing like this had ever happened before. There was anticipation in the air.

There was no counting cars this Sunday. No hymn contest. The place was packed, folks skin to skin in the pews, children and backsliders and the pure of heart all jammed in there together, fanning themselves with biblical scenes and Madison Funeral Home advertisements.

Even the Millers were there, Rennie and her mother and sisters sitting in a row in their witch clothes, their hair twisted into hard, tight knots at the back of their necks. Rennie was holding Babygirl in her lap, looking sort of bothered and distracted. I even saw her swat Babygirl on the leg once, trying to make her stop kicking her foot against the pew. Cadell was there too, the only one among his brothers wearing a necktie, which hung down past the zipper of his pants like a bright blue noose. He acted like nobody ever told him he was a poor boy, like he thought he owned that Baptist church. I never saw a boy love himself so much in my life.

Right offhand I could not think of anybody in Pinetta who was not there. It would have been a good day for the government to take a census count.

The Baptist preacher looked grief-stricken as he stood before us. He was old and pale on a good day, but today he was as white as biscuit dough rolled out and waiting to be cut. It looked like his wife was trembling where she sat up on the front seat, fanning herself ninety to nothing.

The preacher welcomed everybody and we sang a couple of hymns that broke the sound barrier. We did everything out of order, made the announcements, took up the collection, asked for personal testimony – and for once not a soul had any – said the Lord's Prayer, then the preacher, who was dripping with perspiration by now, said, "I know y'all are curious about what brings you here today. We got some mighty unusual circumstances." He looked like he wished he'd had the good sense to retire before now. Like his time had run out but he'd been too busy to notice. "I ask that everyone of you remember this is a house of God, and act accordingly." He cleared his throat and looked where Jack Longmont sat beside his wife, Jewel, who was dressed in black like a woman in mourning. It was clear somebody had died.

"Mr. Longmont," the preacher said, "I'm gon turn things over to you this morning." He looked at Mr. Longmont real hard. "You sure you want to do this, Jack?" he asked quietly, like he thought maybe the rest of us couldn't hear him. Then he sat down next to his shaky wife and bowed his head so low it looked like he might roll out of the pew.

Mr. Longmont walked up to the pulpit. His hair was greased into place just perfect. He had on a shirt and tie and probably a big dose of Aqua Velva like always. We sat too far in the back to smell him. "Thank you all for coming today," he said, like he really hated the fact that we had come. His voice cracked and he paused a second, gripping the pulpit like he was thinking about tearing it up out of the floor. "It is a dark day in my life." He looked out at the congregation, and every eye was focused on him. "I don't know if a thing like this can be made right or not," he said. "They say confession is good for the soul. I don't know but one way to find out. Jewel" – he nodded at his wife, who was sitting with a handkerchief over her mouth – "come on up here."

Jewel just sat there like she wasn't about to make a move. She sat there so long the preacher finally got up and went over and took her by the arm. He led her up to the pulpit and handed her over to her husband, then shook his head and sat down.

"My wife has got something to say to you people," Mr. Longmont said. "I ask you to hear her out. Then I ask you to forgive her, which is what I'm going to try to do. Come on now, Jewel," he said. "Say what you need to say."

Jewel Longmont stepped up to the pulpit and took a deep breath. Her husband took a step back, stood with his hands clasped in front of him, the way ushers do after they take up the collection. He just stood right there behind her, like a shadow that didn't fit right. Jewel took another deep breath. You could have heard a termite chew wood.

"What is this about?" Daddy whispered to Mother.

"Shhhhhh," Mother said. "Listen."

Mrs. Longmont looked up from the podium solemnly. She looked out at the lake of faces glistening in front of her. Then she just dove in. "Some of y'all are my friends," she began. "Some of y'all don't know me too well, but I am here today to ask your forgiveness – all of you."

People sat up straight. Jewel Longmont was good to look at even in all black with two eyes swollen nearly off her face. One eye purple like a wasp had bitten her.

"Jack has asked me to tell you that I have betrayed my husband and my children. . . ." She lost her way then, looked out at her daughter, Marie, who seemed in complete shock, like a person who has been in a terrible car wreck but couldn't begin to tell you how it happened. "I am so sorry," Jewel Longmont whispered. Her voice got hung and broke off.

Nobody moved a muscle. The roomed heated up like a furnace, folks waiting for whatever came next.

"Go on, Jewel," Mr. Longmont said. "Tell it all. Tell what you done."

She took a deep breath and held her head up so high it made her neck beautiful, like a marble column or something. "I want to confess that I have been foolish. . . . I have loved . . ." She shook those sentences off like they were invisible hats she was trying on that were way too small for her head. "I have been with the wrong man," she said. "Loved the wrong man."

A low rumble spread through the sanctuary. It was like people weren't sure what to do, like they weren't sure they'd heard her right, like she was standing up there peeling off her clothes one garment at a time and nobody could think of anything to do but sit there and watch her nakedness. It was like a religious striptease.

"Who was it?" Daddy whispered to Mother. "The man?"

"How do I know?" Mother said. "Shhhhh."

"I never meant for it to happen," Jewel Longmont said. "Sometimes your heart just plays a trick on you, you know?" She waited a few seconds, like maybe she thought half a dozen women in the room would know exactly what she meant and stand up and say so, confess to tricks their own hearts had played on them. But nobody said a word. Nobody's head nodded, *Yes, honey, you tell it now. Yes, darling, so true, so true.* Just a bunch of pairs of marble eyes, hard like that, fixed. So Jewel had to give up and go on. "Next thing you know," Jewel Longmont said, "you have broken your promise to love and obey."

The air was gone out of the room. One by one people began shaking their heads. The only movement in the room was heads shaking – all kinds, some *I cannot believe what I am hearing and can't stand to hear no more,* some *tell me more, tell me every blasted detail,* some *that is a good-looking woman up there who has nearly cried herself sick,* some *see there, all the money in the world can't buy your way to heaven – but can buy you a big heartache.*

"Tell them you're sorry, Jewel," Mr. Longmont said. "Go on now."

She didn't look at him. She looked straight ahead. "I've asked Jack to forgive me and I pray that he will. But I'm prepared to suffer for my sin. I know a sinner has to suffer."

"Who was it?" a thin voice called out from the back of the church. I looked around to see it was Cadell Miller, who was technically too young to ask. Rennie reached out and swatted at him and it looked like she was saying a cuss word. His question set off an echo in the room, grown people saying, "Who was the man? Who was he? Tell us."

"This is nobody's fault but my own," Jewel Longmont said.

Jack stepped up beside his wife. "Go on, tell his name," Jack said. "Tell them who it was."

Jewel looked pleadingly at her husband. "Please, Jack," she whispered. "You promised."

"Tell them." His voice was like a clap of thunder. "Tell them his name."

Jewel shook her head like she could not speak the man's name, like it would kill her to speak it. Like saying his name would make the floor catch fire beneath our feet. Like she was trying to save us all by not telling us the truth.

"Tell them!" Jack Longmont pounded his fist on the podium. "You tell them!"

It seemed like the roof might pop off the place, like the church was swelling to just short of exploding. But Jewel Longmont stood tall and still – and dead silent.

"You know who it was?" Jack Longmont screamed at the congregation. "You know who led my wife to the gates of hell? Butch Lyons, pastor of the Methodist church! Butch Lyons is who."

Just then Marie Longmont sprang up from her seat and ran sobbing to the front of the church and threw her arms around her mother and then Jewel Longmont just sort of melted into a puddle in her expensive black dress.

All hell broke loose. People sprang out of their seats. People clogged the aisles, trying to get out of the church, like they thought any minute lightning might strike and set the place on fire. Everywhere were knots of Baptists and Methodists trying to untangle themselves from the news, trying to get over to the fellowship hall, where they could think things over and drink some punch. The preacher had to go get Mr. Longmont and try to steer him down from the pulpit, maybe even out of the church, maybe even to the Longmont Fellowship Hall, where so many people were going, like coins spilling out of a pocket with a bad rip in it.

"Good Lord," Daddy said. "Jewel and the damn preacher?"

Mother sat like the news was ice-cold and had chilled her to the bone. "It's not true," she said. "It can't be." But I knew she believed it.

I saw Rennie run out of the church with Babygirl, she had tears splashing everywhere. This news must have been awfully hard on Rennie. I knew she idolized Jewel Longmont. I wanted to catch up with her, but the crowd had the doors blocked, everybody shocked and noisy and not sure what to do next.

"Refreshments in the fellowship hall," the preacher shouted from the pulpit. "Let's gather in the fellowship hall for prayer and refreshments, people." But the crowd was stirring around now like a swarm of dirt dobbers after someone had come at their nest with a broom handle.

I could not help watching Marie. She was wrapped around her mother like a Band-Aid on a bad sore. Mr. Longmont was trying to pry her loose, but he couldn't. "Come here," he said. "Come here to Daddy." The preacher had to pull him away.

Jewel Longmont was holding Marie, talking to her real quiet, and Marie's head was jerking up and down with her sobs. I told myself I would be nice to Marie Longmont for the rest of my life – no matter what. I saw Rosemary trying to get to Marie, swimming upstream through the crowd. She paused once to wave to Sowell, who stood beside me, stupefied.

It seemed like seeing Marie so upset had made Jewel Longmont calm down and turn cool. She seemed suddenly clear-headed, clear-eyed, like a woman who finds herself in the eye of a hurricane, that one safe, still spot in a place where everything has gone spinning out of control.

Sowell could not take his eyes off Jewel Longmont. He watched her like he had new appreciation for her. Like besides being beautiful and rich, she had that sort of character that he thought was better than being beautiful and rich. "What are you staring at?" I asked him.

"Look at Marie. She's all tore up."

"I guess you would be too," I said, "if it was our mother."

"No, I wouldn't," he said. "It wouldn't bother me a bit."

Sowell was one of those outer-space-type people, if you know what I mean. He was always far off and dreamy and would always say the thing you did not expect and you were not sure you ought to believe.

The preacher led Jack Longmont out the side door right where we were standing. He was crying like a baby. Daddy patted him on the shoulder just like I'd seen him do at a funeral when a person was burying a loved one. "Jack," he said. That was all.

"He made me do it – confess," Jewel said to the people standing around staring at her – like us. "I didn't want to put you people through this."

"The poor man is out of his head," Mrs. Ingram said. "He's grieving the worst I ever saw."

Jewel Longmont walked out of the church with her arm around Marie and her sons trailing along behind her like slack-tailed dogs on a weak scent. We heard later that they went into the fellowship hall and Mrs. Longmont talked to anybody who would talk to her, answered any questions she could, except about *you know who,* gone home to Madison.

"Who the man was is not important," she was reported to have said. "It's who the sinner is that matters. And the sinner is me. I'm not blaming nobody else."

I had wanted to go to the fellowship hall too, like the rest of the people, but Mother absolutely refused. She said, "We are going home, Berry." She went stone silent and stayed that way.

As we started across the churchyard on the way home Mrs. Freddy came over to us and hugged Mother. "I'm so sorry,

Ruthie," she said. Mother's eyes filled up with tears. "I know you believed in Butch. We all did."

Mrs. Freddy hugged me too. "Hey, Berry, honey," she said. "This is awful, isn't it?"

"Yes, ma'am," I said.

"You look after your mama now." I watched Mrs. Freddy and her husband, Bye, make their way through the crowd and into the fellowship hall, where I wished we were. I had Mrs. Freddy's baby powder smell on me after that hug.

Parked right there next to the fellowship hall was that sad excuse for a truck Mr. Miller drove. Rennie was sitting in the front seat beside Mrs. Miller. She was crying herself sick and there was nothing Mrs. Miller could do to soothe her. She just kept patting her back like she was trying to help her cough something up.

On the walk home Daddy said, "I swear, there must be more to Butch Lyons than meets the eye." Mother didn't respond. "Jewel Longmont." Daddy shook his head. "I wouldn't have thought Butch Lyons was in her league."

When we got home Mother got the dinner out of the oven. Meat loaf, mashed potatoes, gravy, creamed corn, green beans and also Jell-O salad with a can of fruit cocktail dumped in it. She popped open a can of refrigerated biscuits on the countertop and handed them to me to lay out in a cake pan. She told Sowell to pour everybody some tea. She told Wade to put out the plates and silverware. We all obeyed, following her silent example, except when Sowell said, "I don't know what everybody is so upset about. People act like it's the first commandment that's ever been broken in Pinetta."

"Sowell, don't talk smart," Mother said.

"Either Mr. Longmont forgives her or he don't," Sowell said. "That's all."

"That's not all." Mother slapped her pot holder down on the counter. "A good man has had his career ruined, Sowell. A good Christian man, God's servant, who was no match for Jewel Longmont."

Daddy piped up just then from where he was sitting at the table, reading the newspaper while we got dinner on. "I don't believe Jewel had to hold a gun to the preacher's head, Ruthie, if that's what you think."

"Y'all eat dinner without me." Mother walked into her bedroom and closed the door and put on the lock. We could hear her when she threw herself down on the bed, the squeak of the springs, that first sob when it broke.

"Why is she crying?" Wade asked.

"Women like to cry," Daddy said. "You might as well go on and learn that while you're still young. Nothing a woman likes better than a good cry, son."

When the biscuits came out of the oven we all sat down to eat. "Anybody around here hungry besides me?" Daddy took up the platter of meat loaf. "Y'all have some and pass it."

We ate like starved people. Like the food was forgiveness – and after what we had witnessed today we wanted to stockpile enough of it to last the rest of our lives, because there was no telling what might could happen that would make us in serious need of it.

~

I love gossip. Even people who say they hate gossip, I think they love it too. When you live someplace like Pinetta, where there are not many people and not much happens, you need gossip a lot more than other places. You depend on it to make you think you are in a real place, with other real people, living real lives. If people did not stay busy talking about each other and exaggerating things out of all proportion and retelling the worst stories they know again and again, then you would feel lost and lonely. I would. Nobody says you have to believe gossip if you don't want to, but there is no law against enjoying it. That's not a actual sin. Pinetta went gossip wild over the next days and weeks. Everybody guessed what happened and invented the necessary details to make their version believable. Some of the stories had Jewel naked and running around the yard while Jack Longmont chased her with his gun. Some had Pastor Lyons running bare-assed all the way to Madison, where his mother lives. Some said it was not actually Pastor Lyons who done the deed, but a look-alike just passing through, trying to sell his wares at the Longmonts' grocery store. Some said they didn't blame Jewel for anything she might ever do, not living with a man like Jack Longmont, who was more like a bankroll than an actual husband. Other people said Jack Longmont should have shot Jewel when he had the chance, since once a habit like hers develops, there is no putting a stop to it. Oh, people talked. They made up stories and repeated them as if they came from the mouths of Marie Longmont and her humiliated brothers. They discussed how the children had all been forever ruined by the antics of their sinner parents.

It's not that I don't have sympathy for people. I do. But the excitement of the scandal was better than Christmas. I swear. The anticipation of what might happen next made everybody happy to wake up in the morning, eager to talk to their neighbors, curious to see what news the day would bring. If anybody ever tried to say he wasn't interested in the Longmont family drama – and I don't know of anybody who ever did – he would be laughed out of town as the biggest liar of all.

Gossip was nothing new to Rennie. Although, in this case, she was left out of it as a central player, which must have been annoying to her. She was, however, a firsthand witness to the collapse of the finest family in town. It must have been encouraging to her, knowing that even the best-dressed, best-fed people in Pinetta could stoop to low and hateful ways. That must have given her some comfort.

Ever since Jewel Longmont had gotten wind of all Rennie's trouble with her crazy daddy, she had taken pity on her. Jewel Longmont regularly invited Rennie to stay over at their house and keep Marie company or do some small tasks like organize all the canned goods in her kitchen cabinets or work a few hours at the store, organizing all the canned goods on the shelves. It was like Rennie was born to organize other people's belongings. Jewel paid Rennie decent money for her efforts, and Lord knows Rennie needed it, although people said Rennie spent nearly every penny she got on Babygirl, who was not even old enough to notice or appreciate it. They said you could see Rennie at the Longmonts' store combing through the jars of baby food, teething rings, little story books and hair barrettes. They said there she was, just wasting her money, the way poor people always do.

But Jewel Longmont admired Rennie's unselfish devotion to Babygirl and said so more than once. To prove her admiration and further aid Rennie in improving her circumstances, Jewel regularly gave Rennie her old dresses, used shoes, faded undergarments and nightgowns and also her leftover face cream, broken lipsticks and other beauty potions. As far as Rennie was concerned, Jewel Longmont was like her own personal gold mine. She out-and-out worshipped Jewel Longmont and everybody knew it.

According to Cadell, Jewel Longmont was wrong to unload her giveaway clothes and used luxury items on Rennie, no matter how much Rennie loved them and wanted them, because it created a wild ruckus when she went home, hiding her worldly possessions in a sack under her skirt or wearing them stuffed like a lumpy second skin underneath her plain black dress. Her daddy, always on the lookout for any excuses to raise hell, threw a full-fledged fit if he found out Rennie had come home with any halfway decent-looking clothes or self-improvement doodads. He didn't care that it didn't cost anybody a single penny, that Rennie was getting something for nothing – which most people like. It was not that he had too much pride to accept other folks' castoffs either. He was known to drive his tin-can truck any distance required to pick up whatever broken, torn-up thing anybody was discarding – rusted-out wringer washing machine, busted car tires, broken windows, dead batteries. He saved people the trouble of hauling stuff to the dump. He didn't care how useless a thing was – he wanted it. No. It wasn't pride that caused him to go head-to-head with Rennie. It was more that he could not bear his family – especially Rennie – to have a minute's relief from their pure misery. He acted like any sort of momentary happiness was the greatest sin of all. He acted like he was a disciple of suffering, like he worshipped suffering and was planning to bear witness to it all his life.

Consequently Mr. Miller flat refused to allow Rennie to wear the clothes Jewel Longmont gave her. That's how hateful he was. Rennie would have to hide out in the woods dressed in her decent hand-me-downs, or dress in the outhouse and walk the back path to the road or wait until she got to school and change her clothes there – or at somebody's house when she asked to use their toilet facilities. Once Mr. Miller got so mad over Jewel Longmont giving Rennie an expensive red dress with a black patent-leather belt – it was practically new too – that he snatched it out of her hands and ripped it to shreds.

Cadell was the one who told this. He said his daddy was double strong when he went into a rage – like his fury gave him supernatural destructive powers. Cadell also said Rennie got so mad seeing that red dress destroyed like an old dishrag before she even had a chance to try it on that she went hysterical and tried to kill Mr. Miller with her bare hands. She clawed his face until it bled and pulled a fistful of his hair out of his scalp and spit a glob of mucus in his eyes. Her brothers had to pull her off the old man. Cadell swore it was the maddest he ever saw Rennie, that it was one time she was totally fearless. He said he would hate to ever mess with Rennie when she got like that – furious enough to kill. He said his daddy was so taken back by the fierceness Rennie brought forth to make her point that he went totally silent for maybe the first time in his life. Not that it changed anything.

Afterwards Cadell said Mrs. Miller took that ripped-up dress and cut it into quilting squares with vague plans to make something useful out of it – an item that had brought Rennie and her daddy to deadly blows. I, for one, would love to know what in the world she made that red dress into. I hate to think. Mrs. Miller was not known for her needle arts by any stretch of the imagination.

After that red dress incident Rennie tried to stay away from home even more than usual. She had become sort of a regular at the Longmonts' house. She like to say she worked for the Longmonts. She was not actually a maid or anything, but more like an all-around helper. And so that's why on the night that everything happened between Jewel and Jack Longmont, Rennie was as near to an eyewitness as there was. Because she was there. It was like she had witnessed history unfolding. People begged her to tell them what she saw, what she knew. Ordinarily, Rennie would jump at a chance to be in the spotlight and run with it. But in this case she seemed to get no real pleasure from telling the story. She seemed to try hard to shrink the story down instead of puffing it up like she did most stories. This just made it all the more interesting.

Rennie said that on the night of the big trouble Jewel Longmont had one of her bad headaches and had taken some aspirin and sipped down a glass or two of whiskey before going upstairs to sleep with Marie. "This were not unusual," she said. "Mrs. Longmont seemed like she rather sleep with Marie than Mr. Longmont about half the time. When she got those migraine headaches she always slept upstairs with Marie. On this night they went to bed early too."

Rennie said she was downstairs alone, watching their snowy TV as quiet as she could so she wouldn't wake up Mrs. Longmont or Marie. She said maybe she fell asleep in the chair, wearing only her underwear, which she usually slept in or maybe she had on one of Jewel's old nightgowns. She said she wasn't sure. She couldn't remember now – exactly. That one detail is lost. I didn't know what it mattered – what Rennie was wearing – but ever since she'd been under Jewel Longmont's influence she had taken heightened interest in all aspects of clothing. But none of us cared a thing about clothes, so we said, "Never mind that, Rennie. Go on. What happened then?"

It was late when Jack Longmont and his boys came home

unexpected – and drunk – from another one of their failed hunting trips. Rennie said she heard the jeep come up the drive and she woke up, startled. She said Mr. Longmont and his boys had a bad habit of sneaking into their own house when they came home late late, after a night of drinking and who knows what. She said she didn't want them to find her half naked in her underwear – which she could not now remember whether or not she was actually wearing. She claimed she was snatching up her clothes, trying to get dressed before they snuck into the house like thieves. But before they got up to the door she heard a terrible banging around and loud shouting on the front porch.

"My blood froze solid," Rennie said. "It turned to ice. It sounded like they was tearing the house down out there. Men hollering. Lord." When she heard the first shot fired, she screamed from the pure shock of it, like maybe the bullet was aimed at her. Before she could make herself go to the window and look out, Jewel Longmont came running to the door, wild-haired, in her nightgown, shouting, "Marie, you stay upstairs in your room. Don't come down here." She flung the door open just as the second gunshot sounded. She was screaming, "Jack, for God's sake, stop it. You're going to kill him."

By the time Rennie got up the nerve to look out the window she said all she saw was the shadow of a shirtless, barefoot man running toward the road, and Jack Longmont firing his gun in that general direction, yelling, "Run, you goddamn son of a bitch." Rennie said she couldn't make out who it was, but she heard a car engine start up out by the highway and the man screeched off into the night without even turning on his headlights. Rennie swore she never saw who it was. "Can't say for sure," she insisted. "Maybe somebody passing through, trying to steal something." This was where Rennie usually paused and waited to be urged on, begged to continue her firsthand account. We always obliged her.

"Lord, Lord," Rennie said. "After that man run off, Mr. Longmont turned his gun on Jewel, aimed that gun right at her and accused her of every sin he could think of. He was like a raving maniac, firing gunshots at his own house, scaring hell out of everybody. He was a crazy fool with that gun, I'm telling the truth now. His own sons scattered like cats, and Jewel fell to the floor, yelling, 'Jack, put that gun down. Let me explain.'

"But he was way too drunk to listen, too mad," Rennie said. "Mrs. Longmont thought he was likely to kill her – her own husband now – if he could. Them boys thought so too. Thank God they was drunk enough to have a little false courage, to try to save their mother where she was huddled on the floor by the front door, begging Jack to stop, stop, same as a little child begs. Ray, he was the first one to do something. The liquor made him bold. He come up behind his daddy and jumped on him. Then the others come too. The three of them held their daddy on the ground and wrestled his gun away. It's a wonder none of them got their brains blown out – it was such a snarl of grunts and swearing, everybody rolling and grabbing at that gun. All this time Mr. Longmont is just yelping all this hateful stuff, calling Jewel a bitch in heat and a goddamned belle cow and every ugly thing he could think of an animal nature. I mean it when I say it was terrible."

Rennie could tell a story. There was no way not to listen. You'd have to take a gun to your head – and pull the trigger – to stop yourself from listening. It would be the only way. There was nobody who got bored or wandered off once Rennie started telling something. It did not matter how many times you'd heard the story. I myself would have to be struck by lightning before I would even consider missing out on one of Rennie's eyewitness reports.

Rennie said when the boys finally let their daddy up and brought him inside the house he was like somebody from Chattahoochie, the insane asylum, snorting and banging his fists against the walls, kicking at anything in his path. He was like a rabid, slobbering dog. Like a bull charging at a red flag. Jewel couldn't do a thing to soothe him. "I can explain this, Jack," Jewel kept saying. "He came to look after –"

"You liar," he shouted. "I look after you. Me. Nobody else."

"Listen to me, Jack," she pleaded. "It's not the way –"

"You slut," he screamed. "You goddamned whore."

"Jack did not shoot Jewel – not with his gun," Rennie said. "But his words pierced her soul like bullets and killed her dead. I mean it." This was the way Rennie told it. Her exact words. "I saw it myself," Rennie said. "That those words were the death of her. Jewel was already busy dying right there before our eyes – and then Jack Longmont walked over and slapped her so hard she fell to the floor and her eye swole up like she'd been stung by a yellow jacket."

When Ray Longmont told Sowell the story later, he said that this was right about the time when Rennie began to wail hysterically, like she was the one taking the whipping. Ray said nobody could get Rennie to hush. He said she didn't stop her sobbing for days, until she about drove everybody even crazier than they already were.

Of course, Rennie leaves this part out of her version. But I still believe it.

Rennie said that night after Mr. Longmont finally passed

out cold they put him to bed downstairs. She and Marie and Jewel Longmont all slept upstairs – the three of them tangled into Marie's bed – with the door locked and a chair pressed against it. Ray, who maybe was not quite as drunk as his two brothers, sat outside their door with his gun across his lap just in case his daddy decided to barge into the room and mete out some justice of his own or to claim what was rightfully his or to commit a murder that nearly any judge in northern Florida would understand and acquit.

Rennie told and retold this story, never changing a single detail. "I was there," she liked to say. "I saw what went on."

Not everybody was inclined to believe Rennie's version of that terrible night, even though she was the nearest thing to a sober eyewitness. Rennie's reputation as a liar was a cause for some concern. Especially the part where she swore again and again that she never actually saw Butch Lyons run from the house – not exactly. Just a dark figure of a man she did not recognize – a stranger. This detail came close to ruining the whole thing. That's why everybody resisted believing her on this one point. It needed to be Butch Lyons running half naked from the house if the story was to have maximum shock value. Anybody else, a stranger for example, would diminish the pleasure folks got from the incident. See, in Pinetta, we didn't really care what strangers did. We weren't that interested in strangers, and rarely encountered them. No. We preferred that our gossip concern folks we actually knew and dealt with regularly. We gravitated toward the familiar. Especially in matters such as this.

Rennie ignored the doubters among us. Like me. She blamed Mr. Longmont for everything. She said he had been drinking like a fish for days the way he always did on hunting trips, which might explain why he nearly always came home empty-handed and had developed an embarrassing reputation as the worst hunter in Pinetta – which was really saying something. Rennie swore Mr. Longmont conjured up nearly the whole thing in a drunken stupor. "You can ask them boys of his," she said. "Ask them. They'll tell you."

But, of course, nobody was about to be that rude.

When Jack Longmont found out that Rennie was refusing to identify Pastor Lyons as the true culprit and evildoer, he attributed her moral failure to poor home training. "Everybody knows Rennie wasn't raised to tell the truth. She wouldn't know the truth if it bit her in the ass. But I know what I saw. I looked the man right square in the eye and there was no question about it – the man was goddamned Butch Lyons."

Not many folks felt like arguing the point.

So day by day the story came together like a homemade quilt, the kind my grandmother and her country neighbors made in Alabama, a crazy quilt they called it, where each person brought a scrap or two, the more irregular shaped and odd patterned the better, and they all sat around fitting the scraps together, forcing them to fit, stitching each piece to the next so that before long all the pieces came together one way or another and made one big whole thing. A crazy-looking thing.

And it was a useful thing too.

~

Mother acted funny after Jewel Longmont's church confession. She tried hard to hold all her disappointment in, but it seeped out, all day, everywhere, like some kind of sadness you could almost touch with your hands, like you could break off a piece if you wanted to and keep it in a drawer in your room underneath your folded shirts.

For a while, nearly every afternoon when we got home from school, instead of trying to make us rest like she used to, Mother took to lying down herself and taking what she called a nap. She had never done that before. Now it seemed like something she looked forward to. She would close the door to her room, take off her sandals, and lie on her side with her eyes wide-open – every day. It worried me to death.

Weeks went by before I got the nerve to go into her room and lie down beside her. She let me. I put my arm around her and she held on to my hand, squeezed it, then just kept breathing, and I tried to breathe in unison with her. She was not asleep though. Finally I said, "Mother, why are you so sad?"

She rolled over and looked at me with her glistening eyes like she was so surprised that anybody had noticed she was sad – when the truth was, her sadness was driving Sowell and Wade out of the house and keeping them out as much as they could arrange. It was only Daddy who pretended not to notice that Mother was grieving just as bad as if somebody had died.

"Why?" I said.

"Berry, baby," she whispered, like she wanted to make sure nobody would overhear us, even though there was nobody else in the house. "You're going to be a woman one of these days and you're going to find out that things are more complicated than anybody ever tells you when you are just a girl growing up. So I want to tell you right now," then she stopped and looked at me for the longest time.

"What?" I said. "Tell me."

"When you get married," she said, "even if you love your husband, even if he is a good man – you can get, you know, you can get . . . mighty lonely."

I nodded my head. I knew how that was. It was that way with brothers too. "Are you lonely?" I asked.

"Yes," she whispered. "I love you and the boys. You know that. I love your daddy. But it was Pastor Lyons – Butch – who kept me from noticing how lonely I was." She closed her eyes and shook her head, then looked at me again. "Does that make sense?"

I shrugged my shoulders because I wasn't sure if it made sense or not.

"He made me feel like I was pretty and alive and interesting."

"You are," I said.

"I used to go practice those hymns and he would just sit and listen and smile and I don't know what to say about it, but it got to be real important to me. And now he's gone. I haven't heard a word from him. Nobody's heard a word from him."

"Maybe he'll come back."

"I guess Jack Longmont will kill him if he comes back."

"I guess Jewel Longmont must have been lonely too," I said.

"I guess so." Mother pulled me against her chest and hugged me in a way that I loved, a sort of desperate hug. "You are way too young for me to be talking to you this way, Berry. I'm so sorry."

"I'm not," I said.

~

Daddy was on the committee to hire a new preacher at the Methodist church. The committee – which was Mr. Wilmont, Bye Freddy, and Daddy – had mailed a termination notice to

Butch Lyons at his mother's house in Madison. They got no reply.

Now and then somebody would swear he saw Butch Lyons's car out on some back road late at night, but nobody much believed it. He got to be practically a legend around Pinetta in just a matter of weeks. People assigned to him everything that their wildest imaginations would allow, like that he went around Pinetta late at night looking in windows, trying to see other people's wives sleeping, trying to see them in their nightgowns. People said they woke up some mornings and saw his tracks in the flower beds beside their bedroom windows. People said if anybody ever saw his car around Pinetta late at night, which everybody could recognize easy, they'd better get away as soon as possible, hurry and report the sighting to somebody who could do something about it. Jack Longmont, maybe.

It would be months before the Methodist Association sent us a new preacher. Meanwhile, we had makeshift sermons on Sundays, different people taking turns at the pulpit. It was boring mostly, but sometimes really funny too. Daddy took more than one turn giving a sermon. His heart was in it. The trouble was, most people had already heard Daddy's sermons since he didn't ordinarily require a pulpit to deliver one. A sermon could erupt out of him at any given time and often did.

Some Sundays we would get a seminary student who would come up from south Florida and preach to us. These seminary preachers looked about Sowell's age and nobody took them seriously at all, but everybody was real polite to them and invited them to dinner and wished them good luck doing God's work. We just sort of let them practice on us – you know, as a favor, while we waited for a real preacher.

~

Almost two months crawled by. Mother seemed to be getting herself together. At least, that's what I thought. She seemed like her ache had turned to irritation – which was better. We were alone in the house when she came to me with her plan. "Berry, honey," she said. "Can you keep a secret?"

The next thing I knew, I was pretending to be sick to my stomach. Practically all the time. I was staying home from school, lying around in bed all day. When Daddy and the boys got home from school, I was refusing food and Mother was taking my temperature and lying about what the thermometer said and I was going into the bathroom and pretending to throw up in the toilet. It was very exciting. I surprised myself at how good I was at faking sickness. Mother said it was a talent that could come in handy in a woman's life and she was glad to know I had the aptitude for it. She said I was excellent at faking. I could tell she was really proud of me.

But she was the most amazing one. She could be an actress if she wanted to. I swear. I believed her being the worried-half-to-death mother as much as anybody else and I knew for a fact that the whole thing was just an act. It was like we had secretly turned our own house into a stage and we were actresses and there was a thrilling play going on, but the audience – Daddy and my brothers – were not paying attention, which made our performances all the more convincing to us. I loved it all. Mother and me with such a dangerous scheme.

Nobody thought it was a bit odd when Mother finally decided that she needed to take me into Madison to see a doctor and get something for my stomach. "It might be female trouble," I heard her tell Daddy. "Berry is that age, you know." Even

Daddy took the announcement that I was going to the doctor with no questions asked. He kissed me the morning Mother and I were due to drive into Madison and said, "Berry, baby, you cooperate with the doctor now. See if he can't do something to make you feel better."

"Yes, sir," I said. But I was already feeling better.

After Daddy left for work on foot, Sowell and Wade walking to school with him, then Mother dressed like she was going to church and I dressed nice too and we got in the car, just the two of us. It was wonderful. It felt like we were going on a vacation instead of just driving into Madison and trying to find Butch Lyons's mother's house.

Mother had gotten Mrs. Lyons's street name out of the phone book. She remembered things Butch had told her about the place, how it might look, a white house with a screened porch across the front and two palm trees in the yard. She had seen a picture of Butch Lyons when he was young and about to go off to the military. He was standing beside his mother in front of a palm tree, "looking so handsome he almost set that photograph afire," Mother said. Mother swore she would recognize the house when she saw it. She said, "I'll be able to feel it, Berry. You know what I mean?"

"Sure," I said.

But finding the house was not as easy as we'd thought it would be. Most every house in Madison was white. Palm trees were everywhere among the pines, scrub oaks and great oaks. It was harder to find a house without a porch than one with a porch. No house seemed to give Mother *that feeling,* which was our primary guide.

We finally had to stop at the drugstore, which was part of the plan anyway. We wanted to get a Rexall bag to take home with us to pretend the doctor had sent us there to get medicine. Mother bought some milk of magnesia, and some junior Kotex pads, and a sanitary belt and she also bought me three Archie comic books, and one Nancy and Sluggo, which was a special treat, like a reward or something for all my good cooperation. "These are for later," she said. "When we get back home." She also bought a Superman comic for Wade and a Dick Tracy comic for Sowell. And a new fingernail polish for herself.

Afterwards we sat at the lunch counter and she ordered grilled cheese sandwiches with lettuce and tomato and two cherry Cokes and two orders of french fries. While we ate, Mother chatted in her very friendly way with the woman behind the counter wearing nurse shoes and a hairnet. "I don't guess you know a Mrs. Loretta Lyons, do you?" Mother asked the woman.

The woman was wiping off the counter where a customer left a plate so clean it looked like he'd licked it and left her a quarter, which she put into her apron pocket.

"I know some Lyonses around here," she said. "But I don't know nobody named Loretta."

"She'd be an older lady," Mother said. "Somewhere around sixty, I guess."

"Might be Mary Lyons's mama," the woman said. "Mary's mama had a bunch of kids. I bet she's nearly sixty by now."

"Where does she live?" Mother asked.

The woman took out the ink pen from her apron pocket and drew some directions on a paper napkin with little boxes for houses and arrows going everywhere. "Here," she said. "This is the best I can do."

"Thank you." Mother put the napkin in her purse and left the woman a fifty-cent tip, which was a lot.

We got back into the car and followed the map, which led us out the highway just a little bit, like we were going to Tallahassee. When we found the house we both went into a momentary panic. *That's it. The house.* We had looked for it so long that it was sort of scary to actually find it. Mother drove right by it the first time, went out of sight down the road, pulled the car over onto a dirt road and took out her lipstick and hairbrush and worked on herself, looking in the rearview mirror. I noticed her hand was shaky. "How do I look?" she asked me.

"Good," I said.

"Comb your hair, Berry." She handed me her comb.

"What are we going to do now?" I asked. My stomach had that floaty feeling.

"We'll do what we came to do." Mother was so nervous she had sweat dark rings on her blouse. "Talk to Butch." She waved a comic book like a fan aimed at her underarms. It didn't help.

When we finally pulled into the yard of the house I got so nervous my stomach was churning. I was scared I might throw up my grilled cheese. It wasn't nervous dread. It was nervous thrill.

"You come with me," Mother said. "But let me do the talking."

We walked up the steps and tapped on the door. A man opened the door and hollered for a woman who was back in the kitchen, I guess. She came out, wiping her hands on a dish towel. "Mrs. Lyons?" Mother said. "Are you Loretta Lyons?"

The woman looked her up and down, like she was trying to place her but couldn't. "Loretta is my sister-in-law," the woman said. "She lives in town."

"Can you tell me where?"

"Sure I can," she said. "You know where the courthouse is?"

We got the directions and rode back into Madison. It gave us a chance to calm down. We found the house without a bit of trouble. It was small and neat. There were those two palm trees we were looking for, one of them leaning so bad it was propped up with a board. There was the screened porch like Mother said. And there was a cement duck with six cement ducklings lined up behind her along the edge of the driveway – which we were not expecting and which I understood without being told were cute but not tasteful.

We stopped the car out front and Mother gazed up at the front door for the longest time, like maybe now that we'd finally found the place she was going to change her mind completely, put the car in reverse, and take us on back home to Pinetta where we belonged. "This is it," she said.

"Do you want me to come with you?" I asked.

"Sure I do, baby. You're my moral support."

We walked up the drive like this was an official church visit of some kind. Mother carried her purse over her arm. She walked like somebody who ought to be carrying a pair of white gloves in her hand. We knocked on the door to the porch, but nobody came, so we opened the screen and walked across the porch to the closed front door and knocked on it. Then we waited. It seemed like a long wait, but it wasn't. I heard the footsteps coming to the door, the way the porch rattled with each step, the way something glasslike rattled inside the house too, which I would later see were figurines, too many to count, sitting on a small bookshelf with no books in it, just figurines, by the door.

When the door swung open Mother was prepared, I think, to smile and ask for Mrs. Loretta Lyons. She pressed her lips together to freshen her lipstick and cleared her throat and stood at the door with her hands crossed in front of her, her purse dangling from her arm and me, her secret-keeping daughter, beside her. But when the door was opened wide enough, there he stood – Butch Lyons – looking like a giant in the doorway. It took him a second to realize who Mother was. I think I was a good hint. "Good Lord," he said. "Ruthie?"

"Butch?" Mother seemed like she'd had the breath knocked out of her, she put her hand on her chest, as if to check whether or not she was still breathing, to see if her heart was still beating. "Goodness, I didn't expect to find you here. I was looking for your mother."

"My mother?"

"To ask her where you were. To see if she would help me find you."

"No need for all that," he said. He filled the whole doorway. Behind him the house seemed cool and dark. "Y'all come in." He reached for Mother's hand and I saw him squeeze it. Mother could not take her eyes off him – nor him her for a few seconds. Then he looked at me. "Hey, Berry. How you been, honey?"

"Okay," I said.

He led us into the sitting room, which had fancy furniture and doo-dads everywhere. "You all sit down," he said. "Let me get you something to drink."

"No," Mother said. "We're fine. Honestly. We ate lunch at the Rexall." None of us made a move to sit down. We all stood in a small, tense circle. They looked at each other. I looked around the room. It was figurine heaven in there, tiny people and animals frozen into happy poses.

"I wasn't expecting company," Butch said.

"Maybe I shouldn't have come," Mother said. I was afraid she was losing her nerve after everything we'd done leading up to this one moment.

"I'm glad you came," Butch said. "I can't tell you how good

it is to see you, Ruthie. I figured you'd gone the way of the rest of the folks in Pinetta and kind of written me off."

"No," Mother said. "I had to find you. I had to see you for myself."

"Well, I guess I'm not much to see at the moment."

"I thought I'd hear some word from you," Mother said. "I thought you'd get in touch."

Butch took her elbow and looked into her face like it was a mirror and he was trying to see what he looked like in her eyes. "Sit down," he said. "Let's all sit down."

Mother and I took seats on the sofa in the middle of the room and Butch pulled the piano stool over to the sofa so that he was sitting across from Mother, his knees practically hitting hers. He held one of her hands in both of his. "What you must think of me, Ruthie."

"Are you in love with Jewel Longmont?" Mother asked. It was so like her to stab at the heart of the thing right away.

"No," he said, "I'm not in love with Jewel. Not like you mean. But she is a fine woman, Ruthie. Believe me. She did her best to save me."

"Save you? If you ask me, she ruined your life."

"No," he said. "She did the best she could to save me."

"If you say so." Mother pulled her hand away from his and gripped the latch of her purse like maybe she was thinking of dipping inside her billfold and giving him a couple of dollars. It was clear she thought he was pitiful at that moment.

"So what are you planning to do?" Mother changed the subject from Jewel Longmont. "Where will you go?"

"I've put in for a reassignment," he said. "I'm waiting to hear. A new church someplace. A fresh start."

"I see."

"I know all this must be hard for you to understand, Ruthie. I wish I could explain it to you, but I can't. Not right now."

"When?"

"Someday, maybe. It depends . . . on lots of other people."

"On Jewel?"

"She's one of the people, yes."

"I thought so."

"Ruthie, Jewel could use a friend right now. People are wrong about her. They don't understand a woman like Jewel."

"But you do?"

"Yes. I think so."

"But you are not in love with her?"

"No," he said. "I respect her. I respect the hell out of her."

I thought I would faint when he said *hell.* It made me know instantly that, yes, he was guilty as accused, guilty of everything people said, the way he could slide in and out of preacher talk and cussing. If Mother and I thought we were such all-fire great actresses play-acting ourselves over to Madison on this devious errand, what made us think Butch Lyons wasn't just as great an actor as we were? Maybe better.

"As long as you're all right," Mother said. "That's the important thing." No sooner had she spoken the words than a sob broke loose from someplace deep in her chest, and she buried her face in her hands and began weeping uncontrollably. It nearly made me cry to see it. "Mother," I said as I put my arm around her, "it's okay."

I looked at Butch Lyons. He had gone pale and looked like he was lost in the moment, confused and scared and more upset than Mother was, but he was not allowed to cry. "Tell her it's okay," I said.

"Ruthie," he whispered. "Precious Ruthie." He stood up and

pulled Mother to her feet and she just kept crying, like she was trying to stop, like everything had gone too far and she could not get things back to where they should be.

"Berry." Butch looked at me. "Let me talk to your mama a minute – alone?"

I stood in the middle of the room, unsure what to do.

"Just step out into the hall, honey," he said. "I need to talk to your mama grown-up to grown-up." But I was afraid to leave her, so I just stayed put, like the cat had got my tongue.

"Ruthie," Butch said, "tell Berry it's okay."

Mother pulled away from him and wiped her eyes with her hands and stood up as straight as she could. "Berry, you wait for me in the car. I'll be out in one minute." When I hesitated she said, "Go on now."

I walked into the hall and pulled the door almost closed behind me. Then I opened the front door so they would hear it open, but I didn't go out. I stepped quietly back down the hall and watched them from the crack in the door. I was safe spying on them because I was the furthest thing from their minds.

Mostly they just stood there, hugging. I heard him whisper over and over, "I'm sorry, Ruthie. I'm so sorry." I could not hear what Mother said except when she said, "I thought you cared about me, Butch. Me?"

"I do, Ruthie. I swear to God. I care more than you know."

"You have a funny way of showing it." She reached in her purse for a Kleenex. "Don't try to tell me God works in mysterious ways. That's God's excuse, Butch. Not yours." She blew her nose. I could tell she was nearly through crying – for now.

"You're the only person in Pinetta who cared enough to try and find me, Ruthie," Butch said. "I appreciate it too. I swear. More than you know."

"I did it for my own peace of mind," she said, which wasn't entirely true.

"Well, then I want to ask you to do one more thing, Ruthie. For me."

She looked at him with her balled-up tissue in her hand. "What?" she asked.

"I want you to go out of your way to see about Jewel and Rennie and little Marie. See that they're okay. This has been hard on them. Way too hard – and none of it is their fault."

"What is it you want me to do for them, Butch?"

"Just show them a little kindness, Ruthie. That's all. Can you do that?"

"Kindness is my middle name," she said sarcastically. "You know that better than anybody." She ran her fingers through her hair, which was already messed up.

"You are a beautiful woman, Ruthie Jackson." Butch smiled at her like he really meant it. A chill ran over me just hearing him say it. I froze for a minute, overwhelmed by the power of such a sincere compliment – even if the compliment was not paid to me and I knew already that nowhere in my future did such a sentence lurk. It was a truly fine moment to witness. "You are a mighty beautiful woman," he said again.

So that was what Mother had come for. That one sentence. I knew it just as well as if I were Mother. The moment he spoke the words, I knew that was what this whole thing was really about – hearing him say that, being allowed to believe he meant it. I believed it. I certainly did. His voice was true.

On that note I slipped out the front door and hurried to the car and got in, which was like getting in an oven, but I was used to that. I sat and waited for Mother. I debated reading my Archie comics, but I wanted to save them until I got home and could read them in my bed – alone in the room. I was nearly melted by the time Mother finally came out of the Lyons house. She hurried down the walk, looking right and left like she hoped nobody saw her who could later be called to court to testify. She got in the car and slammed the door so hard I thought maybe she was mad, but she wasn't. "Okay, Berry, honey," she said. "Let's head for the barn."

On the ride home she was quiet. So was I. When we were less than a mile from our house Mother said, "This is our secret, Berry. Right?"

"Right," I said.

"If your Daddy asks, we saw Dr. Eckemeyer and he said there was nothing wrong with you except that you are becoming a young woman. Right?"

"Right," I said.

"I love you, Berry. You know that, don't you?"

"Yes," I said.

When we finally pulled up in the driveway Mother said, "Do you think you might like to invite Marie Longmont over one afternoon?"

"Maybe," I said.

"Good," Mother said. "You think about it."

~

As it turned out, I didn't have to invite Marie Longmont anywhere, because Sowell did. He invited her to the end-of-the-year Good-bye Night at Pinetta School. It was technically a graduation dance, but you didn't have to graduate to go and nobody called it a dance since so many people were against dancing. This way if you just called it one thing it stopped mattering if it was really another thing. This way even people who didn't believe in it could participate fully. The people who disapproved of dancing could just pretend they didn't know it was going on. Pinetta people were good at that. The Good-bye Night was boy ask girl. Some years there were not enough girls to go around. Some years there were too many.

We were shocked out of our minds when we found out Sowell had asked Marie. Mother and Daddy both acted like it was the most mature thing Sowell had done up to that point. They seemed so interested in the details of everything and immediately began referring to Marie as "Sowell's little girlfriend." He did not object to this either, which was the weirdest thing of all.

I got the crazy idea that Jimmy might invite me to the Good-bye Night. He was still sort of my best friend. And Lord knows I was about the only friend he had at all, strange as he was. I thought even if Jimmy didn't think up asking me that Mrs. Ingram, his mother, would. I thought maybe she would make him take me. But the idea never seemed to occur to her either. I had to make a fool of myself and bring it up like the desperate girl I was. "Are you going to the Good-bye Night, Jimmy?"

We were sitting out in the car carcass in his yard. He was reading something boring and old-timey. "Who's asking?" he said.

"Me. Who do you think?"

"You sure Cadell Miller didn't put you up to asking me?"

"Cadell? What are you talking about?"

"You think maybe Cadell will go to the Good-bye Night?" Jimmy asked.

"No," I said. "You know the Millers don't go to anything. Not anything to do with dancing for sure."

"Then I'm not going either," Jimmy said. "If I have to dance with somebody, I want it to be Cadell. He's smart. He's the only person I feel like dancing with."

I snatched the book out of Jimmy's hand. "Are you crazy?" I said, which was a rhetorical question since I already knew he was. "You can't dance with Cadell. Number one, he's not allowed to dance. And number two, he's a boy, stupid."

"Noboby else I want to dance with," Jimmy said.

"You're a freak," I said. "You know that?"

"So what?" He grabbed for the book.

"What have you been reading?" I asked him. "What is messing up your head so much? You need to get your nose out of those books or you are going to end up a oddball with no friends at all."

"I'm friends with the people in the books," he said.

"What people?" I shrieked.

"The characters, dummy. The people the books are about?"

"That's crazy," I said. "The people in the books aren't real. You can't be friends with people who aren't real."

Jimmy yanked the book out of my hand. "Yes, they are. They're real. The people in the books are more real than you are – or me either. They're as real as real can be."

"You're pathetic," I said. "I guess you know that."

"So what?" he said. "I don't care."

It made sense why Jimmy stayed to himself so much. He was not right. He was off. I guess he didn't want people to know it, even though everybody already did. Nobody but me would bother to sit out in the go-nowhere car with him by the hour and act like he was a regular person. He ought to appreciate that.

"So I guess you don't want to take me to the Good-bye Night, then?" I asked.

He looked up from his earmarked page. "What?"

"Me," I said. "The Good-bye Night."

He shook his head. "No," he said. "I told you I'm not going."

"I hate you." I slapped at his arm. "You're hateful."

Jimmy looked at me like I was the crazy one. That's what crazy people do, try to make you think you're crazy too, as crazy as they are. But in my case, I was nowhere near as crazy as Jimmy Ingram.

"You ought to ask Cadell about people in books," Jimmy said. "He knows. He reads about people in the Bible and says they are as real as anybody in Pinetta. Ask him."

"Shut up," I said. "I don't care what Cadell thinks. Or you either."

I am proud to say that as miserable as I was to get rejected by Jimmy, who, technically speaking, should be the one getting the rejection, I didn't cry a single tear. I went and laid down on my bed, couldn't find my cat right then, so I just laid there and chewed my fingernails to the quick.

Several times before the Good-bye Night Marie walked home with Sowell to our house after school and just sat around with us in the hole in the weeds, drank some sweetened tea, ate some pimento cheese sandwiches. Marie was sort of quiet but seemed to like being in Sowell's company. Seemed to like listening to what he said with no regard to whether or not any of it was true.

I don't know who told Rosemary about Sowell asking Marie to the Good-bye Night. Maybe it was me in a hateful moment. But probably it was Jimmy in an ignorant one. I guess Rosemary saw us clustered around out in the weeds, sitting with our legs dangling in the hole, talking about nothing anywhere close to interesting. She came bounding across her yard like she was on her way to put out a fire, the closer she got the faster she ran. I can still remember how she looked – her face blood-red, her squinted eyes, her grinding teeth, her yellow hair curling on her head, going wild with frizz. She was mumbling.

It was rare to see anger so openly displayed – it was like seeing somebody stark naked. You cannot turn your head from it. Most people knew how to keep their anger in the back pocket of their pants, stitched into the hemline of their housedress, stuffed in a secret compartment in their purse – somewhere you could get at it if you needed to, so that you were never entirely without it. But it was not like Vitalis that men slicked onto their heads, or the lipstick women used to paint their smiles – so obvious. Everybody had some anger – I thought maybe the Bible said so – but with most people you'd have to strip-search them to find it. But not Rosemary Ingram. Anger was one of her traits, like milk skin, curly hair, those long second toes on each foot. I knew Sowell was in bad trouble.

The news of the invitation was especially terrible for Rosemary because of what she had been letting Sowell do when her mother wasn't home. She would take Sowell into the bathroom in their house, acting like she had a splinter in her hand that she needed him to help her get out with the tweezers and peroxide or acting like she had got a speck of something invisible in her eye and she knew he was the only one who could spot it. Then she would take her shirt off and let him touch her breasts and suck them.

That wasn't all either. It was like she would let him do anything he wanted to and he got more and more inventive every time. Some days she completely undressed herself, panties and everything, and she let Sowell watch her do it. Then she took his hand and guided it around like he was a blind boy or like she was giving personalized guided tours. This went on a long time. One day he wanted to unzip his pants – so he did. Rosemary stayed in the bathroom a long, long time playing with his you know what, his *thing* – kissing it and stuff. She said Sowell just took it out of his pants and sort of handed it to her, like a present or something.

The reason I knew this was because Rosemary always told Jimmy and me what they had done. She liked to tell it. She would wait for Sowell to go home – watch him strut across her yard – then tell us and sometimes her sisters the details. "It's what you do when you love somebody," she was fond of saying. She spoke with such absolute authority that it didn't occur to me to doubt it. Sometimes her sisters fought with her and gave her the kind of reputation speeches mothers usually give and threatened to tell on her, but as far as I know they never did.

I will admit that Sowell was always on the lookout for a chance to get into Rosemary's house and be alone with her in the bathroom. When Mrs. Ingram went off someplace – especially if she took some of the other girls with her – you could see Sowell sort of circling the house, making himself seen, making it known he was available for any splinter removal that might be required.

They would stay in there a long time. I knew because more than once Jimmy and I were watching TV while this was going on. I was nervous because I knew they were not supposed to have people in their house when their mother wasn't home. I didn't want to get caught by Mrs. Ingram and turned over to Daddy. But Sowell, he acted like he didn't care.

Sometimes when Mrs. Ingram was at home Wade and Jimmy and I would see Sowell and Rosemary go out to the hole in the weeds. They would jump down into the hole and disappear. If we tried to sneak up on them, Sowell would threaten to pound us into the dirt, to make a puddle of mud out of us. Sometimes he got Wade to stand guard a good distance away, lookout duty he called it. Wade took this seriously and Sowell paid him in ingenious ways – drawing him pictures of jet fighters dropping bombs or old-time warriors with swords poking each other's eyes out.

We mostly stayed away from the hole when Rosemary and Sowell were there. Jimmy was afraid of Sowell for one thing, plus I don't think he wanted to get a real view of his sister with her clothes off, in case they were off.

I was more curious than he was, but I don't know why since I had seen Rosemary without her clothes more than once already. Sometimes she walked around her practically all-girl house naked. She might be dripping wet, walking from the bathtub to her room, or she might be stark naked sitting on the bed in the girls' bedroom, painting her toenails. Her nipples were as white as her skin. They had hardly any color to them. I noticed that. Her breasts were pretty big and you could tell she just loved them, loved people to see them and mention them. She was always touching them. I liked Rosemary best when she was naked. That was when she was most interesting. Maybe Sowell thought so too.

Rosemary tried to kill Sowell the afternoon she found out he invited Marie to the Good-bye Night. I guess she assumed that he would invite her, that she'd earned it with her pounds of flesh. She ran up and took a flying leap at him from behind, knocking him into the hole. She went at him the way our yellow cat went at dogs who had the bad judgment to growl at her. She was scratching and clawing, hissing worse than a snake. "I hate you, Sowell Jackson," Rosemary kept saying. "I hate your guts."

I believe she really meant it.

Sowell, of course, acted like he was completely surprised by her violent reaction. Like it was the last thing he was expecting – Rosemary to be upset over a stupid Good-bye Night. He looked genuinely bewildered. "Rosemary, what in hell is wrong with you?" he said over and over.

Rosemary jumped on Sowell again and knocked him to the ground and they rolled around in the hole. He was totally shocked and tried to shield himself and get away. But her fingernails were all over him, digging into his flesh. She was making these sounds in her throat while she went at his face and neck like what she wanted to do was remove all the features from his face. She was trying to jab her knee in his private place and in between the clawing and scratching, she slapped him – hard. I knew he was hurting. Even when he rolled over on top of her and pinned her to the ground, she was still trying to kick him. She was crying so hard I think he was truly afraid.

"You get ahold of yourself, Rosemary," he ordered, like an order was just the thing she was going to respond to. "I mean it," he shouted.

"Go to hell, Sowell Jackson," she said. "Just go to hell."

He had to sit on her the longest time because if he let up even slightly, she would go at him again, like her plan was to rip him to pieces or die trying. He was sort of trapped down in the hole with her. We were there to witness it. Including Marie Longmont, who I guessed at this point in her life could not be shocked by anything that happened. She watched in silence, as if a fight was of no great interest to her.

Jimmy and I were yelling, "Let her up, Sowell. You have to let her up."

"Not until she calms down," Sowell said. "Not until she gets hold of herself."

Rosemary spit in his face.

"If I was the kind of boy that hit girls," Sowell said to Rosemary, "I would whip your sorry butt."

"Try it," she said. "I'd like to see you try it." She spit at him again.

"You do that again," Sowell warned, "and I'm through being a gentleman."

So she spit in his face the third time.

"One more time and I'm going to knock the hell out of you."

She spit again, a spray of spittle we could see when it landed. Before he leaned his head down against his shirtsleeve to wipe his face like he'd done the other times, he drew his fist back and socked Rosemary in the mouth so hard it sounded like he'd killed her. I swear she went limp. She put her hand to her mouth and blood was everywhere. "You asked for that." Sowell climbed off of her. "You begged."

Rosemary laid still, crying in jerks, her mouth bloody and now her hands bloody where she tried to cover her mouth. She rolled over on her side and curled up as tight as a roly-poly.

Sowell climbed out of the hole and he was so mad he was crying. Tears were running down his face and he would not look at anybody. He walked across the yard home and did not say come or go to Marie, who sat there like a girl in a trance.

Jimmy helped Rosemary up. No matter what else she might be, she was still Jimmy's sister. No matter how hateful she could be to him, he always claimed her. I liked that about Jimmy. Rosemary had a gash in her lip and chin. Her teeth were blood-red and there were strings of spit hanging out of her mouth. She was sweaty and dirty and her hair was crazy and her eyes were swollen. "Your brother is a bastard," she said to Wade and me. "I hate his guts."

She looked at Marie and for a minute I thought she was going to attack her. There was such a flash of fire in her eyes. "You can have Sowell Jackson," she said. "I wouldn't go anywhere with him if he was the last boy on earth."

Marie was pale and silent.

"He's just hoping you're a slut like your mama," Rosemary said. "That's the only reason he asked you to the stupid Goodbye Night."

We watched as Jimmy helped her navigate out of the hole and as she was limping home she turned and yelled to Marie, "You two deserve each other!" She was still crying a little bit.

"Man," Wade said, "Sowell is going to get it now. Hitting a girl." He took off toward the house to find Sowell. For one thing, I think he wanted to help him and protect him. For another thing, I think he wanted to make sure that if there was any more violence in store, he didn't miss it. Wade was a violence enthusiast.

Marie and I were left alone together at the hole. We sat in silence for the longest time, each of us sort of clawing at the soft dirt with a small stick, unearthing nothing. I felt like I'd inherited a fancy car that I didn't know how to drive. Only it was a girl, and if she had been a car, she would have shown signs of having been recently wrecked, crushed fenders, dented chrome, you know – so that you couldn't be sure how much of a safety risk she was. "Sowell will probably be back in a minute," I said.

She didn't respond, just looked out across the weed patch, away from the houses, tilted her chin and closed her eyes and seemed to be off in a sad daydream or something. I didn't know what to do with her. It wasn't like we didn't know each other. We'd been in school together since the beginning of time, but she was a year older than me and in the summers she went off to Baptist church camps and on other vacations to Silver Springs. Her daddy sold a lot of rattlesnakes to Ross Allen, the snake handler, down there. She had also been to Daytona Beach, Panama City and Atlanta. I'd never been any of those places. Just to Alabama to see my country grandparents and to Georgia to see my town grandparents. That was all. Right this minute that seemed to matter.

"I hear Sowell is taking you to the Good-bye Night," I said.

"He is the sweetest boy at Pinetta School," Marie answered. It was like an official announcement. "He's the only one I like. The rest of them are mean and silly."

I stared at her like maybe she had missed what just went on, Sowell punching a girl in the mouth, busting her lip. "Sowell is not perfect, you know." I felt like it was my duty to give her a balanced perspective.

"Are you going to the Good-bye Night?" Marie picked up a clump of red clay and was crumbling it in her hand.

"Nobody invited me," I said. "Not that I was expecting anybody to."

"Too bad," she said.

"I can go with my daddy, you know, serve punch or something if I want to, but I don't."

"Oh," she said.

"I'll go over there with Mother probably. She likes to go and look at everybody. We do it every year. See how everybody looks. Then we'll come back home."

Marie seemed not to be listening. She seemed to be thinking her own thoughts that didn't have a thing to do with the stupid Good-bye Night. "Rosemary sure was mad," she said. "She has a bad temper."

"She loves Sowell," I said. "It makes her do all kinds of crazy things. She's done worse things than what she did a minute ago. Believe me."

"I guess she hates me now."

"Maybe," I said. "But I guess she'll get over it."

Marie let her handful of red dirt fall into the hole, slowly, like it was being measured by touch. She watched it float down, making a coarse, grainy dust cloud.

"I saw you at church that day my mama confessed." She spoke in a dreamy voice. "You were standing next to Sowell."

"I was. I guess that was the worst day of your life." I held my breath in case it was the wrong thing to have said. It was one of those sentences that just said itself.

She nodded and let out a deep breath. "It was like one day people liked Mama and me and the next day they hated us."

"People are stupid," I said.

"What did you think?" She turned to look at me. It was the first time all day she had looked me square in the eye. Her eyes were such a pale blue that they looked almost lavender, but the sadness in them made you think that the color was not beautiful, that it was a distortion of what natural blue eyes should be, maybe what hers had been before everything happened.

"I don't know," I said.

"Yes, you do," she insisted. "You know."

"Everybody says your mother is beautiful," I said, reaching. "And she is."

She nodded like she would accept that. "What else?"

"What she did was real hard – I would die if I had to do it. I know it embarrassed the life out of her, you know, for everybody to know about her and . . . you know."

"Preacher Lyons?"

"Right." Marie was crumbling another dirt clump, getting another cloud ready to let go of.

"And your daddy was up there, yelling at her. I really hated that. Then when your daddy started to cry . . . I don't know. I was thankful it wasn't me and I promised myself I'd be nice to you – forever – after all that."

"Did Sowell promise that too?"

"No," I said. "Sowell doesn't promise stuff."

She let the dirt fall, sort of shaking it gently as she released it, making the dust swirl as it fell. "Nobody told me she was going to confess to anything," Marie said. "I didn't know what she was going to do until she did it that morning."

"Well," I said – and I knew I shouldn't have – "if it makes you feel any better, my mother has done some stupid stuff too – concerning Pastor Lyons."

"She has?" Marie looked hopeful for the first time all afternoon.

"Sure. I bet lots of women have."

"What did she do?"

"I can't say. I promised I wouldn't."

"Well," she said, "all I can say is, you better hope she doesn't decide to confess in front of the whole world."

It was the worst possible thing I could imagine. "I'd kill her," I said.

"Well, if you didn't," she said, "probably be lots of other people who'd want to."

Sowell never came back out to the hole. I guess we waited a good hour before giving up on him. I walked Marie most of the way home, at least as far as the gas station. This is strange to say, but she liked me. I could tell. It was just a feeling, but it went all through me and I knew with absolute certainty. It was an excellent feeling. Not one I had had much experience with. I didn't ask myself why Marie liked me. I didn't know if the feeling was just for today or forever. But there was nothing to do but enjoy it while it lasted.

"Tell me what your dress looks like," I said when we got to the gas station. She gave me a free pack of Life Savers. I guess she got everything free.

She described a dress that sounded like it was out of *Grimm's Fairy Tales.* I didn't even try to visualize it. It was blue – that was all I could remember. She ordered it out of a catalog and they sent it from Atlanta.

"Berry," Marie said, "promise me you'll come to the Goodbye Night with your daddy or your mother or somebody. Rennie's coming. You don't want to miss seeing her all dressed up."

"Rennie can't come," I said. "Mr. Miller won't let her. There's dancing."

"She's coming. She told me. My brother Ray is bringing her."

"She must have a death wish," I said.

"Maybe she has nothing to lose." Marie smiled.

On the walk home I felt bathed in sweet, soft air. I sucked on my Life Savers and was light-stepping and deep-breathing and strangely content. When I got home I found Sowell lying in his cavelike bottom bunk, pretending to do his homework but mostly drawing all over his notebook, pictures of men in action poses.

"What did she say about me?" he asked when I sprawled out on my own bed.

"She likes you," I said.

He smiled and looked genuinely relieved. He rolled over on his back and rested his forearm on his forehead and went silent again.

~

I didn't know it was possible for Sowell to look as good as he did on the Good-bye Night. Mother got him a new suit in Madison even though Daddy told her not to. He got a new shirt and tie and new shoes and he looked as good as a boy in a magazine. His hair was thick and tried to curl out of control, but it had a natural part in it that looked perfect. He put on some of Daddy's Old Spice and a pair of Daddy's cuff links and I was not ashamed to claim him for a brother.

Mother drove him to pick up Marie. Daddy had to be at the school an hour early to see about things. Sowell adamantly refused to let Wade and me ride along when they picked up Marie. But Mother told him not to be ridiculous, of course we were going. What was he thinking? So we cleaned up too, made ourselves presentable and we all set out for the Longmonts'.

I knew Marie wouldn't care if Sowell brought his brother and sister – not to mention his mother – with him, that she might like us to see her in her Atlanta dress. We sat in the car while Sowell went up to the door. Jewel Longmont opened it and hugged Sowell's neck and then looked out at us bunched up in the car and waved us hello, then waved us to come on inside, and we did. Sowell looked ready to kill us.

Marie looked wonderful. She looked a lot older than she was in that blue dress. It was not the elaborate-sounding thing she had described now that I saw it. It was simple, simple. As blue as her eyes, and her dark hair was combed into a pageboy and she had on lipstick as red as her mother wore. She looked older than Sowell I thought. The way he was looking at her I think he thought so too, like he was definitely in over his head and couldn't be happier about it.

"Hey," she said to us.

"Marie, honey," Mother said, "you look as pretty as a picture."

"Thank you," she said.

"Jack wants to get some pictures," Jewel said. "Marie, you and Sowell go in the living room there and let your daddy snap some pictures." Marie walked toward the living room and Sowell followed her like a shy puppy. Wade followed him.

"Come on," Jewel said to Mother and me, "come back to the kitchen and I'll get us a cold drink."

Her kitchen had wallpaper in it. It was like a Yankee house or something. Our house had sand-painted walls, rough to the touch. I had never seen a wallpapered room before, a design with little kettles and rolling pins and spoons all mingled in with a flowery vine. It was brown with bits of yellow and green. It was the sort of thing that if you lived there, I bet you'd study and memorize the pattern and soon it would be etched in your mind and would come to you anytime you thought of home.

Jewel took out an ice tray and ran it under the faucet, then cracked it open. She got out four glasses and filled them with ice cubes. She seemed as nervous as a cat – a friendly cat. She got a couple of RCs out of the refrigerator and popped the caps off on a bottle opener fastened to her kitchen counter. I was impressed. Her hand shook while she poured the RC, which fizzed and threatened to overflow.

"It was mighty sweet of Sowell to invite Marie," she said. "She is really tickled."

"She looks real pretty," Mother said.

Jewel looked at me. I could tell she was at a loss, whether to express sympathy on my behalf or not. "Berry, sweetie," she said, "I bet this time next year half a dozen boys at Pinetta School will be trying to take you to the Good-bye Night."

I was paralyzed, trying to think what to say. I knew I turned red, because it was like Jewel Longmont was telling an out-and-out lie and we all knew it.

"You know what they say?" Jewel looked at Mother. "The late bloomers, those are the girls who end up being happiest."

"I don't know," Mother said. "Maybe."

"First to bloom, first to fade," Jewel said. She was jumpy as a cat. "Here," she said, handing us our RCs. "Sit down."

We pulled out chairs at the kitchen table. It had plastic place mats at each place, scenes from snowcapped mountains. I wondered if they had been ordered from Atlanta. There was also a salt and pepper shaker set – a green Aunt Jemima was salt and a red Aunt Jemima was pepper.

"Jewel," Mother said. "I'm real sorry I haven't gotten over here to see you before now. I want you to know I've meant to." She spoke these sentences like they were rehearsed lines.

Jewel nodded, like she didn't believe Mother but she appreciated the thoughtfulness of the sentiment anyway. "It's like I've got leprosy or something," Jewel said. "I know it's not easy for people."

"Pinetta is a small town," Mother said. "In fact, it's so small it doesn't even qualify as a town. Your gas station is all there is here – that and the school and the two churches. That's not a town, is it?"

"Not hardly." Jewel seemed to me like a woman craving a cigarette. Like Mrs. Ingram gets when she's out of cigarettes and has to send Jimmy to the store after some.

"A small town is not . . . well, I don't know. I hope Ford and me will move to Jacksonville one of these days." I had never heard Mother say that before. "There's not room enough to breathe in a little place like this."

"You're telling me." Jewel smiled halfheartedly.

"All this will blow over in time," Mother said.

"Yes," Jewel said. "Well, I hope I live to see it."

"Look," Mother said, "why don't you come over to my house next week and have a cup of coffee. I'll make cinnamon rolls. It'd do you good to get out of this house."

"Just you and me? Nobody else?"

"That's all – us and the percolator."

"No sermons? I don't think I can stand any more attempts to save my soul."

"I won't preach about anything if you promise not to confess to anything."

Jewel's laugh was sour-edged. "Monday, after I get the kids off to school."

"Mama, they're ready to go." Wade came in the kitchen, looking all around. I think the wallpaper stunned him too for a minute. He looked sort of horrified by it.

"Here, baby," Jewel said. "I poured you a RC right over here, honey."

Wade made a beeline for it. "They're ready to go," Wade said. "Now."

I was scared of Mr. Longmont. He was friendly-acting and all, but it just seemed like he was simmering underneath his smile, like there was some kind of invisible anger that didn't show in his face, but you could feel it in the air around him, like heat coming off his skin, the loud smell of his Aqua Velva. Or maybe it wasn't anger. It could have been sadness or the residue of humiliation. I don't know. Maybe he had thought the truth would set him free – but it didn't. And that was really the betrayal he couldn't stand.

I noticed that he never looked square at Jewel. Nor she at him. They were like a couple of voluntarily blind people going through the familiar motions they'd been practicing all their lives.

Jack Longmont went in the house when we drove off, but Jewel stood on the porch until we were out of sight. Marie watched her with a worried expression.

"Where are your brothers?" I asked.

"Earl and Ray already left for the Good-bye Night," Marie said. "And James is out back, working on his truck."

"He's not going to the dance?"

"He likes to stay home," Marie said.

We let Sowell and Marie out at the school cafeteria, which had been transformed into a tropical paradise. We could see the palm leaves and the crepe paper draped from the ceiling and the tissue-paper flowers on the tables. Daddy was standing at the door, like a guard. He waved to us.

We watched Sowell and Marie walk up to the door. "The tension at the Longmont house was so thick you could cut it with a knife," Mother said.

"Mr. Longmont gives me the creeps," I said.

"I'm worn out," Mother said. "I feel like I've run a mile."

We went back home and ate tuna fish sandwiches for supper and waited until nine o'clock to go back. That way everybody would be there and the dance would be going full steam and we could be less conspicuous. Mother put on a good dress that showed her figure and pinned up her hair and I put on a dress too. I brushed my hair and put Vaseline on my lips. "This is the last year I am doing this," I told myself. "What do I want to stare at everybody for?"

When we arrived Wade went straight for the refreshment table. Mother found Daddy and I heard him whistle when he saw her. Later on they would dance together and everybody would stop and stare at them – shocked that the principal could dance, and would, even though he did it every year. Afterwards everybody would clap and cheer and act amazed. Except me.

The lights were dim in the cafeteria. Mrs. Freddy's husband, Bye, was playing the records on the loudspeakers he had rigged up around the room. She looked like a million dollars in a red dress with a scoop neckline and pearl earrings. She was standing near him with a cup of punch in her hand and a smile on her face. She winked when she saw me and waved her pinkie finger as she took a sip from her drink. If I could have danced with anybody I wanted to, she was the one person I would have chosen. I was about as bad as Jimmy. Only not really.

I was looking for Sowell and Marie. For one thing, I wanted to see if Sowell knew how to dance. I was weaving my way to the back corner of the room when somebody tapped me on the arm. "Hey, Berry," a familiar voice said.

I turned to stare at Rennie in a black dress – but not the usual one. This one was fancy and low-cut and made you think one wrong move and her breasts might get loose – just like in the movie magazines they had at the beauty parlor in Madison. I'd studied the pictures when I went with Mother to get a permanent wave. I was pretty sure Daddy didn't allow people to wear dresses like this to school activities. I bet Rennie was the first girl who ever tried. Rennie's hair was pinned up on her head, but by now had begun to come loose and fall around her face in curly strings. She stood with her hands on her hips and I watched a drop of sweat run from her neck down to the dark line between her breasts. "It is hotter than Hades tonight, idn't it?"

"Rennie," I said. "You look about perfect."

"I bet you're surprised to see me here." She grinned.

That was not the word for it.

"Jewel Longmont give me this dress." She turned in a circle so I could see it. "Shoes too."

"You look like a movie star," I said.

"I feel like it."

"Does your daddy know?"

She laughed. "What he don't know won't hurt him, will it?"

"What if somebody tells him?"

"Then I'll cross that bridge when I come to it. Besides, it's your daddy I'm worried about."

"My daddy?"

"He tried to get me to go home. Can you believe that? He said, 'Rennie, I know dancing is against your religion.' But I told him it's not my religion, it's my daddy's religion. My religion includes dancing. I personally believe in it. I told him, 'America is a free country, isn't that right?' He said, 'Do your mother and daddy know where you are tonight? That's all I want to know.' And I said, 'Sure they do.' "

"He doesn't want you to get in trouble," I said. "That's all."

Rennie laughed. "Oh, Berry, if you only knew your daddy like I do."

"He's not as mean as he acts," I said. "It's just his job."

"He don't like all these boys lining up to dance with me," Rennie said. "He acts like I'm doing something wrong. He don't have the right to act like that, does he?"

"Who did you come with?" I asked.

"Mrs. Longmont made her boy Ray bring me. I told her it was okay with my daddy. Ray is over there at the punch." I glanced in that direction and, sure enough, there he stood, sweat-soaked, guzzling cup after cup, like a very thirsty boy. "They spiked the punch," Rennie whispered. "Just now. Ray and Earl did."

Earl had brought Rosemary Ingram. His arm was around her. She stood beside him, laughing while he gave her a sip of punch out of his cup. You could see where her lip was busted. She was wearing a dress Mrs. Ingram had made for Rosemary's older sister Jeannie. I remembered seeing the fabric spread out on the kitchen table when she was cutting out the pattern last year.

"Hey, Berry!" Marie came up behind me. "See, I told you Rennie would be here tonight. Look at her here. Can you believe it?"

"Not hardly," I said.

"You'd of thought the queen of England was here tonight when Rennie came walking in," Marie said. "Your daddy nearly fainted. Everybody did. 'That can't be Rennie Miller, can it?' people said."

"I'm dancing with every boy here," Rennie said. "If they don't ask me, then I'll ask them."

"She danced with Sowell." Marie smiled.

"Where is Sowell?" I asked.

"Over there." She pointed to the punch bowl. "That's where all the boys are." Sowell was standing next to Earl, who had Rosemary wrapped around him, her pale arms like a pair of snakes climbing his trunk.

"Look!" Rennie said. "Your daddy is dancing with your mama."

I turned around and, sure enough, there they were, dancing to

Sam Cooke singing about a chain gang. Mother was a jitterbug champion in college. Now Daddy was twirling her around, and she was good. He was pretty good too. People were whooping and hollering. Even Sowell was watching without any apparent agony on his face.

I could hardly take my eyes off Rennie. She looked like a dark, dark version of Sleeping Beauty, just after the kiss had awakened her. She looked radiant and happy and made me marvel at the way all she had to do was imagine something and the next thing you know, it was happening.

"I didn't know you liked Ray Longmont," I said.

"I don't like him," she said. "It's just that my real boyfriend couldn't bring me tonight."

"You have a real boyfriend?"

Rennie smiled like a dark angel. "He's grown."

"Is he a soldier?" I asked.

"Well, you could sort of say that. He wants to take me away to Jacksonville."

I stared at Rennie long and hard. I had the funniest feeling she was lying.

We only stayed maybe thirty minutes, then Mother pried Wade loose from the refreshments and came to get me. "Let's go, Berry," she said. Sowell was holding Marie's hand, about to lead her back out to dance. "Sowell," Mother said, "you ought to dance with your sister one time." He looked like she'd suggested he marry me.

"No," I said. "I don't want to dance." I hurried to the door before there could be any further discussion. If you ask me, Mother's good intentions are going to lead her straight to hell – and probably the rest of us with her. I think she is lucky sometimes that nobody hauls off and hits her square between the eyes.

It had begun to rain, a good hard rain, so we made a dash for the car and got soaked. Daddy drove us home so he could keep the car. He started the engine and the windshield wipers. I loved the sound the windshield wipers made, their best efforts so momentary, so useless. "You all see your mama out on that dance floor?" Daddy said. "Wasn't she something?"

"I saw Sowell dancing," Wade said. "He looked stupid."

"Your brother is a nice little dancer," Mother said. "He looked precious."

"He looked stupid," Wade repeated.

"Sowell takes after his daddy," Daddy said. "That boy likes those slow dances where he can snuggle up to the girl."

Mother swatted Daddy. "Ford!" she said.

"The boy is no fool." Daddy grinned.

"I couldn't believe Rennie was there," Mother said. "Her parents will have a fit."

"She swears they know," Daddy said. "If they had a phone, I'd call them up. She has danced every dance. These country boys don't know what to make of her all dressed up like that. As good as she looks, they're half scared of her."

Daddy drove us as close to the back door as he could. We jumped out and made a run for it. Our yellow cat was under the porch, drenched and crying. Mother saw her before I did. She squatted at the edge of the porch and reached for her, but our yellow cat would never come to Mother, even when she pleaded. "Berry," Mother yelled. "Get your cat, honey."

I climbed under the porch and our yellow cat came right to me and she was shaking all over. She was scared to death of thunder. We saw Daddy's red taillights blur away in the black rain. "Bring her on in the house," Mother yelled to me. "She'll drown out there."

It had rained a lot of times before, but Mother had never let me bring the cat in the house before. She got a towel and wrapped her up. "Bless her little heart," Mother said. "Did you feed her tonight?"

"Yes," I said. I never forgot to feed her.

"She's terrified." Mother rubbed the cat with the towel while the cat tried to get away. "She wants you." Mother handed her to me.

I held our yellow cat up on my shoulder like she was a baby. Mother stood at the back door, looking out at the rain. "This is going to be a bad storm," she said. "My daddy always said a cat knows the weather before it happens. He said a cat can sense a storm coming. Look out there."

The rain was coming down like a torrent of nails. The sound was loud and relentless, like there was a work crew of men above us trying to hammer the roof down. The lightning looked fancier than usual too, like golden blood vessels running through the sky's black body. Every time it thundered we all froze for just a second. Our yellow cat cried out and stuck her claws into my shoulder. "We haven't had a storm like this in a while," Mother said. "It's going to be a mess getting those children home from the school tonight."

I took our yellow cat to my room and arranged her in a towel cave on my bed. Then I put on my nightgown and got in bed beside her. Wade was in the kitchen with Mother. I turned off the light and just laid in bed, looking out the window at the storm. It was getting worse by the minute. I wrapped my body around the cat and she seemed comforted by the sound of my beating heart. That's what they say – that animals like to hear a person's beating heart.

I felt like crying, but I didn't.

When Wade came to bed he got in with me because he was afraid of the storm. "Don't roll on the cat," I whispered. He was asleep in a matter of minutes.

~

The next thing I remember was Mother shaking me. "Berry," she whispered. "Wake up. It's after midnight. Your daddy is not home yet." I peeled myself out from between Wade and the cat and stumbled into the kitchen, where Mother had brewed a pot of coffee and had been working on an old crossword puzzle that was way too hard.

She poured me a cup of half milk–half coffee and put a big spoonful of sugar in it. "Here," she said. "I'm worried sick. I need you to keep me company. Look out the window," she said. "There's a big tree branch down in the yard. It's off the china-berry tree. The wind is whipping through here like crazy."

I sipped my coffee and tried to come to life. Every minute or two the lightning crashed so hard that it seemed like the world was catching fire for a few seconds. "Lord," Mother said. "Where is your daddy?"

Mother busied herself making us some toast even though we weren't hungry. We were the only house with a light on. The whole world looked black. "I have called the school half a dozen times," Mother said, "but there's nobody answering."

"They'll be here soon," I said. And it was like I had powers or something, because at that moment we saw the car headlights swimming up toward the house.

"Thank God." Mother walked out on the porch where the rain was blowing so hard she had to hold on to the doorframe.

Daddy and Sowell got out of the car with their suit jackets up over their heads and ran up to the porch. "This night is not fit for a fish," Daddy said.

"Where have you been?" Mother's voice was frantic.

"We had a heck of an ordeal up at the school with all this rain," Daddy said. "I just now got the last child picked up. Then Sowell and I had to take Marie home."

"Who is that in the car?" Mother asked. I looked and, sure enough, there was a black figure leaning against the window in the front seat.

"Rennie Miller," Daddy said. "Seems she doesn't have a ride home tonight."

"Ray Longmont got drunk," Sowell said. "He and Earl and Rosemary went off without Rennie. They were supposed to come back for her, but they never did. She's been waiting over an hour."

"I'm going to have to run her out to her house," Daddy said.

"Just let her come in here and spend the night," Mother said.

"She won't," Daddy said. "She's been crying to go home. I think there is going to be some serious trouble when Rennie gets home – she confessed that her daddy didn't have any idea where she was. I think I better be there when her daddy finds out what she's done."

"He'll wear her out," Sowell said.

"Maybe not this time," Mother said. "We don't know."

"Everybody knows it," Sowell said. "Her old man beats the hell out of her for any little thing. He's liable to kill her for this."

"Sowell, you get in the house and get on some dry clothes," Daddy said. "Look after your mama until I get back."

"This is crazy, Ford!" Mother said. "You can't go out there in this weather."

"Got to," he said.

"Don't be stupid," Mother said. "Trouble can wait until morning."

"You didn't see Rennie crying," Daddy said. "I promised her I'd get her home and talk to her daddy, and I'm going to do it."

"That's ridiculous," Mother said.

"It's just rain, Ruthie," Daddy said. "A little rain never hurt anybody."

Daddy made a dash back out to the car and Mother stood yelling, "Ford! Ford!" but the rain was so loud he couldn't hear her.

"Come inside," I said. Mother stayed on the porch, watching the car splash out of the yard toward the road. I had to take her by the arm and pull her in the house.

"God, I wish your daddy had good sense," she said.

Sowell insisted that Mother go to bed. He said he would wait up for Daddy. I think Mother was just mad enough to do it. She took some stationery into her room like she was going to write a letter and closed the door. Then Sowell went in and laid down on his own bed.

Wade was asleep in the middle of my bed, so I got up on the top bunk. The minute I settled in, I remembered the cat. I got up and searched for her, but I couldn't find her anywhere. "What are you doing?" Sowell said.

"The cat is in the house," I said. "I can't find her."

"Get in bed," he said. "She'll find you."

Outside, the storm was threatening to lift the house off its foundation and blow it into another county. The windows were rattling like bones. "Move over, Sowell. I'm going to lay with you," I said.

He scooted over against the wall and I lay down beside him in his sheet cave. It was like a little house under there. "Tell me about the Good-bye Night," I said.

"Best night of my life," he said.

"What else?"

"That's all," he said. "Just the best night of my life."

I fell asleep and slept on and off, except when it sounded like the roof was coming off, like the Germans were dropping bombs on the house. I'd see Mother get up and walk through the house, turning on lights, like she needed to see for herself that the place was still standing. I would lie awake until I saw her go back to bed.

When the tree fell on the living room, crashing through the roof, I didn't even know it. It wasn't until Mother started screaming that we all leaped out of bed and ran for her. She stood in the living room, where the trunk of the tree had come through the ceiling and lay like a dead body across the floor. It had crushed the good chair, which was folded nearly in half around the trunk. Rain was pouring in. "Get what you can," Mother yelled, taking pictures down off the wall. She was like a wild woman, grabbing things.

"Get out of there," Sowell yelled. "The roof could give way any minute." But she acted like it was extremely important that she save our throw pillows and record player and lamps. Sowell had to go in there after her and drag her out.

"Just a few things," she said. "Let me get what I can. Berry, help me."

It seemed too late to me. Everything was drenched and swollen with water.

Sowell pulled Mother into the kitchen with her arms loaded. "It's not worth it!" he yelled. "It's just stuff."

"The picture album!" she said. "You've got to get the picture album!"

Wade and I took the stuff from Mother's arms while Sowell went back in the living room to retrieve the picture album. When he came back he handed it to her and said, "Here. Take it." He closed the door to the living room. "Don't anybody go in there," he said. "The floor or the ceiling, either one could give way."

"I don't know what kind of people can sleep through a night like this," Mother said to us. It was like we had revealed terrible character flaws. "I couldn't have closed my eyes for all the money in the world." She looked like a woman who hadn't slept in days and might never sleep again. And who also had the most disappointing children in the world.

"Where's Daddy?" Wade said.

The phone lines were down. Mother had tried to get a radio station early that morning, but the electricity was out too. There was nothing for us to do but wait for daylight. Every time Mother would think about that tree crashing through our living room she would almost start to cry. But Sowell would not let her go in there no matter what. "We're all going to sit right here in this kitchen," Sowell said. "Berry, get Mama some coffee."

"The coffee is cold," I said.

"Don't matter," he said. "Pour her a cup."

Wade ate cereal out of the box and I called for the cat, but she never came. I got worried she had been in the living room when the tree fell. I got worried that she was crushed to death underneath it.

When the sun came up good there was a knock on our door. We all jumped up and went to find Mr. Ingram standing there in the drizzling rain. "Looks like you folks got some damage," he said.

It was the first time we had ventured out onto the porch. We looked around us. It looked like a giant egg beater had gone through the world, scrambling everything.

The Ingrams' old car was flipped up on its side against a tree, tree branches were everywhere and the hole in the weeds was full to overflowing, you could see a little river coming from it toward the house. Bikes and clothes off the line were strewn around along with people's lawn chairs and tools. The Burdetts' carport they had built out back had crashed in on their car. Also their tool shed was tipped over. And their swing set.

"Nobody hurt in there?" Mr. Ingram asked.

"We're worried sick, but we're not hurt," Mother said. "Step in here out of the rain, why don't you."

"Thank you, ma'am." He stomped his boots to shake loose what water he could.

"Ford is not home yet," Mother said. "He drove out to the Miller place in that weather last night. I'm about beside myself."

"That's a bad road out there," he said. "Needs paved."

"We're looking for him to be back anytime now," Sowell said.

"The worst ain't over," Mr. Ingram said. "We got us a hurricane coming."

"Must have been the hurricane last night," Mother said, "tearing through here."

"No, ma'am," he said. "That was just the getting ready for

the hurricane." He was scaring Mother to death. "Why don't y'all come over to the house? Wait with us for this rain to stop."

"No," Mother said, "we'll wait here for Ford."

"Suit yourself," he said. "You mind if I take a look in there where that tree hit?"

"Sure," Mother said. "Sowell, show him."

Mr. Ingram stood in the living room doorway a long time, shaking his head. "That's a bad one," he said. "There's nothing can be done until this rain stops. Son," he said to Sowell, "you keep them out of here now. That roof could give way."

"Yes, sir," he said.

"How's your house?" Mother asked.

"We got more leaks than we do pots," Mr. Ingram said. "And I got a bunch of girls scared to death of thunder, they're in there crying up a storm all their own. But we didn't have much damage. Knock on wood."

When Mr. Ingram left he said, "I'm going to walk on down here and see how the Burdetts fared. I'll be back home directly. If you all need anything, you send Sowell over there after me."

"Thank you," Mother said.

"You sure you wouldn't rather wait it out over at our house?"

"I'm sure," Mother said.

It continued raining all morning. Even midday it was as dark as evening. We saw neighbor men splash by with flashlights in their hands, looking up underneath houses, trying to hammer down loose shingles and boards. Mr. Burdett came by, looking for his hunting dog, Brownboy. He loved that dog.

I looked high and low for our yellow cat. All I could think was that she had snuck out the door when Daddy and Sowell had come home, but we had missed noticing. That had to be it. She was nowhere. It gave me a sick feeling, but Mother said, "Honey, cats have a good sense of protection, that's why people say they have nine lives. I bet she's up under the house right now. She's probably safer than we are."

When I mentioned our yellow cat a few minutes later Mother snapped, "I don't want to hear another word about that cat, Berry. Now that's enough."

Mother's nerves were raw.

We ate peanut butter crackers and played cards at the kitchen table. But it didn't really take our minds off things. When it got to be late afternoon and Daddy was not home it occurred to me for the first time that maybe he was dead.

At six o'clock that night Mr. Ingram came back and brought Jimmy with him. Jimmy was carrying half an orange pound cake his mother had sent – like cake was just what people needed with their house caving in on them and their father missing and a hurricane on its way.

Mother took the cake from Jimmy and thanked him like she'd been sitting around all afternoon just wishing for a slice of orange pound cake. She was pretending everything was just fine.

"You folks need to come on over to the house now," Mr. Ingram said. "You don't need to be over here by yourselves with this hurricane coming. It looks to me like your husband has got hisself stranded out at the Millers'. You need to wait with us. The wife is going to make some sandwiches."

"No," Mother said. "We're going to stay right here."

"You already got a tree through the roof," Mr. Ingram said.

"This is as safe as anyplace else," Mother said. "There's no telling what a hurricane will do."

"If I was you, I'd think about these children," he said.

"I am," Mother said.

Mr. Ingram left, shaking his head, clearly disapproving of Mother's decision. But he wasn't a man inclined to argue much with women. "Let's go, Jimmy," he said.

Before he ran out to follow his daddy Jimmy whispered to me, "Rosemary got drunk last night. The Longmont brothers brought her home passed out. She's been throwing up all day. Daddy says as soon as she feels better he is going to wear her fanny out."

"He won't," I said.

"He might," Jimmy insisted.

"No," I said. "He won't. He never does."

It surprised me the way I sounded. Like somehow I thought Mr. Ingram was less than he ought to be since he did not whip his children – and rarely even threatened to. It made me think less of him. I knew Jimmy was ashamed too to have a father who was not man enough to take a belt to any of his children.

I watched Mr. Ingram walk home through the gray drizzle, a large, slightly bent man who watched each step his booted feet took. He was a man who looked down just naturally, but especially now with the storm coming, the earth already slippery and waterlogged. He was a man who studied the ground beneath his feet, understood his personal landscape, where the path was, and tried hard not to stray from it. He looked as out of place as a mountain in Pinetta, a tired man walking home to a house full of women, *the wife,* he called her, *the girls,* and being trailed by his green stalk of a son, whose distracted stride was long and fast and no two steps in the same direction.

Where was Daddy right now? I had kept the idea pushed down all day. But, *where was he?* He knew the roads around Pinetta better than just about anybody. He knew shortcuts and back roads and paths that were hardly fit for cars. He was usually a man who could find his way where he was going – and back.

Thirty minutes later Mr. Burdett came by. He said pretty much the same thing Mr. Ingram had said, "Come wait with us."

But Mother's decision held. "We're fine right here."

Poor Mr. Burdett had still not found Brownboy. "I reckon that dog could of run all the way to Miami by now, the way a storm scares him," Mr. Burdett said.

I loved a man like Mr. Burdett who would roam around in the messy weather looking for a lost dog, calling him again and again, "Brownboy! Here boy, come on home now!" It gave me a little jolt of lightness.

Mother locked up the door when he left.

"Mr. Burdett don't give up easy," Sowell said.

"*Doesn't,* Sowell," she said. "*Doesn't* give up." She got us each a Christmas candle out of the back of a cabinet and lit it. She told us to get our pillows and spreads and we would all sleep on the kitchen floor together, put our heads underneath the table as a precaution. It felt like a extraordinary occasion. "We'll play cards all night," Mother said, as if we needed to be enticed.

Florida people were generally used to storms. Most people had stories to tell about hurricanes or tornadoes or floods at least. There was a strange excitement in the danger. Not much bravado, just an acceptance of the perils of nature as the divinely inspired way of things. People facing storms had the opportunity to contemplate their lives, to prepare for the possibility of death – which most likely would not happen – but the exercise was a good one. It made people grateful instead of bitter. Afterwards, even if everything was ruined, you could feel good just being alive. *Spared* is what people would say they were. *Spared* meant chosen, special, with purpose. How many people could say that about themselves? It was like something to look forward to.

We played cards by candlelight late into the night. Gin. Mother mostly won. Sowell's heart wasn't in it. He wasn't paying attention. Even Wade could beat him. We ate carrots and pickles and slices of white bread with preserves. The food in the refrigerator had begun to spoil. It was beginning to put off a smell.

The thunder was insistent, like door knocking that would not let up. It seemed about making us let something inside – and we didn't want to. We refused. The early thunder was almost polite, distant and just as comfortable as hearing your name called at suppertime. But the later thunder had lost all patience, given up on convincing us and decided to threaten us, like a maniac who'd knock the door down by banging his head against it if he had to. It made me understand that we don't always get to decide what we let in and what we keep out. A door is just an idea.

"When will Daddy be home?" Wade asked when Mother had ginned what seemed like the hundredth time.

"Could be anytime, honey," Mother said. "Might be first thing tomorrow after this hurricane passes through." She said this like she had adopted it as her official statement, which differed significantly from her personal opinion. Somewhere along the line she had decided not to worry out loud in front of us anymore. She had decided to be brave.

"I wish he'd come on," Wade said.

"He'd be here now if he could," Sowell said. "If he's not here, there's some reason why. Maybe Mr. Miller shot him or something."

"Sowell!" Mother looked like she might slap him.

"Everybody knows Mr. Miller is crazy," Sowell said. "His own kids are scared to death of him."

"Don't talk like that to your brother," Mother said.

Sowell looked at Wade, the candlelight putting gold flecks of fear in Wade's serious eyes, so Sowell retracted his statement. "Naw," Sowell said. "I'm kidding. Either his car broke down or the road went out. That's all."

Wade put down his hand of cards, an *I quit* sort of gesture. He put his head on his pillow like he had things to think about that couldn't wait. For a boy that loved violence so much, he did not love it to involve his own family.

"That's it, Wade, honey." Mother ran her fingers through Wade's hair that was too short to run your fingers through. "See if you can't sleep some." She glared at Sowell, who lifted his shoulders in an apologetic gesture.

Mother put her cards down on top of Wade's. Sowell and I did too. Like a surrender. The whole time we'd been playing cards I kept thinking, *What if you win a card game, get gin every time – so what? What have you actually done?* There was no thrill in it that I could see. Winning was just as flat as losing to me. It was nothing. I was glad when we stopped playing.

We all just laid quietly, listening to the whistle of the wind, to the hammering of the rain against the windows, which rattled and shook like they were within seconds of shattering. It was relentless, the force of the dark world outside. It made us feel both safe and unsafe. It made us know we were a family, a real family, gathered on our pallets on the floor under the kitchen table, touching each other, breathing together, being afraid and brave and imagining everything terrible and good.

"Berry." Sowell nudged me after we had laid quietly awhile. His voice sounded like it had the beginnings of something different in it.

"What?" I whispered.

"You ought to let your hair grow long. I bet you would look good with long hair."

My hand went involuntarily to my head and I touched my short, sweaty hair. It was cut in what Mother called an "easy style." It was really more like a "no style," but I had never minded. For years Mother had cut my hair herself with the blunt kitchen scissors. She could practically do it with her eyes closed.

"Maybe," I said, and tucked a strand of hair behind my ear.

When the hurricane came through that night we had all gone silent and into ourselves in an unsatisfactory, artificial sort of sleep. We woke to the crashing of things against the side of our house, metal things, we didn't know what. Wade's candle fell over and ignited the edge of his quilt. We all pounced on the flame with our bare hands, beating it out. "Blow out your candles," Mother ordered. I think she suddenly visualized the house catching fire on top of all the other impending disasters. "Everybody hold on," Mother yelled as the house began to quiver.

We did.

Once, we had gone to Tallahassee to take Daddy to the airport. He was flying to a principals' meeting in Knoxville, Tennessee. We stood for the longest time after his plane had lifted off and became less than a speck in the air, less than a period at the end of a very smart sentence written across the sky. He had vanished, just like that. Afterwards we stood and watched other planes land, from Atlanta and Dallas and Washington, D.C. We stood outside on a walkway and went deaf inside the roar of each plane, the gusts of hot air nearly blowing us off our feet. Our hair just about blown off our sideways heads. It was intoxicating, the sense of a shrinking self, the sense of sudden powerlessness we had watching those steel birds hit the runway, blow up a dust storm big as a rain cloud. It made us know something small about ourselves.

It felt that same way now, the sound of the hurricane like a fleet of planes landing on our roof and in our yard and everywhere around us. We were mute inside the noise, the rumble of the larger world about to crush our smaller, inadequate one. The house trembled, and we trembled with it. Outside, there were metal sounds like if planes were crashing all around us or like if God was banging pots and pans together in an angry fit.

Inside the house we were all but voiceless, our eyes tightly shut, Mother moaning, "Dear God, dear God, dear God . . ."

The ripping was so fast. I swear we could hear the pinching sound, the squeak of the nails being pulled out of the wood, then it was like the whole house shifted down a little and there was a yank that knocked the kitchen chairs over on us – we were suddenly drenched. It felt like the house was lifted a second, a second that felt like forever – then it dropped down and it was lighter than before. Afterwards things were strangely still, the trembling stopped and we listened to the noise roll away, like a giant bowling ball scattering houses like pins.

None of us moved. We lay there as if waiting for the hurricane to change its mind and turn around and come back to finish what it had started. We held on to each other, gripping clothes and skin, our fingernails buried in the flesh of the family, nearly drawing blood. "Be still," Mother said. "Stay still."

It was soot dark. The silence nearly as frightening as the noise had been. We were breathing like people who had run a long way, not like people who had not moved a muscle in what seemed like a lifetime. "Just wait a minute," Mother whispered.

We had just begun to exhale a little, to remember who we were and where, when there was a scream unlike anything human. Before we could turn in the dark to face it, it was on us, claws and all, a scream like something hellish. Sowell slapped at it, knocked it so hard it made a thud and landed on me.

"Damn cat," Sowell shouted.

Our yellow cat fixed herself to my back, her claws like screws into my skin. I tried to reach for her, to roll over, but she twisted and there was nothing I could do but jump up fast and try to stop screaming, "Get it off me. Get it off." Wade and Sowell leaped up too, and Mother, and knocked the table on its side. My glasses fell off and Wade stepped on them twice, we heard the crunches, and Sowell was trying to pry the cat loose from me, but she resisted.

"She's bloody," Sowell said.

I didn't know if he meant our yellow cat or me. Mother kept saying, "Shhhh, honey, it's just your own cat." Even though our yellow cat had never liked Mother, I think she recognized her voice, because she released a little and she let Mother pull her off of me and talk baby talk to her. She had a gash over the side of her head, one ear hanging by a bloody strip. "Poor baby," Mother was saying.

The kitchen door was blown open, but we hadn't noticed until the water began to come in, and the strange air, and we looked and saw that the porch was blown off our house, some of the nails and boards sticking out like things in shock, like little weapons, knives, spears, swords ready to injure.

"Porch is blown to hell," Sowell said. "Look out here." We all stood in the kitchen doorway and looked out at the missing thing. We looked at absence as though it was an impossible thing to believe, that something could exist one minute and not exist the next. It was sickening and exciting. We were the kind of people that counted on things staying where they were – even people – things being permanent unless somebody made some conscious decision to the contrary. But there was no decision made tonight.

We could see the remains of our porch where it had slammed into the Burdetts' house, part of it. The rest was strewn everywhere, white boards like giant matchsticks dropped in the yard, huge white bones of a skeleton that had risen from the grave and fallen apart in the process.

Neighbors began to call out in the darkness. Flashlights came out like heavy, somber fireflies and shone around the yards in long yellow streaks. The voices were like a music that was not of this world. A dark, beautiful, human music that came from a low place at the back of the natural voices, beneath them somewhere. It was so deep, the sound of the voices.

"Mrs. Jackson, you and the kids okay?" It floated to us where we stood still clumped in the doorway, the cat in my arms now, wet and bloody and wide-eyed in the darkness. "Mrs. Jackson?" The voices were coming for us, washing toward us, like boats with sentences for paddles, coming to the place where we had nearly drowned in our own fear.

"Mrs. Jackson? You hear me?"

But Mother couldn't answer. We looked at her, waiting for her answer, waiting for her to wave and say, "Over here. See, we're all still alive." But she stood as still as a statue with her arms around the shoulders of Wade and Sowell. Wade had a fistful of Mother's skirt in his hand. We just looked out at the night, the debris that could not be identified until tomorrow, if ever. The ruinedness of everything, the brokenness and the thrill of it all twisting into a big feeling that got stuck inside us and would not melt fast enough for us to make it into words.

"We're okay," Sowell yelled at the men making their way toward us with their yellow lights. "Nobody hurt." Sowell sounded like a man to me. His voice sounded like somebody I had not met yet. "Scared the hell out of us. That's all." I was in love with Sowell then, having a voice for all of us when we had none for ourselves.

When the men got to the place where the porch had been, they shone their lights on Mother's face and I swear to God, she looked really beautiful. She looked lit up and pale and perfect except for her hair, which was wet and wild and all over her face. Her clothes were stuck to her body like a fabric sort of skin with flower patterns in it. We all looked at her the way you look at a beautiful woman lying in a casket waiting to get her final reward. Which she deserved.

"Mama," Sowell said. "You go with Mr. Ingram now. He's going to take you over to his house. Berry and Wade too. You go on now."

At that moment we would have done anything Sowell told us to. We were like people who had given what strength we had over to him so that he would have enough to do what needed to be done.

I slept with Rosemary and her sister Jeannie. Well, I didn't actually sleep, I lay beside them, wishing to sleep but not imagining how it would ever be possible again. At one point Rosemary put her arm around me and whispered, "Everything is going to be okay, Berry. Don't you worry." She snuggled up beside me and her skin was hot and she still had the slightest smell of vomit about her, but her heart was beating strong and true and I knew it was a decent heart after all – I could feel it ticking against me.

It had been Rosemary who had put Mercurochrome on the cat scratches on my back. Then some gauze and adhesive tape. She did it as lovingly as a nurse.

Then together we tried to look after our yellow cat, which was sleeping in a broiler pan with a towel in it next to our bed. Mrs. Ingram said our yellow cat would need her ear stitched on with needle and thread, but nobody could hold her still enough to do it. So we taped it on the best we could and cleaned her gash with peroxide, which made her go crazy. Now she was asleep. Mrs. Ingram had given her some whiskey with an eye dropper.

The kitchen light stayed on all night. Mrs. Ingram and Mother whispered and prayed and drank glasses of black-looking Mogen David wine. Outside we could hear the cooperative shouts of the men, sounding like they were having a fine time, exploring the damage in the darkness, shouting in a way that made me think they were strangely happy. That the excitement was worth everything they had lost, because losing things was nothing new to them – but a bit of excitement was.

I had laid beside Rosemary, clutching my broken eyeglasses in my hands all night even though Mother had tried to take them from me and throw them away. The lenses were crushed into spiderwebs and the frame was broken. I held on to them anyway because they'd become such a part of me, like my face or my spine or something. I knew better than to ask Mother, "When can you take me to Madison to get new glasses?" But that was what I wanted to ask. I wanted to ask, "How soon can we turn me back into who I am supposed to be? A girl who can see."

Before daylight I was dressed and sitting in the kitchen with Mrs. Ingram, who'd made Mother lie down on the sofa to sleep. "Bless her heart," Mrs. Ingram said.

When the sun was up, Mr. Ingram woke the whole house when he came in followed by Mr. Burdett, both of them stamping their boots and shaking water off like dogs do. "We got a real mess out there," Mr. Ingram said. "The school is gone too. Blowed off the roof. Most the walls gone."

"The schoolhouse roof is over in the yard at the Methodist church," Mr. Burdett said. "I never saw such a mess. Paper all over the place. It looks like somebody dumped a truckload of confetti over there."

"Makes me think of Germany," Mr. Ingram said. "When I was overseas."

"Good thing school is out," Mr. Ingram said, "because that school is gone."

It didn't seem to me that they were talking about the school as itself but as a symbol that meant Daddy. The school gone. Daddy gone. He was the school, wasn't he? Would any students be there if he wasn't such a vigilante in seeing to it? Pinetta School and Ford Jackson were married in my mind. They were the same two-sided thing.

"We're going to have to get some help out there," Mr. Ingram said.

It was noon before Mother woke up. She sat bolt upright, her face still imprinted with the wrinkles from the quilt, her hair smashed flat on one side. She shot up like a jack-in-the-box and put on her shoes. She walked into the kitchen and rummaged through her purse. I thought she was looking for bobby pins. "Where on earth are my keys?" she said.

I took her purse out of her hands and dumped it out on the table to find the keys.

"It's no time for you to be going home, Ruthie," Mrs. Ingram said.

"I'm not going home," Mother said. "I'm going to find Ford. Where's Sowell?"

She walked out the door before Mrs. Ingram could stop her. She was down the steps and had sloshed halfway across the yard when Sowell and the others, who were trying to tack some tar paper over the hole in our living room roof, saw her. Sowell scrambled down the ladder and made a run for Mother. The other men followed him.

"Come with me, Sowell," Mother said. "We got to find your daddy."

"The road is out, Mama," he said. "There's no road."

"Well, we got to try," she said. "I need you to come with me."

"Daddy's got the car," he said.

The neighbor men were down off our roof now and circled around Mother. I think they recognized she was a woman with her mind made up. The kind of woman that can scare men – especially when the men are in a pack and in full agreement on the right thing to do. One man can argue better than a group of them. A group of men goes silent when a woman insists on something.

"I need one of y'all to drive me out to the Millers'," Mother said.

They looked at her like she was crazy. But there was no use in trying to change her mind. The next thing we knew, Mr. Burdett was in his truck with Mother and Sowell beside him, trying to start the engine, but it wouldn't turn over at all. It didn't even struggle to start. "Battery is wet." He got out of the truck, slamming the door behind him. He walked around to the front of the truck and popped the hood. "Lord God." He stepped back like a man who'd seen the devil.

Sowell jumped out of the truck too, and Mother did. Wade and Rosemary and I ran over to join them. Rosemary screamed when she saw what the men were staring at. Snakes. It looked like hundreds of them, knotted like a ball of yarn all around the engine.

Even Sowell – snake man – looked horrified.

"This rain washed them out of the ground," Mr. Ingram said. "They seeking higher ground."

"Do something," Mother said. "Get them off."

"How you propose we do that?" Mr. Ingram was clearly irritated. "I ain't sticking my hand in that nest of snakes."

Everybody looked at Sowell, but he didn't volunteer. "Good God" was all he said.

It was an awful thing to see, like ropes that tie themselves, then forget how they did it and can't undo it. It looked like a baseball when you peel the skin off of it and underneath are all those strands circling into a big knot. These were not matching snakes. They were every variety, rattler, rat, racer, black, garden, coral, corn, cottonmouth, any kind you could think of. Harmless and harmful joining forces.

Jimmy had run to his yard and looked under the hood of their sideways car and shouted. "There's snakes under here too." We went to see, yes, snakes, but not as many. Like people at a sideshow we went sloshing from automobile to automobile, calling to the women and children in every house to come look under the hood – and every engine made people scream. Every engine was strangled with snakes.

"Y'all look out every step you take," Mr. Ingram said. "There's not a snake left in hell after this storm. The water has drowned them all up and out."

I couldn't see very well without my glasses. I couldn't tell if the sight was worse because of it – or better. "Watch your step," people said. "Get some boots on. There's snakes everywhere."

From that moment on, I never took an unguarded step.

Mr. Burdett had marched into his house and gotten his pistol. He came out carrying a box of bullets in one hand and his gun in the other. It was better than the Florida State Fair when people tried to shoot wooden ducks that swam by on a piece of machinery. Mr. Burdett loaded his gun. We all stepped back, repulsed and attracted.

"You gon shoot out your gas line," Mr. Ingram warned. "Shoot a hole in your carburetor."

"Y'all step back." Mr. Burdett aimed and shot a large black snake right in the head. That started the whole knot of them squirming a little. He shot a second snake, looked like the bullet went through two heads and we couldn't tell if the knot was tightening now or loosening, but it was moving, like a whole thing – a body. Third shot and a small snake dropped to the ground. People screamed. I did. But we were also partly laughing, not because this was funny but because we were funny creatures – humans – and this was a moment when we all clearly knew it.

"Shoot them all," Wade said.

"Daddy, can I shoot the snakes under our hood?" Jimmy begged Mr. Ingram.

Mother had turned away from the spectacle and was headed

toward our porchless half house. Somebody had put a piece of flimsy plywood at an angle up against the entrance so you could walk up it – if you could balance yourself – and get in the door. I guess she knew nobody would be setting out after Daddy on this day.

It didn't matter. While we were still standing around the truck engine, we saw a rider on horseback coming up what once had been the road. He had on a hat too big for him and was riding bareback. For a split second I prayed to God that it was Daddy. We turned to watch the horse and the rider weave their way toward us through the fallen trees and the calamity.

"Who's there?" Mr. Ingram yelled.

"It's Cadell Miller here." He took off his hat and waved it. We all looked around for Mother, but she was gone. Cadell walked the horse right up to where we stood staring. "I set out this morning, looking for Rennie. Daddy sent me after her."

There was a stunned silence before Sowell said, "Rennie is not here. What makes you think she's here?"

"I just came from the Longmonts'," Cadell said. "She was supposed to be over there. But they said she'd been to that dance instead and that Mr. Jackson was supposed to get her home."

"Daddy's not here," Sowell said. "We hadn't seen him since he set out to take Rennie home."

Cadell looked like he was thinking this over. Like it had not been spoken in a language he clearly understood. He dismounted his horse, which was almost as skinny as Cadell himself. He nodded hello to me, like I was the only person he recognized, even though he knew everybody there and they did him. "Where you think they're at, then?" He had on a pair of too-big shoes caked with red mud. No socks either.

"We were trying to get this truck started," Mr. Burdett said.

"Mrs. Jackson has got herself worked up. She wants to go look for them, but between us we don't have a car that will run."

"Look a-here." Mr. Ingram nodded toward the truck engine and the stunned snakes.

Cadell stared at the engine the longest time. It did not look like something that surprised him. It seemed almost like something he had been expecting. "It's the end times," Cadell said.

"What?" Wade asked.

"The end times. It's the end times. Out of the Bible."

"It's just snakes," Sowell said. "It's not any end times. All it is, is snakes."

"Let me talk to Mrs. Jackson," Cadell said. "Where is she at?"

Cadell tied his wet, bony horse to the fallen branch of our chinaberry tree. I was wanting to ride that horse, but I didn't say so.

Inside the house Mother looked startled to see Cadell. I think she thought what we all thought for a second, that he'd come to tell us Daddy was dead. "Hey, ma'am." He took off his hat. "I been looking for Rennie. They tell me she's with Mr. Jackson."

It was like Mother couldn't decide whether to hug him or to slap his face. "Sit down, honey," she finally said. "If you can find anything fit to sit on."

Cadell uprighted a kitchen chair and sat in it. Mother stopped what she'd been doing, cleaning out the refrigerator, putting rotten food into a paper sack. She sat down too. The rest of us stood, like we were a paying audience.

"Mr. Jackson set out late Saturday night to drive Rennie home, Cadell, honey," Mother said. "I told him the storm was too bad. We hadn't seen him since."

"Mama has took to bed over this," Cadell said. "Rennie

missing again. We thought she was at the Longmonts' up until this morning. I don't want to go home and tell Mama don't nobody know where my sister is."

"I bet we could find them if we could get a car started," Mother said. "I'm scared they got in an accident, an electric line came down on them or something. Mr. Jackson knows his way around Pinetta. No way for him to be lost."

"Well . . ." Cadell looked down at his hat in his lap. "I rode over here and didn't pass the first car stopped or going," he said. "There is no stalled car nowhere."

"They got to be somewhere," Mother said.

"Rennie's been acting funny," Cadell said. "She's about worried Daddy to death lately. I got to find her and get her home where she belongs before anything gets worse."

"What you mean acting funny?" Sowell asked.

"Oh . . ." Cadell looked sheepishly at us watching him. "You know, talking a lot about Jacksonville, how she's going off to Jacksonville."

"Jacksonville?" Mother stared at him.

"Mama is afraid she run off with a man."

Mother turned ashen. "A man?"

"She was talking that way, Rennie was. Course that don't mean she done it. Rennie is known to turn a pretty lie when she needs to."

"You're not thinking she ran off with Mr. Jackson, are you?" Mother looked suddenly exhausted. "That is ridiculous, Cadell. It's absurd."

"Yes, ma'am," Cadell said.

It was too late for Cadell to ride all the way back out to his place. Mother insisted he stay for supper, which he seemed more than glad to do. It was nothing, supper. Pineapple slices on stale white bread. But there was plenty.

After Cadell ate enough for two or three Mother said for me to let him walk with me over to Rosemary's house to get our yellow cat. She was none better, had laid in that broiler pan all day. Rosemary looked after her the best she could. Had put some Vaseline where our yellow cat's skin was scraped raw. Now her fur was greasy all over. She looked worse for the care.

"She's hurt bad," I told Cadell. "Her ear is off."

Cadell touched her ear so easy with his dirty fingernail. She looked at him but didn't move. "Sleep is the best medicine there is," Cadell said. "I know that. You got to let her sleep."

We carried her back to our house and took her in the kitchen, where Mother was wiping out the refrigerator with Clorox, trying to get rid of the smell that was haunting our house. She let us try to feed the cat some crackers soaked in sour milk, but the cat was not interested. "You got to pet a sick animal," Cadell said. "You got to keep on petting them if you want them to get well."

"Why?" I said.

"It's something that comes out of you and passes into them," he said. "I ain't saying what. Nothing you can't see. But I've watched it work, rubbing a sick animal, it's like a medicine of sorts." Cadell didn't have to tell me to pet our yellow cat. It was my instinct. I petted her a long time, until she was dead asleep.

I saw that Cadell was staring at me. It made me feel so ugly. "What do you think you are staring at?" I said.

"You don't look like yourself," he said. "Something has changed."

"My glasses broke," I said. "That's all. I can't hardly see my hand in front of my face."

"No," he said, "something else."

"There's nothing else," I said.

It was Rosemary who came over and asked Cadell if she could ride his skeleton of a horse. Cadell seemed to think it over, then shrugged his shoulders and said, "Sure, I guess."

Next thing we knew, Cadell was giving rides to people one at a time, him on the front and Wade or Rosemary or one of the Burdett kids on the back. He would take them in big circles around the house.

"Let me ride by myself," Rosemary begged.

But Cadell said, "No, this horse ain't broke that good."

Sowell was working with the men, hammering some tarp over some busted windows on the Burdetts' house. He had no interest in horse riding. The men had given up on getting their cars started and gone on to other labor. They had decided to wait the snakes out. Mother and Mrs. Ingram and two of her daughters sat on their back steps and looked out at us riding the horse. I didn't know what Mother told Mrs. Ingram. Probably said, "That Cadell Miller is crazy, thinks Ford has gone off with Rennie." She probably laughed her fake laugh. I could imagine it.

"Don't you want to ride, Berry?" Cadell said.

"Not really," I lied.

"Come on," he said. "Everybody else took a turn. The horse won't bite you."

"I need my glasses to ride," I said. "I can't hardly see."

"You don't need your glasses." He reached out to me, leaning to yank me up. "Come on."

Wade gave me a boost and I was suddenly on horseback behind Cadell, holding on to his rag of a shirt. "Git up," he said to the horse and off we went at a slow lope.

"What is this horse's name?" I asked.

"Name's Roy," he said. "He don't actually belong to me."

"Who does he belong to?"

"You know Clyde Greene, don't you?"

"I didn't know he had a horse."

Cadell dug his heels into Roy's side and he took off with a sudden leap. "Bet there's lots you don't know." He smiled. "A rich girl like you."

"I'm not rich." I dug my hands into his belly, just trying to stay on. There was nothing but him to hold on to. I was bouncing everywhere. "Slow down," I said.

"Let's have a look at that tore-down school they was talking about," Cadell said.

"It's too far," I said. "It's too dark."

"Hold on." He slapped Roy's neck with the reins, and we were galloping now. I thought for sure I would fall off. I was scratching Cadell with my fingernails.

"Slow up," I yelled.

"Bounce the same as I do," he said. "Like this."

I tried to, sort of pretended to be his shadow on that horse. He held on to the reins in one hand and Roy's mane in the other. I just held on to Cadell, bounced against him, smashed almost flat against him, and it was nice. I wished we could keep on for a long time. The air was wet and almost cool, but I was sweating where my arms and legs rubbed up against Cadell.

Without my glasses the world went by in a blur. It was like looking through the bottom of a jar – everything curved, no lines anymore. I liked it, the way we just stirred into the mess around us, galloping down what was a half-washed-out road, until we came to a fallen tree and had to slow up and walk Roy around it. Roy didn't want to go around it.

We kept on coaxing Roy until we came up on the school. What was left of it. All I could think of was Daddy seeing this sight, his school, his life in shambles this way. There were desks and tables thrown out in the parking lot, their legs broken, and there was a layer of wet paper all over everything, like a soft crust. It was the most terrible thing to see. Everything crushed and muddy and useless.

"You want to get off and walk around?" Cadell said.

"No," I said. "Don't you either."

"I am too." He slung his foot forward and leaped off Roy. He held the reins and walked me around the school. Snakes had climbed up on bookshelves and one was draped over a basketball net whose pole was bent in half. I just stared at things.

Cadell walked us right inside what used to be the cafeteria. There were still wet strings of crepe paper draped over crumbled walls. The red paper had bled in the rain and left blood-looking streaks on everything. "Why don't you get off and walk around?" Cadell said.

But I shook my head no and he did not insist.

"This here is a lot of money gone to waste." Cadell picked up a swollen textbook and looked at the curled cover. "Ruint." He dropped it back down. "I wouldn't want to be your daddy about now." He looked at me like he hadn't meant anything by it.

I ignored him.

"Where you guess your daddy is about now?" Cadell said.

"I don't know," I said. "I'm scared he's dead."

Cadell looked at me hard. "He ain't dead."

"You really think he's run off someplace with Rennie?" I asked. "Are you really that crazy?"

"What's crazy about it?" Cadell said. "I heard your daddy say once that Rennie was a beauty."

"So what?"

"Well, maybe he got overcome by it."

"You're stupid," I said. "You know that?"

"I'm a lot of things" – he smiled – "but I ain't stupid."

"What are you, then?" I said.

"Well, if you really want to know, I'm pretty smart. I know things – by blood. My blood knows."

"What are you talking about?"

"You know what I'm talking about," he said.

And I did.

Underneath the edge of the fallen roof where a drainage pipe was crumpled like a paper straw was a soaked baseball glove. Cadell went to it like it was something wounded. He lifted it gently out from under the collapsed eve and looked it over for damage. "Look here." He studied it. It was dark and shrunken, misshapen by the water it had been lying in. It was so distorted that he couldn't get his hand inside it. I watched him try, determined, but his fingers couldn't find the slit in the fleshy leather, couldn't push their way in. It looked like he was rubbing on a drowned creature, probing and coaxing – obscene like that. "I'm keeping this," Cadell said.

"Fine by me." I couldn't imagine that anybody would care. Not even Daddy when he came back to this world of destruction. I bet a missing baseball glove would be the last thing on his mind. Who but a poor boy would want something so ruined anyway? That's what I was thinking.

Cadell found other things too, library books, staplers, a

thermos, one lady's shoe, a set of metal coat hooks, a pair of child's underpants. Each thing he set carefully inside a cabinet under a fallen wall – someplace drier. I watched him like an eavesdropper, like each thing he said to me he was really saying to himself, or God. He was like a boy who'd stumbled on a soggy gold mine. "This man's trash is that man's treasure." He handed me the swollen baseball glove like it was an injured animal. "Hold this." He climbed back on Roy, this time situating himself behind me. I balanced the wet glove between my legs. "Getting dark," he said. "We best go."

I liked riding on the front of the horse much better, holding on to Roy's mane and seeing where we were going – more or less. I walked Roy all the way home, letting him mostly lead himself. I never kicked him or smacked him with the reins, so the going was slow and felt more like plodding. It could make a person sleepy, the side-to-side motion on the swayed back of a tired, bony horse.

When we were about halfway home, without warning Cadell put his arms around me like maybe he needed to hold on to something or else he might fall off the horse. I jumped at the suddenness of it, his hands on my skin – nearly knocked his baseball glove to the ground. Afterwards, with his arms loosely locked around me, I tried to breathe in a normal way. We didn't talk at all, just rocked back and forth, hypnotized by Roy's slow sluggish rhythm.

"What would you say if I told you you were right pretty, Berry?" Cadell said.

"I'd say you were a liar."

He laughed. "I didn't say you were no raving beauty, or nothing." He squeezed me tighter around my middle, he opened his fists and his palms were hot against my wet shirt, my ribs. "What kind of berry you named after anyway?" he said. "Sweet blackberry? Sweet strawberry?"

"Chinaberry," I said. "Those hard green kind so bitter they make you spit."

He laughed. "Your mama didn't name you after nothing bitter."

"She did so."

"Well, I don't care then. I sort of like you, Berry. Do you like me?"

"No," I said.

He pulled me back against him real easy and breathed on my neck. "Yes, you do," he whispered. "You like me and you know it."

"Your blood tell you so?" I asked as sarcastic as I could.

"It sure did."

"Well, your blood is a liar too, then."

Mother was mad when we got home because she had not said we could go anywhere in the first place. Now it was dark. "Berry, don't you think I got enough to worry about?" she said. "Maybe Cadell doesn't have good sense, but I raised you to have some."

I told her I was sorry, but I wasn't.

We all slept at the Ingrams' house again that night. Cadell on the living room floor with Sowell, Jimmy, and Wade. Me with Rosemary and Jeannie. I said prayers for Daddy most of the night. But I was pretty sure God wasn't listening. There's ways you can tell. I thought people must seem like beggars to God. That was why I always tried to bargain with him instead, you know, this for that, I'll do you a favor if you'll do me one – a business agreement. I thought God would respect that more.

By the time I woke up the next morning Cadell was up and gone. Mrs. Ingram said he'd left on horseback before daylight. I bet he was going back to the school to scavenge what he could. I bet he couldn't sleep for wanting to get over there and carry on like it was Christmas morning or something.

Nobody was expecting Jack Longmont to drive up in an old jeep he used for hunting. If you asked me, he just liked to show off, let people see what all he had which was so much more than everybody else – for example, he had the only vehicle that was running – even if it did look like something from the junk heap. He blew the horn and nearly everybody in the neighborhood streamed outside to see what he wanted. It was drizzling again too, water still just deep enough to ruin your shoes.

"They'll be sending some emergency relief out here," he said. "I got word from Tallahassee. We got the Department of Corrections on its way with some manpower to clean up these roads and do what they can at the school."

"It's about time," Mr. Ingram said.

"Got a crew coming to work on the electrical lines too," Mr. Longmont said. "We ought to have power in the next couple of days."

"Hallelujah!" Mrs. Ingram said. "I need a pot of hot coffee in the worst way."

Jack Longmont looked at Mother. "Mrs. Jackson, I understand your husband is missing?"

"Yes" was all Mother said.

"And the Miller girl too?"

She nodded yes as if she were too tired to tell the story again.

"I'll take your boy, Sowell, with me," he said. "We'll set out to look for them. If they're anywhere around here, we'll find them."

"They got trees down in the roads everywhere," Mr. Burdett warned.

"Well," Mr. Longmont said, "we'll do the best we can."

"Can I go?" Wade begged, but Mother ignored him. It was just a jeep ride he wanted.

"I'm going with you, Mr. Longmont." Mother put her hand on the hood of the jeep like she was taking an oath – or as a symbol that he should not move that jeep an inch until she was in it, seated next to him. "You wait a minute," she said.

"You'd be better off to stay here," he said, but not like he really meant it.

Mother went inside and put her wet hair in one of Mrs. Ingram's kerchiefs and put on her ruined shoes and got in the jeep with Mr. Longmont. Sowell was in the back.

"Berry, you look after Wade," she said to me. "Wade, you mind your sister, you hear?" she yelled to him. *Fat chance,* I thought. I watched Wade turn from her and walk toward the Ingrams' house. Rosemary put her arm around him and led him inside. He let Rosemary put her arm around him too, which surprised me.

We all watched Mr. Longmont, Mother and Sowell jerk away in that scrap-metal jeep, Mother holding on to the scarf she'd tied around her chin. Sowell staring straight ahead like a boy on a mission. Mr. Longmont, looking strangely happy, waving to us as he steered them out of the yard, out to where the road should be.

"Lord, I hope they find your daddy," Mrs. Ingram said to me. "This is awful, isn't it, honey? Not knowing."

With Mother gone, Mrs. Ingram took over and gave us all tasks to do, which was mainly to roam all our yards and collect debris, anything ruined that could be thrown away. She said to make a big pile out where Mr. Burdett burned his trash and that night if the weather allowed, we'd set a match to it and have a bonfire. For some reason, that inspired us. Even Wade.

By lunchtime we had gathered a pile of stuff the size of a small house and Wade and some of the Burdett boys kept working on it well into the afternoon. It seemed to me like their plan was to set the whole world on fire.

Our yellow cat's eyes were crusted over. I got the crust off with a wet tissue and I crumbled baby aspirin into bread and she ate some of it. Most of the afternoon I sat on the back steps of the Ingrams' house and let our yellow cat sleep in my lap, her head hanging off my knee. She woke up now and then and looked around her like she wasn't sure where she was anymore – if this was still the world or if she'd gone on to some other realm. She lapped up a little water from a saucer. She was already feeling bony, but she seemed better than she had been.

Mrs. Ingram fixed some graham crackers and peanut butter and sat down beside me on the steps. Rosemary and her sisters had gone to take sandwiches to the men who were working on our house. "Berry, honey," Mrs. Ingram said, "I believe that old cat of yours is getting better."

"She's not old," I said.

"Let's see if she'll nibble some cracker." She put some under the cat's nose, but our yellow cat wasn't interested, so Mrs. Ingram ate it herself. "This has been a time, hasn't it? I've never seen the like."

"Me neither," I said.

"I sure wish Butch Lyons was here – you know, Preacher Lyons. Now is the time a congregation needs its preacher."

"I'm glad he's not here," I said.

She looked startled. "Why, honey?"

"I don't like him," I said.

"All of us sinners need forgiveness – even Preacher Lyons." She patted my arm.

"No," I said.

That evening when Mr. Burdett set the trash on fire it was spectacular, partly because he had doused it in gasoline first. Otherwise, he said, it'd be too damp to burn. It was a glorious sight, like a moment of hell and finding out hell was not all bad. Even the heat felt good. We stood around that fire like people worshipping something. Without my glasses it was like living in a world without details, but the fire was something I could see, like I could see inside it, see the flash of faces there in the flames. The men passed around a bottle of whiskey while the fire leaped up over their heads into the night. They were tired and quiet, but happy, I think. Not so worried anymore. It was funny how a man-made fire comforted men. The same way bodies of water did, good land, a clear sky. It seemed like these things were their true religion. It made me think of Communion, when we drank the grape juice at church and pretended to be fortified by the blood of Jesus, which would stain your teeth, your clothes, if you spilled it – leave its mark on you. This fire was the first real light any of us had seen in a while. It seemed holy.

I sat cross-legged on the ground with Rosemary and Jeannie and watched the trash burn, our yellow cat still sprawled in my dirty lap. On and off all day I had thought of Cadell's arms around me, his hands hot and open on my ribs. I thought of him whispering lies into my ear. *Not no raving beauty,* he'd said. *You like me,* he'd said. I had called him a liar, but now I wasn't sure. I kept wondering if he cleaned up some – a lot – maybe he would be something, but it seemed impossible, really. And if he was something, then what would he want with me?

When I was younger Sowell used to put his hands on me, but that was a long time ago now. I tried to think when anybody had last had their hands touching some part of me. Not Daddy's good-night hugs, or those harmless kisses he gave me on the mouth, his stubbly beard scratching me. Not his hand on my backside when he whipped me. Not that way. Like Sowell used to do at night after we were put to bed, touch me because he was curious, because he wanted to see how I was made and how it felt to put his hands on my butt, or belly, or the soft inside part of my thighs. His hands swarmed all over me, his fingers brave explorers and I was the wilderness. I didn't mind. He would say, "Come here, Berry, let's me and you wrestle. See if you can get loose?" It was an invitation I craved. I never turned him down. It was only ruined when Wade wanted to play too, and Wade was so rough and always turned the thing into a fight.

I was thinking about this, about Cadell Miller with the smart blood, who thought my daddy had run off with his sister just because she was a beauty. *What's crazy about it?* he'd said.

"Look, Berry." Rosemary nudged me. "They're coming back."

I turned to see Mr. Longmont's jeep headlights bouncing toward us at a distance. "Please God," I said. I put my cat up on my shoulder like a sleeping baby.

By the time Mr. Longmont maneuvered the jeep into the yard we were all gathered in a half circle waiting for them. As they approached I counted as soon as I could three – not four – people. But without my glasses I didn't trust myself. "Anybody with them?" I asked Rosemary.

"No," she said.

"Any luck?" Mr. Burdett yelled to the vehicle even before it stopped. He held the bottle of liquor in his hand, pointing it at them as they neared, like it was an offering.

"From the road it looked like somebody's house was burning down," Mr. Longmont said. "Like to scared Ruthie here to death. The sight of that fire."

"That's all I need," Mother said. "To come home to my house burned down."

"No luck, I guess," Mrs. Ingram said.

"We searched the best we could," Mr. Longmont said. "The main roads as far as we could get. It's some serious damage out there. But no sign of them. Nothing."

"Things are tore to pieces all around," Sowell said. "Looks like they dropped the atom bomb on us. Water everywhere, man alive."

Mother got out of the jeep and Mrs. Ingram went right to her. The way the light from the fire flashed across Mother's face, her eyes looked dark, sunken. Like it was not what she'd seen that changed her face that way, but what she had not seen. What she might never see.

"We won't give up, Ruthie," Mr. Longmont said. "We'll look until we find them."

Mother turned and looked at him, but her face was barely softened. "I appreciate it – your help," she said. "Sowell, you get Wade and Berry and y'all come to the Ingrams' now." She walked off, not noticing whether Sowell was obeying her or not. He wasn't.

As soon as Mother was out of earshot the men said, "What you suppose come of them two – missing like that?"

Mr. Longmont shook his head. "It might be hard to find somebody out in that mess out there," he said. "Somebody injured or something. But I tell you what worries me. No car. Not a sign of that car anywhere."

"There's not but so many ways to get out to the Millers'," Mr. Ingram said. "It's not but so many places that car could be."

"*If* it was going out to the Millers'." Mr. Burdett lifted the bottle to his lips.

People fell silent a moment, thinking about this. They looked at Sowell and Wade and me with slight embarrassment.

"If they're alive and want to be found," Mr. Longmont said, "we'll find them."

"Maybe they don't want to be found," Mr. Burdett said. "Maybe they never intended on it."

"Hush up." Mrs. Burdett startled everybody, since she was usually so quiet half the time people mistook her for a deaf-mute. "Don't talk like that in front of these children now. Sowell," she said, "son, you take your brother and sister inside now."

We walked to the Ingrams' house in silence, knowing they would stand out there at that fire and discuss us – our father and Rennie – well into the night. They would discuss them the way you discuss lawbreakers or lovers – or the newly dead.

"You think we'll ever find Daddy?" I asked Sowell.

"Yeah," he said. "But I don't know where."

"You don't think he's dead, do you?"

"Maybe," he said.

That night while I was tangled in the bed with Rosemary and Jeannie, Rosemary punched me and whispered, "Listen, Berry, I don't know if I should tell you this or not." Then she waited.

I just laid there with my eyes open.

"I know you're not asleep," she whispered. "You can forget I told you this if you want to, but Rennie used to talk, you know, at school. She used to say she had this *grown* boyfriend. *Grown,* she always said. That's the only way she described him."

"So?"

"So, excuse me for saying so, but your daddy is grown."

"So are a lot of people," I said.

"But none of them are missing," Rosemary insisted.

A tiredness came over me, like a wall gently falling, crushing me beneath the soft wreckage. I felt like I might close my eyes and be gone altogether. Just vanish underneath the weight of Rosemary's words.

"All I'm saying is, if you don't want a snake to bite you, then don't step on it," Rosemary said.

"What does that mean?" I said.

But she was mad now. She rolled over and with her back pressed up against me she let out an exaggerated sigh. "Forget it, Berry. Just go to sleep."

That night I dreamed Daddy and Rennie were at the Longmonts' store, buying cold drinks and peanuts. I dreamed they got in the car and drove off. Rennie was laughing. I ran behind the car, trying to stop them, trying to make them wait for me – but they were going too fast. Daddy waved to me in the rearview mirror.

By the end of the week we had moved back into our own broken house. The porch was still torn off, but there were makeshift steps going into the kitchen and the living room roof was repaired enough to be safe until we could get to town and get the materials we needed to finish it off.

Mother went at the house with a bottle of Clorox and a box of Ajax. She scrubbed anything that didn't move out of the way. Twice more she'd gone with Mr. Longmont for a couple of hours of searching, some back road usually, some spot where he thought maybe a car could wash out of sight into the woods or tumble down a ravine or something. Each trip she went a little more reluctantly than before. Every time she came home a little more changed.

Jewel Longmont came over and brought a box full of groceries from their store. The electricity had finally come back on, so she and Mother made a pot of coffee and drank it – the whole pot – in one sitting. Then they made a second pot. They made me think of women swallowing poison – who couldn't get enough of it. The way they talked, each word more bitter-edged and bewildered than the one before it. Mrs. Longmont, sad because her husband was alive and well and ruining her life and Mother, sad because her husband was dead or missing and ruining her life. It was like two women who wished to God they could change places – change men and circumstances. But who, more than anything, wished they could move away from Pinetta, where everything had gone wrong and kept on going wrong. "How on earth did we end up in Pinetta, of all places?" Jewel Longmont said more than once. "This little nothing of a place."

"There's worse places, I guess," Mother said.

Jewel Longmont leaned over her coffee cup and looked at Mother close. "Like where?"

This made Mother laugh. She laughed like you get a lawn mower started, just a couple of sputters at first, but then one of those sputters catches, fires up, and soon the motor is roaring. That was how Mother got started laughing – Jewel Longmont too. It was like they went crazy laughing, couldn't hardly breathe, gasping air like a couple of fish, slapping their hands on the tabletop, twisting in their leaning-back chairs, threatening to tip over any second, tears pouring down their faces.

It would be years before I understood the way laughing substituted for crying when women were being watched.

"What are they doing in there?" Wade asked. He and Sowell had come down the hall to see.

Sowell shook his head. "They're hysterical," he said. "It's nothing."

It took a while for them to wind down. They each took up paper napkins and pressed them to their mouths, trying to smother the laughter, like putting out a wildfire. "Good Lord," Jewel Longmont said, "pour some more coffee." Mother did. They sipped themselves back into the real world, like waking up from a short nap or something.

"Can I ask you something personal, Jewel?" Mother lowered her voice to a whisper. "Do you ever hear anything from Butch?"

Jewel Longmont blew into her coffee cup, took a tiny sip, and settled her eyes on Mother's, the way you put your hand on top of somebody else's, that light touch. "Do you, Ruthie?"

"Once," Mother said. "That was all."

"Me too."

Mother nodded like she understood, like she was almost sorry for Jewel Longmont – to mess up her life over Butch Lyons, then only hear from him once. It made Butch Lyons seem so low.

I liked to think it made Mother glad she wasn't the one who'd messed up her life that way.

"Jack has been real helpful to me," Mother said. "I guess you know that."

Jewel Longmont smiled at Mother. "Don't worry, Ruthie.

The more he's over here, the less he's at home. I guess I ought to thank you for that."

"Really?"

"Really," she said. "You're doing me a favor keeping him busy. Really."

That night after Mrs. Longmont left, Mother heated up cans of chili and corn and applesauce, made us a delicious hot supper. It was like, thanks to Mrs. Longmont, she had talked all the poison out of her system – for the moment. "Eat up," she said to us, "there's plenty."

I began having dreams about Daddy nearly every night. I dreamed he was in a swamp and alligators were eating his legs off where they floated in the edge of the water. I dreamed he and Rennie were dead and sunk to the bottom of a swamp in our car, their windows rolled up, the radio still playing. I dreamed they had taken a wrong turn and gotten so lost they couldn't find their way home – that they were studying a map of the world, but Pinetta wasn't on it anyplace. I dreamed somebody shot and killed them. I dreamed they shot and killed themselves. I dreamed everything – except Jacksonville. I did not dream them off happy in Jacksonville.

~

When the truckload of convicts drove up we greeted them like they were war heroes. Trustees, they were called, but it wouldn't have mattered if they weren't. Being men – even criminals – with strong arms and backs, that was enough.

Sowell saw the first truck. It stopped out near the road in front of our house, like a canvas-covered cattle truck full of men in prison uniforms. That truck was followed by a second flatbed truck with a bulldozer on it. "Help's here!" Sowell yelled into the kitchen door. We all went out into the yard to see.

We watched with wonder while they set up a camp in the clearing directly across from our house. Before the hurricane there had not been a clearing there – just sandspurs, scrub pines and more jungle. There were two men with small guns on their hips and large guns in their hands who supervised while the convicts erected a huge white tent and unfolded rows of wooden-legged cots inside it. It felt like the circus had come to Pinetta – or a tent revival. Or like the conquering army had arrived to set us free. By early afternoon the bulldozer was fired and loud and went slowly about knocking trees over, shoving trees out of the way. It was as good as any magic we could imagine.

It was evening before the convicts were made to put their leg-irons on. We watched from our front steps as two, three, or four men were chained together for the night, their chains linked to a longer chain that was locked on one end to the back of their truck and on the other end around the trunk of a giant oak. The convicts wore what looked like pajamas, mostly white in the late-evening light because time had faded the black stripes to a pale gray that almost vanished when the sun went down.

It was the most thrilling thing I had ever imagined. These men setting up a little world of their own across the road from ours – these men whose job it was to save us. I lay in my bed, our yellow cat limp and drowsy beside me, and looked out the window at the pumpkinlike orange lights coming from inside the convict tent. I tried to imagine myself inside there, what a relief it would be to be chained to my bed. What a misery. I could not ever remember feeling as safe as I felt that first night when the convicts camped out across from us. They left their yellow bulldozer parked in the road, ate food that was cooked on the back of their truck and served up to them in metal bowls, then laid down on their cots and slept while we slept. Except for the men with the guns. I imagined they never slept. And I was grateful. It was the first good night's sleep I had had in a long time.

The next morning I knew something had changed – for the better. For one thing, the sun was up hot and bright for the first time since the storm. It would bake some of the wetness away – make the world into a big steam bath, eventually leaving the edges of everything dry – at last. For another thing, it was the sound of the bulldozer that woke me. I looked across the road and saw the men lined up at the edge of the road in their chains, ankle-deep in mud with shovels in their hands, digging a drainage ditch alongside the road.

By midmorning I was dressed in my shorts and calypso top, standing barefoot at the edge of my yard with our yellow cat in my arms, watching the men carve what looked like a giant grave into the red clay. Together they made a pattern like so many legs on a caterpillar, moving in unison, *stab, lift, swing, breathe, stab, lift, swing, breathe.* The red clay was raw as wounded flesh. It looked bloody, like the men were performing surgery on the earth right in front of me.

I waved to them, but they were not freehanded enough to wave back. I sat in the sandspur grass and watched them all morning, especially one particular convict. He was young and bold enough to whistle. Sometimes he sang out to the other men, *Oh baby, baby, let's dig us a ditch!* The other men smiled a little, but mostly ignored him. He looked out of place there on the side of the road, sweat dripping off him like he was rained on. His clothes were already soaked. But still, he had half a smile on his face as he *stabbed, stabbed, stabbed* at the wet clay earth. He was what I would call a golden boy. His hair almost as blond as mine, only curlier. I knew in my heart he could not have committed any crime. He had to be a mistake that the government made. His eyes were as blue as the Gulf of Mexico.

I guess he noticed me watching him because he finally yelled, "Hey, girlie, come over here and talk to me a minute." I stood up and stared at him, clutching my cat, unsure what to do.

"You don't need to be scared of me, girlie," he said. "I been a choirboy before I come to prison." The other men laughed and I thought they were looking at me hard – testing me – to see if I had any courage or not. The men with the guns were sitting on the back of the truck at the other end of the line. The bulldozer was a ways off down the road, moaning as it struggled to put the road back where it had been. I held my groggy cat close to my chest and walked across the newly scraped road to where the men were working.

"That's a nice cat you got, Prettygirl," the golden boy said. "What's her name?"

"Doesn't have a name."

"Well, what's your name, then, little girl?"

"Berry."

"That's a pretty name for a pretty girl." He smiled.

"I'm not pretty."

"Who told this little girl she wasn't pretty?" he said to the other convicts. "Y'all tell this child she is as pretty as a picture. Go on, tell her so."

They smiled and nodded at me and mostly grinned at the boy talking the talk. He was like a light shining – 100 watt.

"My name is Raymond," he said. "Pleased to meet you, Miss Berry. This here is Eddie and this over here is Marcel." He motioned to the men on either side of him. "We're at your service, honey."

"What are you doing on the chain gang?" I said.

The men grinned, shook their heads, suppressed a laugh, and kept their rhythm just perfect. *Stab, lift, sling, breathe.* Raymond looked at me and winked. "Love," he said. *Stab, lift, sling, breathe.* "Bet you didn't know you could get sent to prison for love, did you?"

"No," I said.

"All I ever did was love somebody just a little too much. And look a-here where I am. It don't hardly make sense, does it?"

"No," I said.

"You know what I wish you'd do, Prettygirl? I wish you'd go home and get us something cold to drink. You think you could do that?"

"I guess."

"Your mama got some ice in there? You got some Kool-Aid or something?"

"Sweet tea," I said.

"Yeah." He grinned. "Can you be a good girl and get us some sweet tea on ice?"

"I guess so." I ran home, knowing they were watching me, knowing they were depending on me. I put the cat down on my bed and hurried into the kitchen to break open an ice tray. Mother had gone with Mr. Longmont up to the school to get what she could of Daddy's paperwork and books. I had the kitchen to myself.

When I walked back to the men on the chain gang they looked surprised to see me, like the last thing they were really expecting was sweet tea. I hugged the glasses and tried not to spill it before I got to them. They paused, putting a momentary kink in the ditch-digging line, and took those cold glasses of tea and slurped them down in record time. Eddie – he was sort of crazy,

Raymond said – poured the last part of his tea on top of his head. It would be sticky and draw gnats and flies to his hair, but I guess he didn't care.

"Berry, you are a mighty fine girl," Raymond said. "We thank you, honey."

They handed me the empty glasses and started back to work and I just stood there, not wanting to go home. "Who did you love too much?" I asked Raymond.

He shook his head, like he was suddenly remembering how it was – the pain of all that loving. "A woman not much bigger than you," he said.

"What happened?"

"She was no good. You ever love somebody and then just find out that they're no good?"

"No," I said.

"Well, I hope you never do, honey," he said.

I went and sat in my yard where I'd been in the first place, and all day, in the bald sun, I just sat there and watched them build a road that would lead us out of Pinetta.

Mr. Longmont brought Mother home with several armloads of stuff. She stacked it neatly in her bedroom closet, "until your daddy gets back," she said. Then Mr. Longmont sat down in our kitchen and Mother gave him a glass of sweet tea and I thought he was very creepy, the way he looked at Mother, the way he wanted to help her when his own miserable wife could probably use a little help herself.

That night I watched the convicts out my bedroom window until I finally fell asleep. I kept seeing the strong, tan face of Raymond calling me *Prettygirl,* saying it more than once. I could see the word come out of his mouth, his lips and teeth making the word especially for me. It felt like I was learning about the importance of lies, how they can be good for you, and maybe you need them from time to time and you don't always have to sort sentences into piles of true and not true. Just because something is not true doesn't mean you have to throw it away. Maybe you could just enjoy a lie now and then, let it feel good on you, like a soapy bath made of words, or word lotion that you could smear all over yourself, feel soft and smooth afterwards.

When Cadell said, "Berry, you are pretty," everything in me wanted to revolt, fight him and prove his lie, but I didn't, I just let him put his arms around me and hold on and pretend that what he said was true. I did it for him. And me too. But today, I don't know, Raymond was boy-looking, but he was man enough to be in prison, wasn't he? He knew things to do and say, and even if he was offering up a lie, maybe I should be grateful because I bet that was all some men had to offer. Maybe it should be appreciated.

This was the other thing – Cadell and Raymond are two different people. If they both said I was pretty – even if they didn't really believe it themselves – maybe saying it could make it true. Maybe all the truth really was, was everybody agreeing on something, like saying it enough made it so. Maybe if I could believe it myself, then it would happen – like magic. It was not really that I longed to be pretty so bad. I swear. It was just that I longed to be real. In Pinetta it seemed like being pretty was the one thing guaranteed to make a girl real.

I'd look for Raymond again tomorrow. I'd notice if he noticed me. I'd wear something nice.

* * *

The next morning I woke to our yellow cat stretching, clawing my thigh. She jumped off the bed and went to the kitchen like she was looking for food. It was a good sign. Mother let her stay inside all the time now, with Daddy gone. It was like we'd made a trade, a cat for a father. Like our yellow cat was supposed to fill up the empty place Daddy left. Like maybe she would keep us from missing him. I had managed to keep our yellow cat alive like I'd promised God. I hoped he could say the same thing about Daddy.

Deputies from the sheriff's department had come by to see Mother twice. Some of the neighbors must have reported Daddy missing because Mother never did. She was still waiting for him to drive up in the yard with a perfectly good explanation. The deputies asked a million questions about Daddy's possible whereabouts. When they left, Mother cried herself silly, shut away in her bedroom. She had tried to tell them that something terrible had happened, an accident of some kind, that it was not like Daddy to do anything irresponsible.

"Sounds to me like heading out into a hurricane in the middle of the night is pretty irresponsible." The deputy was so rude. "I'm sorry, ma'am, but if there'd been an accident I think there'd be some sign of it someplace. There'd be a car at least."

"Were you and your husband having any kind of trouble?" the other deputy asked. That did it. Mother turned her back on them, marched into her bedroom without a word, and closed the door behind her. There was nothing for them to do then but leave. The deputies walked over to the Ingrams' house and questioned them next. Then the Burdetts.

Every few nights Sowell walked over to the Longmonts' to see Marie. It was a pitch-black walk and a wonder he didn't get lost or bit now that there was no real road to walk on and the snakes were washed out everywhere. Nights – late – he came home and scratched on the window screen to wake me up to unlock the kitchen door and let him in. Sometimes it was so late I didn't know how late it was – whether it was today or tomorrow. I went like a sleepwalker in my nightgown and unlatched the door and he came in, sweaty, his hair curled and his feet muddy. He took off his shoes and sat them on a newspaper until morning, when he would clean them off good. He was quiet, but content in a way that embarrassed me. As soon as I knew he was inside and the door locked again I started back to bed.

"Berry," he said, "you can see through that nightgown you've got on."

I looked down at the gown. It was a sleeveless cotton gown just like I'd worn all my life. Mother wore one just like it. It was the coolest thing we knew of to sleep in – cooler than nothing at all since the cotton would soak up your sweat as you slept. That was what Mother said.

"I can see right through it," he said.

"Then don't look."

"I mean it, Berry. You shouldn't go around in a nightgown people can see straight through."

"People?" I said. "There's no people."

"What about Wade?"

"Wade doesn't care."

"Well, I care," Sowell said.

"Next time you come home in the middle of the night I'll just stay in bed instead of getting up and making you look at me in this nightgown."

"A little modesty never hurt anybody," he said. "That's all I'm saying."

Sowell wasn't saying this like "Berry, you have a nice body under there, which you should not let people stare at," like I bet he would say to Marie – or even Rosemary. He was saying it like "Berry, you should not make people look at your body since it is so awful to look at. You should hide it if you have good sense – if you don't want to scare people away."

The rest of the night I slept with my hands over my breasts, which already were nearly as big as Mother's, which of course were not that big. I could feel my heart beating inside them. They were hard as knots with the softest skin over them and when I touched them something shot through me and I felt it like a gentle kick between my legs.

Sowell woke up every morning holding himself, I'd seen it again and again. If he didn't, he woke up and touched himself first thing, almost before he opened his eyes, like he needed to be sure it was still there, like he needed tactile proof. Did he think I liked witnessing his morning ritual? He acted like it was as normal as yawning, his thing swollen to the size of the small flashlight I used to read in bed sometimes. He handled it like that's what it was too – a shining light. I never said, "Stop it, Sowell, you're disgusting me." But he was.

I needed to get my new glasses. I needed to put them on and look at myself in the mirror. It was like every night when I slept all my angles went soft, all my straight lines began to curve and I was padded where I used to be bony. When I woke up in the mornings I was unsure who I was at first – but all I had to do was look across the room at Wade and Sowell sprawled in their bunk beds in their underpants to remember. I thought this happened like moving into a new house happens, which I had never done before either. Just about the time you finally began to get comfortable inside your modest little house of a body, sort of know where all the rooms are and what to do in each one, then suddenly you were not in that familiar little box-house body anymore. You were in a split-level or something. You had all these modern conveniences that you didn't have the slightest idea how to use – and which, left to your own devices, you would not call conveniences. So that was what had happened and continued to happen – my inside self was relocating in a new and supposedly improved outside self. It was supposed to be roomier here, but it didn't feel that way. It felt more like something unfurnished, hollow rooms with an echo that reverberated all day, every day.

When I got my new glasses I would lock myself in Mother's bedroom and study my body in the mirror. I didn't want to, but I needed to see for myself what was wrong with my body. The glasses doctor said that the shape of my eyeballs is what kept me from seeing. They were oblong, instead of round. I suspected that might be a theme with me. That my eyes were not my only misshapen part.

I might not have minded all this too much if I was sure I would turn out to have a body like Mrs. Freddy's in the end. It was perfect, if you asked me. And she was perfect in it. But what if I turned out to be like Mrs. Ingram, whose body was more of a hotel than a house, all her children having temporarily resided there, kicking and twisting, then finally checking out, leaving the place the worse for wear. Just one of Mrs. Ingram's breasts looked like it could have fed most of the children in a starving country, like she could be a one-woman relief service – and probably would be willing. That was why everybody liked Mrs. Ingram, because she was bighearted and the rest of her was sized to match. But I didn't want to be big. I wanted to be hard to notice.

Meanwhile, I didn't know what all was wrong with Sowell. But something was. In between the nights he hiked over to Marie's house to worship her, sometimes, by force of habit, he went over to the Ingrams' to see Rosemary. He pretended he was going over to watch a little television, but he didn't fool me or Wade.

Since the storm the hole in the weeds was nearly destroyed. There was still more than a foot of standing water in it, and all the edges had gone to mud. It had lost all definition, all the perfect pockets dug into the side walls barely more than dents. Now it was mostly a mosquito-hatching hole. Mr. Ingram himself had sprayed poison into it and around it, trying to cut down on the infestation, and he had warned us all to stay clear of it. So Sowell and Rosemary had taken to sitting in the Ingrams' old car, which had been righted again and the tires removed, so that it sat up on cinder blocks, which made the Ingrams look like poor people – TV or no TV – like they could not afford to have the car hauled away, piece of junk that it was. Inside it the upholstery was bloated and cracking and it smelled like terrible mildew, the black crud beginning to climb all along the roof and seats. But Sowell and Rosemary seemed not to mind. We could see them sitting first on the car hood, then later in the front seat. I thought it was wrong, wrong, wrong.

"We're talking, Berry," Sowell explained to me.

"Like heck you are," I said.

"We're not breaking any laws," he said.

"It's not laws I'm worried about you breaking. It's Rosemary's heart. She does have one, you know."

Now that Rosemary and I had slept together all those nights I felt some responsibility for her. She hadn't bothered me about Sowell the whole time, like she used to before. She was nice to me, sometimes slept with her arm around me and whispered, "Don't worry, Berry." She doctored our yellow cat without being asked. And tried to take up for Wade when he needed it – especially if it was against Sowell. So what if she thought Daddy and Rennie had run off together? I forgave her that. She was just an incurable romantic that way. She believed in love. Found evidence of it everywhere – even where there was no trace of it. That wasn't so bad, was it?

"You've got to play harder to get, Rosemary," I'd told her one night when Sowell was off visiting Marie. She'd come to see about our cat, hoping to see Sowell too.

"Why?" she asked.

"Sowell likes that," I said. "That's why he likes Marie. She is a goody-good."

"He only likes her every other night," she said.

"He only likes you every other night too."

"Well," she grinned, "that's a start."

Rosemary was hopeless.

Even Rosemary's mother had said to Sowell once, "What on earth are you and Rosemary talking about for hours on end in that old car?"

"Nothing much." Sowell shrugged his shoulders.

Mrs. Ingram smiled, but I don't think she was as dumb as she acted. I think she wished Sowell loved Rosemary about as bad as Rosemary did.

~

It was a decent walk down to where the convicts were working on the road now. I guess that meant they were making progress. I walked all the way down there barefooted, careful not to get far off the freshly dozed dirt. When he saw me coming Raymond said, "Looky who's here." He smiled like he was really tickled to see me, even though I came every day. The convicts had their chains on and were spreading gravel with rakes, everything clanging.

"Hey," I said.

"Prettygirl," he said. "You're up early."

Not only was I up early, but I had taken extra care to dress in an improved way. When we stayed with the Ingrams lots of mornings I wore Rosemary's clothes instead of going home for clothes of my own. Her clothes were nothing like mine. For one thing, Mrs. Ingram made most of them, and for another, the great majority of them had been handed down sister to sister. They were patterns you would not expect, sewn up in fabrics you would not expect by Mrs. Ingram, who did not have time or inclination to be a perfectionist. Sometimes the buttons didn't match. Sometimes she had never gotten around to putting the zipper in – maybe she was waiting until she next went to Madison, where she could buy a zipper to match, or maybe her daughters got too much in a hurry to wear their new skirt and matching top and did so before it was entirely finished. The waistband pinned. The facings tucked into the arm holes. But somehow, despite all this, the clothes were beautiful to me. Thrilling in a way, like wearing a whole history or something, dressing each morning in a long story that might never end, and when you put the outfit on you became a chapter in that story. The fabric was always so soft because it had been washed nearly to the unraveling state, the colors gone soft too. I loved dressing myself in Rosemary's clothes. It was like it made me if not Rosemary exactly, then somebody more like her. It was like if you wore somebody else's clothes, you could be somebody else. Maybe that was what I liked. I had on a pair of culotte short shorts with rosebuds all over them and a tummy tickler top with a bigger version of those same rosebuds. It was faded too, like those roses they talk about that fade on the vines, unplucked. I thought I looked better than usual.

"Your mama know you're down here like this?" Raymond asked, not commenting on my outfit – but I was sure he'd noticed.

"Not exactly," I said. "She's got a lot on her mind."

"What about your daddy then?"

"My daddy is missing," I said. "He left the night before the hurricane hit. Nobody can find him. He might be dead."

Raymond, Eddie and Marcel looked at me hard, like maybe this was the first thing I'd ever said that they found truly interesting.

"Nobody's dead until you got a body to prove it," Raymond said. "It's the law."

"Some people think he ran off," I said. It felt strangely pleasant to be saying this, like since they were convicts, they of all people would understand how to hear this. It would not shock them. "With a girl," I said.

"What girl?" Raymond said.

"One of his students. He's the school principal."

"The school principal?" Raymond smiled. "Lord, when I was in school," he said, winking at me, "that couple of weeks – our old principal was so sour he couldn't have got no old lady to run off with him, never mind no girl. So your daddy is a principal, huh?"

"Yes," I said.

"Does your mama think he run off?" It was Eddie asking. Usually he did all his talking with his eyes, the way they were always swimming around in his head, looking things over in a slippery way.

"No," I said. "She thinks he's been in an accident."

"Sometimes women know this stuff," Eddie said. "They have a sixth sense. My mama did."

"Maybe," I said.

"So it's just you and your mama now – all alone?" Raymond asked.

"And my brothers," I said. "Wade and Sowell."

"Well, that's a sad story, Prettygirl. It sure is," Raymond said. "Mighty sad."

"Thank you," I said.

I was afraid to sit on the stack of downed scrub oaks and pines because I knew how snakes liked to lie in log piles. I stood up awhile, then sat in the sandiest spot I could find because I didn't want to get red clay on Rosemary's culottes. I was sitting there, minding my own business, watching Raymond and the others work and sweat and spit. They were good to watch, satisfying somehow, men doing work that really needed done. Especially Raymond. I guess he was the first boy I ever saw that I thought was beautiful. He was too. Not just his good looks, which were so clear, I mean clear eyes, clear skin, even his sweaty hair looked clean and soft and was stuck in a handsome way to the sides of his face and the back of his neck. Even sweaty as he was, it didn't seem like sweat as much as shine, pure shine. Everything he did you had to notice. I did. I wondered if he had a girlfriend. Did she write him letters? Did she come to visit him on visitors' day? What about his mother and the rest of his family – who were they? Did they love him like they should?

I was thinking all of this, imagining Raymond in a happy home where he had been well raised, wondering what misunderstanding had led him here to this moment in time, this one dot on the map of the world – where he was raking gravel on a Florida chain gang in the hot morning sun, like a common criminal, when it was clear he was meant for better things.

"Hey there, missy." One of the men with the guns walked up to where I was sitting. He put one leg up on the log pile and rested his shotgun over his knee. He needed a shave bad, but his hair was combed neat and looped behind his ears and he wore an official hat and a badge on his sweat-soaked shirt. "You don't need to be over here talking to these fellas, honey." He nodded toward Raymond. "They're bad men," he said. "Done some mighty bad things."

"I know."

"You go on home then, honey. Your mama wouldn't want you here."

"She doesn't mind," I said.

"These boys got work to do. They can't be stopping to talk now, girlie."

"I'm not bothering them." I didn't say, "This is a free country, isn't it?" but I thought about it.

"Suit yourself," he said. "But Raymond here, don't let him fool you. Underneath that smile of his is nothing but trouble. You're smart enough to know that, aren't you, girlie?"

"Yes, sir," I said.

When the guard walked off I felt guilty, like I'd betrayed Raymond, listening to the guard talk bad about him. I didn't really know just exactly how bad he was.

"Did you accidentally kill somebody?" I asked Raymond.

"Do I look like a killer to you, Prettygirl?" He smiled. I understood instantly what a ridiculous question that was.

"Eddie, here," Raymond said. "Now Eddie is a killer. Ain't that right, Eddie?"

Eddie looked at me and nodded. His hair was soaked and stuck out in little points all over his head, like his head was a target and too many arrows had been fired into it and now they were stuck there pointing in every direction at once.

"Eddie's unbalanced," Raymond said. "Ain't that what the doctor said, Eddie, when you was on trial? A unbalanced man turned killer. Now if you ask me, Eddie looks like he might be a killer too – no offense, Eddie – but he's got that unbalanced look, don't he? There's never no telling what will upset Eddie, what will get him real unbalanced and make him do something crazy. Ain't that right, Eddie?"

"I didn't kill nobody that didn't need killing," Eddie said. "I got a bad temper. You can ask my mama."

"I guess them dead people would certainly say so," Raymond said. "But Marcel and me, no, now, we ain't killers. Marcel, he's a thief. He'd steal from his own self if he had anything worth stealing, ain't that right, Marcel? He's good too. About as good as they come. Lord knows how much stuff he stole before they caught on to him. But Marcel, he wouldn't hurt a fly, would you, Marcel? He's as gentle as can be. But I tell you what, the day they let him out of here he's gon steal a car as fast as he can, the first car that comes down the road. It's for the pleasure that he does it. That's all. Pure pleasure of it."

"Naw," Marcel said. "Ima straighten out."

"Yeah," Raymond laughed, "you gon get religion, ain't you, Marcel?"

"What about you?" I asked Raymond. "What did you do?"

"I told you already, honey. Just loved somebody a little too much. It was this heart of mine got me in trouble. I swear. You don't need to be scared of me. You're not, are you, Prettygirl – scared of me?"

"No," I said. I wasn't a bit scared of him. If anybody asked, I might have said I loved him.

It was enough of a shock when I heard Mother calling me. She sounded like a blue jay, that insistence in her voice. "Berrrry! Berrrry!" But what shocked me more was to see her standing out in our yard, hands cupping her mouth while she called – because she was wearing a pair of white shorts. She walked all the way out into the road in those shorts and kept yelling for me, her pale thighs as naked-looking as a pair of breasts. The minute I saw her my heart began to race. I had a feeling something awful was happening, seeing her barelegged out in the yard that way. "I got to go."

"Is that your mama?" Raymond asked.

"Yes," I said.

"Lord, Lord," he said, "ain't she a sight." He stopped dead still and shaded his eyes with his hand, looking at her. So did some of the others.

I had taken off running by now. I just barely heard Raymond yell, "Prettygirl, you bring your mama down here with you next time, you hear me? I'd like to talk to her. Damn if I wouldn't."

"What's wrong?" I panted when I got to where Mother stood in the road waiting for me, her eyes squinted, her hair gone limp in the wet morning air. The skin on her bare thighs as white as freshly poured milk.

"Berry, what on earth are you doing down there with all those convicts?"

"Nothing," I said. "Talking."

"What is that you've got on?"

"It's Rosemary's."

Mother looked at me like I was the mysterious one, when she was the one standing outside in a pair of short shorts like she had never done before in her life. "Why are you wearing shorts?"

"It's hot," she said. "That's why. Come on in the house."

I followed her inside, not knowing what I might find there – maybe Daddy, I thought. But instead, there sat Sowell and Wade looking like two boys on their way to a hanging. Sowell was staring at Mother's legs and Wade was trying not to look. "What's going on?" Sowell asked.

"Sit down, Berry," Mother said. "I want to talk to all of you." I took a chair next to Sowell.

"Look," Mother began. "Your daddy has been gone awhile now. Nearly a month."

"Not that long," Sowell said.

"Almost," Mother snapped.

"Are you giving up on him?" I asked.

"Nothing would make me happier than to see him drive up in the yard right this minute, but the truth is, I've stopped believing that is going to happen."

"You don't know," Wade insisted.

"That's right," Mother said. "Nobody knows. But I can't live every day waiting on something to happen that might never happen. The sheriff doesn't hold out much hope. According to all he can figure, your daddy has vanished of his own free will. Maybe that's true, maybe it's not. But I have to get on with things. We all do."

"What things?"

"Life," she said.

When we heard the horn blow outside I recognized it immediately as Mr. Longmont's jeep. It gave me a sinking feeling – like I was standing in a puddle of quicksand. "What's he doing here?"

"For your information, Berry," Mother snapped, "he has come to try to drive you into Madison to get your new glasses. So I don't think you need to be rude." She walked to the door and waved to him. "Just a minute," she called. Her voice was like a silver aluminum foil, assemble-it-yourself Christmas tree – everything about it fake, but still it shone bright. "We'll be right there," she sang out.

"You're not going in those shorts, are you?" Sowell asked.

"What if I am?"

"You're acting like Daddy is dead." Sowell's voice shook. "You don't know for sure."

Mother turned to face him, her eyes like a couple of bright, well-placed ornaments. "But I know for sure I'm not," Mother said. "I don't know where your daddy is, but I know this, *I'm not dead.* Is that what you want, Sowell, me to act like I'm dead?"

"Don't you miss Daddy?" I asked, trying to pry Sowell loose from the spot he was frozen into, like he'd just found out Mother killed Daddy – and she did it by refusing to die herself.

"Yes," Mother said. "Of course I miss your daddy. Now, Berry, you change clothes and come on. Jack's waiting."

"Jack?" I said. "Why do you have to call him Jack?"

"It's his name," Mother said. "That's why." She walked into her room and began changing from her shorts to a dress fit to wear to Madison. She put on perfume too.

I put on my own clothes – plain, plain, plain – and turned back into my own self. It was a letdown. "What does Mrs. Longmont think about her husband coming over here every day?" I yelled to Mother in the next room. "Does she know?"

"Of course she knows," Mother yelled back. "She says she is grateful to have him out of the house. She says I'm doing her a favor, keeping him busy and out of her hair. There is no love lost between those two," Mother said. "Isn't that right, Sowell? Doesn't Marie tell you so?"

When Mother and I walked out to get in the jeep Sowell and Wade were standing in the kitchen like a couple of zombies. They stared at Mother like they had no idea who she was or what she was doing in our house. Sowell especially was looking at her that same way I'd seen him look at Rosemary when she did something particularly tasteless.

"Sowell, you look after Wade. And, Wade, you mind Sowell. I'll bring y'all a comic book."

"We don't want any comic book," Sowell said.

"Well, suit yourself," Mother said with a poison smile. "We'll be back later this afternoon – and your sister will have picked out a nice new pair of glasses."

I sat sideways in the back of the jeep. Mother sat up front next to Mr. Longmont. The jeep was loud and jerky. I held on to the roll bar and pretended I wasn't there. We had to drive right by the chain gang and I felt like a fool. Raymond and Marcel both waved to me, but Eddie just stared with his watery fish eyes. I saw the way they studied Mother, but she never looked their way. Mr. Longmont sounded his horn and waved to the guards who were leaned up against a shade tree, supervising things. They nodded and touched their fingers to the brims of their hats.

Mother tied a scarf around her hair and leaned back in her seat like she was a rich woman and Mr. Longmont was her personal limousine driver. Every now and then he looked over at her and smiled. She was acting like she thought she was a movie star or something and Mr. Longmont was going along with it. Like all she needed was a lit cigarette in a long cigarette holder, smoke wafting around her face like a gray cloud. I didn't say a word nearly the whole way. I was wishing for Daddy.

Suddenly I longed to be in a car Daddy was driving with his elbow out the window, the radio dial on the countriest music he could find, something about a cheating heart, something he could sing along with, the way his face would appear in the rearview mirror periodically to spot-check our behavior in the backseat – *Were we slapping at each other, mumbling insults under our breath?* I liked Daddy beside Mother in a car, him driving her where she was supposed to go, the indifferent way she leaned against the car door, knowing good and well she was not a movie star. Mother said she missed Daddy, but she wasn't acting like it. She was acting like she believed he was off someplace with Rennie, eating in a restaurant nicer than any he ever took her to and so she had no choice but to get even with him.

Raymond was right. You cannot believe a person is dead unless you see his dead body. You have to see it with your own two eyes, touch it maybe and feel the absence in that touch. I could not imagine Daddy dead. Wasn't he the sort of man who had made something of himself, would always keep at it, making more and more of himself, even try to make something of us if we would let him? Who was I going to be without him? I'd always been Ford Jackson's girl, or the principal's daughter – I was that more than I was my own name. He was my connection to the world of things that mattered, the world where people took notice and took action. Didn't he say sometimes that Sowell, Wade and I were the best kids in the world – that he knew it for a fact? Didn't he try to make us be just that – the best kids in the world? We were still trying – at least Wade and me were. I hoped that wherever Daddy was he knew that. We were not going to let him down – even if Mother did.

It was good we were in the jeep. A regular car wouldn't have been able to weave on and off the broken road, take the mud and crater-size holes the way the jeep could. It was rougher than if we'd ridden horses all the way. We were thoroughly rattled and shaken when we finally got to Madison, which looked practically deserted, like a steamy ghost town where the only thing moving was the heat shimmying up off the paved road. Mr. Longmont liked the roughness of the trip, I think, the way he made it into not a joy ride, but a courage ride. He liked nearly slinging us out of the vehicle, nearly tipping the thing over on its side, so Mother had to gasp now and then, grab the sleeve of his shirt and hold on. It was a miracle I didn't fall out the back. I doubt they would even have noticed.

The new eyeglasses I picked out were not pink. The lady said I had an oval face and I should choose something that would complement my face. Lord knows I tried. Mother went inside with me to see the eye doctor and help me make my choice. Mr. Longmont waited out in the jeep. He smoked cigarettes, which I had never seen him do before. He leaned his head back and blew the smoke straight up into the air like he'd prefer a cloud over his head than right in front of his face, blocking the view. I tried on all the frames they had, since they didn't have many. Mother was not much help since she swore I looked nice in every pair I put on. I finally picked out a pair of light blue cat-eye glasses. The doctor said they had a new kind of glass now so that I could see things through my side of it, but it would not magnify my eyes to the size of God like my old pair did. My eyes wouldn't look swollen like the eyes of a monster green horsefly anymore, he said. He promised that. "These new glasses will be real becoming on you, Berry," the doctor said. "You'll look like a young woman in them." Mother paid him and he said we could pick up the glasses in a week.

Jack Longmont didn't take Mother and me to Rexall for lunch, which Mother and I always liked to do. Instead, he took us to a real restaurant where they specialized in frying up frozen seafood. It was delicious, if I did say so. Sowell and Wade would have loved it. Hush puppies, french fries, tartar sauce and everything.

While I was munching away, Mother excused herself to go to the ladies' room. Mr. Longmont watched her walk across the room like it was a favor she was doing him. Then he turned to me, the smell of his Aqua Velva engulfing me. "Berry, honey," he said, "I know how hard this has been on you and your brothers, with your daddy missing and all. I just want you to know that you don't need to worry, I'm going to do everything I can for your mama. I want to help her through this thing."

He waited for me to say thank you or something, but I had a mouth full of fried shrimp and a lump in my throat.

"Anything you kids and your mama need," he said, "all you got to do is ask."

I nodded, tried to swallow, looked around desperately for Mother to come back.

"I got a girl of my own." Mr. Longmont smiled. "I know girls need things. Marie keeps me knee-deep in bills, but I'm glad to do it. That's what a father is for, I say."

I died listening. I went to heaven and back. I went to hell

and back. I flew around the restaurant like a fly who couldn't find anywhere to light. Mr. Longmont was setting off alarms inside me and they were ringing so loud I thought he was going to mention them, say, "Berry, is that your stomach growling? Sounds like a damn ambulance coming."

When Mother finally came back to the table with fresh lipstick on and a fresh smile to go with it, I excused myself.

"Here, Berry." Mother handed me her purse. "Comb your hair and freshen up a little while you're gone, honey."

By the time I got to the bathroom I was shaking like a leaf. I locked myself in a stall and tried to think what to do. Mr. Longmont was so creepy. I thought he was ten times creepier than Eddie and Eddie had killed people. Eddie had those eyes like a couple of fish that swam all through his liquid head. Mr. Longmont had eyes like the barrel of a gun, pointed at you, probably already cocked. What would he think if he knew about Mother coming to Madison to see Butch Lyons that time? What would he think if he knew she had hugged Butch Lyons and cried all over him and acted like he was breaking her heart? He had already lost one woman to Pastor Lyons – I bet he couldn't stand to lose another one that way. Then he would have to give up on acting holy altogether.

I dug through Mother's purse, looking for change. I found a dime and put it in my pocket. I washed my face and ran a brush through my hair and even patted the tiniest bit of Mother's powder on my face where it was so red and startled. Then I snapped her purse closed and snuck out of the bathroom, followed an arrow down the hall toward the kitchen to a pay phone. I flipped through the phone book, looking for Loretta Lyons's number. House with two leaning palms in the yard.

House full of glass figurines that shook with every step taken. I inserted my dime and carefully dialed the number. Maybe I was secretly hoping nobody was home. I didn't know what I would say until I heard a man's voice on the other end.

"Is this Butch Lyons?" I asked.

"Speaking."

"Hello. This is Berry Jackson, Ruthie's daughter – from Pinetta." Then the sentences just came one after the other, like things falling. "I guess you know Pinetta got hit by a hurricane. It blew down the school, but the church is still standing. I don't know if you're still a preacher or not, but if you are, maybe you ought to be making some home visits like preachers are supposed to. Daddy and Rennie Miller are missing and unaccounted for. Mother is about to go crazy. I just thought you might like to know."

"Berry? Berry, honey, is that you? Where are you?"

But I hung up the phone as carefully as I had lifted it. If he ever said I called him up, I would swear he was lying. People would believe he was lying too. I took a deep breath and walked back to the table just in time to see Mr. Longmont gazing into Mother's teary eyes, his hand patting hers on the tabletop. He cleared his throat when he saw me coming. And Mother dabbed at her face with a paper napkin.

Before we started the drive back Mother ran into the Rexall to get Wade a comic book. She also got Sowell a hot rod magazine that had lots of elaborate-haired girls in tight sweaters sprawled out all over the vehicles and gleaming engines. "He thinks he's too old for comics," she explained to me.

I slept most of the way home, which cannot actually be true because the jeep was like a bucking bronco, we slipped and slid and dove into every rut in the road, but it felt to me like I was asleep. Like this whole day had been a bad dream.

~

Half the able-bodied men and boys in Pinetta had begun gathering at the school each day, salvaging what they could, clearing away the wreckage. The county had sent its superintendent to look things over and he declared the school a total loss. Since then folks had decided it was okay to help themselves to about anything they could find. It was like an all-day scavenger hunt, but it was called a cleanup effort.

All along people brought Mother any official papers they came across that might be important. She thanked them and added the mud-caked papers to the damp boxes in her closet.

The superintendent had also stopped by our house especially to see Mother and offer condolences. She treated him about like he was another deputy sheriff. "We'll keep Ford on the payroll through the end of the summer," the superintendent said. "At that time we'll have to make some decisions."

"I understand," Mother said.

That same night at supper she casually asked us what we would think of moving to Eufaula, where our grandparents lived. "Wouldn't you like to live in a real town for a change?" she said.

Every day I woke up to the sounds of the convicts stirring across the road, the smell of their coffee and the clanging of their cups and plates, the sounds of men groaning, fussing, shouting, and the guards issuing orders. "Count off!" a guard yelled at the appointed time. I liked that part. Raymond was number seventeen. There were thirty-three men in all. They didn't actually call out their numbers like they were supposed to, it was more like guttural sounds that meant *go to hell.* That was what it sounded like to me.

"What is so fascinating about those convicts?" Mother asked me one morning at breakfast.

"Nothing." I tore a shredded wheat to pieces and dropped it in my bowl.

"They call her Prettygirl," Wade said, his lips shining with butter. I felt myself redden. So Wade had been spying on me? I really hated him sometimes.

Mother stared at me a long time, like she was looking for a distinguishing mark to verify who I was but she couldn't find one. She broke her bacon in half and dipped it into her runny eggs and never took her eyes off me. "Berry, honey," she said. "There's a reason those boys are on the chain gang."

"I know that."

"They don't get to see many girls."

"So?" I pressed my shredded wheat into the bowl with my hand, crushing it.

"So, you be careful."

"I am."

"Wade," Mother said, "you go on and get dressed. Let me talk to Berry a minute." When Wade walked by I stuck out my foot and hit him in the shin as hard as I could. If Mother hadn't been sitting right there he would have smacked me. As it was, he mumbled, "Berry is a rat face."

"Berry, I know it must be nice to be sweet-talked a little bit." Mother held a toast crust in her hand. "Even if it is by convicts."

"They don't sweet-talk me," I said.

"Honey, in time there will be plenty of boys who'll say sweet things – and mean it."

I stared at her the way you stare at a liar.

"Boys that you can believe, honey. You know . . . trust."

"I trust Raymond," I said, drowning my cereal in milk.

"Who's Raymond?"

"A boy on the chain gang. He's not a criminal," I said. "He's nicer than any boy I ever met."

"Oh, Berry," Mother said. "Just saying what you want to hear doesn't make a boy nice, honey. Remember that. It's easy to say things. But lots of men lie – even if they're not convicts – sometimes they lie even when the truth is on their side. So you be careful."

"You be careful too," I said. "Just because Mr. Rich-Man Longmont says what you want to hear doesn't make him nice either. Does it, Mother?"

She took a bite of bacon. It crunched as she chewed. She shook her head like I was the biggest disappointment of her life.

I usually tried to take Raymond, Eddie and Marcel something good to eat – something they didn't get from the government, like sandwich cookies, peanut butter crackers, dill pickles, whatever I could find and wrap in waxed paper.

Here was what I had learned about Raymond so far. He had two older brothers that were wild as bucks – those were his words. His daddy was dead. His mama was a pure angel, but she had remarried a long-distance timber-truck driver who was Satan himself. Raymond's words again. His stepfather ran his brothers off one by one, but not without a hell of a good fight. Then it was just him, the youngest, left with his mother and that sorry devil. That was how his trouble started, he said.

He ran away from home and lived with a girl once – she was older than him, had a child already. Her name was Sharon and she did her best with him – but he couldn't stay with her because he kept on worrying about his mother. That trucker liked to slap his mother around and Raymond was afraid one of these days he would kill her dead. Even now he hated to get a letter in the mail. Couldn't hardly stand to open it, see what it said. Usually threw his letters straight in the trash, unopened. "That SOB better hope he dies before I do," Raymond said.

One of his brothers went on to become a trucker himself, over in Dothan, Alabama. The other one moved to someplace in Tennessee. The last they heard, he was married.

Raymond never had any sisters. He was glad too. Said that would be just one more thing to worry him to death. And he had enough worries like it was.

My favorite part of the story was where he could not stay with Sharon. I was pretty sure Sharon didn't deserve him.

Near the end of the next week ten of the most trustworthy convicts got off the chain gang, and Raymond was one of them. I couldn't have been prouder of him. They got assigned to work on the school every day now that it was not much more than a pile of bad memory. One of the guards marched them over there early every morning. When they arrived they were unchained. It was their job to clear the site so that construction of a new school could begin. I thought it was an honor that Raymond was chosen as one of the ones who could be trusted without his chains. They picked Marcel too. But not Eddie. Eddie looked about ready to have a fit over it too – Raymond said so. I could picture those swimming eyes of his like a couple of sharks circling in his dark thoughts.

It was a thrill to have Raymond turned loose. He looked ten times handsomer without those chains on his legs. He walked normal now, like a regular man. He could work as hard as anybody. Nobody could say Raymond was afraid of hard work. The convicts worked right alongside the good people of Pinetta. Together they had lifted parts of the fallen roof to see what they might find under there – like maybe Daddy's and Rennie's dead bodies. Mother said people in Pinetta had wild imaginations because it was one thing they could afford. "Imagination is free," Mother said. It took all the men to do it, lift the pieces of fallen roof. There was nothing underneath them but the remains of one more classroom, and one more, and one more.

The scraps nobody wanted were stacked and strewn in a fat teepee of a pile, which would be beautiful when they set it afire. The bulldozer was due to come when the lot was as clear as the men knew how to make it. Then the bulldozer would scrape a perfectly flat surface to build the new school on. It was going to be real modern, people said. A regular showplace.

A thing like this was exciting in Pinetta, anything involving a bulldozer, anything involving tearing down and building back. As it was, several times a day people took time out to gather in the road just to watch the bulldozer push things out of the way and make a flat surface so the road could be regraveled. Pinetta people were the kind who appreciated anything that helped keep the world flat.

Since the Methodist church was across the road from the demolished school, the Methodist ladies started serving hot coffee and cold drinks to the men working over there all day – convicts too. I noticed Raymond drank as many Orange Crushes as they would let him have. It was a real test of their Christian compassion. But then he could thank the ladies with a smile that made them know they had done the right thing. His white teeth, that way he sort of winked when he smiled. It proved to them that generosity was a true virtue. Next thing you know they were scooping him up a big cup of ice to pour his drink over. When he took his break with the other convicts under the branches of a huge oak tree draped in Spanish moss, I always sat beside him, both of us balanced on a bulging root that shot out from the tree like a pointing finger. He smiled at me like it was just what he was hoping I would do, sit beside him. "Come on, Prettygirl," he said. "Me and Marcel saved you a place."

He was so nice to me, it broke my heart.

"He's handsome to be a criminal," Rosemary whispered. We were standing at the drink table getting a refill.

"He's not a criminal," I said. "He's a victim of circumstance."

"What circumstance?" she asked.

Suddenly it occurred to me that the worst thing that could happen would be for Rosemary to get interested in Raymond. How in the world could I compete with her? She would probably have her shirt off in a heartbeat – or worse. Lord no, I had to prevent that. "He killed a girl," I said. "Slit her throat."

Rosemary looked at me with horror. "Why?" she whispered.

"She was undressing in front of him," I said. "You know, sort of teasing him."

"And he slit her throat for it?" She looked appalled.

"It's a long story," I said.

Next thing you know, the Baptists – not ones to be outdone in matters of conspicuous Christian service – decided to serve the workers a hot meal each day, go one better than the drinks the Methodists were providing. The Baptist women came in droves and set up food all up and down the long picnic table in the churchyard. It was as good as you'd find at an official religious covered-dish supper. So the Methodist women started cooking too. It was like an all-day feast. Nearly everybody in Pinetta made a showing there at least once a day. Plenty of people stayed all day, helping out what little they could, then just standing around, watching and comparing tales of their personal devastation at the hands of the hurricane. I usually stayed most of the day too. Walked over in the mornings and back home in the evenings, like I had a job to do.

Cadell and some of his brothers were nearly always there. They got rides in the back of the Wilmonts' truck. Like a lot of other people, they set aside small piles of stuff they thought was good enough to keep – salvage, you could say. Water-soaked books, splintered desktops, bent-legged folding chairs and whatnot. "That over there is the Miller pile," somebody would point. "Put it over there." I don't know what Cadell thought they would do with all that stuff when they got it carted home.

His favorite things, next to the baseball glove, were three small American flags he had dug out from under crushed chalkboards. He said he would get Mrs. Miller to wash and iron them, and stitch the parts that were torn, and then he would hang one on the front of their house, save one to put on his car antenna whenever he got a car – and the other one he didn't know what to do with, so he'd just save it.

While I was sitting beside Rosemary on the back of the Wilmonts' pickup truck, legs dangling – me dressed in Rosemary's clothes, her dressed in mine – both of us sitting there like a couple of harmless lies with smiles on our faces, I was watching Raymond work like a dog – a beautiful dog – when Cadell strolled over that way he always did, big strides, shoulders back, arms swinging. Walked like somebody who owned things – or was at least planning to. He sat on the tailgate beside me. "Hey there, Berry," he said. "How you been?"

"All right."

He just sat there like a bump on a log until Rosemary left to go get another cup of ice. As soon as she was out of earshot Cadell said, "I hear your mama has give up on your daddy. Is that so?"

"No," I said.

"That's what I heard."

"Well, you're liable to hear anything."

"Mama won't give up on Rennie." Cadell kicked the back of his shoe against the truck tire, knocking mud off it. "She'd be better off if she would. Sitting there all day, looking out at the road like she thinks somebody is going to come driving up, bringing Rennie home any minute."

"We all got to keep hoping, Cadell."

"Tell you what I hope," he said. "I hope Rennie don't come home. The way Daddy is disgraced over this thing, I hate to think what he'd do if she come back now. Only way for her to come back home after all this is in a wooden box."

"Don't talk like that," I said. "It's hateful."

"Rennie shouldn't have gone to that damn dance," he said. "Daddy is right about that. Look what come of it."

"It's not because of the dance, Cadell. Rennie was beautiful at that dance. It's because a natural hurricane tore through here."

"It's because she disobeyed," Cadell said. "You don't obey God, you pay a high price for it."

"Your daddy idn't God, Cadell. You kill me, talking like a preacher. You do."

"If you ask me, I say let's keep hoping they ain't dead. But let's give up on hoping they're coming back."

About then we saw Jack Longmont's jeep pull up with Mother sitting in the front seat as big as day. She got out carrying a cake and waved to Mrs. Ingram, who was standing at the picnic table helping keep the food organized and sampled. Mother had on that same pair of white shorts and flip-flops. The way people looked at her, she could have been stark naked.

Cadell watched her as hard as I did. "If you ask me," he said, "she don't look like a woman waiting on her husband to rise from the dead."

Before I could reconsider the instinct I reared back and slapped Cadell's face hard as I could.

I went home earlier than usual that day – miserable. Mother saw something was bothering me but had no idea it was her. "What's wrong?" she asked me twenty times.

"Nothing," I said.

"You okay? You sure?" she kept on. "Seems like something is on your mind."

"Leave me alone," I said. "I just want left alone." This was the wrong thing to say, because Mother cannot leave people alone. She cannot leave well enough alone either. She cannot let anything be – ever. So now she was hovering around like a giant housefly, driving me crazy. I tried to get in bed and close the door and go to sleep. But every few minutes she stuck her head in there and said, "You got me worried, Berry. Did something happen? Did you get your feelings hurt? Are you upset about something? You can tell me," she insisted, "whatever it is. It'll do you good to talk it out."

I couldn't answer these questions. One answer would just lead to fifty more questions. Mother is like that. She has to know. It is a full-time job to keep her from knowing what would not do her any good to know. With Daddy gone, it's *my* full-time job. I am worn out too. I am just about exhausted. I tossed and turned on my bed, called my cat, who would not come, and just sweat myself into a sorry state of mind.

Mother – who is famous for her bad ideas – got the bad idea to let Jimmy come in the house, into my room, to see about me. This is the kind of stuff she does when she gets worried. Her judgment goes from bad to worse. She lapses into pure terrible judgment. "Berry is moping around, Jimmy," I heard her say. "She won't tell me what's wrong. But maybe you can lift her spirits a little. You think so?"

"I guess," he said.

"She could use a little company. Company is the best cure for the blues, don't you think?"

As if Jimmy would know anything about curing the blues. He'd had the blues since the day he was born.

"I bet Berry will be real glad to see you," Mother said in that singsong way of hers.

If she only knew how dead wrong she was.

Jimmy sat on the foot of my bed – he was wearing boy clothes at least – and picked at his toenails, peeling off the pearly pink polish Rosemary had put on just days before. She did it because he begged. Already it was chipping and looking tacky. Besides, his feet were dirty. They smelled.

"Put your feet off the bed," I said.

He slung his feet over the edge of the bed and leaned against the wall. "What's the matter with you?" he asked. "You sad because your daddy is . . . gone?"

I did not want to discuss the matter. Not with Jimmy or anybody. "I just want left alone," I said. "That's all."

"Well, if your daddy *is* dead, Berry, there is a good side to it."

I stared at him.

"People always love the dead more than they do people alive. If your daddy is dead – people will start to think the world of him."

"People already think the world of him," I insisted. "He don't have to die to get a good reputation – if that's what you mean."

"He'll turn into a saint," Jimmy said. "It's human nature. Nobody likes to say nothing bad about the dead. Even I think better of your daddy now. I forget all them times he whipped y'all and hollered at people. All I remember is that time when my daddy was gone to his brother's funeral over at Alligator Point and I got that bad fever – remember? – and your daddy took the day off from work to drive me and Mama to Madison to the hospital. Mama was crying and your daddy was as kind as could be. That's all I'll remember if he turns up dead."

"Why are you saying all this?" I asked.

"Like, say, if you took a gun and shot me . . . ," he said.

"I wouldn't ever shoot anybody," I said. "Not even you."

"Like, just say I got you really mad . . . and I deserved to be shot . . ."

"You deserve it all the time, but I still don't do it."

"I'm giving an example," he yelled.

"*What if I shot you?* That's a stupid example. I never fired a gun in my life."

"Okay. Forget about you shooting me and all. Never mind. Just say, what if I ran out into the highway and laid down in front of that bulldozer out there and it went over me, crushed me flat, turned me into one of those slaughtered polecats or possums that get run over in the road late at night."

"What are you talking about?" I shouted.

"Dying," he said. "Like if I died."

"You are not going to die," I yelled. "You haven't even graduated high school yet."

He glared at me a split second and then went right on. "Okay, then," he said. "Say I hanged myself. Say I didn't want to live no more and I took a piece of clothesline and made a noose around my neck –"

"Stop it," I said. "That's stupid. You're crazy."

"What I'm saying is – if I was killed, then people around here would start to love me. They wouldn't think I was a bit strange anymore. They would understand about the dresses and would not let nobody speak ill of me wearing them dresses. Don't you see? They would make me into a angel in their heads. They would improve their thoughts of me because that's how you honor the dead. Even you would, Berry. You would probably get crazy about me. You would cry your eyes out when they buried me in the ground – and you'd be sincere about your grief too. Everybody would."

I could not take my eyes off Jimmy. He was enjoying imagining his death so much that it got my full attention. He was smiling and everything. "So, what is your point?" I finally asked.

"My point is maybe your daddy is dead. Probably he is. And maybe he's glad too."

"Why are you such a freak?" I yelled. "For once, why can't you just be normal?"

"Like you?" He raised his eyebrows, turned them into question marks over his eyes.

"Why don't you just leave me alone," I said. "I don't want my spirits lifted."

"Listen. I'm trying to tell you something, Berry. Death is magic. It can transform a person like nothing else. Your daddy too. It can make him into some kind of hero."

"My daddy doesn't need transformed, for your information. He just needs to come home." I felt a surge of grief come up in me right then, threaten to spill out. My voice went dry.

"You missed my point, Berry." Jimmy spoke gently. He put one of his nasty feet back up on the bed and went back to scratching the scraps of polish off his toes.

"I get your point," I insisted. "But it's not the right way to think, Jimmy. It's evil."

He shook his head and acted disappointed in me. He had gall – even if he was nuts. "You don't understand anything, do you, Berry? I feel sorry for you. You'd think a principal's daughter would be smarter."

I looked at him hard. He was trying to aggravate me – and at the moment that wasn't very hard to do. "Look, Jimmy," I said, "people are not all longing to be dead. Not normal people. Death is not some kind of good news either. Dying does not make people happy. Why can't you get that through your thick skull? If Daddy is dead" – I paused and took a breath – "then no matter what you say, you cannot make me happy to hear it."

"I'm not scared of dying," Jimmy said. "We're all going to die."

"Why don't you go home?" I said.

"You think too small, Berry. That's what's wrong with you." He got up to leave, shreds of his toenail polish all over my bed like pink bugs. I felt like leaping up and scratching his eyes out. But I didn't, because I thought he wished I would.

"I'm not giving up hope," I said. "You can't make me."

"Suit yourself."

Before he slammed the screen door on his way out of the kitchen, I yelled, "Besides, boys don't paint their toenails anyway." But the door was banging shut and maybe he didn't even hear me.

Jimmy scared me sometimes. I mean it.

After she heard Jimmy slam out of the house in that rude way of his, Mother came back to my room and peered in. "You feeling better now?" she asked.

I swear Mother forces you to lie to her. She practically begs.

"Just dandy," I said.

The next afternoon I walked home alongside Raymond and the convicts. The guard didn't make them put on their chains to walk home in the evenings since I guess he thought they were too tired to run away. Marcel said he was asleep as soon as his head hit the cot, but not Raymond. Raymond said he had to go over things in his head first – you know, wind his way down into sleep like it was a treacherous path that led to sleep and only the sure-footed found their way.

"You want me to get you a book to read?" I asked. "You could read yourself to sleep."

"They put the lights out," he said.

"I got a flashlight," I told him.

"No, they'll start thinking I'm up to something. Probably take it away and neither one of us will ever see it again. Besides, I don't need to read nothing. I can make up my own stories."

Then an idea came to me. "You know what I'll do?" I said. "Right before I go to sleep I'll shine my flashlight out the window. I'll flash it four times, then five times, that will mean G-O-O-D N-I-G-H-T. Okay?"

"Sure," Raymond grinned. "I won't close my eyes till I see it, Prettygirl."

* * *

On the nights Sowell walked to see Marie he usually came home with candy bars for Wade and me that Marie got from their gas station store free. She sent me a Baby Ruth and Wade a Payday. We got to where we counted on Sowell to bring that candy home, especially me, since I liked to give my Baby Ruth to Raymond.

I didn't exactly wait up for Sowell, I just slept light and listened for him to come in the kitchen door. We'd stopped locking it since he'd made such a big thing out of me in my nightgown. Now he just felt his way in the dark, took off his shoes, sometimes his shirt and pants, and laid down in bed with his arm slung over his face. Once I knew he was home, then I usually relaxed completely and let myself dream something. But this night he was crying when he came in.

It was not like girls cry. It was like boys do, who don't want to make any sounds to go with the feelings. Sowell laid on his back in exactly the same position as always, but I could see he was shaking sobs loose. Even in the dark I could see his face was wet and his eyes swollen. *It's Daddy,* I thought. *Sowell knows something.*

I got up from bed and took a few steps across to Sowell's bunk. "What is it?" I touched his shoulder as light as if he was a fire I was sticking my finger into.

He turned his head and waved his hand for me to go away.

"I know you're crying," I whispered, trying not to wake Wade. "Is it Daddy?"

He shook his head. "Go back to bed." His voice was full of that emotional gravel men rake out over their sentences to cover the pain in them.

"I won't tell," I whispered. "I swear to God."

Sowell rolled away so his back was to me. He was scaring me. It made me know suddenly, clearly, how much we all depended on Sowell to hold together – so that the rest of us could too. Since Daddy had gone we looked to Sowell to prove to us that the world was still twirling around the sun like it was supposed to. We made him prove it over and over again, day after day. He did it by keeping on, keeping on, no matter what. I laid down beside Sowell on his bunk, just as straight and still as he was. He was breathing in shudders. "What?" I whispered. "I'm not moving until you tell me."

I don't know how long it was that we laid in silence. Maybe two minutes, maybe twenty. Just about the time I thought Sowell had dropped off to sleep, he rolled over on his back and stared at the wire springs of Wades's upper bunk and without once looking at me said, "Marie."

"What about her?"

"She's moving away. Her and her mama."

"Where?"

"She won't tell me. Her mama doesn't want her daddy to find out, so she won't let Marie say." Sowell sighed like it was the most hideous injustice of his life. "Like I would tell him," he said. "Like she can't trust me."

Jewel and Marie Longmont – leaving Pinetta. It was like if people decided to tear down the Baptist church or something, which had the finest – the only – fellowship hall. It was special. It was not something that should get torn down, just like the Longmonts, who owned everything, were special, not people who should move away.

"When are they going?" I whispered.

"Tomorrow morning. They'll be gone before sunup. Might

be gone already. They were planning to leave when school let out. Then the hurricane hit. They had to wait on the roads to be cleared enough. Get everything ready. Mrs. Longmont is leaving Mr. Longmont a note, you know, to explain."

This was as strange as if Sowell was trying to tell me somebody was moving to Pinetta of their own free will and bringing their new and strange family with them. People didn't move to Pinetta – and people didn't move away. They were born here, grew up here, died here. Except preachers, who sometimes gave up, sometimes got run off. We were the newest people in Pinetta and we'd been here since Daddy became principal, before Sowell and I were even born. So it was nothing taken lightly – coming to or leaving Pinetta. Leaving especially had the connotations of sin.

"Marie is the only thing in Pinetta that means something to me," Sowell said. "With her gone . . ." His voice trailed off.

"She must really love you to tell you a secret like this," I whispered, believing it.

"You know what makes it worse?" Sowell said. "She blames Mother."

I felt myself fold in when he spoke, spitting those words. "It's Mother's fault. Marie's daddy always hanging around Mother, driving her around in that damn jeep. Marie says it's humiliating Mrs. Longmont."

"Mrs. Longmont told Mother she didn't care – that Mother was doing her a favor."

"I guess that's a lie too," Sowell said. "God, Berry, you should have seen Marie." Sowell's voice cracked. "I never saw anybody cry like that and there was nothing I could do." He shook his head like he was trying to get away from the moment. Like he was saying *no* to something too tempting.

"I'll tell you one damn thing," he said. "I'll find Marie. Wherever she goes."

I could not have moved from that spot unless somebody picked me up and carried me. I laid in silence beside Sowell until at last I fell into a dark, drunken sleep.

It was Mr. Longmont's jeep clanking through the yard that woke us up. He was driving like a man on his way to put out a fire. Mother wasn't even awake yet. When he started nearly pounding the back door down, I saw her go across the hall and look out to see who it was. "What on earth?" she said. She ran back to her bedroom to get her robe. "Just a minute," she yelled. "Hold on."

I was up by now too, dressing. But Sowell just lay in bed with his eyes closed.

When Mother opened the door Mr. Longmont came inside like a gust of wind. He held a letter in his hand and was waving it around like it was a white bird and he was having trouble keeping it from flying away. "She's gone," he said. "Both of them. Gone."

Mother sat in a kitchen chair and watched him circle the table. She looked dizzy and blank.

"Here." Mr. Longmont shoved the letter in Mother's face, nearly slapping her. "Read this."

Mother held the letter low in her lap and looked down to read it. It was a long letter, pages and pages of good-bye, I guess. Pages and pages of why, maybe. Mother's face went as pale as the paper in her hands. She was ghostlike in that chair in her wrinkled robe and wild hair, slow reading something that was technically none of her business. When she finished reading she just sat still with the letter resting in her lap and stared out the kitchen window with a bewildered look on her face. Mr. Longmont was rubbing his hands together, running his fingers through his Vitalis hair, and shaking his head in disbelief.

"What am I supposed to do?" Mr. Longmont said. Then he looked right at me and said it again, "What am I supposed to do?"

"Sit down, Jack," Mother said quietly. "I'll make coffee. We'll think of something."

He stood in place like he hadn't understood her.

"Sit down," she said again. "Right there. Sit."

When I left the kitchen Mr. Longmont was sitting at the kitchen table with his elbows propped up on it, holding his head like he was afraid it might roll right off his shoulders. He was making a vise out of his big hands, squeezing his head, his eyes closed tight, his straight teeth biting first his top lip, then his bottom one – as if that could keep him from saying whatever he was afraid he might say.

Now Sowell and I were virtually prisoners in our bedroom. Wade was still sleeping like a rock. I knew Raymond would wonder where I was. I knew he was expecting to see me first thing in the morning with a Baby Ruth in my hand.

Sowell was lying in bed playing dead – waiting.

I guess more than an hour passed before Mother came into the bedroom and said, "Sowell, get dressed and come in here. Jack wants to talk to you."

After she left, Sowell laid in bed a long time like he was thinking over whether to do it or not. Finally he got up, put on his messed-up clothes from the night before and walked into the kitchen barefoot, without combing his hair.

"Sit down, son," Mr. Longmont said.

"No, sir," Sowell said, "I'll stand."

Then Mr. Longmont proceeded to interrogate him, *Did he know . . . ? Did Marie ever say . . . ? Was Mrs. Longmont . . . ? Had he seen . . . ? Did Marie mention . . . ? Did Mrs. Longmont tell him . . . ? Did he notice . . . ? Did Marie seem . . . ? Had they said . . . ? Could he guess . . . ?*

It was terrible. Sowell stood like a boy before a firing squad, proclaiming his innocence. *No, he knew nothing. No, he had been told nothing. No, he saw nothing. No, he had no idea where they might be. No, Marie hadn't told him anything.*

When it was over and Sowell came back to the bedroom he looked wild-eyed. He looked like he needed to break something, like the door off its hinges, the windowpanes, Wade's neck or mine. I didn't know what he might do.

"You kept your promise to Marie," I said. "That's something at least."

He shook his head and slammed his fist into the bed.

I made my getaway then, walked through the kitchen past Mother and Mr. Longmont, who were circled around their cups of coffee, speaking in low, hard voices as I passed. Mother looked at me but said nothing.

I was fairly certain they hadn't believed Sowell. It was hard to believe him since his face was so red-splotched and his eyes swollen to look like a pair of puncture wounds on his face. He didn't look like a boy who knew nothing. He looked like a boy who knew more than he ever wanted to. I was pretty sure they knew he was lying his head off – mostly.

There was no Baby Ruth for Raymond – not even any buttered toast with blackberry jam – when I ran up to the school site.

"Everything okay, Prettygirl?" Raymond asked.

I stood alongside the convict crew as they loaded a drag with brick remnants, sweating already, breathing like horses, groaning when they lifted collectively. I had missed walking to school beside the convicts that morning like I usually did, their legs harnessed in the chains while they walked to the site, which made a certain music almost like church bells, the harmony of their stepping in unison, swinging out the chains with an odd movement of their legs, breathing in, breathing out – together, like a voluntary human machine, only it wasn't voluntary. Which was an easy thing to forget. And it wasn't a machine either.

Something happened to the men when they wore the chains. It was like a lot of men who did not belong – loners, lost types, losers, in Raymond's case, a lover – stopped being individuals who didn't belong the minute they put on those chains. They transcended just simple belonging and became absolutely essential to each other. It was like lots of bad individuals hooked together made one good whole out of themselves. People watched them go across the fields and down the road in the early mornings, almost like dancers, their chains clanking out the strange good-morning music, their voices echoing a non-word with each measured step, sounded like singing, *Yeah, yeah, damn, yeah.*

"What's wrong, Berrygirl? You look like you seen a ghost." Raymond rubbed the sweat off his face with the tail of his shirt.

"It's nothing wrong," I said.

"That your mama come around here in that jeep?" he asked.

I nodded yes.

"Well, she is pretty," Raymond said. "You can tell her I said so. There's worse things than a girl following in her mama's tracks, girlie, idn't that right?"

"I guess."

"I think you take after your mama," he said. "I can see a likeness."

"I can't," I said. "Nobody else can either."

It wasn't even noon before the talk started. Ray Longmont came up to help out and just casually mentioned that his mother and sister had left town for good, gone who knows where. The way he said it wasn't much more than if he'd glanced up at the sky and said, "Looks like we might get rain." He was one of those people who acted like everything in the world weighed exactly the same and none of it weighed much. His mother sleeping with the preacher, his daddy trying to kill his mother, his truck getting a flat tire, his supper getting cold – it was all the same. Just inconvenient. He drank some lemonade, took off his shirt, and went to work like somebody was paying him – and then it started, the talk. *Gone, gone, gone* . . . the word flew around like a butterfly people were trying to catch with long-net sentences.

"Not Jewel Longmont?"

"Why on earth? And took her girl, Marie?"

"This will kill Jack dead."

"If you want Jack Longmont, you need to look over at Ruthie Jackson's house. Man acts like her shadow."

"It's no wonder Jewel up and left. Bless her soul."

"I believe Jack Longmont has stretched kindness a little further than it's meant to go. I see his jeep over at the Jacksons' a good part of every day."

"You don't guess that's what's got Ford Jackson missing, do you? It ain't impossible, is it?"

All day it was like this, the whispers that set in when I came close, the voices that carried to me across the yard. *Jewel, Jack and Ruthie, poor Ford, Jewel gone, Ford gone too. Ruthie and Jack liable to run off next.* The names were arranged in every sequence possible, but the adjectives were mostly the same, tried on this name, tried on that name. *Poor things. Gone. Gone. Gone.* It was like people were thinking Mother and Mr. Longmont had plotted against Daddy and Jewel Longmont from the beginning, tried to run them off, and it was just now coming clear. Mother and Mr. Longmont had gone from being objects of pity to some kind of evil perpetrators. I was getting sick listening. I was feeling like that time when I got that tetanus shot in Madison, like it was poisoning my blood or something.

Jimmy hung around the schoolyard all day. Not actually helping do anything, just sort of slinking around, eating with his dirty hands, sitting off somewhere, reading some water-warped book he'd dug up. "Your mama ought to stop going around with Mr. Longmont," he said to me.

"It's a free country," I said lamely.

"Not really," he said. "It's not really a free country."

"What are you talking about?" I asked. "Mrs. Freddy told us it's a free country in the second grade. Every teacher has been saying so ever since."

"Just them saying so don't make it true."

"I guess you know more than the teachers do then. Is that what?"

"I know your mama ought not to be running around with Mr. Longmont."

"What you want me to do about it?" I said. "Lock her in the house?" Was Jimmy stupid? Didn't he know I had no control about anything my parents did. Not Daddy disappearing. Not

Mother wearing shorts and whispering stuff to Jack Longmont. Did Jimmy think I ran the world?

"You should ask Cadell," Jimmy said. "Cadell can tell you what the Bible says."

"If I want to know what the Bible says, I'll ask a preacher," I said. "When did you start worrying about what the Bible says?"

"Cadell knows a lot about hell," Jimmy said. "He knows everything about it."

"I bet he does," I said. "Since he's on his way there."

I disappointed Jimmy – just the way I was disappointed him. He disappointed me too. I don't know the exact moment this happened – that we lost our grip on being best friends, that the way we used to be just slipped away from us and vanished. I watched Jimmy walk back to the shade tree where he would spend the day in and out of the shadows, just watching this world and passing judgment on it, but not actually living in it with the rest of us. If you ask me, Mrs. Freddy had not done him a favor teaching him to read way back in the second grade. Now he had gone off into that imaginary world where everything was more exciting and interesting and mostly survivable. If you ask me, he had lost touch with real life. Which wasn't right.

When the Wilmonts' truck drove up to the school with Cadell in the back, it was the last thing I needed. "There's your little boyfriend," Raymond said.

I did the best I could to ignore Cadell. He was out of that truck and scanning his eyes over everything. I didn't even have to look at him to know he was looking for me. I wasn't hard to find either. "Well, well," Raymond said, "look who's coming your way, Prettygirl."

Cadell had the good sense not to come too close. I was keeping my eyes glued to Raymond. "Berry." Cadell stood with his feet apart, hands in his pockets. "I'm sorry what I said about your mama."

I ignored him completely. Maybe he would just say his piece and go. "I shouldn't of said it." He stepped closer. "You was right to slap me."

Why was Cadell like that? Always saying or doing the unexpected thing. Now I had no choice but to look at him. There he was – all face and hands and feet. His eyes burning bright and raw. "I got something to show you," he said. "Come over here a minute."

"Not now," I said.

"You gon take interest in this," he said. "Come on."

"Maybe later."

"If you don't come over here an look at this, then I'm gon have to drag it over to where you are and it's gon draw a lot of attention. You don't want that, do you?"

"What is it?" I said, getting a little nervous.

"Come see," he ordered.

I got up reluctantly and started toward Cadell. The last thing I could afford was another big hullabaloo made out of something concerning me. Mother was bad enough, but Cadell – I just couldn't take it. Raymond winked at me as I passed, his head glistening with sweat and red dirt.

I followed Cadell to the Wilmonts' truck, where he reached in and took out a burlap sack. "Come on," he said, "follow me around to the back of the church."

Nobody, except maybe Raymond, seemed to notice us walk past the food tables to the edge of the yard, then follow the path back behind the church, where it was deserted. "This better be good," I said.

"Guess what I got in this sack?" Cadell leaned against the wall and smiled a fifty-cent smile.

"A snake?"

"Hell no."

"Then what?"

He took my hand and said, "Put your hand in here," he said. "It won't hurt you."

I stuck my hand in the sack mostly just to get this whole thing over with. Inside was the softest lump of something I had ever felt. "Feels nice, don't it?" Cadell said. "Take it out."

I put both my hands into the sack and lifted out the tiniest baby kitten. She was white and her eyes were still pink as a rat's eyes. She was too little to mew or anything.

"The runt," Cadell said. "Daddy told me to drown her, but I said to myself, 'No, I bet Berry would like a nice cat like that, since hers has got sick and might die.' "

"My cat is not going to die." I held the kitten up against my neck, her tiny legs paddling against the air. "This kitten is too young to be away from its mother."

"She didn't have no choice," Cadell said. "You take good care of her and she'll be the prettiest white cat in the world. Her mama has got the longest fur you ever saw, like a rabbit or something."

I should have slung the kitten at Cadell and said, *I do not want your stupid kitten.* But I did want it. I wanted it bad.

"I knew you'd like it." Cadell leaned his head toward the kitten on my shoulder like he was going to rub his face against her fur. But then he put his mouth on my neck and slid his wet lips up the side of my face until he had his mouth on mine and he was pressing himself into me. If I had had my glasses this never would have happened. I could see what was coming when I wore my glasses.

"Stop it," I said, pulling back. I wiped off my mouth with the back of my hand, still clutching the kitten, who was trying to swim in my hot hand. "What do you think you're doing, Cadell?"

"Seeing if you're going to slap me again." He grinned.

"I got better things to do than spend my life slapping you." I grabbed the sack out of his hands and started back to show Raymond the kitten.

I could feel Cadell's eyes drilling holes in my back as I walked away. What had he been expecting, that when I laid my eyes on that tiny, half-alive cat I would be so smitten with Cadell that I'd just let him slide his wet mouth anywhere he wanted to? Did he think that what he had just done was a kiss? No. A kiss was the thing I imagined doing with Raymond. It would be exquisite. First Raymond would say sincere things, then he would come closer and closer until he was breathing on me, and I would stand still, afraid to move, while he put his arms around me and pulled me close to him and I could feel his heart beat through his hot skin. Then he would kiss me and it would be like a small and perfect death. I would come loose from this world once and for all.

When Raymond saw the kitten he was upset. "That cat needs its mama, Berry."

"I'm its mama now."

Raymond shook his head. "Poor thing, don't hardly stand a chance."

It bothered me that he said that. I put the kitten in my shirt-tail and carried it to the food table. Mrs. Ingram immediately set to work dipping the tip of a cloth into milk and letting the kitten suck it. She said, "Berry, let me see about that kitten for you, honey." She took it away from me and settled herself on a bench with the kitten in her lap and let it suck the milk-tipped rag as long as it would. "What are you going to name it?" she asked.

I looked at the balled-up cat trying to suck anything that touched her face, sucking the air itself. She looked not much bigger than a wet dandelion. "Her name is Desire," I said.

Mrs. Ingram looked at me and shook her head like she thought that name was all wrong for this tiny cat. "It don't fit her," she said.

"It does," I said. "Because she has so much desire to live. Don't you see?"

Rosemary was the only person I knew who had as much interest in healing the sick as her mother did. When she saw the kitten she begged to hold it, and finally Mrs. Ingram had to let her. Every time I came by to check on Desire, Mrs. Ingram said, "It's not good to handle a sick cat too much, honey," and she wouldn't let me hold my own cat. It wasn't until I took her home that night that I got to have her to myself, feed her with an eye dropper.

Our yellow cat was healing up. She mostly stayed in the house now. I thought maybe she would love Desire and want to adopt her, but she didn't. She came by where I had Desire sleeping on a towel on my bed and smelled her several times, but that was all. She didn't love her or hate her, either one, as far as I could tell.

What I am about to tell will make it seem like Sowell wasn't really as heartbroken over Marie as he claimed. But I swear he was. I bet if you could look through his skin, you'd see his heart was shattered like a dropped cup, everything in it spilled out.

The first night after Marie was gone Sowell tossed and turned in bed awhile, let out sighs that sounded like truck tires going flat, then finally kicked his damp sheet off, pulled on a pair of shorts and left the house.

It wasn't my usual habit to spy on Sowell, but in this case I was worried about him. As soon as I heard him go out the kitchen door I snuck into the kitchen and saw him start across the yard to the Ingrams' house. It was late. Most of the lights were off, but I could see him go to the side of the house where the girls' room was and scratch on the screen, maybe say something, call Rosemary's name or whistle like a bobwhite. I don't know. I watched until I saw her climb out of the window. She had on one of my plain sleeveless white shirts and a pair of shorts.

They walked past the hole in the weeds, which stood now like a vacant grave in our midst, and went down a path that was too small for cars and was mostly overgrown. I wouldn't walk down there for all the money in the world. It was swampy and full of snakes and who knows what. People said if you kept on far enough down that path you would come to quicksand and I believed it. But I guess Sowell and Rosemary were low on choices.

The next morning Desire was worse. I didn't know if we had overfed her or if we were starving her to death. Maybe she was just too shocked to be without her mother, to be alone in the world. When Mother saw her she said, "Berry, I don't think that kitten is going to make it."

"Mr. Miller was going to kill it. Cadell was trying to save it from his daddy."

"Sometimes the mother cat herself will kill the runt."

"That's so hateful," I said.

"You just be prepared for the worst," Mother said.

It was like that had become our family motto or something.

When Sowell had come home in the wee hours he had marks all over his neck where Rosemary had nearly sucked the life out of him. In the morning light they looked like bruises. He acted like he wished they weren't there, trying to put talcum powder on them like maybe that would cover them up. I think it was Rosemary's way of making her mark, saying to the world, *See, no matter what Sowell says about Marie, he is partly mine, here's the proof.*

While everybody else would be trying to ignore his purpled throat, Rosemary would be the one to draw attention to it. I knew for a fact that she would tease him about it in front of all the men working in the schoolyard. It would make her happy to see Sowell with her mouth print all over him, it would please her to see him embarrassed over it. She was sick like that.

There was nothing Mother could do with Sowell really. At breakfast she stared at him with a mix of surprise and disgust. "What is that all over your neck?" she asked.

"Nothing," he said as he slammed out the back door.

I missed walking to the school with the convicts for the second morning running. I was afraid to leave Desire alone. Mother didn't have Mrs. Ingram's natural affection for sick animals. She might put out a bowl of milk for the cats, but that would be it. She was not one to spend the day dipping the tip of a handkerchief into milk so a rat-size kitten could try to suck on it. It fell to me to do. I tried to do everything exactly like I had seen Mrs.

Ingram do, but Desire wouldn't suck. I pried her tiny mouth open and injected some milk from the eye dropper, but it just ran back out the sides of her mouth. She lay as still as a rock. I talked to her, made fake purring noises, stroked her tiny body, everything I could think of.

"Get our yellow cat," Wade said after watching my futile efforts. "Maybe that little cat will think it's her mother."

Our yellow cat was not unwilling. I wrapped her moderately cooperative body around the kitten and put the kitten's face next to the cat's heart and the kitten actually moved a little, made those swimming motions again. Our yellow cat seemed willing to lie still, let the kitten squirm beside her, but nothing more. I set a bowl of milk next to them so it might entice them in some way, and at the very least should let them know that I was trying my useless best.

Midmorning Mother said, "Berry, you are worrying those cats to death. Leave them alone."

When I thought I had made their accommodations perfect I left them in our darkened bedroom and walked over to see Raymond and Marcel and the others.

But Cadell was the first person I saw. He was loading lumber scraps in the back of the Wilmonts' truck. Who knew what for. "How is that little white cat doing?"

"Bad," I said.

The guard who watched the convicts was named Mr. Bruce. He had gotten to know my name and was nice to me. He didn't care if I sat and watched "the crew," as he called them, work until they dropped. Mr. Bruce blew a whistle when the convicts got a break and he blew it again when it was time to start back to work. Twice a day he walked them into the woods so they could relieve themselves. Otherwise, he would yell, "Hold it," whenever they asked for "time out," which meant to pee. Usually they could hold it. Even if they couldn't, it wasn't because of wetness around their crotch that you could tell – since their government-issue clothes were soaked and stuck to them like adhesive tape from early in the hot morning. No. It was just because of the smell.

"These boys is a good lesson," Mr. Bruce said to Cadell and me. "Watching them makes you think twice before becoming a jailbird, don't it?"

"Yes, sir," we said. But it wasn't true.

"Shoot," Cadell said when the guard left. "All it is, is like the army. You follow orders. They give you food and bed. You do your time and then you're out."

"It is not as good as the army," I said.

"Depends on how desperate you are," Cadell said. "Three squares and a roof overhead. That ain't all bad."

"They don't chain your feet in the army."

"There's worse things," he said. But that was crazy. Cadell was one boy that I knew would not last ten minutes on a chain gang, not the way he liked to lead the way and explore everything. He would bust up on the chain gang. Go insane. He didn't have a good disposition like Raymond.

Just as I knew she would, Rosemary was making a fuss over Sowell in front of everybody, saying, "Son, son, looks like somebody been kissing on you." The men around Sowell smiled – probably wishing they had their necks covered with that kind of proof – but Sowell just kept pushing that wheelbarrow like it took every ounce of his concentration.

"Somebody must be mighty sweet on you," Rosemary said. "I wonder who could it be?"

Anybody watching would think Sowell was stone deaf. The more Rosemary went on with that, getting louder and sillier, the stonier Sowell got. The other men and boys laughed and egged her on, but Sowell didn't even look at her until the very end, when it seemed like she was finished with the teasing. The look in his eyes wasn't irritation either. It was a look that made it perfectly clear that he would be back at her bedroom window tonight and she better be ready because he would make sure that whatever happened last night that she liked so much would happen twice tonight. He was like a man counting the minutes.

I bet if Marie could have seen how he was acting she'd be glad she was gone from him.

When the sheriff's car drove up to the school work site nobody thought that much about it. But when the deputy got out and asked, "The Jackson children over here?" people went silent.

Mr. Burdett nudged Sowell and said, "Son, they looking for you." Sowell dropped the wheelbarrow handles and stood there without his shirt, wiping his face off with a bandanna he had tied around his neck as feeble camouflage.

Wade was playing around with some boys up in the churchyard, but the sheriff's car drew him like a magnet. He walked toward Sowell, who stood his ground. Wade was trying to stand in Sowell's shadow, I think. I stayed sitting on the ground, Indian-style, silent.

"Over there." Somebody pointed to us – mostly Sowell. "That's the Jackson boy right there."

"What can I do for you, mister?" Sowell asked as the deputy approached. It occurred to me that the deputy might arrest Sowell, charge him with taking indecent liberties with Rosemary or a plot to kill Mr. Longmont – or Mother. Maybe he was being arrested for lying so much.

"You Ford Jackson's son?" he said.

"I am," Sowell said.

"We located your daddy's car," he said.

I felt myself slip a little, the ground sort of shift under me and tremble slightly.

"Where was it at?" Sowell asked, like this was any other ordinary conversation.

"Jacksonville," he said.

"Jacksonville?" I shouted. It was like he said the one word that would break me open in the worst way.

"I been over to see your mama," he said. "She wanted me to come around here and get you kids and bring you home."

I had never ridden in a sheriff's car before. Especially not a Jacksonville sheriff's car. Everybody stared at us while we got in – Sowell in the front, Wade and me in the backseat. Wade was grinning like a fool.

I waved to Raymond, but he just stared at the whole proceeding like it was something more awful than he had dreamed, to see me in cahoots with the sheriff, to see me get in that car without the least bit of kicking and screaming. I felt sort of like a traitor too.

I saw all those Pinetta faces, gone pale in the insufferable heat of the afternoon, their eyes round and curious, watching us, the Jackson kids, like – at last – we had done something notable.

"Shit," Sowell said when we saw Mr. Longmont's jeep parked in our backyard. "What's he doing here?"

"He's looking after our poor pitiful Mother," I said. "What else?"

"She's not a widow woman," Sowell said. "He acts like she's a damn widow woman."

"I guess he's hoping so," I said.

"If Mother marries Mr. Longmont, do we get to live in his big house behind the gas station?" Wade asked. He said it like he was hopeful. "They got a TV."

"She's not going to marry him," I said. "She's already married."

The deputy didn't comment. He let us out and we went in the house like we were company coming to visit. Mr. Longmont met us at the back door. "Your mama is in the bedroom," he said, "lying down."

We walked down the hall single file to Mother's bedroom. She was lying on her side, waiting for us, with the lights out. We entered quietly and sat on the foot of her bed, the springs begging for a little mercy under our shifting weight.

Mother propped herself up on her elbows and looked into our dirt-streaked, sunburned faces, "What did the deputy tell you?"

"They found Daddy's car in Jacksonville," Sowell said.

She nodded. "That's right." Her hair was smashed flat on the side of her head where she had been laying. It looked like somebody had hit her with a board.

"So Daddy is somewhere in Jacksonville?" I felt a surge of anger. "All this time?"

Mother reached for my dirty hand and squeezed it. It was almost sweet the way she did it. "They found his car," she said, "not him. A couple of boys were trying to sell your daddy's car in Jacksonville. Said they found it deserted on the side of the road. The sheriff thinks they stole it. But the boys claim they never saw your daddy and don't know his whereabouts."

"Do you believe them?" Sowell asked.

"The sheriff believes them," she said. "He says these boys he arrested are just petty thieves, not, you know . . . they wouldn't hurt anybody."

"Any sign of Rennie?" Sowell asked.

"A pair of high-heeled shoes on the floor of the car," she said. "The ones Mrs. Longmont loaned Rennie. Jack identified them."

"Can't you make him go home?" Sowell whispered. "Why's he have to be here all the time?"

"This is hard on him too, Sowell," Mother said, her eyes meeting Sowell's full force.

"Oh, I get it," Sowell said. "Misery loves company. Right?"

"Do you want to hear the rest or not?" Mother said.

"Go on," Sowell said.

"Your daddy's car was damaged. They don't know whether it was wrecked before the boys stole it or afterwards. So your daddy and Rennie might have been hurt in an accident. They're checking all the hospitals again."

"So we don't know any more than we did before?" I said.

"Not really," Mother said. "We just know where the car is."

"Right," I said. "Jacksonville."

I didn't know what it would take to make Jack Longmont go home. He sat in the kitchen like it was his job to stand guard over us, when really I think he was just afraid to go home and see how gone his wife and daughter really were. I avoided the kitchen because Jack Longmont was like a kudzu vine planted in there, overtaking everything. I went into my room to see about Desire. She was lying still, stretched out, not in a ball like usual. I knew instantly that she was dead. I touched her matted fur and she was cold and sort of frozen into position. Her eyes were closed. She had such a lonely expression on her face, like she had been alive, then dead, so fast that she never had a chance to understand anything.

"Sowell!" I cried.

But it was Jack Longmont who got to the bedroom first. His shoes as loud as a wood ax across the wooden floor. "What is it, Berry?" he said. "What's wrong?"

I pointed to the towel on my bed and the dead kitten. For a minute he just stared at it like he didn't understand what it was. He kept looking at me instead, like he was waiting for me to explain death. Then he stepped to the bed and lifted the towel with the kitten in it. "Poor little thing," he said.

Sowell and Wade were saying, "What happened? Did your kitten die, Berry?"

"Give it here," Sowell said to Jack Longmont. "Me and Wade will bury it."

"Come on, boys," Mr. Longmont said, "you can help me."

I watched out the window while Mr. Longmont dug the hole. Sowell wanted to do it, but Mr. Longmont took the shovel out of his hand and stabbed it into the dirt in the flower bed under my window where we buried nearly everything that died. Two scoops of dirt was all it took.

Wade wrapped the kitten in waxed paper and folded the edges with his fingers so it looked like a piecrust. He worked on it with great seriousness. When Mr. Longmont was ready, Wade laid the waxed paper in the hole and Mr. Longmont raked the dirt back into the hole with the shovel, then smoothed the spot with the sole of his shoe.

I watched all of this, waiting for the sadness to come. I thought it would make me cry to see that kitten buried, but no tears ever came, no feelings at all. "I'll have to tell Cadell," I said when the kitten was buried, but nothing else. I waited at the window after Sowell and Mr. Longmont left, and watched Wade arrange a pile of gravel over the grave in the shape of a sloppy cross.

"You want to say a prayer or something, Berry?" Wade asked.

"No," I said.

"You want me to say one?"

"You can if you want to."

"I guess not then," he said.

That night I slept with our yellow cat in my bed like usual. I was sort of disappointed in her inability to save the white kitten. I thought all she'd had to do was love it. I didn't think she'd really tried. It was like now that she had finally gotten inside the house she wanted to be the *only* cat in the house. That seemed wrong to me – greedy or something.

Sowell was gone someplace with Rosemary. He'd put on some of Daddy's Old Spice before he left. I guess he thought Daddy wouldn't be needing it anymore. Next thing you knew, he was going to be wearing Daddy's white shirts and lace-up shoes.

Wade had read himself to sleep. Sometimes I let him read out loud to me. He liked to read science things about the planets and stars. He would lie on his top bunk with his head almost out the window and try to locate things in the night sky, struggle to make the actual stars fit the drawings in his book. He seemed to be really counting on outer space. Had dreams of going there. Was hoping for intelligent life somewhere out there, light-years away. I personally didn't think the stars were that interesting. When I looked at them no real questions came to mind.

I flashed my good-night code toward the convict camp, its

orange lanterns hanging like eerie jack-o'-lanterns. Nine perfect flashes that spelled out something only Raymond could understand. I imagined him lying on his cot in his underpants. They let the convicts sleep in their underpants if they wanted to since it was so hot. I knew because some mornings I saw them when they got up and went to the latrine out back. Men in their underpants didn't bother me. I think it was because I shared a room with my brothers and I'd got used to it.

I thought about Raymond sweaty and restless on his cot and wondered if he was thinking about me. I pretended he was thinking that when they set him free he would come back for me, drive into Pinetta in a nice car and knock on my door and I would be more grown by then and I'd look a lot better than I did now. He'd tell Mother and Daddy that he loved me. He'd say he'd started to love me that first day when I came out to the road, carrying our yellow cat in my arms. He'd say how sweet I was to bring him those Baby Ruths and to flash him a personal message from my bedroom window each night. He'd say, "That was what kept me going. I swear to God." He'd be completely reformed from any wrongdoing.

He might even go to church with us, and folks would remember him from how hard he worked on the road and the school after the hurricane hit. They'd shake his hand and welcome him and say, "You have paid your debt to society, son." Rosemary would think he was the handsomest thing she ever saw and I would finally tell her he didn't really slit that girl's throat like I said. Then maybe we'd get married – right there in Pinetta Methodist Church. We should have a new preacher by then. If Daddy was back, he could walk me down the aisle. If he was not back, maybe I'd ask Sowell to do it. (No matter what, I would not let Mr. Longmont do it. He might own everything in Pinetta, but he didn't own me.) I would not run away with Raymond though, you know, elope. I wanted to do things the right way.

Sowell woke me up when he came home in the wee hours. The way he shook me fit right in with what I was dreaming and I could have gone right on thinking he was Raymond if he hadn't kept saying, "Wake up, Berry." I couldn't stand somebody to say *wake up* to me. That used to be Daddy's job, getting us up each morning for school, getting us to the breakfast table so we could all eat together before he left for work. It came hard to me, waking up. Daddy had a way of scaring me into it.

"What do you want?" I said.

"Me and Rosemary saw you flashing that Morse code out the window. You can get yourself in a lot of trouble that way."

"There's no law against it," I said.

"What message you sending?"

"None of your business."

"Rosemary said she bets you're saying *I love you.*"

"Tell her to mind her own business," I said. "She's got more than enough of it."

"Berry, you need to stay away from those convicts," he said. "You're asking for trouble."

"I guess you would know, wouldn't you, lover boy?"

Sowell punched me, but it didn't hurt. I hit him back. Then he climbed into his lower-bunk cave and I heard him mumbling. I put my pillow over my head and went back to sleep, but my dream was ruined.

In the morning when I woke up, our yellow cat was in bed with Wade, which bothered me more than I could say.

* * *

Mother had started "lying down" late into the mornings. Some days she didn't get up and begin to stir around until nearly noon. Mr. Longmont was at our house at daybreak practically every day. He made coffee in our kitchen and carried Mother a cup and they sat in her dark bedroom, her lying like a dying woman in her housecoat, the one she'd bought a long time ago to take to the hospital with her when Wade was born. Since then it had just hung in her closet in case – as she put it – she ever went anyplace nice. Now there she was, lying around in it, the bow tied at the neck, while somebody else's husband brought her her morning coffee and sat on the foot of the bed, talking about the meaning of life or something. I think they were trying to plot some path into the future, like they were both living half lives at best now and something needed to be done about that.

Wade and Sowell and I got our own breakfast. I made cheese toast. They ate cereal. We were quiet as a house full of mice. When Mother saw any of the three of us go down the hall she always called us into her room. I think she wanted to force us to look in there and see that there was nothing wrong going on. "Come in here a minute," she would say. "Jack was just telling me about . . ." It didn't matter what. It was like she was trying to trick us all into liking each other, but what was really happening instead was that we were all liking her less and less. I think she could feel that, which was what made it so hard for her to get up in the morning and face the long, hot day ahead.

"Berry," she said. "Jack is going to be an angel and drive me into Madison to pick up your new glasses today. Don't you want to come with us?"

"I'd rather stay here," I said.

"Suit yourself," Mother said. "But don't you think you should thank Jack? He's going out of his way."

"Thank you," I said.

"Sure, Berry," he said. "It's my pleasure."

That was exactly the problem. Everything was Jack Longmont's pleasure. What about our pleasure? Why couldn't he go home and let us have a moment's pleasure?

That morning when I walked to the school with the convicts I told Raymond and Marcel what had happened to Desire. They listened like it was fairly important. "Well," Raymond finally said, "I could of told you that was going to happen."

"Some things ain't meant to be," Marcel said.

"Besides," Raymond said, "there's worse things than dying. Plenty worse things."

"That must of been a sick little cat," Marcel said, "to use up all her nine lives in such a hurry."

"I don't think she knew she had nine," I said. "She didn't have time to find out."

"Don't worry about it, girl," Marcel said. "The world is full of cats. You'll get another one."

Marcel didn't understand. He was inclined to say things like "there's more than enough trouble in this world," "there's more than enough cats in this world," "there's more than enough idiots in this world." Like that. He could fit these sentences into nearly any conversation. True sentences that didn't mean anything at all.

The cleanup job at the school had taken longer than first anticipated. But now it seemed that the end was in sight. Raymond and Marcel were digging a shallow trench around the scrap pile so that it could be set on fire later in the afternoon. "There's talk we'll be moving our camp at the end of the week," Raymond said.

"Where to?" It gave me a sinking feeling.

"About twenty miles closer to Madison," he said. "More roadwork down there."

"Myself, I like working on a school," Marcel said. "Churches and schools – that's my preference."

"He means he's going to miss those churchwomen serving that food," Raymond said.

"Amen," Marcel said.

"Especially that one. Over there. In that green dress. See there." Raymond nodded.

"That's Mrs. Freddy," I said. "She's married."

"Don't I know it." Raymond smiled.

Mrs. Freddy had come to serve food nearly every day. She didn't seem too upset about her classroom being blown away. In the beginning you could see her tromp through the debris looking for something she could recognize, but she didn't break down over it or anything.

She called our house now and then to see if there was any new word on Daddy. Sometimes if I answered the phone she would say, "Berry, honey, how's your mama holding up?"

"Good," I always said, which was a bold-faced lie.

"You know I thought the world of your daddy – still do," she said. "Me and lots of other folks."

"I know it," I said. What else could I say?

Mrs. Freddy was always extra nice to me. Sometimes when she saw me sitting around watching the convicts work, she said,

"Berry Jackson, come over here and talk to me a minute." Maybe she gave me a slice of cake or something. We'd sit on a overturned tree at the edge of the schoolyard. "So," she said, "I guess your family has been having a pretty rough time."

"Not too bad," I said.

"You look different without your glasses," she said.

"Everybody says that." I ran my finger around the edge of my cake where the icing was.

"Your family will be sort of like this school here," Mrs. Freddy said. "It might get a little torn up for a while, but it will get built back and be stronger than ever."

That's the kind of stuff Mrs. Freddy always said. It was the teacher in her, I guess. She tried to be cheerful and encouraging at all times. But I didn't mind. "You sure are growing up, Berry." She smiled. "I remember when you were just a little first- and second-grader in my classroom. Now look at you. You're nearly as tall as me."

It was true. But I wanted more than that. "I wish I was as beautiful as you."

She looked completely startled. Like maybe nobody had ever said she was beautiful before. She stared right at my face. "Why, Berry, what a nice thing to say to an old married lady." Then she tried to laugh. Afterwards she could hardly take her eyes off me. I could tell that deep down she sincerely liked me. Maybe even loved me slightly.

So now I had a warning – Raymond would be leaving soon. "Moving camp," he called it. It was like if they sent a notice saying the electricity was going to be turned off for a while – only it was going to be turned off forever. I knew Raymond didn't like letters. I guess he worried he would get one saying his mama was dead. But maybe he would let me write to him care of the prison. Maybe if I promised to send him only good news – even if I had to lie my head off and make stuff up.

It wasn't easy to tell Cadell the white cat was dead. I knew he would blame me, think less of me. Maybe he would think I hadn't really tried. Maybe I hadn't. I searched him down, which wasn't hard. He and two of his brothers were at the food table. I bet those churchwomen had to run them off from there over and over. I bet those Miller boys swarmed that table like flies.

"Cadell," I said, coming up behind him, "I got to talk to you." He turned around to face me. His brothers did too. "Over here." I pulled him away from them, by his shirt sleeve. I led him all the way to the steps of the church. "Okay." I stood facing him.

"Well, what is it?" he said.

"The kitten died. I tried to keep her alive, but I couldn't."

Cadell looked at me a long time like I was telling him my daddy had died. I think that was what he was expecting. A bigger death of some kind.

"We buried her," I said. "I'm real sorry."

"Me too," Cadell said. "I know you done your best, Berry."

"Maybe not," I said.

"You did," he said. "I know it."

Maybe I don't like Cadell much, but I will say that he had a touch of magic about him. The way he could say the opposite of what you were ready for. Make you feel sort of light-headed and actually like yourself for a split second.

We walked back toward the food table together without saying much. Finally Cadell said, "Things will get better, Berry. You wait and see."

"I know it," I said. But I didn't.

"I see how you're lovesick over that jailbird," Cadell said. "I never thought I'd see you mooning over a known criminal. What you like so much about him?"

"He's nice," I said. "That's all."

"What was his crime?" Cadell said.

"Love. That's what he says."

"That's a new crime, far as I know," he said. "But I reckon people has died from it. You're not about to die from it, are you, Berry?"

"I'm nowhere near dying," I said.

"That fella is no angel, you know, Berry. As long as you know he's no angel."

"I know that."

"If he wants to go to hell, fine and dandy, but don't let him take you with him, Berry."

"Nobody is fixing to go to hell," I said.

"Sure they are," he said. "Most of us on our way right this very minute."

"Speak for yourself," I said.

Mother and Jack Longmont drove up to the church just after noon. Mother brought a cooled pot of pork and beans and wieners baked in brown sugar. Mr. Longmont carried it to the table for her, which got everybody's attention. At least Mother had the decency to wear a regular dress since she and Mr. Longmont were on their way to Madison to get my glasses. It gave her an air of moral improvement.

Mrs. Freddy hugged Mother and said, "Oh, Ruthie, I've been thinking about you."

"They found Ford's car," Mother said. "I guess you know."

Mrs. Freddy nodded. Of course she knew. Everybody in Pinetta knew everything that happened. "Jack has been nice enough to drive me around since I'm without transportation," Mother said. "He's been real kind."

Mrs. Freddy nodded like she understood.

"We're on our way to Madison," Mother said. "Berry needs her glasses."

"Sure she does," Mrs. Freddy said. "Of course."

"It's odd, isn't it?" Mother said, looking around at the church where up until a few weeks ago she had played the piano, pounded out song after song with such fury and passion, "how everything changes."

"I know you miss Butch," Mrs. Freddy said. "He was the one person who would know what to say to you at a time like this."

"No," Mother said. "Butch wouldn't know. Not really."

"Well, I miss him," Mrs. Freddy said. "I forgive him and wish he would come back. The church is almost dead without him. Bye is talking about transferring to the Baptist church, but I can't do it, Ruthie. I've been a Methodist all my life. I can't just bail out because things have happened."

"No," Mother said, "that wouldn't be right."

It was Cadell who yelled, "They fixing to light that stack of lumber. Y'all come on and watch."

Pinetta people loved fire. We passed it off as good entertainment, watching a fire burn – something even hotter than our daily lives, something so beautiful and potentially destructive. The men liked thinking it was something dangerous that they could control. Maybe it was the only thing.

At Cherry Lake, after an evening of swimming in the snake-infested waters, Daddy used to make us a blazing fire to roast hot dogs and marshmallows. We would sit on the ground in our wet swimsuits stuck to us like tissue paper, our hair drying in unnatural curls and points, the mosquitoes biting and the crickets shrieking and we would unwind black coat hangers we'd brought from home. We'd slide the hot dogs on the curly ends and stick them into the fire until they were cooked or our wire handle was too hot to hold. The hot dogs always ended up blistered and blackened and covered with soft ash, but we said they were delicious, wrapped in a slice of white bread. I loved having my family gathered around a fire. It seemed so religious or something. Scalding our tongues with hot white marshmallow like taking Communion – all our faces lit up, full of the flicker of the Holy Spirit. When we were gathered around a fire in the darkness it always made me believe in things.

I don't know how it was decided that Marcel would be the one to light the match to start the fire. "Back up, now, folks," Mr. Bruce said. He held his gun up sideways in front of him like he might shoot us if we didn't back up. "This fire is going to jump out now. You kids get back."

We all stood at a careful distance while Marcel put the match to some dry paper. He lit several pieces and started small fires that seemed to join forces and then – *poooof!* – like an explosion the fire took hold and made a huge mushroom of flames sort of like a bomb. Everybody cheered. Why do people smile at fire that way? Wade, for one, looked almost delirious with satisfaction.

The crackling sound started and it was thrilling to watch the flames eat the wood, the plaster, the books. Maybe that was what people liked about fire – its fierce hunger and the way it raged until that hunger was satisfied. Now and then you could hear glass burst and fly out like a spray of diamonds. We were all like hypnotized people, standing just out of reach of destruction. "It's beautiful, isn't it?" people said. "Look at that."

Nobody noticed the snakes that crawled out of the fire, smoked out of dark slots between the wooden boards where they had probably nested for days. We weren't watching the ground, but the sky, how high the flames shot, the smoke that signaled to the world that we were, after all, not lost. I barely remember the sound – I'd heard it before – that death rattle, but it blended with the crackle of the fire and so I went unwarned until I saw Raymond's face, his eyes, the way he suddenly charged at me, screaming my name, and instead of moving I froze like a salt statue and he dove into me and pushed me so hard it knocked the breath out of me and I fell to the ground just feet from the fire – saved. I was saved.

The rattlesnakes bit Raymond. Two of them, one strike each. People began to scream. Mr. Burdett reached right into the fire for a stick to beat them with. Mr. Bruce yelled, "Get back. Get back." He put his gun to his shoulder and fired four shots at close range. The snakes twisted themselves up off the ground like poisonous plants growing, each shot making them jerk and tangle themselves together, then fall to the ground and lie still, like two lazy snakes, still moving, but not as fast.

Mr. Burdett took his stick and, using the ember end to strike them with, slung the two snakes back into the fire to fry. They were still writhing until they disappeared entirely. Devoured by the flames.

Raymond had fallen to the ground after the snakes bit him. He held the places on his leg where he was bitten. I crawled over to him, panicked. "Somebody help him," I called out. But I didn't need to.

Already Mr. Burdett and Mr. Wilmont and Cadell himself

were dragging Raymond into a clearing and calling for help getting him into the bed of Mr. Wilmont's truck. Women were grabbing tablecloths to spread in the back of the truck. Mrs. Freddy brought a dish towel and the men tied it in a knot around his thigh just above his knee and inserted a stick to make a tourniquet out of it. I watched as the men lifted Raymond and carried him, his arms tight around their necks. He looked scared.

Mother ran and grabbed me so hard I would have bruises later. "Berry," she said, "thank God." She shook me by the shoulders and looked me over. "You almost got bitten," she said.

"We need to get this leg into a tub of kerosene," Mr. Burdett said. "We'll take him over to the house. I got kerosene there."

"I ain't supposed to let him out of my supervision," Mr. Bruce said. "You go get the kerosene and bring it here."

"We don't have time for that," Mr. Burdett said. "Man can die from snakebites."

Mr. Bruce looked lost in his small choices – either yes or no. It was Mother who decided for him. "That boy saved Berry's life," she said. "I'll be sure he doesn't run off, if that's what you're worried about. Tell him, Jack."

Jack Longmont seemed like a man waiting for his instructions. He stepped forward, "Look, I'll take full responsibility here."

Mr. Bruce scratched his head under his hatband where his hair was dented. "This is against regulations."

"As far as I'm concerned," Mother said, "this boy is practically a hero. You don't want the death of a hero on your hands, do you?"

"Soon as you get his leg in that kerosene, you bring him back to the camp," Mr. Bruce said.

"Of course," Mother said.

By then Mr. Wilmont was already in his truck with the motor going. I climbed in the back beside Mr. Ingram, who was holding the stick in the tourniquet. Nobody tried to stop me. Mother and Jack Longmont and Sowell and Wade followed in the jeep. I don't know who all followed them – just about anybody who had a car it looked like – it was follow-the-leader, and Raymond was the leader.

When we got to the Burdetts' the men took big jugs of kerosene out from the carport and drug out a metal tub and poured the kerosene into it. I sat with Raymond and described what they were doing. "You're going to be okay," I said. He was as pale as the undershirts hanging on the Burdetts' line. He looked glassy-eyed with fear and didn't speak a word.

Mrs. Ingram was the one to pull Raymond's pants off him. She started with his shoes. Then she had to take his tourniquet off and pull down his pants as fast as she could, then put the tourniquet back. He cooperated the best he could. I couldn't help but stare at his pale legs, his gray underpants so threadbare that I could see through them.

The men carried him to the tub of kerosene and sat him in it. Raymond winced when the bites touched the kerosene. "Oh shit," he mumbled. The places were already swollen into red lumps under his skin. You could see where the fangs went in. Like two neat pinholes. The poison already seeming to travel down his veins, like he had a bad case of hives. He settled himself into the tub with an audience gathered around him, people saying, "That's a nasty bite, son. Somebody should of thought there'd be snakes in that pile of wood. Who's got a sharp knife? Somebody get a razor blade. We gon need to suck that poison out."

The tourniquet had to be loosened and tightened at short

intervals. In minutes a green substance began to leak out of the bites, you could see it, the poison. Raymond laid his head against the back of the tub and closed his eyes. "You all right, son?" Mr. Wilmont asked.

I didn't know what it was about kerosene that drew the poison out, but it was magic to see. Mr. Wilmont dipped a can in the kerosene and tried to collect what poison he could and sling it into the dirt.

Mr. Burdett came out of his house with a bottle of whiskey and offered Raymond some. It made him open his eyes for the first time. He took the bottle and drank hard. When he swallowed, all the veins in his neck protruded. "Have all you want," Mr. Burdett said. "I got more." Raymond kept his mouth on that bottle, sucking out a big gulp every few minutes. The kerosene was terrible-smelling.

"That was a mighty fine thing you done, son," Mr. Wilmont said. "Berry here didn't see those snakes, did you, Berry?"

"No," I said.

"They'd have bit her sure as the day is long – a girl her size, she might not have been able to tolerate it. You could say you saved her life, son. Idn't that right, Berry?"

"Yes," I said.

I was so dizzy I thought maybe I had been bitten. I looked my legs over for marks – but no. I was saved. Raymond had saved me.

When people thought Raymond had soaked in the tub long enough, Mr. Wilmont decided we'd better cut those bites open with a razor blade and try to suck out as much of the remaining poison as we could. Mr. Wilmont was not a doctor, but he passed for one in Pinetta. He had been a medic in World War II. Now he had a reputation and people brought their sick animals and family members to him when they couldn't get all the way to Madison.

Raymond's leg was swelling up. The redness was getting worse. "It hurts, don't it, son?" Mr. Wilmont said.

"Like hell," Raymond said, never moving his lips from the bottle in his hands.

The men lifted his bare leg out of the kerosene and draped it over the edge of the tub. "We got to cut you a little bit," Mr. Wilmont said. "See if we can't suck the rest of that poison out. The more we can get rid of, the better."

We all watched the cutting like it was the most intricate of surgeries. The blood spilled in streams. "Not so deep," Mr. Ingram said. "Don't need to be a deep cut."

"Give me a cloth," Mr. Wilmont ordered and one appeared. He wiped the wound with it, studied it, but seemed not to want to put his mouth to the bite and suck the actual poison out.

In less than an instant I was on my knees beside the tub. "I'll do it," I said.

"No, honey," Mr. Wilmont said. "It's not a job for a girl."

"It is," I said. "It's because of me, isn't it? So let me do it. I want to."

I knew everybody was staring at me. I was so hot I thought I might burn up right there, like somehow I was caught in the blazing fire back at the school. Like it had gotten inside me and was burning up my own personal trash pile of sins. I was glad I didn't have my glasses, glad I couldn't see all those faces peering into my soul.

"Step back, honey," Mr. Wilmont said. "Mrs. Jackson, you want to get Berry, here?"

"I'm not going to step back." I shoved him with my elbow. "I want to do this."

"You want me to get her, Ruthie?" Mr. Longmont asked.

I could feel Mother's eyes on me. It was a cool sensation, like two ice cubes on my parched skin. "Leave her alone," Mother said. "Let her help the boy if she can."

Mr. Wilmont looked two parts horrified and one part relieved that he didn't have to do it himself. "Okay then. It's your girl, Mrs. Jackson. But if she was mine, I wouldn't have it."

The silence was as heavy as if the sky had fallen in on us. No one spoke. People barely breathed. All the faces made one God face in my mind. All the eyes like little planets circling around Raymond, who was the sun. It was just like in Wade's solar system books, all the intersecting orbits, all that insistent spinning.

I saw Rosemary standing next to Sowell. I knew the blurred look on her face – that as many nasty things as she'd done to Sowell in her life, she would never do anything as nasty as this – especially not in broad daylight with people watching, women and children too. It was like she was disgusted with me, thought I was pitiful in a way that made her squint so she would see less of me and what I was about to do. I think she was astonished that I had thought of something even lower than all the things she had ever thought of – and that I would do it to a filthy convict who was practically naked and as far as she knew had slit at least one girl's throat.

Marie Longmont would have been too pretty to be on her knees now. If I had been Marie Longmont the crowd would have rushed to me and lifted me up off the ground and there would have been twenty volunteers to take my place – and the first one would have been Sowell. A beautiful girl was not allowed to get away with certain things – it was the job of all people to protect the beautiful among them. Even a girl like Rosemary had her limits. So I was lucky – for once. Because I was plain enough to get away with an obscenity no pretty girl could. I was plain enough to be forgiven.

"You got to suck right there," Mr. Wilmont said. "See, where I cut here. You gon get blood in your mouth now and kerosene too. But don't swallow. Just suck as hard as you can, then spit it out when you get a mouthful. You understand?"

I nodded.

"If you start to choke, stop. You hear?" Mr. Wilmont wiped Raymond's leg a second time.

I saw that Raymond had raised his head and was watching me. His red-rimmed eyes looked right into mine and it was like the push I needed to go over the edge. I put my mouth on the first snakebite, closed my eyes and sucked on Raymond's punctured leg. It was like kissing him. The taste of it was salty and bitter and the smell of the kerosene did not cover the smell of his own sweat. Mostly it was blood that filled my mouth. It tasted like my own blood when I bit my lip. It made me dizzy. When my mouth was full and I began to choke, I turned my head and spit. I thought I might throw up, but couldn't let myself, so I gagged on air.

"Get the child some water," Mrs. Ingram ordered.

In no time Mrs. Burdett was back with a cup of water. "Here, honey," she said. "Wash your mouth out with it, but don't swallow any."

In all my life people had never watched me do anything before. Not one time that I could remember. Now it was like I was something to see. It was a good feeling, the horror on the men's faces, the way they shook their heads but did not take their eyes off me, the way the women covered their mouths with their hands while they watched. Sowell, who looked at me like I was out in the yard in my see-through nightgown.

I sucked the first cut until not even any blood was coming

out. It was like a dry wound, reddened where my mouth had been. I drank and spit. Then Mr. Wilmont took the razor and cut the second bite and the blood gushed like before. I could feel my stomach turn.

Raymond hadn't taken his eyes off me. His stare kept me going. "Does it hurt bad?" I said.

"You're doing real good," he said.

I closed my eyes and put my mouth on his leg again. All that blood and venom and kerosene. I spit and washed out my mouth and sucked again. Again. Again. I was gone out of myself. It felt like when you hold your breath until you faint, but past that. I was touching Raymond, his bare leg, my hands on his swollen skin, his underpants soaked in kerosene, gone invisible now, his heartbeat so near, pulsing in his leg, I could taste it. His thighs were shaking. And all the people vanished, just their bodies around me like empty shells, the selves in them, gone. There was just Raymond. A convict. A prisoner of love – but not mine. There was just him saving me and me trying to save him. I was happy, maybe for the first time in my life.

When it was over Mother insisted that the men carry Raymond into our house. Nobody much argued with her, especially not since she had Jack Longmont for backup. She went inside and made up a nice bed on our sofa. Good sheets and fresh pillowcases and a quilt my grandmother had made. Mr. Burdett suggested Raymond finish the bottle of whiskey and he nearly had. He was sluggish now, running a fever, his leg swelling to twice its size and already turning purplish.

"Sowell," Mother said, "you and Jack run him a tub and wash him up real good. Get him some of your daddy's clean clothes."

Sowell obeyed her to the letter. When the men brought Raymond inside the house, they carried him to the bathroom like Mother instructed, shut the door so I couldn't see in, and put him into the warm water and bathed him. I would have paid money to do it myself – or at least witness them doing it. It sounded like they were building something, all the noise they made.

I saw Sowell take in the clean underpants and undershirt. Jack Longmont and Sowell carried Raymond out to the sofa and Mother combed his hair for him, making a nice part. She put ice packs on his leg and gave him four aspirin.

"He's going to have blood poisoning now," Mr. Wilmont said. "No way around it. Try to keep his fever down. Keep him drinking so he don't dehydrate. He'll be pretty sick for a while."

Mr. Burdett went home and got a second bottle of whiskey and brought it over. It was supposed to be for Raymond, but Mr. Burdett took the liberty of opening it up and taking the first swallow. For a while Jack Longmont, Mr. Ingram, Mr. Burdett and Mr. Wilmont sat around the living room, drinking whiskey and "keeping an eye on Raymond" while he slept. He had seemed to pass out about the time they got him into bed and, if you asked me, he looked like an angel. I hoped that wasn't a sign that he was going to die.

Mother was worried I had poisoned myself. She made me gargle with salt water and baking soda. Then she sent me in to take a bath while she made a big pot of coffee for the men. Ordinarily she didn't allow any whiskey drinking in our house, but this was unusual circumstances. The coffee was sobriety insurance, I guess. It also kept her busy. She seemed almost happy.

"After your bath, Berry, I'll cut your hair if you want me to," Mother said. "While it's still wet."

"No," I said. "I'm letting it grow."

* * *

We all sat around in the living room, where Raymond was lying with his bit leg displayed out of the covers, propped on pillows. It was looking really bad, puffed up like a balloon, his skin darkening where I had sucked so hard it left marks. "That boy needs to stay put until the swelling dies down," Mr. Wilmont said. "He don't need to be moving around any."

"His name is Raymond," I said. "Raymond Lee."

At one point Mother sent Jack Longmont to tell Mr. Bruce that we were keeping Raymond at our house overnight or until he was better. Then she made sandwiches for everybody and we sat around the living room and ate while we watched Raymond toss and turn and jerk. He was sweating a river, the sheets already sticking to him. "Give the boy another swig of whiskey," Mr. Wilmont said. Whiskey was the Pinetta cure-all.

It was a strange ritual, like a funeral almost, people gathered around the dead or dying, eating everything they could get their hands on. Sowell especially was eating like it was his last meal on earth. In a way it felt like a worship service, an offering, like replenishing our bodies would somehow magically replenish Raymond's. We were eating to save him. That was clear. Tragedy inspired hunger. It required food.

In a matter of hours Mrs. Burdett and Mrs. Ingram and several women from the churchyard brought food by. It gained them entrance to our house, for one thing, allowed them to come inside and glimpse the snakebit convict lying up on our sofa with our daddy's clean underwear on, his hair fresh washed and straight-parted, his breath reeking of whiskey, his eyes closed like a dreamer. He looked like he could be almost anybody's boy.

And they could glimpse me too if they wanted to – the girl

who tried to suck the poison out of a boy on the chain gang. The girl whose daddy was missing, maybe run off, who was not there to stop such a thing from happening.

Mother kept ice on Raymond's head and ice on his leg, like Mr. Wilmont told her to, trying to keep his circulation slow, not let that poison travel too far too fast. "The drunker you keep him, the better off he'll be," Mr. Wilmont said, so Mother let the men keep giving him sips of whiskey. "You need to see if the boy won't eat some saltines," Mr. Wilmont said, "keep his stomach from turning sour." Mother did everything Mr. Wilmont told her to. It was like she wanted to prove that she could take orders as well as give them.

It was late when the men finally went home. All but Jack Longmont. It was clear he had no intention of going anywhere. "You go lie down, Ruthie," he said. "I'll sit up with the boy."

But Mother had better sense than that. She pulled a chair over close to the sofa and brought me the pillow off my bed and our yellow cat for my lap and she said, "Berry will watch after him, won't you, Berry?" I loved Mother right then. "He's sleeping so hard. The rest of us might as well get some sleep too," she said. "Berry can call us if she needs us. Jack, you don't need to stay. You've done enough. You might as well go on home too."

But that was less than a long shot. "The boy *is* a convict, Ruthie," he said. "Besides, you never know if you might need something – need driven someplace." Mother smiled at him and led him into the kitchen, where they talked in their usual whispers. Wade went to bed and so did Sowell. For once he didn't go looking for Rosemary, stalking her like she was a dog in heat.

I turned off all the lights in the living room and sat in my chair and watched Raymond sleep. I wondered if every boy was transformed this way when he was clean and lying in a clean bed. Raymond was in pain, it was clear, but he was also strangely peaceful wearing Daddy's white underwear, wrapped in ironed white sheets, his hair smelling of baby shampoo. When his breathing got too low and regular I put my head against his chest to be sure his heart was beating, or I put my fingers on his lips to see if I could feel breath. He was sweating, so I wiped his face with a cloth and got him fresh ice when he needed it. "Make sure you keep his heart higher than his feet," Mr. Wilmont had said, so I tried to keep him in a sitting position while he slept. I liked the idea of keeping his heart high. It was wonderful to be with him in the dark. To believe he needed me.

I heard Mother finally go to bed. She looked in on Raymond, who was lying still but was not fully asleep. "Bless his heart," she said. She blew me a kiss and went down the hall. Mr. Longmont stayed in the kitchen, smoking a cigarette, which I could smell. I wondered if he was going to sleep sitting upright in a kitchen chair, but no. In a short time I heard him go down the hall to Mother's room. He had taken his shoes off, they were under the table, and gone down the hall in his sock feet. He did not speak to me as he passed the living room and I was glad.

When Raymond was sleeping sound I went to my bedroom and put on my nightgown. I knew it was wrong. On my way back I looked in Mother's room and saw that she was asleep in her clothes, Jack beside her in his, lying like a man in a casket, hands folded over his chest. A respectable distance between them.

Our yellow cat had made herself a place on the bed with Raymond. When I tried to move her Raymond took my hand away and said, "She's all right. Leave her be." Afterwards I did not let go of his hand, just let my hand fall with his. I just held on.

"Any more of that whiskey?" he asked.

I got the bottle and he drank from it. Afterwards he looked at me, sitting nervously in my nightgown. I knew he could see the outline of my breasts, even in the dark. I wanted him to. He looked at me and didn't move, his leg was like a piece of fallen timber between us. I took his hand in mine and put it on my breast, the heat of his sweaty hand so nice. If he was surprised, he didn't act like it. He moved his hand slowly over my breasts. I took my hand away and let him do it. It was the first time my breasts ever seemed like a real part of me, connected to my soul or something.

"Where's your mama?" he whispered.

"Sleep," I said.

"Come over here a little bit then." He spoke softly.

I got out of my chair and sat on the edge of the sofa beside him, my heart kicking hard. Raymond put his fingers in the wet underneath part of my hair around my neck. "I wouldn't never hurt you, you know that, don't you, Berry?" He tangled his fingers in my hair and pulled my face toward his.

"Yes," I said.

"I done some things I'm sorry for."

"I know."

"Don't be scared of me."

"You saved my life," I said.

He ran his hands down my neck and over my breasts. It made me close my eyes, his gentleness, the scratch of his rough hands. I felt him tug at my nightgown, pull it up so that my breasts were bare, and he put his mouth there, tasting them. It felt like I was floating away. He cupped one breast in his hands and began to suck it. He sucked hard, like a starved baby. I thought about that white kitten who'd died, the way it was always swimming in dry air.

Raymond closed his eyes and sucked and kissed and licked me. I was lost in the sweetness and desperation of it – his and mine. Sometimes I watched him with what felt like ecstasy and the next minute it was nothing but cold, hard curiosity. I studied this man with his mouth all over my breasts – how starved he acted, like he was trying to eat me alive, like he wanted to suck the life out of me, like he loved me. I was not myself every second, sometimes I only watched myself from outside somewhere. *Look there at Berry,* I said to myself, *getting loved by Raymond, that handsome boy, grown enough to be on the chain gang.* It was like I was sailing around in the deep, black air, watching us and feeling glad and amazed.

Raymond was getting loud, gasping for air, like he couldn't breathe, like he was underwater or something. His breathing stirred my breathing. Then with no warning he broke into whisper-like sobs. He was crying. I looked at his perfect face, the way he clung to me, and I thought of his mother, the mother he could not rescue, that maybe for a moment I was his mother – and at last he had saved us both from the end he feared. He seemed like a sweet baby to me, no more dangerous than our yellow cat, who pawed at my chest and purred before she settled into sleep.

"What's wrong?" I whispered.

Raymond kept his face buried in my breasts, his tears hot and sweaty where he pressed his skin against mine. "Why are you crying?"

He just held on to me and cried like a man trying to catch

his breath. It was not the way I thought it would be – love. "It's okay," I whispered. "Everything will be okay." I stroked his hair and let him cry.

I knew then, in that small moment, that all my life I would be the kind of woman that inspired weakness in men. It was like my future stretched out in front of me and I could see it, a future of men turning to me for comfort, not passion. Men trusting me more than I wanted to be trusted. Men turning into boys, maybe even babies, in my arms. I would be the kind of woman who loved men into lesser, not finer, selves.

I thought of Mother. The way she always needed a man in her life – but she believed that the man she needed most didn't really exist. She had to have it proven to her over and over again. She depended on the certainty of the disappointment, the one thing she could always count on. Now it was Jack Longmont's turn to prove it. I knew he would prove it to Mother in time, just like he had proved it to Jewel Longmont. I understood that the only man who could ever really let Mother down was one who didn't. Where was he? This man she'd spent her life imagining? I felt a sadness for Mother that made me want to forgive her.

I held Raymond for a long time. I thought of the way they tell you that the sound of a heartbeat soothes, that when you take puppies from their mothers they miss her heartbeat and you have to hold them against your own chest so they can hear yours – or at least try and trick them with a ticking clock wrapped in a warm towel. Maybe that was what Raymond had missed most in prison – putting his face against someone else's skin, listening to another heartbeat, being touched easy by someone, even a girl like me. Raymond was listening to my pounding heart like he was memorizing it.

He was practically a grown man. Not just a boy, I said to myself, not just a boy like Cadell Miller or somebody. I touched the wet curls around his face with my fingers and ran my fingertips over his eyelids. I held him until at last he stopped crying and lay like an empty bucket in my arms, everything spilled out.

He was not asleep, but not really awake. I pushed his face from my reddened breasts and placed his head back on the pillow. It seemed that my breasts had not been real until Raymond kissed them, like I needed the proof of a moment like that. Raymond had put his rough hands on my breasts like a man praying, like a man who believed in women, that women were life-giving, life-saving, life-sustaining, like he was worshipping me. This was what I thought. His fingernails were dirty and his hands torn up from all his labor. I'd noticed that. But in my mind they were praying hands still.

He opened his eyes and seemed almost confused to see me. He watched as I pulled my nightgown back down to cover me. It was damp and wrinkled, like gauze that covers an injury.

"I'm sorry," he whispered, his voice hoarse. I began to stand and he reached for me, grabbed my arm. "You're not leaving, are you?"

"I'm going to sit right over here," I said, "in my chair."

I gave him more aspirin like Mother had told me to and watched him fight his way into a worried, fitful sleep. His swollen leg trembled and I rubbed ice over it until I had soaked the sheets and quilt. He was full of fever – shivering with fever.

But me, a strange calmness had come over me.

Before daylight I went down the hall to change out of my nightgown. Sowell saw me come in and get my clothes, but he said nothing.

Jack Longmont was the first one up the next morning. I heard him put on his shoes and stomp around the kitchen making coffee. Mother still had on yesterday's dress. She made herself busy in the kitchen, frying eggs and bacon. Raymond was asleep but his fever was down a little. His purple leg was extended out of the covers and was the color of an eggplant. "He's not much better," I heard Mother tell Jack.

We had just sat down to breakfast when the sheriff's car pulled up out front. Wade sprang to the window to see. "What now?" Mother said, wiping crumbs from her mouth with her apron. She opened the door and let the deputy in.

"Morning, ma'am, he said. "I come to take Raymond Lee off your hands."

"Sit down," Mother said. "Have some breakfast."

"No, thank you, ma'am."

"Coffee at least," Mother said. "Berry, pour the deputy some coffee. Sit down." She motioned to him. "Right here."

Men had a way of doing what Mother told them. The deputy pulled out the chair and sat down. I poured him a cup of coffee and set the cream and sugar on the table in front of him.

"You can't take Raymond Lee," Mother said sweetly. "Not yet. He's too sick."

"I'm sorry, ma'am, but sick or not, he's a prisoner of the state." The deputy drank his coffee child-style, with enough cream and sugar to kill the taste of the coffee. I noticed that.

"Give him a couple more days here," Mother said. "Please."

"We owe that boy something," Jack Longmont said. "He saved Berry here, saved her life, you know that. That counts for something, don't it?"

"Sure it does," the deputy said. "But the law is the law."

A panic came over me that was not fear, not anger, but more like grief – the threat of a huge grief, like some monster wave you see coming when you are at Alligator Point swimming in the Gulf of Mexico – and you know you can't outjump it, or float over it, or run from it fast enough – so you just stand and wait for it to overtake you, maybe even kill you. You feel it pull you under at the same time it swallows you up and you do some graceless somersault and stop knowing which way the air is, which way to safety, up or down.

I couldn't say good-bye to Raymond – not yet. I couldn't just watch them haul him away, back to prison, knowing I might never see him again. Especially not after what he had done last night. After he cried like that.

"You worried that boy is going to escape?" Jack Longmont asked the deputy. "Is that it? Because with that bum leg of his he ain't going nowhere. And if he tried to – I tell you what, I'd shoot him myself now. And you can count on that."

"Day after tomorrow," Mother said. "Can't you come back for him then? We'll let him go with no fuss, I promise. Just let us look after him until he's better."

"I don't know." The deputy shook his head.

"You're a Christian man, aren't you?" Mother said. "Say?"

Finally, with his arm thoroughly twisted, the deputy left without Raymond. "Day after tomorrow," he told Mother, "I come back for that boy – dead or alive."

"Thank you," Mother said.

The deputy tipped his hat at her when he drove off in his black-and-white car, probably wishing this was more of a black-and-white world.

Mother made Raymond a plate and I took him his breakfast. He was drowsy and couldn't eat much, but he drank black coffee and that seemed to help. Afterwards Jack Longmont and Sowell helped Raymond into the bathroom and he sat in a cool tub for a long time, with his leg propped up. Jack sat in there with him and smoked a cigarette. Mother fixed him a fresh bed – clean sheets, dry quilt.

All day people were in and out – neighbors mostly. Mother put a chicken on to boil for chicken and dumplings and it smelled like heaven itself and Mrs. Ingram brought over homemade vegetable soup and cornbread. The Burdett kids came by wanting to see the snakebites – which looked like a couple of black eyes by now, bulging and purple, blood blinded. Raymond obliged them, pulled the sheet back so they could see. "You sucked that poison out right there, Berry?" they asked. I nodded yes. "Wooooo, I couldn't stand to put my mouth on nothing that nasty," they said. It prompted a round of snakebite stories – everybody in Pinetta had a repertoire of them, owned and borrowed. Nobody ever tired of hearing them told and retold. Poisonous or non-poisonous is one of the major themes of our lives.

I sat in the living room all day at Raymond's beck and call. It felt like we were connected by an invisible secret, and people who moved between us got tangled up in it without even knowing it. I put our yellow cat on the foot of Raymond's bed and he really liked that a lot. She slept on his good foot. He slept on and off all day too, in between visits from the curious and the concerned. A couple of times he got nauseated and tried to throw up, so Mother set a big pan beside his bed and wrapped a towel over his chest and around his neck, like a big bib. "Just in case," she said. His presence in our house took on a holiday feeling – lots of company, lots of food, lots of storytelling, and, in my case, lots of nervous excitement.

Even though Mr. Burdett brought more whiskey, Mother wouldn't let Raymond drink it. She said he didn't need any more and he didn't argue with her. She took the bottle and put it in the kitchen, promising him a "drink before bedtime to help you sleep."

Mr. Wilmont came by and fussed at Mother to keep ice on Raymond's leg. She had to send Wade to the Burdetts' and Ingrams' to borrow ice. They emptied ice trays into a mixing bowl, and Mother put it in the freezer and rationed it out all day long. Jack went over to his store and got cold drinks and fried pigskins and boiled peanuts to offer people when they stopped by. For a long time a group of men sat around our living room in our water-damaged chairs, eating peanuts, dropping the hulls in paper sacks, and telling tales as though there wasn't more than enough work still waiting to be done almost anywhere you looked.

I was not alone with Raymond for a minute – except when he was sleeping. Sometimes, even with a room full of people, he looked at me and winked. Mother asked him once if he thought it would make him feel better to shave his face. He said, "No, ma'am. Not much." Now he had a blond five o'clock shadow.

Any time that day that I so much as closed my eyes – even blinked them – the picture came to me of Raymond's fevered head, his wet face, his mouth on me, so hard, so gentle, as though it were seared on the inside of my eyelids. It was more than remembering – it was rehappening, and sent a hot jolt through me each time, like an electric shock.

We had a house full at suppertime. Neighbors who brought biscuits and honey, sliced ham, butter beans and pickle relish, buttered corn on the cob. Everybody wanted Raymond to eat –

and he tried, but he couldn't hardly do it. Except for the chicken and dumplings. He ate that good.

Over and over people said to him, "Where you from, son?"

"Havana, Florida," Raymond said.

"Havana? Sure enough? They grow good sugarcane over there, don't they?"

"Sure do," Raymond said.

Nobody came right out and said, "What is a nice boy like you doing in prison, son?" They talked about that out in the yard or on their way home, I guess. In Pinetta nobody was too poor to have good manners.

Mr. Ingram did venture to ask, "When you expected to get your release, son?" Like Raymond was in the army or something.

"Got a shot at it in eleven years," Raymond said.

"Eleven years?" Mr. Ingram just shook his head like he couldn't come up with any reply to such a thing. "That's a long time," he said.

"Yes, sir," Raymond said.

I wasn't sure if Raymond was liking all this attention or not. I knew it was wearing him out. I knew his leg was hurting him bad. Several times he asked Jack Longmont to help him into the bathroom and when he stood up on his good leg and the blood ran down into his swollen, snakebit leg, he winced with pain. Sowell tried to carry his leg for him, like it wasn't even hooked on, like it was a separate thing – but that didn't work. Raymond's fever kept up, so Mother put an oscillating fan on him. "Y'all let the boy sleep," she said to the company, but it never quite happened – not until late, late after everybody had finally gone home.

"You don't need to sit up with him tonight," Mother told

me. "You need to get some sleep, Berry. He'll be okay. He can call out if he needs something."

But I insisted on sitting up, pulled a chair up beside his bed like the night before and situated myself in it for the long haul. Jack Longmont had poured Raymond a glass of whiskey to help him sleep and he was sleeping now. Sort of whistling while he slept.

Mother said, "Berry, as long as you're determined to sit up with Raymond tonight, what if I let Jack sleep in your bed?"

"Okay," I said, knowing Jack Longmont would probably hate that plan, thinking he had rather lay on the hardwood floor in Mother's room than in a nice bed anyplace else.

Mother brought me the cat and kissed me – and kissed Raymond's sweaty forehead – and went to bed for the night, turning off the lights as she went. The minute the lights were out, it felt like the house lifted up off the ground, like it was floating on air, like a wooden spaceship in bad repair. I was instantly dizzy.

Maybe Raymond would've slept through the night if I hadn't waked him up. I did it easy, by taking his hand in mine and squeezing just enough for him to open his eyes. There was yellow moonlight outside the windows, but inside it was dark blue all around, that kind of darkness that has tiny sparks shooting through it, like the inside of your own dark head. "You okay?" I whispered to Raymond. "You need anything?"

He sat up a little bit and looked around like he was trying to remember where he was. "You got some water?"

I gave him a sip from the glass Mother had put beside his bed. He took it from me and drank nearly all of it. He took an ice cube out of it and ran it over his forehead and down his neck. "I'm about to burn up," he said.

"You got eleven more years in prison?" I asked. "That's what you told Mr. Ingram."

"At the least." He dropped the ice cube back in the glass and handed it to me. "Why?"

"I was thinking." I took the glass and set it back on the table. "Maybe I could write you sometime, you know. Send you a letter at the prison."

Raymond shook his head. "Naw, Berry," he said. "That's no good. I don't like to get letters and I wouldn't never write you back. It's nothing personal. I just wouldn't."

"Why?"

"I don't like writing," he said. "Never have."

"They're coming to get you day after tomorrow. They're taking you back."

He leaned back on his pillow and closed his eyes.

"What'd you do that was so terrible?"

Raymond took a deep breath and looked at me a long time. There was moonlight across his face. "Somebody died on account of me," he said. "It shouldn't never have happened. It was somebody I loved, you know. It was a accident. But nobody believes that. I loved her more than anything and I thought she loved me too, but she didn't. I can see that now. She loved somebody else more – and he was no good. And it was because of him that everything happened. But I got the blame for it."

"Is that all?"

"That's all you got to know," he said. "Where's that yellow cat at?"

I got the cat where she was sleeping in a chair across the room and handed her to him. He laid the cat on his lap and petted her. "Don't ask me no more questions, Berry."

"Okay," I said. "I'm sorry."

Then it was quiet. He rubbed his hand over the cat and she seemed like she liked it, just stretched herself out and looked as limp and satisfied as she ever had. Raymond's lips were moving like he was talking to himself, but there was no sound at all. He kept watching that cat, his hand real gentle on her. All I was thinking was that Raymond had loved somebody – and it hadn't been me and it wasn't going to be me. Why hadn't she loved him back? It didn't make sense. But in a way I was glad that she had disappointed him that way – because I was sure I wouldn't. Maybe he could appreciate me for that.

"Berry." Raymond's voice was low and dark as the night. "Come sit over here by me."

I did it. I acted like a girl in a trance.

"Unbutton your shirt," he whispered.

I was asleep in the chair when Jack Longmont woke me up the next morning. "Berry, honey," he said, "you go lay down in your bed and sleep awhile. Go on."

I stumbled back to my bed and it smelled like Aqua Velva, but I slept good anyway, slept in my clothes, missed breakfast. I didn't dream while I slept. I just relived my time with Raymond. I felt his hands slip inside my shirt, his hands on my small breasts, making them swell and feel full of hope or something. "You can't tell nobody about this," he whispered into my neck, his breath hot and sour. "They wouldn't nobody understand." He had become like a baby in my arms, the same way he had the night before, the only sounds he made were little non-words, broken whispers, half moans and sucking noises. He didn't cry, but he seemed just as sad and just as starved as when he cried.

He put his arms around me and held me against his face so hard that I thought he might break my back, like my spine might just snap in two. He didn't touch me anyplace else, just kissed my breasts and rubbed his face all over them and even in the dark I could see that his *thing* was hard under the sheet, sticking up like the pole under a circus tent – like Sowell's always does. I was glad to see it. Glad to know. It was good enough for me.

Now it all spun before my eyes like a film flipped off its reel and going too fast, then stopping on this frame, that frame. The pictures were so powerful, better than letters could ever be.

It was noon before I got up. I only woke then because I heard Mrs. Ingram and Rosemary in the kitchen with Mother. While I was changing into clean clothes Rosemary came into my room. "Wake up, sleepyhead," she said. Then she just stood inside the door and stared at me, her mouth open. "What's that?" she whispered.

I looked down at my breasts. There were bright red marks where Raymond had left evidence. "It's nothing," I said, hurrying into my clothes.

"Oh, my God," Rosemary whispered. "Did *he* do that?"

"Don't tell," I said, "promise me." But it was like asking the wind to promise not to blow or the rain to promise not to fall. Telling was Rosemary's nature. You can't make someone promise something that goes against her nature. Of course she would tell. Sowell would probably know before nightfall. Then, one by one, the rest of Pinetta too. But I didn't panic. I don't know why not. I just didn't.

Maybe I secretly wanted someone to know. Maybe I looked forward to the opportunity to deny it and swear on a stack of Bibles that Raymond never touched me – knowing that nobody would believe me anyway. Hoping they didn't. Maybe I wanted people to look at me as if I was a girl with a history that had something vaguely to do with love – with having been loved. For the moment I had what might pass as proof.

Or maybe I did panic, and my panic was like some blood-numbing anesthesia, so I didn't even feel it.

Mother told Raymond she would fix anything he wanted for supper his last night. "Just name it," she said. What he wanted was chicken and dumplings again – which she could just warm up, so she set out to bake him a special cake for his dessert. A good-bye cake. It's like we were all a bunch of disciples getting ready to feed him the last supper – right before the truth flared up in our faces and everything went wrong again. She made yellow cake with chocolate icing and pecans on the top.

Raymond seemed better. He sat up straighter, stayed awake longer, ate more, smiled more. People shook his hand and said, "Good luck to you, son," and "You take care of yourself now," and other sorts of ordinary good-byes as if he were about to leave on a long vacation the next day instead of being locked up in prison again. But Raymond just shook their hands and nodded and played right along with it all. "Same to you," he said.

Mrs. Ingram said, "Berry, you're a lucky girl, honey. Those snakes could have bit you. God works in mysterious ways, don't he?"

I wondered why God had to depend so much on snakes to make his points. It all started with Adam and Eve and now here it was, still going, way off here in Pinetta. I guess nobody would blame me for loving a boy who saved me from being snakebit. Not even God.

"It's been good for your mama to have this distraction, hasn't it?" Mrs. Ingram said. "Get her mind off your daddy for a little bit."

"I guess," I said.

"Looking after that convict has been keeping her busy," she said, "and that does her a world of good, don't you think so?"

"Sure," I said.

I didn't know how it all fit together really – Daddy gone, Raymond here. Maybe Daddy would come back, but probably not. Raymond would be locked up for eleven more years, starting tomorrow, and he might never come back either. All he had to look forward to was natural disasters which allowed him out into the world with a shovel in his hand, cleaning up the mess. He might forget all about us over time – except maybe he would have a couple of scars that would make that hard to do. Maybe people would say, "What happened to your leg there?" Then he'd have to tell them. "Some snakes was about to bite this girl, Berry," he'd say. Then he might remember me. Maybe he'd say, "Berry, she used to let me suck her tits at night, after her mama was gone to bed." Convicts talk ugly like that, but I knew he would remember it nice. He would. I knew he would. I would bet my life on it.

It didn't have a thing to do with Daddy. I wanted to tell Mrs. Ingram that she was wrong. Raymond didn't keep Mother's mind off Daddy. If her mind was off Daddy, then it was Mr. Longmont that caused that. All Raymond did was help Mother prove that she was a good woman, a Christian woman – no matter how else it might look to people. She was probably grateful to Raymond for that. She needed to prove it, I guess. Mainly to herself. There was that fancy cake sitting up on her cake pedestal like an award that was going to be presented to Raymond after supper. Already she had carried it in there and showed it to him so he would have something to look forward to all day.

* * *

Raymond's prison clothes were washed and ironed and laid out for him to put on first thing in the morning. He ate his supper sitting up in his bed and we ate ours gathered around him. The cake was cut like it was a marriage ceremony, not a bit less solemn. Mother gave Raymond a huge piece, bigger than what she gave Sowell or Jack Longmont, either one. He ate every bite of it too. "Y'all been mighty good to me," he said. "I appreciate it too. I sure do."

"I just wish we could do more," Mother said.

"You done plenty," Raymond said. "More than plenty."

When good-byes and good nights were said and done all around, then it was time for bed. Mother insisted I sleep in my own bed. "No need to sit up in a chair all night, Berry," she said. "Raymond's better. Aren't you, Raymond?"

"That's right," he said. "You go on to bed in your room, Berry. You don't need to stay in here. I mean it."

"But I want to," I said.

"I'll sleep better if you don't," he said. "Really will."

It was like he had slapped my face in front of my whole family. I didn't know what was wrong with him. How could he waste our last night this way? How could he say for me to stay away from him? I went to bed feeling sick to my stomach. It was the first time it had occurred to me that he might have any potential for cruelness.

Sowell laid in bed and wrote another useless letter to Marie. It always put him to sleep – writing it, then ripping it up. Wade studied the stars the best he could, twisting his book around at all angles, trying to get his bearings on the heavenly host or whatever it is. In a while he gave up and went to sleep too. But not me. I couldn't sleep.

I could hear Mr. Longmont snore in Mother's room. She

slept with the door open wide, said to us, "Now you come in here if you need anything, you hear? I'm leaving this door wide-open." I guess she knew that there was nothing on God's green earth that could force us to go in there for any reason. It was bad enough to have to look in as we went past, Mother and Jack Longmont sleeping in their clothes like a couple of giant figurines, frozen into stiff, straight positions.

Not only couldn't I sleep, I couldn't even close my eyes. Every time I tried, it started up the movie again – starring Raymond and me – and then it was all I could do to lie still and quiet in my bed. *Don't think about it,* I ordered myself. But that was stupid.

It was way after midnight when my yellow cat jumped off my bed and went down the hall into the living room. I knew she was looking for Raymond, would jump up in his lap and let him pet her. It made me sick to think about it at first, his hands, his warm fingers, rubbing her. Then I started thinking that maybe it was a sign, you know. Maybe from God. I think that many a person has probably missed many a sign from God – and it's better to believe in the sign and be wrong than not to believe at all. Maybe the yellow cat was showing me the way, setting the example I was to follow. What could it hurt? I could wander quietly into the living room and if Raymond got mad, said, "Berry, what the hell you doing in here?" then I'd say, "I came to get my cat, that's what." But maybe he wouldn't be mad. Maybe he'd say, "I been waiting on you. I was scared you wouldn't come. It's my last night, Berry."

I was on my feet thinking this, had to make it out of the bedroom and down the hall so quietly that nobody would twitch, nobody would roll over and wonder what that squeak in the floor was. I walked on air. I swear. My feet hardly touched down. It was like floating.

It was just like I thought, my cat lying in Raymond's lap. There was enough light coming in from the open windows to see that. Raymond had the fan going too, pointed at him but circling like a church choir humming, the sound, stirring the hot air. I walked up beside him as invisible as a ghost, my white nightgown blowing when I went in front of the fan. I was hardly breathing.

"Is that you, Berry?" Raymond whispered.

I was afraid to answer him. This was my house, wasn't it? I could go where I wanted to, couldn't I? But I stood frozen, unable to speak.

Raymond twisted around enough to see me. "It's you," he whispered.

"I came for my cat," I said, my voice false.

Raymond looked away from me, lifted my yellow cat from his lap, and set her down on the floor. He put his hand out. "Come here," he said. I took his hand.

He pulled me to the sofa. "Lie down here." But there was no room. "Here." He puts his hand on his chest. My heart was beating so hard I was afraid it would wake up Mother, my blood circling my body in loud waves. I lay down on top of Raymond real slow, careful not to hit his bad leg. I lay on my side, still and straight. "Why didn't you want me to be with you tonight?"

Raymond put his hands in my hair and pulled my face down against his neck. "You're still a kid, Berry. That's why. You're not grown."

"I don't care."

"It ain't right," he whispered.

We lay there a long time with Raymond's hand in my hair,

sort of petting me like I was that yellow cat. I could hear his heart beating, felt his breath on my face. I was not scared.

"You can't stay here," he whispered. "You got to go on back to bed, Berry." But while he was saying it, he pulled the edges of my nightgown up, all the way, over my head, and I was naked underneath. I sat up then, the light from the open window coming across me like a pale ribbon. I straddled him like a horse and let him touch my breasts. His pants were off, the sheet was between us, but still I could feel him and I thought it meant he loved me. I didn't want to see it or touch it. I just wanted to know it was there – the desire – for me.

Raymond was gentle. He pulled me to him and buried his face in my skin. "Oh, God." It was like all the breath went out of him. He put his mouth on my breast, and my nipple got hard and he sucked it, then I felt his teeth. He bit easy at first, but then grabbed me hard, pushed me down against his mouth and bit my nipple so hard it almost made me cry out in pain. Tears came, a flood of silent tears, and I pushed at his face to make him stop. It was like melted butter between my legs. I felt him push up hard, hurting me. He strained against the damp sheet, pulling me down on him, the sheet rubbing me, burning. The more he struggled to push inside me, the more closed I was. It hurt bad, his trying. It hurt so much. But I didn't cry out. I was afraid to. I bit my bottom lip until I thought it would bleed. I thought I tasted my own blood. I scratched his cheek, dug my fingernails into his skin, hard, hard. But I didn't let him do what he was trying to do. I was too afraid.

It didn't matter really, though. Raymond jerked like when you're asleep and dream you're falling. All his muscles kicked. On the sheet between my legs I felt the hot liquid like glue. Like that paste Mother made out of water and cornstarch. Sticky like that. He groaned like he was hurt bad. Like he might die. He let go of me and I hated him – because he let go. I touched my breasts. There were teeth marks. There was blood.

I was breathing too loud. His breathing was even louder. People will wake up, I thought. I grabbed for my nightgown and put it over my head, trying not to cry. Why was he so hateful? Why did he have to ruin everything? Tears ran down my face and I couldn't help it. Raymond kept shaking his head like he was trying to get rid of some terrible thought that was stuck there. He kept looking at me and shaking his head, shaking his head, like he couldn't think what to say. It was awful. He reached up, held my face in his hands and wiped away my tears with his thumbs, "Oh God, Berry," he said. He sounded ready to cry too. "Please, Prettygirl," he said. "I'm sorry."

"You're ruining everything,"

"I know," he said. "It's what I do, Berry. I ruin things." He put his arms around me gently and pulled me against his chest. "I didn't want to hurt you. I swear to God. You're just a kid."

"Stop saying that."

"Okay, okay." He patted me like I was a little kid who had skinned my knee or something. He was like a daddy, saying, "It's okay. It's okay. Don't cry." He kissed the top of my head. It was the only time he'd ever kissed me. I relaxed then and lay still, curled beside him, away from his bad leg. His touch was warm and easy, the way he ran his fingers up and down my arm, so slow.

I could have stayed there all night. I could have fallen asleep in his arms. He was touching me so gently. The fan was humming too, filling the room with a chorus, *He's sorry, he's sorry.* It was a beautiful sound, the music of forgiveness.

"If I had you for a baby sister," Raymond whispered, "I wouldn't let nothing happen to you. You believe me, don't you?"

What was he talking about?

"Do you believe me, Berry?"

"Yes," I whispered.

"You better go back now," he said. "They might wake up."

I felt like I was lost in my own house, like I didn't know the way to the end of the hall. I stood up and I was shaking. "I love you, Raymond." I didn't mean to say it. It was like asking directions. I was trying to find my way back.

"You're a good girl, Berry." He closed his eyes and turned his face away from me. I felt my way along in the dark, felt my way to the door and went silently down the hall like the ghost of a girl I was.

~

There was nothing we could do. The deputy arrived promptly at eight o'clock the next morning. He drank a cup of coffee and let Raymond eat a plate Mother fixed him before they left. He let him put on a pair of Daddy's work pants that were way too big and one of Daddy's old sports shirts. Sowell helped him dress. He put on his same government-issue shoes. Mother combed his hair for him like he was a child.

There was no place for me in all of this. It was business. It was hurried. We acted like we'd had ten minutes to pack Raymond's things and send him off to summer camp. I was useless, just standing at the edges, staring.

"I hope you'll be kind to this young man," Mother said to the deputy. "He saved my daughter's life – put himself in danger to save her. You'll see he gets medical care at the jail?"

"We'll have a doctor look at him." The deputy was holding his hat in his hands, turning it around and around, ready to go.

"He's a real sick boy." Mother put her hand on Raymond's forehead. "Still got some fever." She treated him like he was Wade's age and not old enough to be locked behind bars.

Sowell and Jack Longmont hoisted Raymond up and braced his arms around their shoulders and helped him limp out to the car. Wade held the doors open. "I want to thank you, ma'am," Raymond told Mother. "You been mighty nice."

Right before they bent him into the backseat of the sheriff's car Raymond looked at me nice and said real quiet, "Take care of yourself now, Prettygirl. You hear?"

"Okay," I said, but my voice was gone.

They laid him out in the backseat of the car. He was leaned up against the side window, his leg out straight. The deputy took Jack Longmont aside to say a few private words, then he slammed himself into the car and put his hat back on. As they drove off, Raymond winked and gave me a thumbs-up sign out the back window. He was not smiling. I watched the car until it vanished – went someplace on the other side of this world, like the moon does. They teach you to keep believing in the moon even if you can't see it.

I went inside and went to bed for the rest of the day. Mother brought our yellow cat and laid her in the bed beside me. She kissed my forehead and said, "Oh, Berry, honey." She moved the hair back out of my face and whispered, "You sleep as long as you can."

Later I heard the commotion when Mother and Jack Longmont left to drive to Madison. I knew they would return with my new eyeglasses. It was wonderful to have them gone.

I went back into the nights and stayed there. My breast was

tender where Raymond's teeth marks were. Every time I closed my eyes I saw his mouth on me, I saw his closed eyes and heard his sobbing. It made my heart raw.

~

My new blue cat-eye glasses came in a matching blue case. When Mother handed them to me I shut myself in the bathroom to try them on. They were almost the color of my eyes. I put them on and stared at myself for the longest time, so long that my face was expanding and contracting in the mirror like something out of the crazy house. I didn't think I looked so bad. Not as bad as in my old glasses. My eyes were not swollen. They were normal. The main difference though was that all the lines were back in things, the edges, the details. Now I could be sure again.

"Sowell," Mother said, "how do you like your sister's new glasses?"

Sowell studied my face a minute. "Better," he said.

~

Cadell rode Clyde Greene's horse, Roy, over to our house in the late afternoon. I was glad to see him, which I didn't think was possible. He was like a pleasant distraction. Maybe he could make me forget about Raymond for a while, take my mind off things. I wondered if I'd seem different to him. If he'd look at me and know. What would Cadell's blood do?

Cadell had a good face, a boy in bad need of a haircut, his long hair pulled back behind his ears, except for some that fell into his eyes. His clothes were soaked from the heat and pasted to him. Even without a saddle Roy was lathered and snorting when they walked into the yard. "Hey," Cadell said when he saw me sitting on the back steps. "I come to see you."

He slid off Roy's wet back and looked at me hard. "I see you got your new glasses," he said. "I was just about to get used to you being blind. They look all right though."

We ran a bucket of water for Roy at the spigot on the side of our house. Roy drank and drank. "Come inside and I'll get you a cold drink," I told Cadell.

" 'Preciate it," he said.

We went inside and got two RCs and sat in the living room on the sofa that until recently had been Raymond's bed right in front of the oscillating fan. "Where's your mama?" Cadell asked.

"She's gone over to the Longmonts'," I told him. "She fixes their supper lots of nights. But also, Jack Longmont told her he had a surprise for her over there. She went to see what it was."

"Well, that's kind of why I'm here too." He was suddenly very serious. "Because I got a surprise for you – you could say that." He looked me in the eye. "But it's nothing good, Berry."

"What is it? Word from Rennie?"

"No," he said. "No word." He drank his RC nearly gone, stalling for time, then looked at me awkwardly. "That convict fellow – he's gone back to jail now, right?"

"Right."

"You miss him?" Cadell asked.

"None of your business. If you come to give me a surprise – then, what is it?"

"You ain't going to like it," he said. "Might not like me after I tell you."

"Might not like you anyway." I smiled.

"It's about that convict."

"Raymond?"

"After those snakes bit him, you know. He saved you from getting bit and all that ruckus. Well . . . see . . ." He drank more RC like he wanted to keep that bottle in his mouth to stop himself from talking.

"What?" It was not like Cadell to play games this way.

"When y'all left I asked that other convict – Marcel is his name – I asked him what had Raymond done to get sent to prison. You know, what was his crime?"

"So?"

"Marcel said Raymond got locked away because he killed his own mother."

Words are funny, the way they come at you full force, then just bounce right off you like bullets off the side of a steel barn. I saw those words coming, I saw the force of them, but they just slapped up against me and bounced away. Words need a place to enter. A lot of people think you got to let words in through your ears, but that's not so. Words can get in other ways – harder ways. They can come in through your open eyes. You can breathe them in. They can work their way through your sweaty skin like ringworms do. They can enter a wound you are trying to heal up. They can just sit on you like a tick you didn't know was there, attach themselves to you and sort of suck their way in.

Once words are spoken, then there they are. They don't just vanish into thin air like some people think. They don't just disappear. They are like parasites that become part of some larger organism, like a small idea that hooks into all your bigger ideas. Words are as real as anything, which is why speaking lies is so dangerous.

"I don't believe you," I said. "Marcel was lying."

"That Mr. Bruce," Cadell said, looking at me so sheepishly,

"the guard, he said it was so, Berry. Raymond run his mother down in a stolen truck, he said."

"Raymond loves his mother."

"I'm not telling this to hurt you worse. I swear to God. I just thought you ought to know. You were so crazy about him and all. I thought it was right to tell you."

"You're just jealous."

Cadell nodded his head. "It's so. I saw how you liked that fellow. I was jealous." He seemed truly embarrassed. He leaned forward as he spoke, his long legs folded beneath his chair, his elbows on the armrests, his fingers laced into a tangle while he talked. "You want to hear the rest or not?"

"Go on," I said. He had already got the words started. He had already spoken the poison into the air.

"Marcel told me this," Cadell said. "Seems there was some big fight one night – Raymond's stepdaddy going at him. Raymond was trying to keep the old man off his mama. It got real bad. Raymond jumped into the old man's truck to make a run for it and his mother ran out to stop him from going off in a truck that didn't belong to him. He just ran right over her, they said. He swears it was an accident – he didn't see her, thought it was his stepdaddy coming after him, it was too dark. But the court found him guilty. It was in the papers. According to Mr. Bruce, the papers said Raymond got revenge on his mama for always taking his stepdaddy's side. He killed her dead, Berry. I thought you should know."

He sat and silently stared at me for a long time. It was practically like one of those contests – who can stare at who the longest. But I wasn't really staring at Cadell. I was staring at Raymond, he was starring in a show in my mind – a horror show. And it seemed all the more tragic to me – Raymond, his life. If it was true, then all it did was make me love him more. There had to be reasons, didn't there? Some kind of explanation.

"I'll go." Cadell stood up and put his empty RC bottle down on the table. "I thought you should know the truth. I'm sorry to be the one to tell it."

I didn't move from the chair where I sat. I was running him out of the house without saying a word, just the power of my hard stare. I listened to Cadell let himself out. Waited until I thought for sure he was gone, then walked to the kitchen and looked out the window. There he was, sitting in the grass under the chinaberry tree, holding on to Roy's reins, looking worse than miserable.

"Why don't you go on home," I yelled out to him.

He shook his head and just sat there some more. Roy was nibbling at spotty little grass patches. He looked uncommonly satisfied and swaybacked beside Cadell, who sat like a dark lump on a log.

"You can't just sit there all night," I yelled.

"Hell if I can't," he said.

Why are people always so interested in messing up love? Their own love, other people's love. It's like people can't stand anybody to really love something – especially another person. They want to provide you all the reasons why maybe you shouldn't, they want to warn you, try to talk you out of it. To ruin it any way they could.

Didn't the Bible say love one another?

Didn't the Bible say forgive and forget?

I thought people were scared to death of love. Scared to give it. But even more scared to get it. Pinetta was a rat's nest of an example. Everybody looking for love – but wouldn't let the people who wanted to, love them. Mother, for one, could write a book. Not to mention Jewel and Jack Longmont. There was poor Sowell writing letters to Marie, who'd forgotten he was alive, while meanwhile Rosemary was circling the house, trying to get her hands on him, trying to love him enough to make him love her back. Even Cadell, simple as he acted – I thought he was scared of love too. Why else would he try to mess things up for me, try to make me think bad of the one and only boy I ever thought much of? And nobody was more scared of love than Raymond. Not even me.

Love made me think of playing hot potato. It you caught it, you tried to get rid of it as fast as you could – it was like nobody wanted to end up holding on to it.

When Mother and Jack Longmont came home they had Wade in the backseat and they were blowing the car horn like an ambulance was coming. I ran outside to see what on earth. So did everybody in the neighborhood. Mother and Wade looked like they'd just won the jackpot. They threw the car doors open and jumped out. "Berry!" Wade shouted. "Jack Longmont got us a television set!"

It was true.

It was like bringing home a new baby, the fuss that everybody made. Sowell came running and helped Jack Longmont carry it into the living room. All the neighbors came too, to watch it be set up and turned on. Even Jimmy Ingram came out, who had become more and more of a home boy. A boring book reader. A preparer of casseroles with secret ingredients. Even he came to see our new TV.

"What's Cadell Miller doing sitting out there under that tree?" Jimmy asked.

"Being stubborn," I said. "What else?"

It was like a party in the house that night. Mother made popcorn and let all the children in the neighborhood sprawl over our floor and watch the shows. That fake TV laughter really killed me. But it was a nice television set anyway.

"Berry, you and Sowell need to thank Jack," Mother said to us quietly. "Go ahead, now."

So we thanked him.

It bothered Mother that Cadell was sitting out in the yard like a hobo. Twice already she had called to him to come inside, have something to eat, watch TV. "No, thank you, ma'am," he said both times. Even Mother knew it was not normal for Cadell to refuse food. "What's wrong with him?" Mother said.

"He came to tell me that Raymond killed his mother," I said, aiming for honesty and nonchalance at the same time. "He wants me to think it was an errand of mercy. That he's some kind of hero. Now he's sitting out there, pouting."

Mother stared at me. "He shouldn't have told you."

I stared back at her. "You believe it?" I asked. "Do you?" I was helping her pop a second batch of popcorn on the stove. It sounded like a shoot-out in the kitchen, like bullets flying. I was holding the handle of the skillet like it was a gun.

"The deputy told Jack so," Mother said quietly. "Said Raymond claimed it was an accident, but his stepdaddy witnessed the whole thing, honey. He swore the boy ran his mother down intentionally." Mother watched me closely as she spoke, like maybe she thought I would burst into sobs and have a breakdown or something. But she didn't know Raymond like I did, so she had more room to doubt.

"That's crazy," I said. "Raymond wouldn't do that."

"All I know is that he was found guilty," Mother said.

"I don't care," I said. "I don't believe it."

I shook the skillet hard, trying to keep the popcorn from sticking. The truth – if it was the truth – was like popcorn inside your gut, small kernels at first, hard and uninteresting, but when the truth got heated up, it popped open, turned into something irregularly shaped that took up more space than you'd planned. It filled you up – all your empty spaces – until you thought you would have to burst or die.

Mother and I poured the popcorn into a big bowl and drizzled butter over it. "I'm going to take this in there," she said. "Berry, you go out there and tell Cadell to come in the house. He can't sit out there all night."

It was a relief to get out of the house. I walked over where Cadell was leaned up against the chinaberry tree. He did look like a starved hobo. When he saw me coming he sat up straight.

"What are you trying to prove?" I said.

"Berry, did you ever think about this . . ." He was tearing the leaves off a tall sweetweed he held up close to his face, skinning it as he spoke. "If Rennie did run off with your daddy, do you know what that makes me?"

"What?" I said.

"Your uncle. It makes me your damn uncle."

I don't know why that struck me as funny. I started to laugh and couldn't stop. I laughed so hard it made Cadell laugh to watch me. "What's so funny?" he kept saying. "What?"

I got to that line where laughing turns into crying, where the tears come – all I needed to do was touch that line, just barely touch it so that I could stop myself. "You're crazy," I said.

"So does that mean you're not mad?"

"I didn't say that."

"I'm not leaving here until you tell me you're not mad, Berry. I mean it."

"First," I said, "you try to tell me my daddy ran off with your sister. Then you have something to say about my mother – who is always nice to you. Now you try to tell me Raymond ran his mother over with a truck. I swear, Cadell, what's next?"

Cadell smiled his half smile, where just one side of his mouth lifted up. His eyes were clear. He tossed his stick aside. "You got good news due you, Berry," he said. "That's for damn sure."

"Okay, then," I said. "So you don't need to sit here the rest of your life. You're worrying Mother to death. She said for you to come inside and watch some TV."

"Naw," he said. "I got to start back."

"It's dark as pitch," I said. "You can't even see the road."

"Roy knows the road." He stood up and slapped Roy on the rump. "Don't you, Roy?"

"You wait here a minute," I said. "Don't go yet."

Cadell watched me disappear into the house. I scooped him up a napkin full of popcorn, then went to my room and got my reading flashlight and ran back out to him. "Here," I said. "So you don't get lost. Last thing we need is somebody else to disappear around here."

He took the flashlight and stuck it in his pants pocket, which was already ripped half off. "Thanks," he said.

"Make sure you bring it back," I said. "It's my reading light."

"Come on and ride with me down the road a ways, Berry," Cadell said.

"Just to the turnoff," I said.

Cadell made his hands into a stirrup and lifted me up onto

Roy. Then he held on to my arm and half jumped, half pulled himself up behind me.

The air was heavy as a wool blanket. It was the sort of air you could hold in your hand. I kept adjusting my glasses on my nose. I wasn't completely used to them yet, the way they fit. We rode without saying much, rocking side to side, Cadell's sticky skin against mine. The night hung over us like a mild threat, like something that might happen but probably wouldn't. The moon was like a scar in the sky.

"You were right, what you said today," Cadell whispered. "I was jealous of that jailbird."

"His name is Raymond. I don't want to talk about him anymore tonight."

"Me neither." Cadell slipped his arms around my middle. I had been holding my breath, waiting for him to do it, knowing he would do it. I didn't jump this time. I just felt him press himself against me, his chest hard against my back, his pounding heart, his hands hot and dirty on my skin. He was breathing the way Roy had breathed earlier in the afternoon, like he had come a long, hard way.

Cadell could never make me forget about Raymond. But I didn't mind if he wanted to try.

~

It had been nearly three months since Daddy and Rennie disappeared. Jack Longmont wanted to help Mother file for Daddy's life insurance, but it was looking doubtful since we had no body to bury.

In my mind I had given Daddy a decent burial. Several of them. Some were dignified. Some had people weeping and gnashing their teeth and flinging themselves on the floor in front of his casket, wailing with loss and grief. I had all the students from Pinetta School file past his casket and burst into tears, remembering the way he had changed their lives for the better.

I had conducted my own silent services, said a hundred whispered good-byes, some prayerful, some angry. It was like gently prying his invisible fingers loose from the tight grip he held on our lives. You had to do it one finger at a time.

More than once I dreamed Daddy was off in prison with Raymond. I dreamed they shared a cell and Daddy was always reading a newspaper out loud to him, telling him what was going wrong in the world, trying to talk him into joining the army when he got out, putting his violent tendencies to good use. I dreamed they kept the radio on a country music channel and on Sundays they listened to gospel. Daddy got letters from home and kept them under his pillow and when he got a chance Raymond snuck them out and read them, every word. I never dreamed what Daddy was in prison for. And I never dreamed his release.

I believed in my heart that Daddy was dead. It didn't seem possible that a man who devoted his life to making people do what was right could do something as not right as abandoning his family. I didn't think Daddy would run off with Rennie either. She would be too much for him. Even Mother was too much for him. He didn't understand Mother, made her mad nearly all the time, but underneath it all I thought he loved her and wanted to be in charge of whatever concerned her. It was one of his primary satisfactions. He wouldn't give it up voluntarily.

Besides, there was something cold inside me, a floating place, that had started up during the storm that first night when

Daddy didn't come home. In the beginning it had been like a sharp icicle that stabbed at me regularly. Now its edges were melting slightly and it just filled an empty space with that hard coldness. If I were Cadell I would probably say my blood told me Daddy was dead. My blood knew.

The school board had hired a new principal. He was moving to Pinetta from Opelika, Alabama. He had a wife but no kids. He told Mother that if we decided to vacate our house, he'd be interested in renting it. This made us instantly dislike him.

Mother had pretty much stopped talking about moving to Eufaula to live near our grandparents. Now she said things like "Jack and his sons are in that big house all by themselves. No woman to make it into a home." It seemed like Mother had decided to think of herself as a widow. I don't think she could allow herself to contemplate abandonment any more than I could. As far as I could tell she had given Daddy a silent burial too.

"Jack has filed for divorce," Mother told us one night at supper. "He'll be a free man in less than a year. He'll be able to start a new life."

Sowell and I never responded to these announcements. But Wade was the one with the great imagination. "If you marry him," Wade said, "can we get free stuff from his store?"

Sowell still hadn't heard a word from Marie. Some nights I watched him write her letters in bed with a flashlight propped on his shoulder. He spent a long time perfecting the letters, knowing they would not be sent. Knowing she would never read a single word. In the end he ripped them to shreds.

I still thought about Raymond too much. Every morning I woke up and had to remember that he was gone now, that the chain gang had moved camp entirely. A construction crew from Tallahassee was due to start on the new school sometime soon. The convict tents were down, the trucks gone, not much more than a spot of dead grass where the tent had sat to remind us that the convicts had ever been here – that and the work they'd done. Raymond was like a presence in his absence. His absence was so big that it overtook everything else.

At night I missed watching the lantern lights across the road, imagining the men bedding down for the night, Raymond lying on his cot with his hands behind his head, sweating himself to sleep, being eaten alive by mosquitoes and no-see-ums. I missed signaling him good night with my flashlight, four-five, four-five. I missed putting him through his paces, an assortment of fantasies each night which mainly starred me, while I searched my way through the scraps of memories he'd left me, trying to find that place where you can finally let go and drift off.

I didn't wake to thoughts like *here I have my room with my brothers, here is another perfectly hot day, here is my house and yard and blue sky overhead.* No. I woke to what wasn't. Raymond wasn't sleeping on his cot, Raymond wasn't marching to work in his chains, Raymond wasn't looking for me, Raymond wasn't saying my name.

~

We were sitting at the kitchen table, eating supper. Mother had made fried chicken and creamed potatoes, so the kitchen was extra hot and the air was thick with grease. Our faces were bright in the heat, our mouths coated with shine, our hair wet and stuck to the sides of our pink faces. We were fairly content.

When they thought the moment was right, Mother and Jack told us that they had an announcement to make. "We have a plan," they said. This explained why Mother had made our favorite supper. We listened while we ate, almost afraid to look at them as they spoke what seemed like a rehearsed dialogue.

"You all know next month is your daddy's last paycheck," Mother said. "Jack has offered to continue to pay the rent on our house until I became legally free, you know, to remarry." That was the word I dreaded – *remarry*. "I've accepted his offer. And we ought to all be grateful for his generosity."

"My divorce will be final in less than a year," Jack Longmont said. "Your mother and I will get married and move you all into my house. I can put you boys to work in the store – maybe Berry too. It will be a good arrangement all around."

"How does that sound?" Mother smiled, her fork aimed at us. "Say?"

No one spoke. We swallowed our milk. We broke the crispy parts off our chicken. We hardly looked at her.

"I asked you a question," Mother said.

Sowell finally spoke up. "Do what you want to."

Mother looked at us like we were three handicapped children and her hopes for our making it in the world were slim. She seemed exasperated. "Fine." She stabbed her fork into her mashed potatoes. "Fine."

~

So this is it, I thought. This is how something unimaginable happened to you, how you ended up headed somewhere you never had any intention of going. It was like life was a long ride on a Greyhound bus and nobody ever told you that the bus would have to stop along the way, that you would have to get off at some unlikely station, board a different bus to keep on going. If you couldn't wait for the right bus, if you didn't have the fare, maybe you would just have to get on any bus, the next bus, and see where it took you. There was no real need to make a plan of your own.

I thought about the way Daddy had always fiddled with maps, plotting and planning and figuring – taking pride in folding the maps perfectly and keeping them in the glove compartment, just in case. He had rather read a map than a book. He liked to figure out the shortest route, the most scenic route, the fastest route, and then estimate the mileage for all options.

But Mother, no. She never believed in maps. She just got out on the road and drove, read any signs she came to, guessed which way to turn, turned around if she was wrong, stopped at gas stations and smiled at the attendants and asked them where she was, told them where she was trying to go, who she was looking for, what the house looked like. They drew routes in the air with their fingers or with the hats off their heads, waving them, explaining. Even with maps in the glove compartment, Mother remained map-resistant, map-proof. It seemed now like I could understand that. She didn't even own a car, did she? She was about like a hitchhiker – wasn't she? – with Daddy gone. Her thumb out, her smile in place. And Jack Longmont, here he comes, first in his junk-heap jeep that travels fine even with no road to go on, and later his pickup truck that sits up high off the road with a paid-for load in the back, and now and then his real nice car, the size of a small blue motel on wheels, that he drives to church and to Madison and whenever he wants to look good going.

So what is the use in being mad at Mother?

~

After supper we had Neapolitan ice cream for dessert. We'd barely scooped the ice cream into the bowls when there was a loud knock at the screened door. We turned to see the source of this annoying interruption, expecting to see Jimmy lurking at the screened door, his buzzed head, wearing some rag of an old dress. But it was definitely not Jimmy.

Mother gasped and dropped a bowl of ice cream on the floor. It splintered into a thousand pieces, flying everywhere. It scared our yellow cat and she shot out of the room, letting out a terrible cat shriek. Mother put her hands over her mouth like she was trying to suppress a scream herself, some cat shriek of her own.

"What the hell!" Jack Longmont jumped from his chair, knocking it to the floor.

Sowell and Wade looked suddenly paralyzed.

There, on the other side of the screen, stood Rennie Miller and Pastor Butch Lyons – holding hands. "Hello!" Rennie called out. "Anybody home?"

The way Jack Longmont charged toward the door, I was afraid he was going to attack Butch Lyons where he stood. I guess Mother thought so too, because she grabbed his arm. "Jack, don't."

"What the hell you doing here?" Jack Longmont demanded.

"What are *you* doing here?" Rennie asked with genuine wonder.

Mother opened the door and just stood there staring at them, this hand-holding pair, Rennie smiling like the happiest girl alive and Butch Lyons quiet, looking at Mother with a message in his eyes that I could not quite decode. "Hello, Ruthie," he said. "How've you been?"

"Couldn't be better," Mother said sarcastically. "Everything is just peachy around here, or haven't you heard?"

"Can we come in?" Butch asked.

"We got news for you," Rennie said.

Mother looked at Jack Longmont as if to clear it with him, as if she were soliciting an unspoken promise that he would behave like a gentleman and make no effort to kill Butch Lyons in front of us, her children. Jack Longmont nodded to Mother, but his face looked hard and murderous.

"Come in then," Mother said. "I guess."

It wasn't until they walked into the kitchen and we saw them in full light that we noticed Rennie looked different, her hair cut short and moderrn, her face made up with a little rouge and a lot of lipstick, her belly beginning to round. She put her hand there when she saw us staring. "Yes," she said, grinning. "It's true." She held up her left hand. "We're getting married." Sure enough, there was a small diamond chip on her swollen finger.

"Married?" Mother's voice was hollow and the word *married* echoed through the house. I think *dead* would have been less shocking to her.

"This marrying disease must be catching," Sowell said to Wade and rolled his eyes.

"We'll explain everything, Ruthie." Butch Lyons looked from Mother to Jack Longmont. "You need to hear this too."

Jack's eyes were like blocks of dry ice, the look on his face dark and chilling.

"Come in the living room," Mother said, never one to let any sort of pending disaster deter her from common courtesy. "Sit down." She looked at Sowell, Wade and me like we were not really people, just messy details cluttering up the moment. "Boys, you can be excused now. Eat your ice cream outside," she says. "Berry, you pour some iced tea for everybody."

Sowell and Wade seemed happy to get out of there. They

didn't balk and beg to stay. It's like they'd rather not know anything if they didn't have to. I'd never understood that about them. They always said I was nosy, but the truth is they lack curiosity of the most elementary nature. It's like a serious character flaw – their basic, overwhelming desire not to know, to never ever have to know. I considered their success in the area to be among their greatest failings.

I was happy to pour the iced tea and serve it because it meant that I got to stay and listen. I heard Jack say, "Ruthie, this is not a damn social call. Let them say what they got to say and get on their way."

"Don't get mad before you hear them out, Jack," she said. But I knew she was already mad. I knew that seeing Butch Lyons hold Rennie's pregnant hand, the one with the ring on it, was a torment to her. I think Butch Lyons knew it too.

They sat down in the living room, Butch Lyons and Rennie on the sofa, Mother and Jack Longmont in chairs across the room from them. There was plenty of empty space in the middle.

"Getting married?" Mother smoothed the skirt of her dress over her knees. "That's news." It was like she was talking to herself, refusing to look at the happy couple. "But the only news I really care about, Rennie, is where is Ford? Isn't Ford with you?"

"I'll get to that in a minute," Rennie said. "First, Butch has something to say to Mr. Longmont." She squeezed Butch Lyons's hand. She was as beautiful as ever – maybe even more so. "Go on, Butch. Tell him."

Butch Lyons looked at Mother helplessly. "It's about Jewel."

"Don't think I want to hear this coming from you." Jack Longmont spit his words.

"You need to hear it," Butch Lyons insisted. Rennie nudged him along with her eyes. Butch fixed his eyes on Jack Longmont.

"The night you came home and thought you found me climbing out that window on to the porch – it wasn't what you thought."

"Bullshit," Jack Longmont says. "I know what I saw. You trying to tell me a man climbing out my window in the middle of the night – a goddamned preacher too – you trying to tell me that's nothing?"

"I didn't say it was nothing. I said it wasn't what you thought."

"Go to hell," Jack Longmont snapped.

"I was there. I admit it," Butch said. "I was trying to sneak out without you finding me. I admit that too. But I hadn't been with Jewel. Jewel was upstairs asleep. She didn't even know I was in the house."

"Like hell." Jack Longmont practically spit when he talked.

"It's true," Rennie chimed in. "It was me that called Butch to come over there. Mrs. Longmont and Marie was asleep. You and your boys was off hunting – so, you know, I was thinking I had the night by myself – and I called Butch to come out there."

"I came over knowing it wasn't right," Butch said. "But I didn't think any harm would come. I thought Rennie and I could have a little time together, you know. Be alone. I should have had better sense I guess, but a man in love . . ."

"A man in love?" Mother said this like an echo. Like Butch would have to repeat that sentence if he had any hope of her ever believing it.

"A man in love." Butch's eyes sort of brushed across Mother's like something was being swept aside, but the others didn't know it. "Well, let's just say love has made a fool of many a good man."

"Obviously." Mother's voice was as cold as the ice tray I was trying to open in the kitchen. You know when you lick an ice tray and your tongue sticks to it – and there you are, stuck, hurting, feeling like an idiot? Her voice made me think of that.

"If you were over at the house fooling around with Rennie – with another woman – another *girl,*" Jack corrected, "then why in hell would Jewel feel the need to protect you? Why would she give a damn? You sneaking into the house like a goddamned criminal."

"Lord, Mr. Longmont, you don't catch on, do you?" Rennie shook her head in what seemed like total disbelief. "Mrs. Longmont wadn't trying to protect Butch. Butch is a grown man and can protect hisself. She was trying to protect me." Rennie looked at Jack like she was his weary but wise schoolteacher and he was suddenly nothing more than a badly behaved schoolboy. She actually scolded him with her eyes and the sharpness of her tongue when she spoke.

"My daddy would of killed me if he found out what I was doing – me and Butch and all – that we was, you know, in love." Rennie glanced at Butch. He didn't smile but he nodded for her to continue. "Mrs. Longmont come downstairs just about the time Butch was hurrying into his pants to go out the window and I was trying to scramble into my clothes too. We was panicked. We was in the living room on the sofa – or we had been. We started off watching some television, talking a little bit. Then next thing you know . . . We never thought nothing like what happened would happen."

"Love is blind sometimes." Butch Lyons said this as if it was some original thought he had just come up with. A good reason of some kind.

Mother glared at him. I know he noticed. It crossed my

mind that she might leap on him in a fit of fury and claw his eyeballs out, rip his tongue out with her bare hands.

"When Mrs. Longmont saw us . . . you know," Rennie continued, "she was bad shocked. 'Good Lord, Rennie,' she said, 'what's going on down here?' She looked at Butch, then me, and, well, I guess she understood. I could tell I had just disappointed her to death. I got scared. I begged her not to say nothing. I said, 'Please God, don't tell nobody. It will ruin Butch. And I swear my daddy will kill me. He will. I know it.' I was down on my knees, begging her."

Rennie paused and shook her head slow, like she was remembering. "And you know what Mrs. Longmont said?"

"I bet you're going to tell us," Mr. Longmont said sarcastically.

"She said, 'Let me handle this, Rennie, honey. I'll explain things to Mr. Longmont and he'll understand.'" Rennie's eyes teared a little and glistened for emphasis. "Mrs. Longmont was a pure angel."

"This is ridiculous." Mr. Longmont stood up. "Ruthie, have you heard enough? God knows, I have."

At first it was like Mother didn't hear him, then she reached for his hand and said, "Just hear them out, Jack. I don't know if they're telling the truth or not, but it doesn't cost anything to hear them out." It was obvious Mother's curiosity had not been fully satisfied. Mine either. I think I get it – this bad curiosity – from her.

Jack mumbled, "Shit," and sat back down.

"Go ahead," Mother said. "Say what you came to say."

"You was like a wild man, Mr. Longmont," Rennie said. "We heard all that scuffle on the porch, then you started shooting that gun. We was scared you had shot Butch dead, killed him. I saw my life was over. If Butch was dead, then I would have to kill myself too. There wouldn't be no other way. So, Mrs. Longmont, she run out there to keep you from killing Butch."

"This is absurd," Mr. Longmont said. "I'm not going to listen to this." But he didn't get up and storm out. He just sat there, doing what he said he was not going to do.

"Mrs. Longmont was trying to tell you what happened, but you were just screaming all this mess and you slapped her, knocked her to the ground, called her all those names. You remember that, don't you? What you called her. She kept on saying, *I can explain,* but you wouldn't let her. It was clear you didn't have not the least bit of interest in hearing the truth."

"Good God," Jack said. "Rennie Miller – a spokesman for the truth. If that's not the end all."

Even though he was smart-talking back, it was clear Jack Longmont was under Rennie's spell now. How had she managed to turn him into one of those behavior-problem boys who needs the belt taken to his backside? It wouldn't have surprised me if she'd pulled out a switch or a paddle and whacked him with it until he had sense enough to be sorry, to say he was sorry. He looked as startled as the boys at school when they know they are in for a thrashing and they know they deserve it too. He looked embarrassed, as if he'd turned to stone at the exact moment of his greatest humiliation.

It was Butch Lyons who broke the spell. "I want you to know, Jack, I offered to come forward and tell the truth. When I heard you wanted Jewel to stand up and confess to something she didn't do – I swear I didn't want her to have to do that. But Jewel insisted on confessing. She wouldn't let me take the blame like I should have. She said it was not the first time she realized how anxious you were to believe the worst of her. She said you seemed almost happy, thinking she had disgraced herself and her family – like you took a strange pleasure in it – her fall from favor. She said when she saw how dedicated you were to believing the worst, she decided to go ahead and let you have at it."

"You were so hell-bent on it." Rennie shook her head.

"It was never Jewel," Butch Lyons repeated. "Jewel was innocent of all you accused her of."

"My God," Mother whispered.

"That day in church when you made Mrs. Longmont confess, I couldn't hardly stand it." Rennie's voice got loud. She paused and pointed a finger at her own chest, tapped her finger in the general vicinity of her heart. "It was for me that Mrs. Longmont lied – to save me."

"You're a liar," Jack Longmont said. But it was clear he believed her.

I picked this moment to walk into the living room with a tray of iced tea, the ice cubes rattling like a bell signaling time-out. "Have some tea?" I offered the tray to each person. One by one they each took a glass and a napkin and looked at me but didn't speak. It wasn't that anybody was thirsty for iced tea, nobody even took a sip. It was just a way to remind ourselves how civilized we were. So I went back to the kitchen and cleaned up the spilt ice cream off the floor. Our yellow cat was already there, licking up as much as she could. I tried to chase her away because I was worried she would lap up no end of broken glass, swallow it maybe, and tear her insides apart. I had to put her outside to save her life. I took a wet rag to mop up the floor. I could see in the living room through the open door.

Mother rattled her iced tea glass, staring into it like there was a fly drowning there. "How did you two get together?" She asked this like she was only mildly curious. But she couldn't fool me. This was what Mother really wanted to know. This was her burning question.

"It was Ford's idea," Rennie said. "When I was staying with you I told him about the trouble at home – I just broke down and told him everything. He got all upset and said I needed to talk to the Baptist preacher. But the Baptist preacher was too old. That man is near about dead. You can't tell an old man like that the things I had to tell. So instead, I went to see Butch. He didn't care if I was not a actual Methodist, just as long as I was a person in need. Right, Butch?"

"Sure." He nodded.

"I just walked over to the church during my lunchtime and said, *Excuse me, mister.*" Rennie looked at Butch and he smiled. "Later on you called him and invited him to the house, remember?"

Butch glanced at Mother, but she didn't meet his eye. Instead, she looked at Jack Longmont, stiff in his chair, his face like a carved statue. He would be no help now.

"Ford?" Mother said. "What about Ford, Rennie?"

"That night of the storm," Rennie said, "Ford was worried about me getting in trouble with Daddy. He insisted on driving me home. We couldn't get down the road to our house, it was washed out, so we had to go the long way, down to the highway and back up that gravel turnoff. The rain was like a river pouring down. It was so bad. Our car stalled out. We were out in the middle of nowhere."

I wanted to hear this story. It was part my story too, wasn't it? I walked into the living room and sat on a stool by the door.

No one seemed to notice me. Rennie was getting distressed telling this, taking long breaths, looking at Mother, pleading for forgiveness and not exactly getting it.

"Go on," Mother said. "Then what?"

"Ford got out of the car to go get help. I begged him not to, I swear. I begged him to wait until daylight. But no, he said being out in that car with me overnight would ruin him. He said people never would get through talking about it. Lord, it was dark. Raining so hard. I never saw rain like that. Ford, he stayed gone forever."

"Ford?" Mother said. "Rennie, when did you start calling him Ford?"

Rennie looked like Mother had slapped her. She blushed. Her blouse was soaked with underarm sweat, which sort of ruined her modern good looks. She glanced at Butch for a split second. "I'm nervous telling this," she said. "I hate to be the one. That's all. You keep calling him Ford, so, you know, I guess I'm just doing the same, calling him what you call him."

Nobody spoke a word. We just watched Rennie falter. "I'm not a schoolkid anymore," she kept on. "Right? I am nearly a married woman. When you're a kid he is Mr. Jackson, but when you're grown, you know, he's Ford. Right? Isn't that right?"

It was clear Mother didn't accept this explanation. Without saying a word, she made everybody in the room know that Rennie's answer was unacceptable. She did this with her eyes like a couple of hot spotlights aimed at Rennie, and the tapping of her fingers on the arm of her chair, both hands at once, drumming. Now she had everybody nervous as a cat – all of us.

"He stayed gone forever – Mr. Jackson," Rennie said with emphasis, trying to get her story afloat again. "I waited and waited, but he never come back. Water was coming up inside the car. So I took off my shoes and decided to wade out of there and look for Mr. Jackson – knowing that rain had washed the snakes out everywhere, I could see them swimming by. I never prayed so hard in my life." Rennie paused to look at Butch.

He nodded a silent yes.

"Mr. Jackson wasn't nowhere," she said. "So I just kept walking in all that rain, walking and praying, walking and praying and finally – I don't know how long it was – I seen a car coming. I got out in front of it and waved it down. I was crying and screaming for them to stop. I scared them, I think. But they stopped. Two vacation people from up North. Delaware, I think they said. They put me in their car and asked me where I was going to." Rennie fished a tissue out of the pocket of her dress and shredded it in her fingers while she talked. "They was acting like they'd take me anywhere I needed to go, you know? Anywhere."

Pastor Lyons put his arm around Rennie and stroked her short black hair.

"So I don't know what made me do it," Rennie said to Mother, "but I said to them people, *Jacksonville.* Take me to Jacksonville.'"

"She was scared," Butch said to Mother. "You can understand that."

"Those people drove all night," Rennie says, "a man and his wife. I laid down in the backseat and slept like a dead girl. They didn't wake me up until midmorning when we got in Jacksonville. I never been to Jacksonville in my life. I didn't have no shoes, so the man, he stopped and bought me some shoes and give me twenty dollars and they drove off."

We didn't get that many vacation people coming through here, most especially not in a storm. There was something about the way Rennie was telling this that wasn't right. It made for good telling, like her stories always did, but it didn't *feel* true. There's a feeling that a true story creates – a physical way a true story lands in an empty place that is just the right size and shape and will not accommodate any variation from that size and shape. It's a feeling like popping a bone back into its socket, or fitting a oddly shaped foot into a well-worn old shoe, or a pair of dentures into the exact mouth they were designed for. The truth has a certain fit, and the way it snaps into place gives you a sense of relief. Even something terrible – if true – provides some relief. Of course, Rennie might not have known this since Rennie was not that attracted to the truth in the first place. Hers had been ugly, so I guess she didn't hold it up – the truth – to be the end all of things.

"But what about Ford?" Mother insisted. "What happened to Ford?"

"I hadn't laid eyes on him since that night." Rennie shook her head. "I swear to God."

"Don't swear, Rennie," Butch Lyons said. "They believe you."

A silence set in like another person entering the room with his own sullen personality.

It was Jack Longmont who finally broke the spell. "This is one hell of a sob story."

"If you don't know anything about Ford, Rennie, then why are you here?" Mother asked.

"I said I hadn't seen him, and that's true," Rennie said. "But me and Butch, we think we might know his whereabouts." She blew her nose on the tissue in her hand. "When I got to Jacksonville, I called Butch to wire me money. He wanted to come marry me right then, right that minute, didn't you, Butch? He's the one told me Mr. Jackson was gone."

"After the storm I got an anonymous phone call in Madison," Butch said. "Saying Ford Jackson and Rennie Miller were both missing."

"Anonymous?" Mother scoffed. She thought he was lying.

I froze for a second. A heat wave washed over me like a red sea – a blood sea. Was he going to say it was me who called him? Did he remember? I waited for him to turn to me and say, "Berry, is there anything you want to say right now? A confession of your own, maybe?" But he didn't. He never even looked at me. Just talked right past me sitting there by the door like a small piece of furniture.

"Where is Ford now?" Mother snapped. "That's all I want to know. Where is he?"

"He's been shot." Rennie looked around, her eyes touching on every face.

"Shot?" Mother gasped. Mr. Longmont tried to take her hand, but she pulled away.

"They got him in a hospital in St. Augustine," Rennie said. "He's real bad." She searched her pocket for a folded piece of paper and offered it to Mother. "Here."

Mother just looked at it, the white notepaper, Rennie's neat handwriting, the worst news of her life folded neatly in half.

"Why would anybody shoot Ford?" Mother said.

"Don't noboby know. They just found him that way – shot on the floor of his rented room. There was no identification or nothing." Rennie explained. "When Butch came to Jacksonville he talked to the police and they tracked down a man in the hospital that fits Mr. Jackson's description. Nobody can be sure, of course, but Butch saw the man, his head wrapped like a mummy. Butch thought it was him, didn't you, Butch? He's real bad. But he ain't dead."

"The police think it's possible Ford shot himself," Butch said. "A self-inflicted wound."

Mother glared at Butch Lyons like she wished she had a gun to shoot *him* with, like she'd love nothing more than to pull a trigger herself at this exact moment. "That's ridiculous. Ford would never do a thing like that. Butch, you know it too. He didn't even have a gun. His gun is in the bedroom in his top dresser drawer."

"I'm just telling you what the police told me," Butch Lyons said.

Mother snatched the note out of Rennie's hand and stared at it, like she was afraid to unfold it and read her fortune.

Butch Lyons and Rennie got up to leave. "I'm sorry as I can be for anything I done wrong," Rennie said. "I hope both of you can forgive me."

Neither Mother nor Jack Longmont spoke.

"We better be on our way," Butch Lyons said. "We got one more stop to make this evening."

"We're going out to the house," Rennie said. "I need to see Babygirl. And Mama and Little Sister. They need to see I'm okay." She ran her hand over her belly.

It was me that showed them out through the kitchen to the back door. Rennie looked at me like she'd almost forgotten who I was. "Hey there, Berry," she said, distracted.

"I thought you were going to marry a soldier," I said.

She looked at me like she couldn't really place me, my face, my voice. "Butch here is a soldier for the Lord, idn't he? You like my hair?" she asked. "I cut it."

"It looks good," I told her.

Rennie took my hand. "I'm sorry about your daddy, Berry. You believe me, don't you?"

"No," I said.

"You think I'm a liar, Berry?" She looked at me hard, her eyes crashing headfirst into mine. "Is that what you think?"

Before I could tell her that there was no relief in the story she told, that it was not an exact fit to the gaping hole torn in the middle of our lives, before I could explain it to her, Pastor Lyons said, "Let's go, Rennie." He pulled her along by her arm. She turned and waved with two bent fingers. She looked at me with a message in her eyes but I didn't know what the message was.

I stood in the doorway and watched them get into Butch Lyons's car and drive off. I guessed Mrs. Ingram would be over here in no time – just to see what Pastor Lyons's car was doing at our house. Just to see if she was imagining things.

Wade and Sowell were outside, sprawled in the metal yard chairs. They were like two people waiting on the stars to come out on an overcast night. "What happened?" Sowell yelled.

"They think somebody shot Daddy," I said.

Sowell and Wade hardly moved a muscle. They didn't come running to hear the story. They just sat in their bouncing chairs and looked up at the dark sky.

~

Jack Longmont cried when Butch Lyons and Rennie left. He cried with his face in his hands, and Mother did her best to comfort him, but she was no good at it. All the rest of the night he sat around, muttering to himself, talking out loud to no one, shaking his head. None of us could stand to look at him.

Mother made plans for us to go to St. Augustine the next day. It was like Rennie and Pastor Lyons had set her on fire with all their bad news. She was like a wildfire blazing through the tinderbox house. Jack Longmont insisted on driving us to St. Augustine, which was wrong of him. So wrong. But he was so pitiful that Mother agreed just so he would stop begging. I'd like to have seen her try to go without him. Fat chance. I was scared he was praying for Daddy to die. It was like he couldn't stand to let Mother out of his sight, not for one minute.

When Mother called the people at the hospital in St. Augustine they told her not to get her hopes up. "It's a miracle he's alive at all," they said.

That was how it seemed to us too.

Mother tore the house apart and put it back together that night. She wanted it right, in case they let us bring Daddy home. "I guess he can lay unconscious here as well as he can there," Mother said. "Idn't that right?"

When Wade and Sowell and I went to bed Mother was still banging around, doing and undoing, listening to Jack Longmont regret in his deep, low voice, his words floating through the house like mosquitoes – not really harmful, but not so harmless either.

I don't like the word *vegetable* when you are talking about a person. A person is not a *vegetable* – even in a coma. They said it was doubtful that he would recover. His brain was damaged by the bullet. His memory was probably gone. He might never wake up. They said these things to Mother on the phone and she said, "I see. I understand."

She lied.

Now we were all beginning the long job of unburying Daddy. Digging him out of the shallow graves we'd put him in. I was doing that. Saying *forgive me.* Begging him to rise from the imaginary grave. Thinking I would spoon-feed him chicken soup, let it dribble down his chin and scoop it up gently and keep on and on, forcing him to eat, forcing him to live. I would give him sips of ice water and read to him from the Bible.

Before I was asleep Mother came in our room to put away a load of clean clothes. "Berry," she whispered. "Your daddy's gun is gone out of his dresser drawer. You don't think Raymond Lee stole it, do you?"

"He's not a thief," I said.

Mother shook her head. "How did I miss noticing it was gone?"

"Maybe Mr. Longmont has got it?" I suggested.

"Don't be silly." Mother ran her fingers through her uncombed hair and scratched her scalp. "I must be going crazy," she said.

"You're not," I said.

She looked at me. "Your yellow cat is going to have to go back outside if we bring your daddy home, Berry. You know that, don't you?"

Late, late Mrs. Ingram came over in her housecoat and brought Mother a bottle of Mogen David wine to help her sleep. Mother drank a bunch of wine too, but it didn't make her sleepy. It made her bold. For once Mother made Mr. Longmont go home for the night. He got mad and slammed the door when he left. She was sleeping in her clothes again – with Mr. Longmont gone I thought she could maybe close her eyes and rest.

I don't know what made me wake up – Sowell and Wade were out like lights. But I heard Roy snorting outside. I felt Cadell's spooky eyes looking in the window. He woke me up with his eyes alone – never spoke a word, just nodded toward the kitchen door and I knew what he meant.

I snuck through the house and opened the back door and there stood Cadell like a bad dream. "Rennie is waiting up at the church," he whispered. "She wants to talk to you before she leaves."

"Tell her to come here," I said.

"She won't. She sent me to get you. But we got to hurry. That preacher is meeting her at midnight to carry her away from here."

"Mother will kill me if she finds out."

"I got Roy out here. Come on."

I followed Cadell out to where he'd tied Roy to the chinaberry tree. Cadell didn't mention that I had my see-through nightgown on. I guess it was too dark for him to notice. We got on Roy and Cadell led him away from the house a ways, then kicked his belly to make him gallop all the way to the church. I held on for dear life. The night was like ink, like swimming in black ink.

Rennie was waiting at the front steps of the church. I couldn't hardly see her since I forgot my glasses. "Thank goodness you come," Rennie said, hugging me. She took my hand and led me into the dark church. We felt our way along the pews until Rennie said, "Right here, sit down." So I did. She turned to Cadell. "You wait outside."

"No," he said.

"Cadell, this is private," Rennie said. "Between me and Berry."

"Y'all hurry up. I ain't got all night." He walked outside and pulled the door to.

Rennie sat down beside me, held my hand and petted it like you do a cat. "I ain't a liar, Berry. Just because somebody has got to tell lies to stay alive – don't make them a true liar."

Rennie's hand was sweaty and hot.

"Any lies I told, it was because I didn't see no other way. And also because I didn't want to say nothing that would bear down on your mama too hard, you know. I lied for her too. You can understand that, can't you?"

My eyes were getting used to the dark. I could make out Rennie's face. She had those puffed eyes you get from bad crying.

Rennie lay my hand across her belly. "Feel that?" she whispered. "This right here is your daddy's baby, Berry."

I snatched my hand away. "It's not. It's the preacher's baby."

"I wish it was," she said. "God knows." She was rubbing the lump in her belly where the baby was growing. "I'll lie on a stack of Bibles if I got to, swear to God Butch is this baby's daddy. But I need one person in this world to know the honest truth. You, Berry. If your daddy don't make it . . . if he . . . you know . . . dies. Somebody has got to know the truth. The baby is your blood."

I shook my head. "You're lying."

"Your daddy ain't all that different from mine, Berry. You know that? He didn't want nobody in Pinetta to know nothing about this baby. He didn't want to break your mama's heart with this sort of news. So he said he'd take me to Jacksonville. Lord, I was happy." Rennie bowed her head like she was about to say a prayer or something. "It wasn't me that shot your daddy, Berry. Don't let nobody tell you different."

"Who shot him then?"

"It wasn't me. Once he got out of the car in that storm, I

mean it when I say I never laid eyes on him again. There wasn't no vacation couple, okay? I lied about that. When your daddy didn't come back, Berry, I got the car started and I drove myself all the way to Jacksonville."

I should have run from the room. I should have gone home to tell Mother. Called the sheriff to come arrest Rennie for the crime of lying.

"You can't drive a car, Rennie," I hollered.

"Sure I can. I been driving Daddy's old truck since I was ten."

"Why are you telling me these lies?" I stood up like I was going to make a run for it, but she grabbed my arm and pulled me back.

Rennie looked into my eyes hard, like she was driving nails in. "I thought your daddy loved me."

"Daddy never loved *you,* Rennie," I said. "He loved Mother."

She blew her nose into a handkerchief. "When I called Butch, he come right to Jacksonville after me. He didn't waste a minute. He says he loves me." Rennie put her face in her hands and wept like somebody out of the Bible, like it was the end of the world. She was scaring me.

Everything Rennie said came into my head in pictures I didn't recognize, like photos out of an album that belonged to a family of strangers. I'd already allowed Daddy to die a bunch of ways in my mind. And now Rennie was adding one more death to all the others.

"Do you hate me, Berry?" Rennie asked.

"You lie too much, Rennie."

"Just because you don't like hearing it, Berry, don't mean it's a lie."

We heard a car pull up on the gravel outside. It didn't have its headlights on. Rennie jumped and hurried to look out. "It's Butch. He's come to get me." She wiped her face on the hem of her dress. I could see the outline of her belly, the small bulge.

"Somebody ought to get some happiness out of all this heartache," she said.

"You?" I asked.

"It's not wrong to want a little happiness, Berry. You can't blame me for that."

We walked out of the church. "Maybe your daddy never did love me, Berry," Rennie whispered. "But I loved him."

"Shut up," I said. "Stop saying that."

Butch Lyons was waiting in the car for Rennie. Maybe she was right about him. Maybe he loved her – maybe he didn't waste a minute. She kissed Cadell on the face – and me. "What I done, Berry, I done because I had to. I didn't see no other way." She took off, running to the car.

Me and Cadell watched them as they drove away. I didn't know where Rennie would go. I didn't know what would happen to her. But I had a funny feeling that I would never see her again. That nobody in Pinetta would ever see her again.

Me and Cadell climbed on Roy and let him slow-walk back through the black night to my house.

"What did Rennie want with you?" Cadell asked.

"You were listening through that door," I said. "You know."

"Not all of it."

"Well, you'll just have to ask your blood the rest of it then."

~

St. Augustine is a nice town. They have the beach. They have lots of restaurants and motels for the Yankee tourists. We got directions to the hospital. It was as hot as Hades. Between the fireball sun and our hot nerves, we were melted by the time we got there. Me and Wade had to sit in the waiting room with a bunch of coughing people. Sowell went with Mother and Mr. Longmont to see Daddy.

Me and Wade hadn't hardly thumbed through the first magazine before the three of them came back, looking white as self-rising flour. They looked like they'd seen a ghost, like they'd turned into ghosts themselves. "Look at them," I said to Wade. "Daddy's dead. I know it."

"It's not him," Sowell told us. "It's not Daddy in there."

"You sure?" we asked.

"Don't you think me and Mama would know Daddy if we saw him? It ain't him."

Mother looked caught up in a big joke – and it wasn't funny. "I don't know whether to laugh or cry," she said.

"They got a man in there all right, been shot. He's near dead," Sowell told us. "But Pastor Lyons is crazy if he thinks that old man is Daddy."

"Poor man," Mother said. "It's pitiful."

"Where's Daddy then?" Wade wanted to know.

"I wish I knew." You could tell by the way Mother said it that she wasn't going to waste any more time wondering or looking. You could tell that Daddy was as good as dead for her.

On the ride home Mother held hands with Mr. Longmont. They put the radio on and she hummed along with it. I think Sowell was mad because Mother seemed so happy. Wade fell asleep stuck to the plastic car upholstery. I just rode along with the window down, the hot air whipping across my face like something slapping me.

~

A hobo came through the neighborhood yesterday. He was the first one since the road was repaired. We saw him coming, walking along the roadside in the weeds since the road was too hot for human feet, the tar melted, the heat shimmying into steam. The hobo had a little dog with him, tied on a rope. It was Wade that hollered, "Hey, mister," and brought the man into the yard. Mother looked him over and fixed him a pimento cheese sandwich and two boiled eggs.

He was younger than the usual hobo. His teeth were nice. I guess he wasn't much older than Raymond, although he was not a pretty man, had no smile. He was not alive in the face. His eyes were dull as old pennies. Even walking around, even sitting on our back steps, peeling those eggs – he was mainly asleep. His little dog was named Blue and the hobo fed him a bite for every one he ate himself. He didn't like to talk. Wade tried to engage him with questions, but he seemed like somebody who had forgot everything he ever knew – or else had never known anything worth mentioning. After he ate and filled up his canteen with water from the spigot he walked off with the rope around Blue's neck tied onto his belt loop. He was odd, this one. He left without our knowing anything more about him than when he walked up. There is no satisfaction in not knowing.

I was thinking when the hobo disappeared that maybe Daddy would come home like that someday, like a hobo whose hunger led him back to our door. I imagined the look on Mother's face when he scratched on the kitchen screen. For all we knew, right that minute he might have been on his way home, walking in the ditch with his thumb out. Or maybe he had hopped a train out to California to think things over, to see whether or not he missed us enough to bother with finding his way back to Pinetta.

I thought about Raymond sometimes and wondered if he ever thought about me. I wondered if I'd ever see him again. So far he had not even bothered to come to me in a dream. But Daddy did sometimes. He never showed his face. He came disguised as a stranger, and I knew it was him only when he started to say things. He said, *A little hard work never hurt anybody.* He said, *Make something out of yourself.* He said, *Women love to cry.* He said, *You and your brothers are the best kids in the world. Don't think I don't know that.*

~

It was Jimmy who told me first, but I didn't believe him. Jimmy had got where he liked to hurt people's feelings any chance he got. There was something wrong with Jimmy. Ever since the hurricane he had acted hateful. He begged Mrs. Ingram to let him go to Tallahassee to live with his aunt. He said he hated Pinetta. He hated the kind of people we had here. He wanted to be a different kind of person from us. He said he would kill himself if she didn't let him move to Tallahassee. He had made Mrs. Ingram cry, talking like this. If I were her, I'd let him go. I didn't see why we needed him around here if all he was going to do was keep everybody crazy. I had stopped believing most of what Jimmy said.

But not Cadell. When Cadell came pounding up on Roy's bare back, both of them lathered with sweat, Cadell leaning forward with that urgency of his, flinging himself to the ground so winded he could hardly talk, it made me listen. "They found your daddy's keys," he said.

"What?" It was all I could think of to say.

Cadell was gasping for air like a caught fish does.

"What?" I said. "What? What?"

"Daddy and Mr. Burnett and them did. They were out there at that stand, deer hunting – you know, out near that quicksand sinkhole where Clyde Greene's daddy went down. They found some of your daddy's belongings, his keys for sure. Daddy and them are on their way now to show your mama. They're coming in Mr. Burdett's truck."

"That don't mean nothing." Sowell came up behind me, listening to Cadell.

"By that quicksand," Cadell said. "Look like those keys come up from the quicksand."

"Could be anybody's keys," Sowell said.

"Naw. It's got his military ring on there, you know, with his initials. They got the school keys on there too. He used to let me unlock the PE closet. I recognize them keys."

"Why don't you go home," Sowell said.

Something true can go over you like fire. Like there is something being branded on your soul by a hot iron in a reckless hand. It wasn't that Cadell's words were the true thing. It wasn't his words that turned my blood to flames, made me feel that I had ashes for bones. The truth – even the truth nobody ever knows – moves all around like a hot wind, bothering everybody, rearranging things. It can knock you to your knees. I thought of Daddy misplacing his keys and making us turn the house upside down searching until we found them. I thought of him jingling them in his pocket on Sunday mornings when he was digging for some change for the collection plate.

"Your daddy wouldn't be the first man to take a wrong step out there," Cadell said. "He wouldn't be the first to go under."

In minutes Mr. Burdett and Mr. Miller and some of his boys pulled up in the truck, and everybody spilled out of their houses, leaving their supper to get cold on the table. They gathered in the buttery light of our hot kitchen to see the keys, which Mr. Miller claimed the quicksand had spit out like a watermelon seed. The people in the kitchen wanted to touch the keys, to tell their own version of what might could have happened, to watch and see if anything they said would be enough to make Mother cry.

I went outside and sat under the chinaberry tree where Cadell had tied Roy to a low limb. I didn't want anybody to see how I was feeling. It wasn't the right way to feel. Sometimes all the parts of a thing do not make a whole. In school they teach about a world where there is logic and explanation. At church they try to make you think God has a master plan and you can participate in that plan if you promise not to mess up your part too much. They don't tell you that even in the best-laid plans, the best-lived lives, there are things missing, lots of things, things you need. Sometimes what is missing may be right in front of your face, but you never see it. It just brushes up against you like the wind, real and invisible. Sometimes the missing thing is the glue that holds everything else in place.

This thought gave me hope.

It's dark when Cadell comes out to untie Roy and ride home. At first he doesn't see me sitting there. When I speak he nearly jumps out of his skin, scaring Roy, making him rear up on his back legs. "What you doing sitting out here like some kind of ghost?" he says.

"Nothing," I say.

I watch him ride off in the darkness. He thinks he knows the way home. He thinks that just because he's made the trip a hundred times that this time won't be any different. He jabs Roy with his heels and takes off in a gallop. I watch them disappear. There is something good in the way Cadell goes about things. I want to tell him so sometime.

It's Wade who finally comes outside to look for me. "Come in the house, Berry." He leans down to pull me up. I'm ready to go inside anyway. The mosquitoes are so bad I can't stand it. If you let them, I swear they will eat you alive.

ACKNOWLEDGMENTS

My deep gratitude to Betsy Lerner at the Gernert Company for her valuable guidance and insight. She is a brilliant writer, reader, and agent. I'm honored to have her represent my work. And to Judy Clain at Little, Brown, whose genuine love of books – including this one – is a gift. I'm fortunate to have the benefit of Judy's wisdom and sensibility. My sincere gratitude to Michael Pietsch for his accessibility and generosity of spirit. I'm also indebted to many other talented people at Little, Brown: Sophie Cottrell and Terry Adams, who extended palpable goodwill; Claire Smith, who communicated faithfully with humor and patience; Molly Messick, who made herself indispensable; Heather Rizzo and Heather Fain, who helped get this book into the world; Marlena Bittner, who proves that there are no coincidences, just degrees of miracle; Shannon Byrne for her high energy; Stephen Lamont for his insights and attention to the manuscript; and finally, my thanks to Peter Mauceri and Craig Young. Without their efforts, all else would be futile and we all know it.

I also thank Sylvie Rabineau and Liza Wacthner, who always keep hope alive.

~

Lately I have come to believe that the accident of birth is no accident. I have lived long enough to be properly thankful for my own childhood. The proof is in those with whom I shared the journey, my brothers, Roger, Wayne, Frank, and Paul, and my sister, Lucy. I like this world better knowing they are alive and well somewhere in it.

My gratitude to our mother, who has always refused to be boring even when we wished she would give it a try – I am deeply grateful for her refusal to yield.

To our father, who died dancing, left this world while the music played on – and who remains as mysterious in death as in life. I am grateful for the bewilderment – both his and mine.

I am indebted to all the people who have been inclined to love me, whether I deserved it or not. And to those who have not been so inclined – including those few who have made me miserable. All came bearing gifts. I'm sorry not to have understood this sooner and appreciated them properly.

Always, my thanks to Dick Tomey, who said, "Happiness is a decision you make." And who has proved it a thousand times.

As Hot As It Was You Ought to Thank Me

A novel by

Nanci Kincaid

A READING GROUP GUIDE

Some Comments

Nanci Kincaid's writes about the origins of
As Hot As It Was You Ought to Thank Me

Berry Jackson has been with me awhile. Her voice came to me over a series of years and still does. I was interested in the way she looked at the world. Her world is Pinetta, Florida, in the mid-1950s. I know it fairly well.

As often happens in my fiction, I hear a narrative voice that begins to tell me a story – and if that voice is insistent enough, then I begin to transcribe it to the page. Second only to a compelling voice is the need for a compelling place. I'm a true believer in the power of place, the way the accident of birth dictates in large part one's view of the world. Place matters. I'm also interested in the vanishing places, voices, cultures that I knew growing up. I'd like to save them on the page if I can so that they won't be lost to me forever. Sometimes it takes pure fiction to make a real place real. It takes an imaginary voice to preserve an assortment of personal memories.

I lived in Pinetta as a small child. It was my introduction to life on Earth – this small, hot, very intense place. I wanted to take the memories from my childhood in Pinetta and offer them to Berry Jackson to see what she might do with them. She took to Pinetta instinctively – as if she were born to it – and so did the other characters who conspired to tell this story. That doesn't always happen – believe me. I always respect any character who cannot be forced, who refuses to be used fictionally in any pursuit other than a search for the truth, by which I do not mean an assortment of proven facts and recorded events, but something more illusive, something unproven, but no less valid. Berry Jackson lifts Pinetta off the map of Florida and relocates it in that fictional purgatory treacherously suspended between memory and imagination. For that, I'm grateful to her.

The small snapshots of memory that I offered Berry were as follows:

* My father was principal of Pinetta School. Smoking was the primary behavioral offense he dealt with. That and the occasional young girl looking for love who had to be stopped in her tracks. There was no back talk, sass, or other form of verbal disrespect from students then. Such a thing was beyond imagination. Although once some boys took chalk and drew naked women on the front of the school. At the time it was as if the civilized world had spun out of control – such an overt pornographic endeavor in Pinetta, a place we considered one of God's primary hot spots.

* We lived in a small two-bedroom white house clustered with five other identical houses, united by our collective unfenced sand and sandspur yards. The neighborhood children spent hours playing in a sizable hole in the ground – from daylight to dusk, if possible. There we learned to fight, tattle, settle disputes, forgive, share food, keep secrets, and most everything else a child needed to know.

* The chinaberry tree in our yard was as near to shade as we knew and we practically worshipped that tree as if it were the

Tree of Knowledge or the Tree of Life. (My oldest daughter's nickname is Chinaberry – after that tree.)

* Pinetta was as hot as Hades – maybe hotter. (Hades was much referred to in Pinetta.) Family photos show me standing in the yard again and again wearing nothing but my underpants, my brothers beside me bare chested in elastic-waisted shorts, one of them always wearing his ridiculous cowboy boots despite the deadly temperature. There was no modesty at the time, since no one had thought of it or taught it yet. Besides, I shared a bedroom with my brothers and that demystified us all.

* Snakes transcended biblical proportions in Pinetta – completely defining my nervous, barefoot childhood. It is no exaggeration to say I never took a single step without looking for a snake underfoot. In the long run I think growing up in such a snake-infested place more or less ruined my enjoyment of the great outdoors. Snakes terrified and entertained. People caught them, killed them, killed them a second time, maybe a third time, some people ate them, many people hung their lifeless carcasses over the mailboxes out by the gravel road, some saved their skins for God knows what. Snakes were the fact of life I thought people had in mind when they referred to the facts of life. Fact number one: snakes.

* The Methodists and Baptists had a ritualized competition of Sunday-morning hymn singing. We learned that singing loud was more important than singing in tune or getting the lyrics right. We were proud to be Methodists because we believed Methodists were dignified and understated, not tacky like the showy Baptists could be – and usually were.

* There was a family we visited whose extreme poverty and odd ways fascinated us and made them the nearest thing Pinetta

had to celebrities. For some strange reason I envied them their fall-down house and bare-bones life. To me, poverty seemed an adventure of sorts – in an otherwise dull world. As far as I ever knew, nobody hated poor people then. They appreciated the contrast they provided. It seemed then that the poor took a certain pride in their poverty too – and flaunted it as though it signaled their superiority.

* I remember hearing about a woman who stood before the Baptist congregation and confessed to the sin of adultery. It was something exciting for people to talk about. The church was the theater of Pinetta. We didn't have a movie theater. And we didn't need it.

* I had a favorite playmate who wore his sister's hand-me-down dresses most of the time. He never seemed to mind. Once we got used to it, nobody was much bothered by this.

* There was quicksand in palmetto thickets all around us – or so we all believed. The terrible stories were sufficient to keep us from wandering too far or exploring the world much beyond our own yards.

* Hobos brought us hit-and-miss stories from the outside world. Our mother fed them sandwiches, which they ate on the back steps while we watched. We were never afraid of them, nor did we disrespect the lives they led. They proved to us that there was a larger world beyond – which they had seen and we had not – and that was always good to know.

* Chain gangs passed through Pinetta from time to time to work on the roads. People did not assume that the convicts were in any way evil – even if they were – no matter what crimes they had committed. Convicts were mostly thought to be wayward boys who'd made terrible mistakes when they were too young to

know better, the sort of boys who would have been better off if instead they'd had sense enough to simply run off and join the army. Prison was like the army for poor boys and bad seeds – a rite of passage, generation after generation, for some families.

* We got our first TV set while living in Pinetta. Our neighbors already had one – and we were envious. We were mystified by the fake laughter. My mother had to explain to us what it was. It was creepy then the same way it is now.

* I remember once standing on the porch with my parents and brothers on a dark, windy evening watching a tornado pass by in the distance. I don't remember anyone being fearful – just excited. You hoped it would not come your way – but you also hoped it would.

* We had a yellow cat too.

This is mostly what I had to offer Berry Jackson. The rest she brought to the story of her own accord. Without her glasses she was as blind as anybody else in Pinetta, but with her glasses she was a true *seer*. Like Cadell, who understood things by blood, Berry too understood things she could not name. She – like her mother and Rennie Miller, and Jewel and Jack Longmont, and Rosemary Ingram and her brother Sowell, and maybe her daddy, Ford Jackson, too – was searching for love. Maybe everybody was.

In a place like Pinetta, you had to make do with what was available, to love what or who you could find to love. Sometimes the search was so overwhelming, the yearning so strong, that you could not see that love was every place you looked, that you were surrounded by it the same way you were surrounded by quicksand. Berry loved Raymond Lee, a boy on the chain gang. She was not his victim. She was not shamed by him in any way – not by what he had done to get sent to prison, "loved somebody too much," or what he had done to her – made her real. She loved Raymond because he let her. And she believed he loved her because she needed to believe it.

Pinetta was a hotbed of snakes and storms and sandspurs and sexual longing. It was a place of bad seeds and fertile seeds. Maybe God was love, we were never sure. To us God was like the sun – a fireball of an eye in the sky, watching our every move, too hot to hide from, too hot to ever deny.

Reading Group Questions and Topics for Discussion

1. Discuss Berry's attitude toward religion and faith. Religion is part of her everyday life, but how does she relate to it? Do you see a lot of religious symbolism in this novel? What about Pinetta's two churches – how do they shape the community?

2. Broadly speaking, this is a story about a young girl's growing understanding of the adult world. How does Berry relate to the adults around her? What does she learn? How does she react to her parents' fallibility?

3. Do parts of this novel remind you of your own childhood? What do you like most about Berry?

4. How does Berry react to people who diverge from what might be considered normal in a small southern town? (The hobos who pass through, for instance, and her friend Jimmy with his proclaimed love for Cadell.) Where do you think Berry's capacity for acceptance comes from?

5. How do you respond to Berry's relationship with Raymond? Does it make you angry, uncomfortable? What do you think about the way Berry handles it? Does her silence betray her age, or does it make her seem beyond her years? Or could Berry simply have done nothing else?

6. Berry's family's reaction to her daddy's disappearance isn't one of dramatic grief. Does this make sense to you? Why do you think the family's response is or isn't appropriate?

7. As a student in Mrs. Freddy's second-grade class, Berry is shocked at the chalk drawings of naked women on the schoolhouse walls. Later she maintains a quiet knowledge of her mother's affair with Pastor Lyons. How does Berry think about right and wrong?

8. Berry calls herself plain, not beautiful like Rennie or Marie. What observations does Berry make of the girls and women around her? Aside from Berry, how would you generally describe the experiences of the women in this book?

9. Some people maintain that writing a novel is as much about creating an atmosphere as it is about telling a story. What feeling does *As Hot As It Was You Ought to Thank Me* give you? How does Kincaid create the mood of this story?

Some Books That Made a Difference

Nanci Kincaid's suggestions for further reading

A Tree Grows in Brooklyn by Betty Smith

I read this when I was maybe ten years old – and was riveted. Brooklyn seemed as far away from my life in Tallahassee, Florida, as Mars did – the people just as alien. In the South of my childhood New York was a code word for sin. It was where people went who could not thrive in the heart of Dixie, who could not embrace the Baptist mind-set – you know, restless-hearted people. There was always an implied element of shame when speaking of someone who took off for New York. We felt sorry for them – embarrassed for their God-fearing families who had done their best but failed. This book confirmed the suspicion that bad things went on in New York. But I was transformed by the knowledge that there were other "real" worlds out there, other girls not so unlike me who lived in dangerous places that I could access by book. This was helpful since nobody I knew traveled much – except maybe to visit their relatives on holidays, who might live as far away as one state over. I didn't even dream of really traveling – especially of ever making my way "up North," where we understood we would not be liked much and would likely be made fun of too. *A Tree Grows in Brooklyn* was also the first "adult-seeming" material I remember reading. It shocked me. It made me feel I should hide the book beneath my pillow. I was pretty sure my parents knew nothing of Brooklyn, what went on there, and I felt I should protect them from such knowledge. I loved the "otherness" of this book.

Huckleberry Finn by Mark Twain

Okay. Here we go. These are my people. I knew these folks because they were my family – the family of nearly everyone I knew. This was reassuring on the cosmic level. What I admire most about Mark Twain is that he wrote about the pain and heartache of the human condition – and made it funny. I laughed so many times but always understood that what I was laughing about was not really funny on the larger scale. That was such genius to me – the ability to tell the ugly truth in a beautiful, amusing way. It is also such a classically southern device – the ability to laugh at oneself, to use humor to mask misery and evil. I realize everybody claims Mark Twain – that he is one of the true American writers – but to me he was totally southern. Maybe, in part, because he wrote about Jim – Huck's best friend, his "inferior" best friend. But mostly because he told the truth in the only way I thought southerners were allowed to do it – with humorous anecdote, self-deprecating humor, and an implied accent. Inspired by the Bible, southerners adopted parables (both oral and written) as the device of choice in exploring the human condition, making it palatable, revealing and projecting moral lessons, and getting a few good laughs along the way. This is why stories are so powerful in southern culture. They were – maybe still are – our best shot at truth telling.

The Autobiography of Malcom X

At last, a black person speaking the truth to a southern white girl like me. I was starved for this book. On some large level I felt changed after reading it. I loved the courage it took to "tell it like it is," as Percy Sledge used to sing. It scared me in the most satisfying way. There was a collision of the absolutely familiar with the distinctively "other." One of the most personally meaningful books I have ever read.

Black Like Me by John Howard Griffin

For reasons similar to those above.

Mama by Terry McMillian

McMillian's first – and best – book. She let me into the house/lives that had always been off-limits to me. I wrote her a letter and thanked her. *Crossing Blood* is very much about longing to witness a life/lives by witnessing the house(s) where it is lived. I thought this book was honest and brave. It shocked me a little too.

Brothers and Keepers by John Edgar Wideman

This was the first book I ever read where I was acquainted with the writer. Since it was nonfiction, it felt like reading a diary – or eavesdropping on a series of personal phone calls. The fury that inspired this book was what I responded to. I thought if Wideman wanted to tell me how the world looked from his vantage point and expected me to listen and care, then maybe I could do the same – and assume that he would listen and care. I wrote the first draft of *Crossing Blood* in his class in Wyoming. Having him as a reader somehow emboldened me to try to tell the truth – even if it might make somebody mad. Before that time I had been under the impression that you had to wait for most of your family – or your parents at the very least – to die off before you could even take a stab at telling the truth. (And I certainly didn't want to be rude.)

In Defense of Academic Freedom by Sidney Hook

A nonfiction book about education in America. I read it when I was working as a secretary at the Tuscaloosa school board in hopes it would lead me to a job as a teacher's aide, which it did. I wrote Hook a letter too and thanked him for his optimism. Amazingly, he wrote me back.

Portnoy's Complaint by Philip Roth

Who were these crazy people? I felt better about myself and the peculiarities of my people, took comfort in the thought that maybe we were not the only culturally specific people worth writing/reading about. I grew up ignorant of everything Jewish. There was one Jewish boy in my school – he was several years older than me. I think his name was Goldberg. His father owned the best dress shop in town. The best I could tell he lived a completely secret life. All I really knew about him was that he was sort of rich – comparatively speaking – had no chance at heaven since he refused to claim Jesus as his personal lord and savior (which at the time was pretty hard to do in the Bible Belt, no matter who you were), could not eat pork (this included barbecue!), and had to marry a Jewish girl someday, although where in the world he was going to find one was a mystery to me. This book suggested a world within a world. I was intrigued and curious. Still am.

To Kill a Mockingbird by Harper Lee

Maybe the all-time best book ever. The narrative voice was perfect in its familiarity, the story classic. Harper Lee, who hails from Alabama, knew how to write deadly subject matter while making you laugh at yourself – and the human condition. And, oh, the voice! The voice!

"Why I Live at the PO" and "The Petrified Man" by Eudora Welty

She writes place as though it were another person – a distinctive and influential character who dominates every story. No one understands the power of place better. I believe in place. It is the true religion of my own fiction writing. "Why I Live at the PO" is perfect. And "The Petrified Man" is even better. I had just moved back to Alabama after six years of living "off," as they say. (In Wyoming, actually.) I drove to Birmingham to hear Miss Welty read "The Petrified Man." I cried like a baby. I sobbed out loud. The woman next to me, African American, a stranger, was so alarmed she held my hand and cried with me. We made quite a spectacle of ourselves. It was not that the story is sad. It's a wise and wonderful story – never self-conscious, never aiming to make a show of itself. I was simply overcome to be "home," humbled to hear the language of my past, my blood, that inner voice always whispering to me that I had nearly trained myself not to hear. It was my longing for the language, the yearning for cross-racial sisterhood, and the reminder that the accident of birth is probably no accident that made me cry. Eudora Welty was a natural storyteller. She had that strong Mississippi accent and stood there onstage with her sweater held on by a dangling chain with metal clasps and her glasses held on by a similar apparatus. She wore a pink polyester dress and Hush Puppies shoes. I was in love with her. She was so real – and I so wanted to be – that she broke my heart to pieces.

The Water Is Wide by Pat Conroy

I loved this book. It's my favorite Conroy book (although he might not appreciate hearing that). I come from teachers, marry teachers, give birth to teachers, and have been a teacher myself –

it's in the blood in one form or another. Teaching is a rite of passage in my family, and so I loved this book the same way I loved the movie *To Sir, with Love* when I saw it in high school. Still may be my favorite movie. I don't apologize either.

A Good Man Is Hard to Find and *Wise Blood* by Flannery O'Connor

If Philip Roth taught me something about what it is to be Jewish, then Flannery O'Connor taught me something about what it is to be Catholic. She writes such a dark world. It was like reading chapters of the hell we are all so afraid of growing up in the Bible Belt.

The Heart Is a Lonely Hunter by Carson McCullers

McCullers grew up a short distance from my mother. I did not really know her characters, though – which surprised me. But I do know a little about the universality of the lonely hunt.

The Moviegoer by Walker Percy

He was a man who wrote about women in an interesting way. When I think of New Orleans, I think of Walker Percy – and the cocktail world he depicted there.

As I Lay Dying by William Faulkner

I first read this when I was seventeen, having convinced myself that it would be "good for me." It wasn't. It made no sense at all, but I never let myself stop (believing in the intrinsic benefits of intellectual punishment). I read page after page of his nonsense until I finished the book, not astute enough even to realize that the narrator changed with each chapter. To say I was an unsophisticated reader is a vast understatement! Since it was obvious

I could make no sense of the book, I tried to "feel" the words rather than understand them. Afterward I waited for lightning to strike. It didn't. Years later, at age thirty-seven, I read it again – reluctantly. And this time I was startled at how the book spoke to me. It was practically my autobiography – and that of half the southern women I knew. Lightning struck – big-time. I think of Faulkner as one of those interesting artists who is genius on the page, but somewhat of a fool in his actual life. I think the work he set down on the page was organically brilliant, but that for the most part he failed to actually understand it in any real way. I have to confess I love this – from a literary standpoint. Organic art of all kinds is my absolute favorite – excessive education can be the death of it too. But Faulker, to me, has come to represent that classic southern man I grew up encountering everywhere who would prefer not to have to know anything if he could avoid it. He would go to great lengths and drinks to avoid being introspective. He could write answers for people like me, even if he never heard my or any questions, wouldn't want to hear them or contemplate their significance. The insight he brings to his work is purely subconscious. So many smart men in the South wish they weren't. They aim at and often perfect the art of "not knowing." Scholars might think I'm crazy. But I stand by my instincts. Faulker understood and revealed so much more in his writing than he knew in his daily life. This is compelling, amusing, and powerful. It is also wildly irritating. And I like to think it is something "pure" that many of us could do if we didn't educate ourselves totally out of the organic realm.

Heart of Darkness by Joseph Conrad

Almost same as above. I first attempted this book when I was eighteen. To say I was bored to tears would be an understatement. I would read thirty pages and then realize that I was not paying one bit of attention, had no idea what was going on, so I quit. Years later, in my thirties, I tried it again and relished every page. Conrad understood something about men that I never will. But he also understood and taught me something about women – and I appreciate it.

Fatal Flowers by Rosemary Daniell

The first book I remember reading with a wayward, sexual female protagonist. It was bold at the time – I thought.

The Liars' Club by Mary Karr

I was fascinated with the mother in this book.

Their Eyes Were Watching God by Zora Neale Hurston

I simply loved this book. My girl, Zora, came from Florida, like me. The other Florida.

The Color Purple by Alice Walker and
All Over but the Shoutin' by Rick Bragg

The first halves of these two books thrilled me to death. I went crazy. *The Color Purple* I read in black and white – and I felt that book. So when Quincy Jones and Oprah made the movie of the same name, all that living color nearly blinded me. It was a great movie too, but not the dark and painful story I had read for myself. *All Over but the Shoutin'* I read out loud to my West Coast husband while we drove through Alabama. I think I freaked him out a little, the way I practically shouted out some of those perfect sentences. I was excited to be reading books that spoke to me so powerfully on many different levels. But in both cases I have to admit I didn't love the second halves of the books very much. They both seemed to become about teaching me something or showing me how a person can transcend a tough life to go on and accomplish things. I'd rather figure that out myself. I am one of those rare readers who does not insist on a happy, triumphant ending to every story. But the voices and gut truth of these books I hold high to this day. (I love Rick Bragg's mother thing more than I can say. It explains Bill Clinton perfectly too – if anybody wants to know.)

Keeper of the Moon: A Southern Boyhood by Tim McLaurin

My friend Tim wrote his early life. I loved it then and love it even more now that he is gone. Tim was the real thing, one of those true die-hard North Carolina tobacco farmers' sons who exalted poverty – took pride in his humble beginnings and the hard times of his family and his life. He understood drama because he lived it. In many ways this book is a love story.

The Grapes of Wrath by John Steinbeck

I'm interested in the lives of the poor. I witnessed some dramatic poverty as a child and it terrified and fascinated me. The characters in *The Grapes of Wrath* reminded me of people I saw all around me. If Steinbeck hadn't done such a good job, Flannery O'Connor might have written these characters.

In Cold Blood by Truman Capote

Am I the only American who will admit to watching crime TV? I confess, I'm interested in crime. I read this book with horror – an exploration, not explanation, of evil. I read it in search of logical explanation – which suggests how long ago it was, since I don't search for that anymore.

I have not listed many current books because it is hard to tell which of them will stay with me and which I will forget. The above books have remained vivid in my mind and I considered myself changed in some small way after reading each of them. The test of time, I guess.

(I see as I compile this list that I gravitate to particular themes – the southern experience, the defeated people, poverty, mothers, race, gender issues, crime and betrayal, and voice – but of all of these, voice is what I love most.)

ABOUT THE AUTHOR

Nanci Kincaid is the author of *Crossing Blood, Pretending the Bed Is a Raft* (made into the film *My Life Without Me*), *Balls,* and *Verbena.* Nanci divides her time between Honolulu, Hawaii, and Austin, Texas.